D0975739

SOUL

of the

SWORD

Books by Julie Kagawa
available from Harlequin TEEN and Inkyard Press
(Each series listed in reading order)

Shadow of the Fox

Shadow of the Fox
Soul of the Sword

The Talon Saga

Talon
Rogue
Soldier
Legion
Inferno

Blood of Eden

Dawn of Eden (prequel novella)+
The Immortal Rules
The Eternity Cure
The Forever Song

The Iron Fey***

*The Iron King**
Winter's Passage (ebook novella)**
*The Iron Daughter**
The Iron Queen
Summer's Crossing (ebook novella)**
The Iron Knight
Iron's Prophecy (ebook novella)**
The Lost Prince
The Iron Traitor
The Iron Warrior

+Available in the *'Til the World Ends* anthology by Julie Kagawa,
Ann Aguirre and Karen Duvall
*Also available in *The Iron Fey Volume One* anthology
**Also available in print in *The Iron Legends* anthology
along with the exclusive *Guide to the Iron Fey*
***The Iron Fey series is also available in two boxed gift sets

JULIE KAGAWA

SOUL
of the
SWORD

ink
yard
press

Recycling programs
for this product may
not exist in your area.

ISBN-13: 978-1-335-18499-3

Soul of the Sword

Copyright © 2019 by Julie Kagawa

All rights reserved. Except for use in any review, the reproduction or utilization
of this work in whole or in part in any form by any electronic, mechanical or other
means, now known or hereafter invented, including xerography, photocopying and
recording, or in any information storage or retrieval system, is forbidden without the
written permission of the publisher, Inkyard Press, 22 Adelaide St. West, 40th Floor,
Toronto, Ontario M5H 4E3, Canada.

This is a work of fiction. Names, characters, places and incidents are either the
product of the author's imagination or are used fictitiously, and any resemblance to
actual persons, living or dead, business establishments, events or locales is entirely
coincidental.

This edition published by arrangement with Harlequin Books S.A.

For questions and comments about the quality of this book, please contact us
at CustomerService@Harlequin.com.

® and TM are trademarks of Harlequin Enterprises Limited or its corporate
affiliates. Trademarks indicated with ® are registered in the United States Patent and
Trademark Office, the Canadian Intellectual Property Office and in other countries.

InkyardPress.com

Printed in U.S.A.

To Misa sensei for all her help. And to Tashya, for everything else.

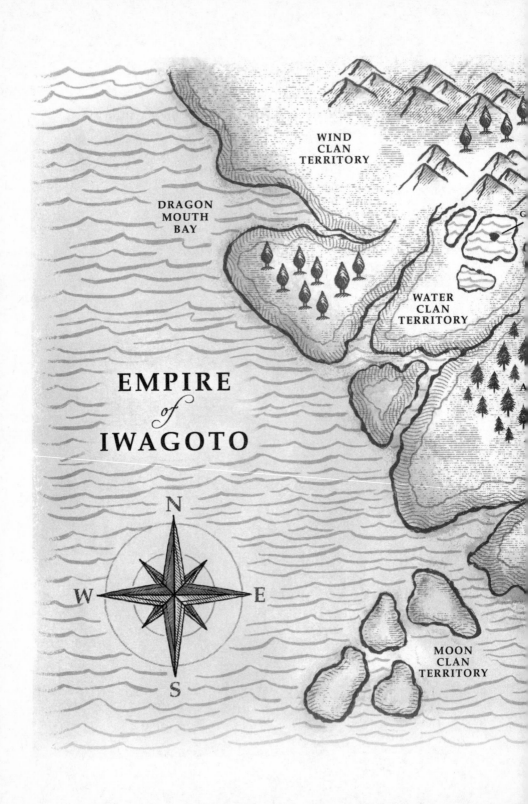

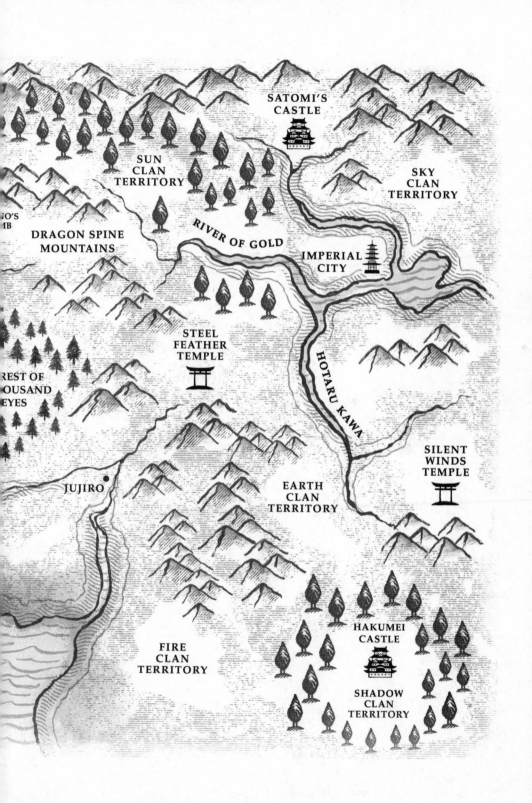

PART 1

1

BIRTH OF A GODSLAYER

One thousand years ago

*H*is throat was raw from screaming prayers into the wind.

The storm raged around him, beating the cliffs and sending sprays of ocean water crashing against the rock. The night was pitch-black, his drenched clothes were icy cold, and he could barely hear himself over the howl of the wind and the roar of the sea. Still, he kept chanting, the scroll clutched tight in shaking hands, the lantern flickering wildly at his feet. His vision blurred from salt spray and tears, but his voice never wavered as he shouted every line on the crumpled parchment as if it was a challenge to the gods themselves.

Crying out the final prayer, letting the wind tear it from his lips and fling it over the ocean, he collapsed to his knees on the stones. Gasping, he bowed his head, his arms falling limply to his sides, the opened scroll fluttering in his grasp.

For several desperate, pounding heartbeats, he knelt there,

alone. The storm bellowed around him, slashing and clawing with foamy talons. His wounds, sustained from fighting a demon horde to reach this place, throbbed. Blood seeped down his chest and arms and over the scroll, staining the parchment pink.

Many yards out to sea, the ocean stirred. Waves surged and roiled, and the surface of the water began to lift as if something monstrous was shifting just below.

With an explosion of spray and the howl of a god, an enormous dark shape rose out of the depths and coiled up into the night. Lightning flashed, illuminating massive horns, fangs and glimmering scales the color of the tide. A rippling mane ran down the length of the creature's back, and a pair of whiskers as long as a ship writhed and fluttered in the wind as the Great Dragon curled in the sky, flowing in and out of the clouds. A pair of eyes like glowing moons peered down at the tiny figure below, and a perfect, iridescent pearl shone like a star in the center of its forehead. With the rumble of an approaching tsunami, the kami spoke.

"Who summons me?"

Clenching his jaw, the man lifted his head. His heart trembled with the knowledge that he should not gaze so boldly upon a god, the Harbinger of Change himself, but the despair and hate-sickness deep in his soul drowned out any other emotion. Swallowing the pain from a throat raw from screaming, he raised his voice.

"I am Kage Hirotaka, son of Kage Shigetomo, and I am the mortal who has called upon the power of the Dragon's prayer." His thin, raspy voice faded into the wind, but the huge creature cocked its head, listening. Its inhuman gaze, carrying the wisdom of eternity, met his own, and he suddenly felt as if he were falling into a bottomless pit.

The warrior placed his hands on the ground before him and bowed, touching his forehead to the rough stone, feeling the gaze of the Dragon on his back. "Great Kami," he whispered, "by my right as scroll bearer, on this night, the thousandth year after Kage Hanako made her wish upon the scroll, I humbly ask that you grant my heart's desire."

"Once more, a Kage calls upon me." The deep, thunderous voice sounded neither amused nor surprised. "Once more, the Shadow Clan toys with darkness and holds the fate of the realm in their hands. So be it." Lightning flashed and peals of thunder shook the clouds, but the Great Dragon's voice rose above it all. "Kage Hirotaka, son of Kage Shigetomo, bearer of the Dragon scroll, what is your heart's desire? What wish would you see come to pass?"

"Vengeance."

The word was barely audible, but the air seemed to still as he spoke it. "My family was killed by a demon," the warrior went on, slowly sitting up. "It slaughtered everyone. My men and servants were strewn from one end of the house to the other. My wife…my children…it didn't even leave anything to bury." He closed his eyes, trembling with grief and rage. "I couldn't save them," he whispered. "I came home to a massacre."

The cold, indifferent observer waiting in the clouds said nothing. The warrior's hand strayed to the sword at his belt, and his fingers curled around the sheath. "I don't want it dead," he rasped, his voice choked with hate. "Not by a simple wish. I will kill the monster myself, drive my sword into its black heart to avenge my clan, my family, my wife." His voice quavered, and the knuckles wrapped around his sword turned white. "But when it dies, I don't want its spirit to return to Jigoku. I want to trap it here, in this realm. To know pain and rage and helplessness. To understand there is no relief, no way for it to return as the demon it was." The warrior bared his teeth. "I want it to suffer. For eternity. That is my wish."

Overhead, the Great Kami peered down through the storm,

lightning flashing off its blue-black scales. "Once spoken," it rumbled, its voice as impassive as ever, "there is no going back." It tilted its head, those endlessly long whiskers fluttering in the wind. "Are you certain this is your heart's desire, mortal?"

"Yes."

Thunder growled, and the wind intensified, shrieking as it beat against the warrior and the rock. The Dragon seemed to fade into the storm until only its eyes and a glimmering gem shone through the darkness. Then they, too, disappeared into the black, as the clouds swirled faster, faster, until they resembled a great whirlpool in the sky.

A blinding streak of white descended from above, striking the center of the rock, mere feet from where the warrior knelt. The samurai flinched and shielded his face as stone shards flew everywhere, cutting his flesh where they hit. When the brightness faded, he peered up and squinted painfully as blood and water ran into his eyes. For a moment, he could make out only a thin, bright shimmer against the darkness. Then his eyes widened, and he stared in awe at what the lightning bolt had left behind.

A sword stood upright in a smoking crater, the point jammed into the stone, its blade gleaming against the darkness. An almost hungry power pulsed from the sword, as if it were alive.

His wounds forgotten, the Kage samurai rose and walked on shaky legs to the weapon, which glowed faintly against the black, as if fed by its own inner light.

"It is done." The booming statement held the finality of death, of a sword cutting the life from a body. Though the mighty serpent had nearly faded once more into legend, its voice echoed through the storm. "Let it be known, the Wish of this era has been spoken, and the winds of change have shifted their path. Let no mortal call upon the power of the scroll for another thousand years. If this realm survives what is to come."

"Wait! Great Kami, what should I call it?" The warrior

reached out and touched the sword hilt, feeling a tremor race up his arm. "Does it have a name?"

The warrior felt the Dragon slide from the world like an eel slipping through a net, returning to its kingdom deep below the waves. One last rumble of thunder rolled out to sea, and on the echo of the wind, he heard the kami's final word.

"Kamigoroshi."

Kage Hirotaka stood alone on the bleak platform of rock, wind and spray still whipping around him, and felt a savage smile cross his face. Kamigoroshi.

Godslayer.

2

THE DEMON OF THE KAGE

Yumeko

Silence fell as Master Jiro finished his tale.

"That demon," I said, as the priest reached for a wooden pipe sitting next to the firepit. "The one that killed Hirotaka's family. Was it…"

Master Jiro nodded and stuck the end of the pipe into his mouth. "Hakaimono."

I shivered, and around the campfire, the rest of the party looked solemn. We had taken shelter beside a trickling brook, surrounded by shaggy pines and towering redwoods, and the air was tinged with sap and the slight hint of frost, as we were still very close to the mountains that bordered Sky Clan territory. Summer was ending, and the days were growing cool as autumn took its place.

Okame sat against a mossy redwood, gazing into the shadows with his back against the trunk and one foot planted on a root. Firelight washed over him, accenting his lean, lanky form, reddish-brown hair pulled into a tail and narrow face uncharacteristically grim. The normally cheerful, outspoken ronin was quiet as he stared over the riverbed, his eyes dark.

"So, Kamigoroshi came into existence through the Dragon's Wish," Taiyo Daisuke mused. The Sun Clan noble sat cross-legged against a log and wore an expression of stoic serenity. Across the fire, Reika shot him an exasperated look. The noble's arms were wrapped in bandages, and strips of bloody cloth peeked from under his robe, mementos from our last terrible battle. He should not be up, Reika had scolded earlier this evening. He should be lying down, resting, before he tore open the wounds she had spent the night stitching closed. But Daisuke insisted he was fine. Even with his once beautiful kimono torn and filthy, his skin pale and his long, silvery-white hair hanging limply down his back, he emanated poise and elegance.

"Yes," Master Jiro confirmed. "Because Hirotaka wanted revenge against the oni that killed his family and the woman he loved. A way not only to destroy the demon but to make it suffer, to know pain and rage and helplessness. He got his wish. Not long after summoning the Dragon, Kage Hirotaka faced Hakaimono on the field of battle and, after a terrible struggle that nearly wiped out a village, managed to slay the demon. But instead of banishing the oni back to Jigoku, Kamigoroshi sealed the oni's soul within the blade, trapping it for eternity.

"Unfortunately," Master Jiro went on, "that was the beginning of the Kage's downfall. The demon drove Hirotaka mad. It did not possess him—perhaps its influence was still too weak, or perhaps it did not know it could do such a thing yet. But, little by little, it broke down Hirotaka's resolve, using his lingering rage and grief to overwhelm him. Until, one night, when Hirotaka finally lost himself and changed the course of the Kage forever."

Daisuke stirred, realization crossing his face. "The massacre at Hakumei castle," he said, looking at the priest. "The interrupted treaty between the Hino and the Kage."

"A scholar of history." Master Jiro nodded in approval. "Yes, Taiyo-san, you are correct. The following spring, there was a meeting between leaders of the Fire Clan and the Shadow Clan, to discuss a marriage between the two families. The rivalry between the Hino and the Kage was growing out of control, and war was imminent if an accord could not be reached. The treaty never happened. In a room full of unarmed diplomats and courtiers, with a typhoon howling outside, Kage Hirotaka appeared and slaughtered every member of the Fire Clan. Not a single Hino survived that night."

"That was the beginning of the second Great War," Daisuke stated. "After the massacre at Hakumei castle, the Hino vowed to wipe the Kage from existence, and they rallied the Earth Clan and the Wind Clan to their cause. The Kage turned to the Water, Sky and Moon Clans for aid, and the resulting war lasted nearly two hundred years."

"Nearly destroying the Kage in the process." Master Jiro nodded again. "Because one man made a wish on the Dragon scroll with hate in his heart and unknowingly invited a demon into his soul.

"That is the story of Kamigoroshi and the Dragon's prayer." Master Jiro blew out a long curl of smoke that writhed away over my head. "Now you know how the sword was created, and how the Dragon's Wish, well intended as it might be, brought ruin and disaster to the empire."

"That's why the scroll was split into pieces," Reika added. The shrine maiden was also sitting on the ground with her legs crossed, the billowy white sleeves of her haori folded to her chest. Chu and Ko, a pair of small dogs that were really komainu shrine guardians, lay curled up in her lap, dozing on the red hakama trousers. "No one knows the exact details, but it's said that as the war raged on, a council of kami, yokai and an order of monks came together to discuss what should become of the Dragon's prayer. They made the decision to separate the scroll and hide the pieces throughout Iwagoto so that something like the last wish could never happen again." Reika's lips thinned. "It was the right choice. The scroll holds far too much power for a single person to be trusted with it. Look at the chaos and destruction it's caused this era already, and the Dragon hasn't even been summoned yet."

Across the fire, Okame snorted. "So, if the scroll is so danger-ous, why don't we destroy it?" he asked with a shrug. "Sounds like an easy solution to me. Toss the thing in the fire right now and let's be done with it."

"It is *not* that easy," Reika said. "And it *has* been tried before. But the Dragon's prayer is a sacred artifact, a gift—or curse if you wish to look at it that way—from the Harbinger of Change himself. Much like Kamigoroshi, if you destroy the Dragon's prayer, it will simply reappear in the world again. Always in a place where it will not only be discovered, but to a person who will unfailingly summon the Dragon and make a wish." The miko's eyes narrowed. "The scroll *wants* to be found, Okame-san. That's why it's so dangerous. If we destroy it now, it could reappear in the hands of the very people we are trying to keep it away from."

Okame grunted. "This is why I don't trust magic," he mut-tered, leaning back against the tree. "Inanimate objects like swords and scrolls should not *want* to be found. They should not *want* anything. How annoying would it be if my sandals decided they didn't want to carry me anymore and wandered off into the woods?" His sharp black eyes flicked to me. "Don't get any ideas, Yumeko-chan."

I giggled at the image, but sobered quickly. "What happened

to Hirotaka?" I wondered, looking at Master Jiro. "Did he ever regain control of Hakaimono?"

The priest shook his head. "Kage Hirotaka was captured and executed by his clan, long before the end of the war," he replied. "By then, he was far too gone, and his crimes too great, to have any hope of redemption. Kamigoroshi, or the Cursed Blade of the Kage, as it would come to be known, was sealed away and vanished from history for six centuries. But such artifacts of evil cannot stay hidden forever. Four hundred years ago, it reemerged alongside the coming of Genno, the Master of Demons, when Hakaimono escaped the sword to possess its bearer. It is unclear whether Genno orchestrated the demon's release, or if Hakaimono simply took advantage of the chaos that came with the uprising, but Kamigoroshi once again carved a bloody path through history until the blood mage and his rebellion were put down.

"After Genno's death," Master Jiro continued, "his army of demons and yokai scattered to the wind, and the land was left in chaos. Kamigoroshi disappeared again for a time, but then, the first Kage demonslayer emerged, able to wield the Cursed Blade without immediately falling victim to Hakaimono." He shook his head, puffing out a cloud of white smoke. "How the Shadow Clan trained their demonslayers to guard their souls against the demon's influence is unknown, but the Kage have always walked the very edge of darkness, knowing they flirt with disaster. And now they have fallen to it once more. Hakaimono has been released, and the land will not be safe until Kage Tatsumi is killed and the demon returned to the sword."

I straightened, my stomach twisting as I stared at him over the fire. "Killed?" I repeated, as the priest's sad gaze met mine. "But...what about Tatsumi? I know he must be fighting this. Is there no way to save him, to bring him back?"

I felt sick, like a millstone was pressing down on my insides.

I'd met the cold, emotionless demonslayer when a horde of demons led by the terrible oni Yaburama had attacked my home, the Silent Winds temple, and I was forced to flee while they massacred everyone there. I'd convinced Tatsumi to accompany me to the capital to find Master Jiro, the only person who knew the location of the hidden Steel Feather temple, because the temple held one piece of the object everyone was looking for.

The Dragon scroll. The thing that could summon the Great Kami into the world to grant the bearer's heart's desire. The item everyone was desperately searching for, was willing to kill for. Including Tatsumi. His clan leader had sent him to retrieve the scroll, and he would have stopped at nothing to acquire it.

When we'd met, I'd told the demonslayer a tiny white lie: I said I didn't have the scroll, but I could take him to where one piece of it had been sent—the Steel Feather temple. What Tatsumi didn't know was that I had that piece of the scroll hidden in the furoshiki cloth tied around my shoulders. And maybe that had been terribly deceitful, but if Tatsumi had known I possessed a fragment of the scroll back then, he would have killed me and taken it to his daimyo. And I'd promised Master Isao I would protect that piece of the prayer at all costs. It was my greatest secret, well…aside from being half-kitsune.

But, Kage Tatsumi had his secrets, too. The greatest one being Hakaimono, the oni spirit that lived in his sword and was constantly fighting him for control. During the final battle with Yaburama, the demon in the sword had finally overwhelmed the demonslayer, and Kage Tatsumi was no longer the quiet, brooding warrior I'd come to know over our travels. Gone was the boy who was fearless and pragmatic, who had no sense of self because his life was dedicated to serving his clan. Who was cold and unfriendly and standoffish, until you learned that it was his duty as the bearer of Kamigoroshi that made him shy away from people. The knowledge that he had to remain in control at all times, or a demon would possess him.

And now, it had happened. Kage Tatsumi had been possessed by the terrifying and wholly evil Hakaimono, and I had no idea how we were going to bring him back.

"There must be another way," I insisted. "A ritual, an exorcism. You're a priest, right? Can't you exorcise Hakaimono and get him to leave Tatsumi?"

Master Jiro shook his head. "I am sorry, Yumeko-chan," he said. "Were it a normal demon, a yurei ghost, or even the spirit of a tanuki, it would be possible. But Hakaimono is not a normal demon. He is one of the four great generals of Jigoku, one of the strongest oni that has ever been spawned. If freeing the sword bearer could be done, the Kage would have found a way, and I am only one priest." He made a small, hopeless gesture with one wrinkled hand. "In the past, it took entire armies of men to bring Hakaimono down, and he still left a trail of bodies and destruction behind him before his rampage was brought to an end."

"We can't worry about the demonslayer," Reika said, her voice firm. "We have to deliver your piece of the scroll to the Steel Feather temple. Let Kage-san's own people deal with what he has become." At my horrified look, her eyes softened, though her voice remained hard. "I'm sorry, Yumeko. I know you and Kage-san grew close as you traveled together, but we cannot waste time chasing down an oni lord. Protecting the scroll is more important." She jabbed a finger at my furoshiki. "Everything we're facing now—Hakaimono, Kamigoroshi, the demons, the blood witch, the possessed demonslayer—it's all because of that cursed scrap of paper. Because humanity has proven that it cannot be trusted with an item of ultimate, world-changing power. We must deliver the scroll to the Steel Feather temple and make sure the Dragon cannot be summoned in this era. That is the only thing that matters."

"Hang on." Okame sat up, frowning. "I admit, the demon-slayer is pretty scary sometimes, and he's threatened to kill me on occasion, *and* he has the personality of a disdainful rock..." Reika glared at him, and he hurried on. "But that doesn't mean we should abandon someone who fought with us against a blood witch and a demon army. How do we know he can't be saved?"

"What is your solution, ronin?" Reika snapped. "Track Hakaimono across the empire? We don't even know where he's gone, and there are still things out there searching for the Dragon scroll. Even if we do find him, what then? Attempt an exorcism? No mortal has been strong enough to drive Hakaimono out once he takes control."

"Oh, I see," Okame shot back. "So, *your* solution is to ignore the insanely powerful oni lord and hope he becomes someone else's problem."

"No, Okame-san. Reika... Reika is right." My voice came out choked, and my eyes blurred with tears. It felt like a mirror had shattered inside me, and the shards were cutting me apart from within. I swallowed hard and continued, even though I hated it. "Getting the scroll to the temple...is more important," I whispered. "The Dragon's prayer was entrusted to me, and everyone at my temple died to protect it. I have to finish what I started, what I promised Master Isao.

"But," I added, as a somber silence fell, "that doesn't mean I'm abandoning Tatsumi. When this is done, after we reach the Steel Feather temple and deliver the scroll, I'm going to find Hakaimono and force him back into the sword."

"Nani?" The shrine maiden sounded incredulous. "Alone? You're no match for Hakaimono, Yumeko."

"I know," I said, shivering as I remembered the terrifying form of Hakaimono looming over me. Looking into his crimson eyes and seeing no hint of Tatsumi staring back. "But Tatsumi is strong," I added, as the shrine maiden frowned. "He's been fighting the demon for nearly his whole life. I'm not going to abandon him to Hakaimono. I have to try to save him."

"Forgive me, Yumeko-san," came Taiyo Daisuke's voice. "But there is something I have yet to understand." He shifted to a new position, and his sharp, intelligent gaze fixed on me. "You are kitsune," he said, and though I heard no malice in his voice, it still drove a cold spear through my stomach. "Why do you care so much for the demonslayer?"

I swallowed. In the battle against Satomi's demons, my true nature had been exposed, revealing my half-yokai blood to everyone. Reika had known, but it had come as a shock to Okame and Daisuke when I'd suddenly appeared with fox ears and a tail. Considering my full-blooded kin were notorious tricksters and troublemakers, and yokai were not looked upon favorably by most humans, they had taken the revelation surprisingly well. Still, I *was* kitsune; while they might accept that I wasn't dangerous, I was still yokai, something they didn't understand. I didn't blame the noble for questioning my motives. I would just have to work extra hard to prove to them that I was still the Yumeko they had always known, foxtail and all.

"Tatsumi saved my life," I told Daisuke. "We both made a promise. You don't understand, you didn't hear Hakaimono…" My voice caught, remembering the demon's taunts, his sadistic amusement as he'd informed me Tatsumi could see and hear everything that was happening. "He's suffering," I whispered. "I can't let Hakaimono win. After I take the scroll to the temple, I'm going after Tatsumi, and the First Oni. None of you have to come," I added, gazing around the fire. "I know saving Tatsumi wasn't ever in the plan. After we get to the temple and the scroll is safe, we can go our separate ways, if that's what you wish."

Across the fire, Okame let out a long sigh and raked a hand

through his hair. "Yeah, that's not going to work," he stated. "If you're going to go chasing merrily after the demonslayer, Yumeko-chan, you should already know I'm coming along. I don't necessarily like the guy, but he's good at chopping things that want to eat us in half." He shrugged and offered a wry grin. "Besides, if he isn't around, who am I going to pester? Taiyo-san just doesn't give the same 'I'm going to kill you' looks."

I smiled, relief warming my insides like tea on a cold night. "Arigatou, Okame-san."

Daisuke's brow furrowed as he gazed at the sword in his lap. "I was unable to protect Kage-san while he was fighting Ya-burama," he said, touching the lacquered sword sheath. "I vowed to keep him alive so I could duel the bearer of Kamigoroshi when Yumeko-san finished her task. I failed, and if Kage Tat-sumi is killed, our duel will be lost." His eyes narrowed, and he looked up at me. "You have my blade, Yumeko-san. I will redeem my past failure, and when the demon has been driven back into the sword, Kage-san will be free to duel me as he promised."

"Baka." Reika snorted, and in her lap, the two canines raised their heads. "Every one of you. You're all talking about saving the demonslayer as if facing down an oni lord is going to be easy. Remember Yaburama? Remember how he nearly killed you all? Hakaimono is far worse. But more important than that..." She glared at me, dark eyes flashing. "Even if you do manage to find Hakaimono without being ripped apart the second he notices you, how do you intend to save your demonslayer, kitsune? Are you a priestess? Can you perform an exorcism? Do you possess spiritual magic strong enough to not only cast Hakaimono out, but to bind him in place long enough to actually perform the exorcism? Because if you don't, if you can't control him, he's going to slaughter you long before you can get close enough to do anything. Have you thought about *any* of this?" Her gaze narrowed darkly. "Do you even know what's involved in exorcising a demon? Or do you think your kitsune tricks and illusions will work on an oni as ancient as Hakaimono?"

I flattened my ears at the verbal assault and the anger radiating from the miko. "Why are you yelling at me, Reika-san?" I asked. "I'm not going after Tatsumi until after I've delivered the scroll to the Steel Feather temple. That's what you wanted, right?"

"Of course it is! It's just…" Reika exhaled sharply. "You cannot simply chase after Hakaimono and hope for the best, kitsune," she said. "Especially when you have no way to deal with him. All you'll be doing is throwing your life away, which does not sit well with those of us who have been trying so hard to protect it!"

"Reika-chan." Master Jiro's voice was soft, a gentle reprimand, and the shrine maiden sank back, though her eyes still flashed with dark fire as she glared at me. With a sigh, the old priest put down his pipe and turned his gaze to mine.

"Yumeko-chan," he began in that same calm, unruffled voice. "You must know that what you are proposing is not only very dangerous, but it has never been done before. Driving out an oni, particularly one like Hakaimono, is not like exorcising a malicious tanuki or kitsune spirit. It is not the same as freeing a person from kitsune-tsuki. I am assuming you know of what I speak."

I nodded. Kitsune-tsuki was fox possession, something that the most evil of my full-blooded relatives, the nogitsune, delighted in. Their spirits could slip into a person and take over their body, controlling them from the inside. What they made their hosts do depended on the nogitsune, but they were mostly depraved, twisted acts for the fox's own pleasure and entertainment. During my training at the Silent Winds temple, I had spent a single evening learning about kitsune-tsuki from Denga, and had alternated between being terrified and quite sick the rest of the night.

Which, I suspected now, had been the intent.

Master Jiro tapped the end of his pipe against a rock, spilling ashes onto the surface. "Hakaimono is not a kitsune spirit, Yumeko-chan," he stated. "He is not a ghost, or a tanuki, or something that can be exorcised with words or pain or the application of one's will. He is an oni, possibly the strongest Jigoku has ever spawned. Whatever became of the demonslayer's soul is locked deep within Hakaimono, and no priest or blood mage in the history of Iwagoto has been able to overcome the First Oni's will with his own. If you decide to face Hakaimono, it is likely that you and everyone around you will die."

I swallowed hard, as a stony weight settled in the pit of my stomach. "I understand, Master Jiro," I told the priest. "And it's all right. You and Reika don't have to come."

"That is not what I am saying, Yumeko-chan." Master Jiro sighed and tucked his pipe back into his obi. "Driving a spirit from a possessed body is taxing and dangerous," he said, "for both the ones performing the exorcism, and the victim himself. To have a chance against an oni of this power, we must be of the same mind. I am willing to accept the risk—"

"Master Jiro—" Reika began, sounding horrified, but the priest held up a hand, silencing her.

"I am willing," the priest went on, "but to attempt an exorcism, we must first bind the demon so it cannot escape and slaughter those performing the ritual. There can be no doubt, no dissention between us." He looked around the fire, at me, Reika, Daisuke and Okame, his expression solemn. "The First Oni is not to be underestimated. If we fail, make no mistake that Hakaimono will kill us all. So we must be in agreement. Is this truly the path we wish to take?"

All eyes were on me now, as if my answer would shape the

decisions of everyone who followed. And for a moment, I hesitated, as the magnitude of the situation settled over me like a heavy winter quilt. Was I doing the right thing? All of my companions were willing to help me, but at what cost? According to Master Jiro, exorcising the demon might not be possible. If we went after Tatsumi, I would be putting the lives of everyone around me in danger. We could all die facing Hakaimono.

But I remembered the night I'd performed for the emperor of Iwagoto, how Tatsumi's eyes had revealed worry and desperation, because he'd been afraid I would be outed as a charlatan and executed. I remembered the way he almost touched me, his hand a breath from my face, when before he had recoiled from any physical contact, as if expecting to be hurt. And I knew I couldn't leave him trapped inside the monster he had become, especially when Hakaimono had gloated that Tatsumi could see and hear everything happening around him and was powerless to stop it.

"I'm sure," I said firmly, ignoring the shrine maiden's frustrated sigh. "Even if it's impossible, even if Hakaimono kills me…I have to try. I'm sorry, Reika-san, I know it's dangerous, but I can't leave him to suffer. If there's the smallest chance to save Tatsumi, I have to take it. But, I swear, I'll get the scroll to the temple first. You don't have to worry about that."

She rubbed her forehead in a resigned, exasperated manner. "As if delivering the scroll is going to be a simple task, as well," she sighed.

"Well, that settles it, then." Okame stood and stretched his long, wiry arms, as if he had grown tired of the debate and had to move. "Tomorrow morning, we take the Dragon scroll to the Steel Feather temple and save the empire from a plague of evil and darkness. And after that, we hunt down Hakaimono to rescue the demonslayer and save the empire from a plague of evil and darkness." He snorted and shook his head. "That's a lot of evil and darkness we have to deal with. I bet life will seem quite boring afterward."

"Unlikely," Reika muttered. "We'll probably all be dead."

Okame ignored that. "I'll take first watch," he announced, leaping gracefully onto an overhanging branch. "Everyone can rest easy, and don't worry—if I see any bandits, they'll be dead before they know what hit them."

"Do not be greedy, Okame-san," Daisuke said, making the ronin pause with his hand on the next branch. "If you see any dishonorable curs attempting to sneak up on us, pray give me a signal so that I may greet them on my feet. And if you see Hakaimono himself, remember that I have a promise to duel Kage-san. I would ask that you not deny me that most glorious battle."

"Oh, don't worry, Taiyo-san. If I spot an oni lord trying to sneak up on us, the whole forest will hear me yell."

He shot us a final grin and disappeared into the branches. As the noble leaned against the log and Reika tucked her hands into her billowy haori sleeves, I cast about for a good place to lie down. I didn't have a blanket or pillow, and even though it was late summer, the night was chilly so close to the Sky Clan mountains. But my red-and-white onmyoji robe was heavy and the material was warm. I curled up in a patch of dry leaves, listened to the hoot of an owl and the rustle of many small creatures around me, and tried not to think too much about Hakaimono. How strong he was. That I had no idea what the five of us could do to defeat an ancient oni lord, much less drive him out of Tatsumi. And how a rather large part of myself was completely, absolutely terrified to face him again.

"Hello, little dreamer."

The unfamiliar voice was deep and lyrical, caressing my ears like a song. Blinking, I raised my head to find myself in a bamboo grove, green-and-yellow fireflies drifting through the stalks like floating stars. The dirt beneath my paws was cool and soft, and a tiny pond shimmered in the moonlight just a few feet away. When I peeked into the water, golden eyes in a furry face stared back, black-tipped ears standing tall against the night.

A low chuckle made the stalks around me vibrate. "I am not in the pond, small one."

I turned, and a shiver raced from the base of my tail all the way up my spine, making the fur along my back stand straight up.

A magnificent fox sat where a pool of moonlight had collected between the bamboo, watching me with eyes like flickering candles. His fur was a brilliant white, thick and flowing, and seemed to glow in the darkness, casting a halo of light all around him. His bushy tail was a plume of silver-white that rippled and swayed as if it had a mind of its own.

"It is not polite to stare at your elders, little cub."

I shook myself, and around me, the grove seemed to ripple, subtly shifting in appearance. Or perhaps it was just a trick of the moonlight. "Who are you?" I asked. "What is this place?"

"Who I am doesn't matter." The white fox rose, his elegant tail waving in the breeze. "I am kin, though a great deal older than you. As for where you are...can you not guess? You are kitsune, it should not be that difficult."

I looked around, noting that the bamboo grove had changed. We now stood in a forest of blossoming sakura trees, their pink petals drifting to the ground like snow. "I'm...dreaming," I guessed, turning back to the white fox. "This is a dream."

"You can call it that." The white fox nodded. "It is certainly closer to the truth than anything else."

I frowned, trying to dredge up a memory long buried in my mind. Of a day in the forest, hiding from the monks, and the sudden feeling of being watched. Of a pair of glowing golden eyes, a bushy white tail, and the sense of longing that came when our gazes met. "I…I've seen you before," I whispered. "Haven't I? A long time ago." He didn't answer, and I cocked my head. "Why are you showing up in my dream now?"

"Your plan to exorcise Hakaimono is going to fail."

The ground beneath my paws seemed to crumble away, leaving me hovering in a void. "What?"

"Hakaimono is too strong," the white fox continued calmly. "In the past, the Kage have attempted to do what you are planning, to force the oni spirit back into Kamigoroshi. It ended in death and disaster. Hakaimono is not a normal demon, and the demonslayer's relationship with the Cursed Blade is unique. Even if you manage to capture and bind the First Oni, the priest and shrine maiden will fail the exorcism, and Hakaimono will kill you all."

I trembled, forcing myself to meet those piercing yellow eyes. *How can you know that?* I wanted to say, but the words froze in my throat when I met a gaze that had seen kingdoms rise and mountains crumble. Those eyes were ancient, all encompassing, and gazing into them was like staring into the face of the moon itself. I looked down at my paws.

"I can't give up," I whispered. "I have to try. I promised Tatsumi that I wouldn't leave him to Hakaimono."

"If you want to save the demonslayer," the white fox said, "relying on humans is not the answer. If you truly wish to free Kage Tatsumi, you must do it yourself. From the inside."

From the inside? Bewildered, I looked up at him. "I don't understand."

"You do," was the cool reply. "You were speaking of it tonight, in fact. Oni are not the only creatures who can possess a human soul."

Understanding dawned, and I flattened my ears in horror. "You mean…kitsune-tsuki?"

"Sacred rituals and exorcism will not work on Hakaimono," the white fox continued, as if oblivious to my dismay. "They are only words. Words of power, yes, but Hakaimono's will is stronger than any human's, and he will not submit. To have a chance of saving the demonslayer, another spirit must confront the oni lord within Kage Tatsumi's body, and drive him out by force."

"But...that would mean I would have to possess Tatsum myself."

"Yes."

Flattening my ears even further, I backed away. "I can't do that," I whispered, as the other kitsune's eyes narrowed to golden slits. "Possessing a human body. It's...evil!"

"Who told you that?" the white fox asked. "The monks at the temple? The ones who tried to limit your kitsune magic, who insisted that you remain mostly human?" His slender muzzle curled. "Kitsune-tsuki is only a tool, little cub. Much like your illusions and foxfire, magic itself cannot be evil. It is how you use your powers that determines the intent."

His words had an eerily truthful ring to them, but they still felt...strange. If it wasn't dangerous, why had kitsune-tsuki been so strictly forbidden by the monks at the Silent Winds temple that I wasn't even allowed to talk about it, lest I become curious? "I've never done kitsune-tsuki," I said. "In fact, I'm not even sure I can. I'm only half fox, after all."

"That does not matter." The white fox shook his head. "Kitsune-tsuki comes naturally to all of us. As I believe your Master Isao once said, it is in your blood. When the time comes, your yokai half will know what to do."

"But... It just feels...wrong."

His magnificent tail gave an irritated twitch. "I see. Then perhaps we should view the problem from a different perspective."

The forest around us disappeared. Petals swirled through the air like they were caught in a typhoon, blinding and suffocating. When I sneezed and looked up again, the soft petals had turned into snowflakes. I stood among the clouds at the top of a mountain, gazing down on the humans' empire, far, far below.

The world was burning. Everywhere I looked, all I could see were flames, consuming the land and spreading everywhere. I could smell ash and smoke, and the stench of burning flesh clogged my throat, making me cough. It seemed I was looking down on the plane of Jigoku itself.

"That is the state of the empire," the white fox said behind me, seated primly on a snow-covered rock, "if you cannot stop Hakaimono."

My legs shook. The howling wind seemed to dig talons of ice beneath my fur and rake them down my back. I stared at the destruction, as the tongues of red-and-orange flames blurred together, filling my vision until all I could see was fire.

"Think on it carefully, little dreamer." The white fox's voice now seemed to come from far away. "Before the flames of war consume the world, consider how choices will affect everyone. You are the only one who can defeat the First Oni and save the demonslayer's soul. I can show you how and give you the best chance of victory when you come face-to-face with Jigoku's strongest oni. But only if you are willing.

"Unfortunately," he went on, as I stood there struggling to breathe, "our moment here is nearly done. You are needed back in the waking world, little dreamer. Just remember my offer, and I will find you again when the time is right. For now, the shadows draw close, and you must..."

Wake up.

I opened my eyes and immediately knew something was wrong. The forest was too quiet; the rustle of small animals was gone, and the insects had fallen silent. I sat up carefully and saw

Daisuke and Master Jiro dozing with their chins on their chests and Reika curled up near the fire with the two dogs.

A man stood at the edge of the firelight, his long shadow spilling over the ground.

At my yelp, Daisuke's eyes snapped open, and Reika jerked upright, tumbling the dogs out of her lap. Seeing the stranger, the dogs exploded into a cacophony of high-pitched snarls and barks, bristling and showing tiny teeth to the intruder, who watched them with cold amusement.

"Hush, now." His voice was high and raspy, and he raised a spindly hand before the rest of us could say anything. "I did not come here for a fight. Do not do anything...hasty."

Movement rippled around us, shadows melting out of the darkness to form a dozen figures clad completely in black, only their eyes showing through the slits in their masks and hoods. Their swords gleamed silver in the moonlight, a dozen razors of death surrounding us in a bristly ring. Shinobi, I realized with a chill. Their uniforms were unmarked; only the stranger in billowing black robes wore the familiar crest that set my heart to pounding: a moon being swallowed by an eclipse. The symbol of the Kage.

The Shadow Clan had come.

3

THE SHADOWS CLOSE IN

Yumeko

*T*he robed man stepped farther into the firelight, and the orange glow washed over him. He was very thin, his face pinched and narrow, and his bones showed through the papery skin of his hands, as if some force had sucked away his vitality. His face was painted white, his lips and eyes outlined in black, as he loomed over us like some terrible specter of death. For a moment, I wondered…were he to suddenly die while his ghost lingered on, would anyone even know?

"Please excuse this intrusion," the man rasped. His stark black gaze, cold and impassive, slid to me, and I shivered. "I hope we have not disturbed anything important."

"Where is Okame-san?" I asked, and the man arched an ink-thin eyebrow. "He would have told us you were coming if he could. What did you do to him?"

The tall man gestured toward a tree. I glanced up and saw

Okame in the branches, bound hand and foot to the tree trunk, a gag stuffed into his mouth. A shinobi crouched on the branch nearby, the ronin's bow across his knees.

"I'm afraid we could not have your friend alerting you," the man said, as Okame struggled against the ropes and glared at him. "We wouldn't have wanted you to get the wrong idea— that we were simple bandits in the night. Worry not, it was a temporary solution."

He raised a hand, and the shinobi who had been crouched on the branch immediately turned and sliced through the ropes tying the ronin to the tree. As Okame started to free himself, growling curses as he yanked out the gag, the shadow warrior melted into the darkness, leaving the ronin's bow hanging from a nearby branch.

The knot in my stomach uncurled, but only a little. There were still a dozen shinobi surrounding us, plus the robed stranger at the edge of the firelight. The scent of magic clung to him, stale but powerful, like some highly poisonous mushroom.

"What is the meaning of this, Kage?" Daisuke asked in a cool voice. The noble hadn't moved from his place against the log, but both hands remained on his sword. "This is Sky Clan territory, and we are mere hours from the Taiyo border. You have no authority here, and no right to set upon us as if we are common bandits. If you cannot produce proper documentation, I must humbly request that you leave."

The tall man gave a ghastly smile. "I'm afraid I cannot do that, Taiyo-san," he said, sounding pleased and offended at the same time. "Allow me to introduce myself. My name is Kage Naganori, and I am here at the behest of the daimyo of the Shadow Clan, Lady Hanshou herself."

Reika straightened. "Naganori?" she echoed.

"Indeed." The man turned his predatory smile on her, making Chu and Ko, now sitting beside her, growl and bare their teeth. "The little girl is perhaps the wisest of the bunch," he mused. "Perhaps the rest of you have heard of me?"

"I haven't," Okame said. The ronin stalked into the circle, bristling like an angry dog, ready to snap at anything that got too close. "I'm still waiting to see why I should be impressed."

"Okame-san." Reika gave the ronin a warning glance. "Kage Naganori is the Shadow Clan's arch-mage, the head majutsushi of the Kage family."

"Yes," agreed Naganori, stark black eyes now glaring at Okame. "But if you desire a show of talent, ronin, I would be happy to indulge your question. Perhaps you would be impressed if I made your shadow dance without you? Or if I commanded the night kami to blind you for the rest of your life?" He raised an open hand. A tiny ball of living blackness hovered over his palm, swirling in the air like ink. "Perhaps a curse of darkness, where all light will forever be snuffed out wherever you go, will be enough to impress?"

"It does not become one of your station to threaten, Naganori-san," came Master Jiro's quiet, calming voice from the other side of the firepit. "Nor did you seek us out to place curses on random ronin. Why have you come?"

Naganori sniffed, dropping his arm and the globe of shadow with it. "As I said before," he continued, "we are on a mission from Lady Hanshou. I apologize for this intrusion, but it was imperative that we reach you before you reached the Taiyo border." The majutsushi turned and fixed me with his piercing stare. "We have come for the onmyoji. Lady Hanshou has requested her presence."

"Me?" My blood chilled. I was still wearing the billowy red-and-white onmyoji robes from the night I had performed in front of the emperor. It had been part of a ploy to get us all into the Imperial palace to search for Master Jiro, as peasant girls, ronin and shrine maidens could not simply stroll through the gates unannounced. I was certainly not an onmyoji, a mystical diviner of the future, but that night, I had found myself in front of the Imperial court and the most powerful man in the country, and if I had failed to convince him that I was what I claimed to be, we would all have been executed.

It had taken a little kitsune magic and more than a little luck, but not only had the emperor believed my performance, he had offered to make me his royal onmyoji. I had respectfully declined his offer, but it seemed the story of the onmyoji girl and the emperor's fortune had spread farther than I'd have liked. I could suddenly feel the scroll beneath my robes, pressed against my ribs, and I twisted my fingers in my lap to keep them from straying toward it. "Why?" I asked Naganori. "What does Lady Hanshou want with me?"

"It is not my place to know. You can ask her that when you get there."

My heart pounded for a whole different reason. Lady Hanshou was the woman who had sent Tatsumi to the Silent Winds temple to fetch the scroll. Had she figured out that I possessed it? No. If she truly knew that I had it, she wouldn't have sent the majutsushi to talk with me; I would have gotten a knife to the throat while I slept.

Still, venturing into the territory of Kage, when their daimyo was actively looking for the scroll, seemed like a very bad idea. "If it's all the same, I'd really rather not."

"I'm afraid I must insist." The majutsushi raised a hand, and the shadow warriors hovering in the darkness took a menacing step forward. Daisuke tensed, and Okame half raised his bow, as the growling from the two dogs rose sharply into the air. "I do not wish this to end in violence," Naganori said, clasping his hands before him. "But we *will* be taking the girl to Lady Hanshou. Those who oppose us will be cut down for interfering in Shadow Clan official business."

"I would be more cautious with your threats, Kage-san," Daisuke said, earning a frown from the majutsushi. "Lady Yumeko is under my protection, and harming a Taiyo is a crime against the Imperial family. I am certain Lady Hanshou does not want to start a war with the Sun Clan."

"Daisuke-san..." I looked at the noble in surprise.

"She's also under the protection of the Hayate shrine," Reika chimed in, and raised her arm, an ofuda strip held between two fingers. Chu and Ko stepped forward, forming a tiny barrier in front of the shrine maiden, their eyes shining gold and green in the darkness. "I'm afraid we cannot let you take her away, even if we must defy the Kage daimyo herself."

"Yep," Okame added, smiling evilly as he fitted an arrow to his bowstring. "Basically, you want Yumeko, you have to go through all of us."

"Insolence!" Naganori bristled, and around us, the shinobi raised their swords. "I will not stand and argue with ronin and commoners." The Shadow mage raised his hands, and the air around him grew darker as even the firelight flinched away from him. "Our Lady sent us for the girl, and if you get in the way of our mission, we will have no choice but to strike you down."

"Wait!" Quickly, I stood up and faced the majutsushi, and the circle of blades turned in my direction. "I'll go," I told him. My stomach twisted with the words, but if the other choice was a bloodbath with shinobi and a Shadow mage, I'd choose the less messy option. Even though meeting Lady Hanshou would probably go very badly for me, I didn't want to drag the rest of them into a fight with Tatsumi's family. There were a lot of shinobi surrounding us, ready to pounce, and those were just the ones we could see. And the majutsushi was an even bigger question mark. I didn't think Naganori's Shadow magic would produce flowers and butterflies, unless they were black butterflies that ate your soul, which didn't seem healthy at all.

And perhaps, when I faced Lady Hanshou, the leader of the Shadow Clan, I would learn more about Tatsumi and how I could save his soul from the monster now possessing it.

Stepping forward, I faced Naganori and raised my chin. "I'll go," I said again. "If Lady Hanshou has called for me, I will go and speak to her."

Tatsumi, I'm sorry. I hope you can hang on until I can find a way out of this.

"Yumeko." Reika stepped forward, causing her dogs to skitter aside. "It is *inadvisable* for you to go right now," she said, raising her brows at me. No doubt referencing the precious secret hidden beneath my onmyoji robes. "If you are going, then I insist upon coming with you."

"You don't have to, Reika-san…" I began. But the shrine maiden gave me a look reminiscent of the expression Denga-san used to make when he caught me in the middle of a prank, so I fell silent.

Daisuke stood slowly and with great dignity, drawing the attention of all. "I, too, must insist upon accompanying Yumeko-san," he said. "I made a vow to protect her, and I will not suffer the dishonor of breaking my word. Where she goes, I will follow. Until the time of my death, or she no longer has need of me."

"And I'm her yojimbo," Okame added. "The bodyguard goes wherever the client does. So I'm coming, too." He smirked at Naganori, as if challenging him to refuse. "No matter what anyone says."

I looked at the majutsushi, expecting him to protest, but Naganori simply smiled. "Such a loyal bunch," he mused, in a voice that was half-mocking, half-suspicious. His gaze slid to me, flat and cold like a snake's. "A shrine maiden, an honorless ronin dog and a Taiyo noble, all willing to accompany you into the unknown. What is the onmyoji hiding to deserve such loyalty, I wonder?"

"Maybe I'm not an onmyoji," I suggested. "Maybe I'm really a kami princess in disguise."

He snorted a laugh. "That I am certain you are not," he said, before letting out a long sigh and waving a hand. Behind him, the shinobi straightened and sheathed their blades in a raspy chorus. "Very well," Naganori said, surprising me. "If your companions are decided, they are welcome to accompany us back to Hakumei castle. Let no one say the Shadow Clan lacks hospitality. You will all be honored guests of the Kage." He smiled again, but it wasn't a very nice smile, more knowing and evilly amused. "I am sure Lady Hanshou will be pleased to have you."

"Back to Kage lands." Reika's brow furrowed. "I hope you brought horses. Shadow Clan territory is on the southern edge of Iwagoto, past Sun and Earth lands. Literally on the other side of the empire. It will take weeks of travel to get there."

"For the uninitiated, yes." The majutsushi's voice was now smug. "Why do you think Lady Hanshou sent me, and not a squad of ashigaru—foot soldiers? Were we to travel by foot, it would certainly take far too long. But we are not traveling by ordinary means." He raised a billowy sleeve, casting a long shadow over the floor. "For those who know the way of shadows, no distance is too far, if one does not get lost in the void along the way."

"Ah," Okame said, giving Daisuke a sideways grin. "There's that cryptic Kage babble I was waiting for."

Naganori's lips thinned, and he dropped his arm. "Come," he ordered, and turned away. "The night is waning, and even on the paths we must take, it is still a long way to Hakumei castle. Lady Hanshou is waiting."

4

A Hidden Talent

Suki

*F*rom the shade of a willow tree in the garden, Suki watched Lord Seigetsu meditate by the pond, hands cupped in his lap and eyes closed, and silently admired his perfect physique. His long silver hair glimmered in the moonlight like liquid metal, his back was straight and his face serene. Even his spotless white robes had settled perfectly around him. A small pale ball perched on the tips of his thumbs, glowing softly and seeming to hover there of its own volition. At his feet, red-and-white carp swirled lazily in the crystal clear water, barely making a ripple on the moonlit surface, and overhead, a sakura tree, fully in bloom, sheltered the figure beneath with brilliant pink blossoms. Not one petal fluttered down to disturb him.

"Isn't Lord Seigetsu amazing?" Taka said next to her. The little yokai sat against the tree trunk, his single huge eye riveted to the figure at the edge of the pond. A wistful smile stretched his fang-filled mouth, and his chin rested in the palms of his clawed hands as he stared at his master. "Everything he does is perfect," the yokai stated. "I wish I had his poise, his grace, his...perfection." He sighed. "Sadly, I will have to be content with 'small' and 'hideous' and 'only slightly useful.' Not that I'm complaining!" he added quickly. "Or that Lord Seigetsu has ever called me those things. I just...have accepted the truth about certain things. Some of us are destined to be lords and leaders." He gestured with a clawed hand to the figure beside the pond. "And some of us are born to be servants, right, Suki-san? Oh, gomen." He clapped both clawed hands over his mouth, perhaps remembering that the girl he spoke to was no longer alive. "I didn't mean to imply... I only meant..."

Suki drifted back to smile at him, shaking her head, and the little yokai relaxed. Taka wasn't malicious, she knew. He didn't have a cruel bone in his body. She did believe he was slightly lonely and didn't get to talk much with Seigetsu-sama, especially when the subject was about their mutual, mysterious benefactor. "Lord Seigetsu saved me," Taka went on, returning his gaze to the figure by the pond. "He took me in when no one wanted me, and has allowed me to travel with him ever since. Sometimes, I wonder why. He doesn't tolerate anyone else following him." He blinked his huge eye. "Well, except you, Suki-san, and you're a ghost, so he can't exactly threaten you."

Suki cocked her head with a frown, but Taka didn't seem to notice. The yokai leaned against the tree with a gaping, toothy yawn. "You worked at the Imperial palace, didn't you, Suki-san?" he asked, startling her with the randomness of the question. His mind worked like that, she'd noticed, bouncing from one thought to the next like an agitated cricket, never settling on one thing for long. She nodded, hoping he would not mention her old mistress, Lady Satomi. Thankfully, the memories of her death, her old life, were becoming scattered and hazy. She had been a maid to the emperor's concubine, but Lady Satomi turned out to be a blood mage, one who practiced the forbidden magic of Jigoku, and she had killed Suki to summon a demon into the realm. Why Satomi had summoned the oni, Suki wasn't sure—something about an ancient scroll—but the moment of her death had been violent and terrifying, and something she didn't care to think about.

She wasn't entirely sure why her soul continued to exist in the mortal realm. According to the ghost tales her mother used to tell her, souls that lingered did so because something tied them to their former lives. Vengeance was the most common reason, a desire to punish those who had wronged them in life. But Lady Satomi was dead, killed by the very man Suki followed now. If it was revenge she desired, wouldn't she have moved on?

Suki shivered. She knew she was dead, and that nothing could really hurt her now, but the thought of drifting aimlessly through the world as a spirit was terrifying. She couldn't go home; her father, Mura Akihito, certainly did not need the ghost of his only child hovering around his shop. Taka was friendly, and Lord Seigetsu *had* slain the horrible Lady Satomi; following them seemed a better idea than aimlessly wandering the land. At least she wasn't lonely anymore.

Near the edge of the pond, Seigetsu rose, as fluid and graceful as sunlight over leaves. His ball vanished into his billowing robes so swiftly that Suki might have imagined it was there at all.

"Taka, come. I have need of you."

"Hai, Seigetsu-sama!" The little yokai practically flung himself across the ground in excitement. Suki hesitated a moment, then drifted after him.

"Yes, Seigetsu-sama." Taka halted at the feet of his master. His single huge eye gazed up at the man in open adoration. "I am here. What do you want me to do?"

The silver-haired man pointed to the ground. "Here, Taka-chan," he ordered. "Sit on the pillow, if you would." Taka instantly did as he asked, plopping himself onto the red cushion and gazing up expectantly. Seigetsu sat down again as well, crossing his legs as he gazed down at the little yokai, the torchlight flickering over his silver hair and Taka's bald skull. "Now, close your eye," he ordered. "And be silent."

The yokai obeyed, closing his eye and pressing his lips together. Seigetsu straightened, and the white globe suddenly appeared in one hand, balanced on three fingers. As Suki watched, fascinated and wary, he reached out with his other hand and touched two elegant fingers to Taka's forehead.

For a moment, nothing happened. The carp swirled lazily in the pond, torchlight flickered and a wind rustled the branches of the sakura trees, though not a single petal showered the motionless figures below the trunk.

Then, Taka's small body spasmed, making Suki jump. It jerked again, violent shudders ripping through the yokai's delicate frame, and his head fell back, fanged mouth gaping. As Suki trembled in sympathy and fear, his eye slid open, completely black and as empty as the void, and she would have gasped in horror if she could.

Seigetsu just smiled. The ball in his hand flickered softly, pulsing with its own inner light, seeming to echo the heartbeat of the yokai in front of it. Seigetsu kept his fingers pressed to Taka's forehead, his face serene even as Taka twitched and shuddered beneath him.

"Tell me of the fox girl," he murmured. "Where is she going? Is she in danger? What will happen to her in Kage lands?"

Taka's mouth opened, a thin, scratchy voice emerging that was so unlike the happy, cheerful yokai that Suki could only stare. "The path is treacherous," he whispered. "Hands reach out, pull them into the mist. Shadows in the walls, under the floor. Whispers stalk the streets, glowing eyes burn the darkness. A living dead woman has a request."

Suki couldn't make sense of any of this, but the silver-haired man nodded. "Nothing terrible so far," he muttered. "And what of Hakaimono?"

Taka shuddered violently, his small hands twitching at his sides. "Death," he rasped, and to Suki's ears, even the harsh whisper sounded horrified. "Death, chaos, destruction. Mountains of bodies. Valleys of fire. Claws and teeth, ripping flesh. Walking bones, blood, pain, fear!"

"Predictable." Seigetsu sighed, though Taka's voice was growing ever more frantic, continuing the litany of horrifying descriptions as if the events were happening in front of him. A thin stream of blood ran from his nose down his chin and spattered onto his hands. "Enough," Seigetsu ordered, pulling his arm back. His deep voice rippled through the air and caused the ground to shiver. "Taka, stop."

The little yokai slumped, his head falling to his chest, as the torrent of words came to a halt. Suki was still trembling, but Seigetsu simply tucked his ball into his robes and brushed out his sleeves, before turning his attention to the yokai again. On the pillow, Taka groaned, stirred and slowly opened his eye, blinking up at the man overhead.

Seigetsu smiled. "Back with us, Taka-chan?" he asked.

The yokai's forehead wrinkled. "Did I...have another vision, master?"

"You did." Seigetsu nodded and tossed him a silk handkerchief. "Quite a terrible one, it seemed. I had to pull you back before you caused real damage to yourself."

Taka caught the handkerchief, frowning, before pressing the cloth to his nose with a plaintive sigh. "I wish I could remember."

"No, Taka-chan," Seigetsu reassured him. "You wouldn't understand the visions even if you could. Put it from your mind. I have already discerned what I needed to know."

"Hai, Seigetsu-sama." The little yokai perked a bit, giving his master a toothy smile. "As long as I can be useful to you, that is all I wish for."

Watching them, Suki was suddenly filled with apprehension. Could Taka-chan see the future, or at least a part of it? And if he could, was Lord Seigetsu using the little yokai for his own ends? The thought made her uncomfortable. Seigetsu-sama was obviously very powerful and could control some kind of magic, just like Lady Satomi. What did he want with the kitsune girl and the demon?

Taking a step back, Seigetsu waved a hand, as if he were ripping something from the air. With a soundless billow, the tranquil pond and gardens surrounding them frayed apart, scattering to the wind like tendrils of colored smoke, revealing a dark, murky forest. The torches disappeared, taking their light with them, and even the tiny glimmers of fireflies vanished like they had never been. In the sudden gloom, Seigetsu's eyes glowed like candlelight as he gazed into the shadows. "Everything is going according to plan," he mused, as Taka scrambled to his feet, the pillow beneath him dissolving into colored mist. "The game is starting to come together, but we mustn't let either of them go too far down the wrong path. It seems the fox girl will be occupied for a time, so perhaps we should keep an eye on Hakaimono, make certain his part in the story is not lost. Come, Taka." He turned away, a brilliant figure in white, silver hair and robes glowing in the shadows. "It is a long journey to Mizu lands, even if we ride the winds. We should get started."

"Can Suki-san come with us, master?"

Seigetsu looked back. His gaze rose to Suki, still hovering at the edge of the trees, and a corner of his mouth curled up.

"I had assumed as much." His voice was like a cool mountain spring, deep and powerful, and Suki felt a shiver all the way from her toes to the top of her head. "She is, of course, important to the story, as well."

5

THE MOST DANGEROUS QUARRY

HAKAIMONO

*T*he Kage had found me already.

"Hakaimono." One of the men stepped forward, glaring at me from where I stood at the top of the temple steps. A majutsushi of the Shadow Clan, clad in black with his face painted white, though I could see the sweat on his forehead, smell the fear radiating from him. His men, a dozen Kage samurai in all, clustered behind him, hands on their sword hilts. I felt a smirk twist one side of my mouth. After all this time, after all our battles, the Shadow Clan had learned nothing. One majutsushi? A dozen samurai? The last time I faced the Kage, I had carved my way through a hundred of their best warriors before they ever put a scratch on me.

I grinned at the dozen humans standing among the stones and overgrown weeds of the courtyard. This was a small temple, shoved away in the foothills below the Tokan Kiba Mountains on the edge of Sky Clan territory. The temple itself was ancient and falling apart; the roofs were full of holes and at least an inch of dust had coated the creaky wood floors. A statue of the humans' revered Jade Prophet sat unhappily alone in the main hall, topped with a few white streaks from the sparrow nest atop her head. I had found this hilarious, and had chuckled at the foot of the statue for a good minute before moving on. From what I could discern, either through disease or attack or because the monks had simply grown old and died, as humans were wont to do, the temple had been abandoned long ago, which was the reason I'd chosen to stop here. I'd been stuck in Kamigoroshi for a long time; the world had changed since I'd seen it last, and I needed time to reacclimate before I started laying waste to cities and soaking the land in blood. Slaughtering a temple full of pious bald men would have been fun, but such massacres had a way of drawing attention, something I was trying to avoid right now.

Unfortunately, it seemed my arrival had already been noticed. Barely three days out, and the Kage were already hounding my footsteps. Persistent bastards. I'd known I would see them sooner or later. They had a whole team of shinobi and majutsushi who monitored the bearer of Kamigoroshi—which at this time had been Kage Tatsumi—making sure the demonslayer stayed sane and in control. As soon as I had escaped, one of them probably scampered home to let the Shadow Clan know I was free again. This little visit wasn't unexpected, but it did mean the Kage were already moving against me.

Then again, a bloodbath was just what I needed to relieve some stress and pent-up frustration. That it was the Kage, the line I had vowed to wipe from existence for their insolence of keeping me trapped in Kamigoroshi, made it that much better.

"Congratulations, Kage," I said, smiling from the top of the steps to the main hall. "You found me." My grin grew wider, showing fangs, and several of them flinched. They had likely never seen an oni before, even one who was human-sized. This was, technically, Kage Tatsumi's body I was using, though now that I was free, some of my demonic features had seeped through. I wasn't as large as my true self, but the horns, claws and ink-black skin were a dead giveaway. I still looked like an oni, which could make even the bravest humans blanch in fear. "Now, what do you propose we do about it?"

Deep inside, a flicker of a subconscious not my own stirred. Kage Tatsumi, the original owner of this body, desperately trying to drive me out, to stop what he knew was about to happen. I felt his presence struggling within, like a fish tangled in a net, and laughed at his feeble attempts to halt the inevitable.

Keep watching, demonslayer. Watch, as I shred your clansmen into little bloody strips and scatter them to the wind, and know there is absolutely nothing you can do to stop me. But keep trying. Struggle and fight as long as you can. I love the way your despair feels. There was a pulse of rage, directed at me, and I snickered. *Just remember, the last time I was trapped in Kamigoroshi for nearly four hundred years. You've been in there three days. It already feels like forever, doesn't it?*

The majutsushi stepped forward. "Hakaimono," he said again, and I had to give him credit; his voice didn't shake, though the cuffs of his sleeves were trembling, very slightly. "By order of Lady Hanshou, you will release the demonslayer, Kage Tatsumi, and return to Kamigoroshi."

I laughed at him. The sound echoed off the courtyard walls and rose into the night, and the samurai clustered together, raising their swords. "Oh, this is new," I mocked, still chuckling as I gazed down at them. "Release the demonslayer, you say? Let him go and willingly return to Kamigoroshi for another few centuries?" I tilted my head in a mock quizzical manner. "And out of curiosity, what do I get if I agree to these demands? Another four hundred years of boredom, despair and slowly going insane?" I shook my head. "Not a great deal, Kage. Your negotiation skills could use some work."

All pretense of civility faded as the majutsushi pointed a thin finger up the steps, his features twisting with hate and fear. "Do not mock me, demon," he spat. "Release Kage Tatsumi and return to the sword, or face the wrath of the entire Shadow Clan."

"The wrath of the entire Shadow Clan, you say?" I echoed. "Human, your clan declared war on me when you sealed me away in this wretched sword a thousand years ago." I raised Kamigoroshi by the sheath, lifting it before me, and the majutsushi fell back from the stairs as if I had brandished a severed head. "I remember Kage Hirotaka," I continued. "I remember his wish to the Dragon—to keep me trapped in this pathetic realm. To suffer endless torment. Well, he got his wish." I drew Kamigoroshi, letting the centuries of hate and rage rise to the surface. "Weak, pathetic, short-lived mortals. You speak of declaring war on me, but you're too late. I've already declared war on the entire Shadow Clan, and I will not rest until every member is purged from existence, until every man, woman and child lies dead in their own blood, and the name Kage is erased from the course of history, forever."

"Monster." The majutsushi's face had gone pale, horror shining from his eyes as he stared up at me. "We waste our time, and our words, with this one. There is no saving the demonslayer."

He thrust a hand toward the top of the steps. A ripple of power surged through the air, and black chains erupted from the stones and coiled around me. They slithered over my arms and chest, cold and constricting, binding my limbs and anchoring me in place. The majutsushi gave a smug smile and turned to the samurai.

"Kill it," he ordered, pointing up the stairs. "Destroy the abomination. Take its head and return the demon to Kamigoroshi. For the honor of the Kage!"

The warriors gave a unified battle cry and charged up the steps, swords raised high. I narrowed my eyes and grasped the sword hilt as the first warriors reached the top of the stairs, even as a tiny voice inside shouted a futile warning to the approaching samurai. *He* knew that the majutsushi's Shadow magic would be useless against one who thrived in the dark.

Keep watching, Tatsumi. Your clan is about to get a bit smaller.

With a snarl, I tore myself free of the chains, and the first two samurai exploded in a haze of blood as Kamigoroshi ripped through their middles and sliced them in two. The halves fell away, expressions frozen in shock, as I beheaded another samurai and stepped forward to meet the rest. They gave shouts of fear and surprise and slashed at me, far too slow. Blood arced through the air and spattered upon the stones, as Kamigoroshi flashed like a whirlwind and the samurai fell away in pieces.

Lowering the sword, I breathed in the bloody mist and looked at the one remaining human, the majutsushi who had called for my head. He stood at the bottom of the steps, eyes wide as he stared at the limbs and bodies of his men, now scattered around me and dripping down the staircase.

"Well." I gazed around in mock curiosity, then turned to the human. "Looks like it's just you and me now."

"Demon," the man whispered as I started down the steps. He thrust out a hand, sending a trio of black darts at my face. I swatted them away, and they vanished into wispy tendrils of smoke. Wide-eyed, the majutsushi backed across the courtyard and I followed, easily keeping pace with his frantic, stumbling steps.

"The Kage will not fall to you!" He waved an arm, and a pair of black, hound-shaped shadows emerged from the darkness and flew at me. I split one on Kamigoroshi and crushed the throat of the second in my fist as it lunged, and the shadow beasts writhed away into nothing.

The man continued to scrabble backward. "You cannot win,"

he insisted, panting. Sweat poured down his face, dripping to the stones, as he raised both hands in a warding gesture. "No matter what you do, your time in this realm is limited."

A net of darkness flew from his fingers, arcing toward me. I ripped it from the air and tossed it aside, as the human finally hit the wall of the courtyard. Gasping, able to flee no more, he pressed back into the stones, trembling, as I stopped a pace away. His face paint was streaked with sweat, the black markings blotted and smudged, and the whites of his eyes showed as he glared up at me. Defiant in the face of death.

"My clan will avenge me," he whispered. "Lady Hanshou knows you have been released, Hakaimono. As long as you walk this realm, the Shadow Clan will not rest. We will purge you from the land, even if we must sacrifice a thousand warriors, shinobi and majutsushi to do it!"

"Lady Hanshou?" I chuckled. "Lady Hanshou set you up as bait, human. She never expected you to win." The human's brow furrowed, and I snorted. "Hanshou knows me... We go way back, your daimyo and I. She is well aware that a dozen warriors and one majutsushi isn't enough to even challenge me. You and your men were a sacrifice to either slow me down, or to test how strong I've become. There's probably a shinobi close by right now, watching us. That's fine. It can take this message back."

I raised Kamigoroshi and brought it down, striking the top of the man's skull and splitting him all the way to the groin. The majutsushi collapsed to his knees, the pieces of his upper body falling to either side, before he crumpled wetly to the ground.

"The Shadow Clan will die," I said to the air, to the hidden shinobi no doubt listening to my every word, and to the trapped soul inside me, raging at his own helplessness. "For every day I was imprisoned in the sword, I will kill one member of the Kage—man, woman and child—until there is no one left. I will raze their castles and cities to the ground, and soak the earth in

54

so much blood nothing will grow there again. And when I reach Lady Hanshou, we will see if an immortal can continue to exist after I've torn the withered heart from its chest and eaten it in front of her." Sheathing Kamigoroshi, I turned and began walking across the yard toward the temple steps. "Take that back to your daimyo," I told the empty air. "Tell her she doesn't have to send anyone after me. I'll see her soon enough."

From the corner of my eye, I caught a flicker of movement on the temple roof, a featureless shadow sliding through the darkness. As it disappeared into the night, I smirked and shook my head. Exactly as I'd suspected. The Shadow Clan, for all their secrets and mystery and claims of dancing with the darkness, was fairly predictable.

Although they had found me sooner than I'd thought they would. Even if this group was just a test, an experiment conducted by their ruthless daimyo to see what I could do, more would follow. After centuries of living with the Kage, learning their ways and their secrets with every demonslayer that took up Kamigoroshi, I knew more about the Shadow Clan than anyone save their immortal daimyo.

The problem was, the Shadow Clan knew *me*, too. A dozen samurai I could deal with. A few hundred became problematic, especially if they sent majutsushi with them. Their newest head mage, a skinny human named Kage Naganori, was an arrogant, insufferable prick but, from what I had seen, powerful. And much as I hated to admit it, Kage Tatsumi was only mortal. His body, though I gave it a bit of the toughness and rapid healing my kind was famous for, was not as durable as an oni's. All it would take was a sword across his throat, an arrow through his heart, and I would be stuck in Kamigoroshi for another few centuries.

Deep within, I felt a flicker of a longing that wasn't mine, the soul of Kage Tatsumi desperately hoping someone would kill him.

So eager to die, Tatsumi? Don't worry, you'll get your wish soon enough. But this time, I'm not going back into that cursed sword. This time, when you die, I'll finally be free.

I raised my head and gazed at the moon climbing slowly over the roof of the temple. The Shadow Clan would die. For trapping me in Kamigoroshi, for arrogantly assuming they could use my power to further their own designs, I would wreak my vengeance upon the entire Kage line. They would experience horror and suffering like they had never known, and in the end, when she was surrounded by the slaughtered remains of her clan, I would personally twist Lady Hanshou's head from her withered neck and be done with the Kage forever. But there was one thing I had to accomplish, first.

I turned and walked across the courtyard, pebbles crunching under my feet, toward the rotten gate that marked the entrance of the temple. I'd have to hurry. It was a long journey to my destination, leaving Sky Clan territory, through Taiyo lands again, and across the treacherous Dragon Spine Mountains that split Iwagoto in half. Traveling through the Dragon Spine was hazardous even in good weather; all sorts of monsters and yokai roamed those lonely peaks, and though the thought of running into a tsuchigumo or mountain hag didn't bother me, it was said the kami of the Dragon Spine Mountains were fickle and sometimes demanded sacrifices. Humans traveling those narrow paths were known to vanish into thin air. I didn't relish the idea of hiking through yokai- and kami-infested mountains, but it would make things difficult for those who pursued me, as well. If any of the Shadow Clan followed me into those jagged, unforgiving peaks, I'd make sure they didn't come out again.

Beneath the gate, where once-fierce stone guardians now lay cracked and broken on the ground, I paused and gazed back at the slaughter in the courtyard. Kage samurai were scattered in pieces up and down the temple steps, and the split body of the majutsushi lay slumped in the dirt. *So easy.* I breathed in the scent of death. *Humans die so quickly. Like snuffing out a candle.*

Tatsumi stirred, his anger brushing against my mind, and I smiled. *Don't worry, demonslayer. You won't have to watch the complete destruction of the Kage. Once I'm free, I'll release you from your misery and send your soul on to Jigoku. This is just the beginning.*

6

THE PATH OF SHADOWS

Yumeko

*W*e followed Naganori to a small, seemingly forgotten cemetery deep in the forest.

"Well, this just gets better and better," Okame muttered, as we passed beneath a crumbling stone torii gate at the edge of the graveyard. Headstones jutted out of the forest floor, so worn and covered in moss that it was impossible to read them. Scattered among the graves, eroded by time, I spotted a few statues of Jinkei, the Kami of Mercy and the Lost. An ancient, somber quiet hung in the air, the feel of a place forgotten by the world, unchanged for centuries. I hoped that all the souls buried here had been able to move on.

"Leave it to the Shadow Clan to make things as uncomfortable as possible," Okame continued, pitching his voice low, so as not to disturb the dead, I supposed. "And here I was hoping for a kago to travel across the empire in comfort and luxury."

Kago were covered litters carried on foot to their destination. I had seen one in the Imperial city, the gold-trimmed lacquered box making its way down a crowded street, an escort of mounted samurai beside it. Sunlight had flashed off the polished wood and golden trim, but all I could think was how tired and hot the four bearers at the corners looked. "But the Kage lands are on the southern edge of the empire, Okame-san," I whispered. "Wouldn't that take a dreadfully long time?"

"Weeks," Daisuke said quietly. His face was serene, but his gaze flicked back and forth, as if he expected ghosts or hungry dead to leap out at us. "Perhaps longer. I was expecting horses, an escort of sorts to the Kage lands. So, why did they bring us here? Why a graveyard in the middle of the night?"

"Because we of the Shadow Clan know darkness better than most," Naganori answered, turning to smile at our discomfort. He stopped in the center of the narrow trail and raised both arms as if to embrace the scene around us. "For the other clans, the night is to be feared, a thing to shut out and keep at bay with light and warmth. But the darkness has always favored the Kage, and we have learned that traveling through the shadows is far quicker than traveling in the light."

"Cryptic," Okame remarked. "So how are we actually getting there?"

The majutsushi dropped his arms and glared. "It is a complicated ritual that would take too much time to explain to the uninitiated," he said. "I will simplify it for you. We will be performing a technique called Kage no michi, the Path of Shadows. In its simplest form, we leave this realm by entering the shadows and emerge on the other side of the country in much the same way. We will arrive at our destination much faster than if we had walked, ridden, or were carried in a luxurious kago over land."

"Then the stories are true," Daisuke said. "Of Kage shinobi passing through solid walls and getting into spaces that should be impossible to breach, because they can melt into the shadows and emerge on the other side."

The majutsushi sniffed. "Those are rumors, Taiyo-san, but like many rumors, they hold a kernel of truth. The reality of shadow walking is much grimmer. You see, in certain areas and on certain days, the curtain between the mortal realm and the realm of the dead is very thin. Graveyards, obviously—" he gestured at our surroundings "—temples and battlefields are places where the dead and the living sometimes mingle. The Tama Matsuri, held every year on the longest night, is a time when our ancestors can cross the veil and step into the mortal realm to visit their living relatives, until the sun rises and they fade back into the world of the dead.

"The Path of Shadows," Naganori went on as I shivered, "bridges the space between Ningen-kai, the realm of the living, and Meido, the realm of the dead. On certain nights, the curtain parts, but we of the Kage have learned to open it at will, just wide enough to slip between. Using this technique, we can travel hundreds of miles in a few hours, though there must be a Shadow mage present to open the curtain once again. The ritual itself is exhausting, and it will take us a few jumps to get to Kage lands, but we will arrive at Hakumei castle in days, rather than weeks."

"Amazing," Daisuke mused, but he sounded concerned as he said it. "I was not aware that the Kage could move so quickly and fluidly across clan borders. It is truly astonishing, if they can move an entire army from one territory to another without being seen."

The majutsushi gave a raspy chuckle. "I know what you are thinking, Taiyo-san. But you needn't worry. The Kage do not use this technique often, and never in large numbers. Attempting to walk the Path with the five of you will be a risk in itself."

"Why?" I wondered.

Naganori gave me a disdainful look. "Because, girl," he began, "walking the Path of Shadows is dangerous, as you will see in but a moment. Meido will be but a breath away, and the spirits of the dead are very jealous of the living. You might hear a familiar voice, calling out to you. You might see a beloved relative, waving to you in the distance. But beware, the call of the dead will lead you to your doom. If you take a wrong step, if you stray from the path, you will stumble into their world. And once you are in the realm of the dead, it will not let you go."

The ice in my stomach spread to my whole body, as Naganori fixed us with a piercing glare. "So heed this warning," he said in a firm voice, "and ignore the pleas of the dead, no matter who you see, no matter what they tell you. It will be hard. Every few years, we lose a majutsushi or a shinobi to the Path. They know the dangers, they are aware of Meido's call, and yet, they step into the shadows and never come out again." His black eyes narrowed, and he pointed a twig-thin finger in our direction. "It will happen to you, if you are not vigilant and don't do exactly as I say. And even then..." He sniffed again and shook his head in resignation, as if the assessment had already been made. "The call of Meido is strong, stronger for the weak willed and undisciplined." His gaze flickered to Okame and me before shifting away. "I expect to lose at least one of you before we reach the Kage lands."

He turned away, and Okame made a rude face to his back before bending close to us. "I don't like this person," he murmured, earning a snort of approval from Chu. "Did you see the way he looked at us, Yumeko-chan? I think we should all arrive at the Kage lands safe and sound, just to spite him."

Master Jiro, nearly forgotten behind us, stepped forward looking grim. "If we are truly going to walk alongside the realm of the dead, we must be careful," he told us. "The majutsushi spoke true—the spirits of the dead are very jealous of the living. Watch out for each other. Do not let each other step off the path. I fear what we might see or hear while we are in the Shadow world."

"And that mage certainly isn't going to help," Reika muttered, glaring after Naganori. "It wouldn't surprise me if one of us accidentally 'tripped' and stumbled off the path while following him."

I cocked my head at her. "Does that mean the Path will be very bumpy, or that Naganori-san will not help us if we do?"

She sighed. "No, Yumeko. Just…be careful around the majutsushi. I don't trust him at all."

The head majutsushi of the Shadow Clan started chanting. Standing at the base of a large stone marker, Naganori held two fingers to his lips and began a low, droning murmur that raised the hairs on the back of my neck. As we watched, the shadow cast by the narrow gravestone seemed to darken, sucking in light until it resembled a strip of the void itself, lying in the flickering torchlight.

Naganori turned to us, gesturing with a pale white hand. "Quickly now," he urged. "The way will not remain open for long. Follow me, close your ears to the voices and do not allow your eyes to stray from the path. With any luck, we will be on the other side of Taiyo lands before the night is through."

He stepped onto the narrow strip of shadow cast by the headstone and seemed to vanish as the darkness swallowed him up.

Okame uttered a soft curse.

Nearly invisible in the shadows, the Kage shinobi watched us, as if fearing we would attempt to flee now that Naganori was gone. I wouldn't say the thought hadn't crossed my mind, but I doubted all five of us would get away even if we tried to escape.

I took a deep breath, driving away the fear clinging to my heart. *This is for Tatsumi,* I reminded myself. *I won't abandon him to Hakaimono. Somehow, I'll find a way to bring him back.*

Setting my jaw, I walked into the narrow strip of shadow, and the world around me faded into darkness.

I shivered and rubbed my arms as I gazed around. It was cold, but not the brisk air of a forest in winter, or the icy chill of a mountain lake. This was a dead, stiff cold, like being buried in the dark, silent earth with the worms, beetles and bones. Around me, there was no breeze, no sound or scent, or any hint of life. It was as if I stood in the center of a narrow, endless hallway, a strip of utter blackness, a path of void winding away into the dark. To my right, I could see the cemetery and Okame, Reika, Daisuke, Master Jiro and the two dogs, but their figures were blurred and faded at the edges. Okame was saying something as he pointed in my direction, but his voice sounded muffled, as if he were underwater, and his gaze passed right through me.

To my left was a solid wall of mist and fog. Ragged tendrils drifted over the path, coiling around my ankles like icy fingers. That cold, dead chill seemed to emanate from the fog and whatever lay beyond. As I watched, a section of mist parted, and for just a moment, I could see a face, pale and hollow-eyed, staring at me from the void.

Panic rose, making my heart flutter around my chest like a frightened bird. My pulse became a muffled thump in my ears and seemed to echo for miles, the only spot of life in the darkness.

"Careful." A voice resounded behind me, and the tall, skeletal form of Naganori seemed to materialize like a wraith. His lips were pressed into a grim line as he stared down at me. "Don't step off the path, or the spirits of the dead will be on you in a heartbeat. They can hear it, you know." He pointed at my chest. "Your fear will give you away. If you cannot control your emotions, they will hound you the entire way." He sighed. "Though I suppose that might be too much to ask, even of one who is an onmyoji. Perhaps a spell would be advantageous. I could always put you to sleep for the journey."

My skin crawled. "No," I told the majutsushi, and took a careful step back. "That won't be necessary."

His lip curled. "Very well. But my orders are to bring you to Lady Hanshou, alive and unharmed. I care nothing for the others, and neither does anyone else in the Kage." He loomed over me and lowered his voice. "Their well-being is dependent upon your cooperation. Make certain you endeavor to arrive safely in the Kage lands, or your friends could suffer the consequences."

I bristled, even as another flutter of fear went through my stomach. For a moment, the urge to use fox magic in not a nice way was very tempting. I had visions of ghostly hands reaching for him through the mist, or his robes suddenly bursting into heatless blue flames. But Naganori might recognize another form of magic; he might even discover I was part kitsune, and I did not want this man knowing my true nature. Nor did I want to put the others in danger, as the majutsushi had just made a very inelegant threat.

"Well, isn't this a charming place." Relief bloomed through me as Okame's familiar, acidic voice echoed through the oppressive silence. The ronin stepped close, his bolstering presence at my back, and I could imagine his challenging smirk aimed over my head at Naganori. "Is this where you spend most of your time, mage? Now I see where your delightful personality comes from."

The majutsushi's chin lifted. "Insolent dog."

"That's what everyone tells me." Okame grinned, as with ripples of color and warmth, the rest of our company emerged through the gloom. Reika whispered a soft prayer to the kami, as Chu and Ko growled and peered out from behind her legs, both dogs staring wide-eyed into the mist.

Naganori drew back, almost seeming to float as he drifted

away. "Follow me," he said. "Once again, I will offer this warning—keep to the path, do not stray from the trail and do not stare too long into the mist. If you do, you might find yourself separated from the path and your companions. The mist has a way of tricking your mind into thinking that you are all alone with the spirits of those who have died. If you cannot ignore them and focus on the path, it will become a reality. Now, hurry. The dead have already taken notice, and I am curious to see how many of you make it through to the other side."

"Stay together, everyone," Reika murmured, and we started down the path, following the majutsushi through the corridor of mist and darkness.

"Yumeko-chan," whispered a voice.

My heart skipped a beat. It was impossible to tell how much time we had spent on the path, hours or days, but it was starting to feel like we had always been here. Like the flat, dead grayness was all I knew, and it was hard to remember anything else.

I turned my head, very slightly, to see a figure standing at the edge of the path just ahead, smiling at me. His face was lined and weathered, he wore wooden geta clogs and a familiar straw hat on his bald head. As my throat closed and my heart gave a violent surge of recognition, the figure chuckled softly and held up a withered hand.

"Hello, Yumeko-chan," said Master Isao.

My steps faltered. Tears sprang to my eyes, but I wrenched my gaze away and hurried on. None of the others seemed to have noticed the monk at the edge of the path; when I looked at them, their own eyes were glassy and distant, their faces pale. Reika's jaw was tightly clenched, and Okame's eyes were suspiciously bright. I spared a glance behind me and saw Master Jiro marching rigidly on, his gaze fixed straight ahead. Daisuke trailed behind, his expression schooled into a blank mask. No one appeared to see or hear the figures in the mist. They seemed caught up in their own thoughts, or perhaps they were seeing faces that they recognized in the fog, as well.

"Fox girl," said a voice, and now Denga-san appeared, walking alongside me down the path. "Running away again?" he said, in his familiar exasperated voice. "Where do you think you're going, exactly? You know running away from your responsibilities won't make anything disappear."

"Go away," I whispered, pinning my ears to my skull. "I'm not listening. I don't want to see you, so leave me alone." Neither Reika nor Daisuke glanced at me, though the ghost of Denga-san snorted.

"That's just like you." He sighed, keeping pace with me as I walked. "Carefree and immoral, just like a yokai. Like a soulless fox." His voice hardened, becoming bitter and angry. "I knew it was a mistake to take you in. From the moment you arrived at the temple, I never wanted you there. And neither did Master Isao."

My breath caught, and tears stung the corners of my eyes. I tried to shut out his words, but they echoed in my soul, cutting and painful. "That's not true," I whispered.

"No?" He sneered, a cutting, cruel expression I had seen him make only once or twice, but it was still painfully familiar. "Master Isao despised you, fox girl. He knew what a yokai could do, even a half-yokai. He taught you discipline and control because he feared the mischief and misery you would bring if you were allowed to run free. Because he knew a yokai could never be trusted."

"No," I protested, and turned to face not Denga but Master Isao, standing a few feet away in the mist. His eyes were hidden in the shadows of his wide-brimmed hat, and he was no longer smiling.

"Fox girl," the familiar figure whispered, shaking his head.

His sad, accusing voice cut into me like the lash of a whip. Raising his chin, he met my gaze, impassive black eyes stabbing me through the heart. "Disappointing," he whispered in a voice of stone. "I had hoped for so much more. We raised you, taught you our ways, gave you everything, and you repaid us by leaving us to die."

It was as if he'd punched me. Denga's scorn and anger I could handle; his words were cruel, but not unexpected. But to hear those words from Master Isao... It was as if he had seen my greatest, most secret fear and had dragged it out to brandish in my face. I sank to my knees, as a hole opened in my stomach and my eyes blurred with tears. Denga appeared behind the head monk, as Jin and Nitoru stepped to his other side. Their reproachful gazes bored into me, heavy and accusing, though none were as terrible as Master Isao's pitiless glare. "I'm sorry," I whispered, as images of that night swirled through my head. Flames and demons and blood, and the lifeless bodies of the monks sprawled on the temple floor. Tears crept down my cheeks and stained my robe where they fell. "I wanted to save you..."

"You left us to die," Master Isao repeated. "We gave our lives to protect the scroll, as the demons tore us apart, and you did nothing. You deserve to be here, with us. Why should we have died, and you lived? Come, Yumeko-chan." He raised a hand, palm out, beckoning me forward. "Come with us," he urged, "and all is forgiven. You can start over. It can be as it was before—no fear, no pain. I know you must be lonely, a half-kitsune all alone in the world. Forget your troubles, and your duty. Forget the scroll, Yumeko-chan. You belong here, with us."

Forget the scroll?

Blinking, I looked up. Master Isao stood there, hand outstretched, a gentle, forgiving smile on his face. Denga, Jin and Nitoru stood behind him, but now their expressions were eager, hopeful.

Almost hungry.

A chill went through me, and I drew back, watching the monk's smile turn to a puzzled frown. "Master Isao…" I began, feeling as if my mind was mired in cobwebs and just starting to clear "…would never tell me to forget the scroll. His duty was to protect it, and he died to ensure it would not fall into the wrong hands. He and the others gave their lives to make sure I could escape, because their responsibility to the scroll was everything."

Master Isao scowled. "I died so that you could live," he hissed, taking a step forward and making me shrink back. His face changed. Now he looked like a pinched old woman, lips pulled back from her yellow teeth as she glared at me. "Ungrateful child," the woman spat. "You belong here with me. I gave up everything for you—my love, my health, my happiness. And you ran away to live your life with that insignificant merchant nobody. Disgraceful! And after everything I did for you."

I blinked at her, shaking my head. The woman continued to rail at me, her voice a droning buzz in my ears. Behind her, I could see other forms in the mist, but the figures I had thought were Denga, Nitoru and Jin were now people I didn't recognize. I had the dawning realization that the woman hadn't been saying anything different, and she had not changed her image to look like Master Isao. But somehow, I had seen and heard exactly what I had feared, the secret guilt deep inside coming to the surface.

I blew out a breath in disbelief. *They weren't real*, I told myself. *Master Isao, Denga, Nitoru, Jin—they weren't here at all. I just saw what I expected…what I've always feared.*

The woman continued to rail at me, accusing me of being a horrible daughter and forgetting her, of not visiting her grave as often as I should. She certainly didn't recognize me as a stranger, and a kitsune at that; it seemed the dead saw only what they wanted, as well.

They're not malicious, I realized. *Just unhappy. Maybe it gets very lonely in Meido while they're waiting to move on. They see the spirits of the living as people they knew, and it reminds them of when they were alive.* I wrinkled my nose. *Though you'd think Naganori could have mentioned that.*

Carefully, I rose and bowed to the distraught spirits, sobbing at me beyond the wall of mist. "Safe travels to you," I murmured. "May you find what it is you are looking for, so you can move on." Then, I took a deep breath and turned my back on the spirits of the dead. They howled and cried, begging me not to go, but I stepped away, and their pleading, sobbing, cursing voices faded into background noise. Closing my ears to the clamor, I shook myself and looked around for the others.

I was alone on the dark path. I couldn't see Reika, Okame, Daisuke, Master Jiro...even Naganori had disappeared. My heart gave a violent lurch as fear and panic spiked, and I gazed wildly around for any hint of the familiar.

"Yasuo?"

The whisper drifted out of the darkness, causing relief to flood my veins. I took a few steps toward the voice and saw a familiar figure materialize in the distance.

Okame-san. I nearly called out to him but stopped myself, seeing the faces of the dead watching me through the mist. Not wanting to attract their attention, I began striding toward Okame, moving as quickly as I could without making any noise.

"Okame," I called in a loud whisper, but the ronin ignored me. He stood at the edge of the path, gazing at something in the fog. A few feet away in the mist, I suddenly saw the pale figure of an old man, who pointed an accusing finger at the ronin at the edge of the mist and snarled something I couldn't hear. Okame's shoulders were hunched, his head bowed, and a quiet sob came to me over the whispers of the dead.

"I'm sorry, Yasuo." Okame's voice was choked. "Forgive me."

No, Okame. Don't listen! Fear stabbed at me again, and I began to jog toward him, but it was like running toward something in a dream. No matter how I tried, I couldn't seem to close the distance, though I could clearly hear his voice, shaking and tormented, drifting to me through the shadows.

"It was a mistake, brother. I didn't...I didn't realize what would happen. I know I can't ever make it up to you, but..." A pause, as the spirit on the other side said something, and Okame's voice came again, resigned and heavy with guilt. "Yasuo, if joining you is the only way to put your spirit to rest..."

"Okame, no!" I put on a burst of speed, but I was still too far away to reach him. "That's not your brother, Okame!" I cried in desperation. "Your brother isn't talking to you, it's just an angry, lonely spirit who wants your soul! Don't let it trick you into joining it in Meido!"

The spirits of the dead hissed at me, crowding the edge of the path, their voices rising into the air. Okame finally turned his head, his bleak, hollow gaze meeting mine through the darkness.

"Yumeko-chan," he murmured, as the spirit in front of him gnashed its teeth. "I'm sorry," the ronin said, making me frown in confusion. His eyes were bleak, but he still gave me that wry, crooked grin of defiance. "It looks like I can't go with you to the Steel Feather temple," he said. "My brother, Yasuo, has demanded that I stay with him. I have to put his spirit to rest."

"No, Okame-san. Listen to me." I hurried forward, pleading. "That's not your brother. It's not Yasuo. Would your brother demand that you stay here, in the realm of the dead? Really look at him, and tell me what you see."

The ronin shook his head. "It doesn't matter, Yumeko-chan," he said dully. "The truth is I betrayed my brother, and he died because of it. Yasuo is right." Okame faced the spirit again and took a step forward. One more step would take him off the path into the mist. "I should be here, with my brother and all

70

the men I betrayed. It was my duty, and I abandoned it. I abandoned him." He took a short breath, as if steeling himself, and raised his chin. "I'm the one who should be here, not them."

I cried out and reached for him, knowing it was too late, that he was too far away. Ghostly hands reached through the fog and latched on to the front of his jacket. He did nothing to stop them, and they dragged him off the path, into the mist beyond.

"Okame-san!"

There was a blur of white and blue, and Daisuke appeared, lunging forward and grabbing Okame by the collar just as the ronin was pulled into the fog. Planting his feet on the path, the noble yanked backward, bracing himself, eliciting angry cries from the mist beyond. I hurried forward, heart pounding, as Daisuke pulled the ronin halfway out of the fog. Pale hands and arms clutched at Okame, trying to drag him into the land of the dead.

"Spirits," I heard Daisuke grit out as I reached them and grabbed Okame by the sleeve, joining in the deadly tug-of-war. "I know you are angry, that you grieve, that you are jealous of those who still live. I apologize, but I cannot allow you to take this one just yet. Forgive me, but he is needed here!"

He gave a mighty yank, and the hands clinging to Okame tore loose. The three of us tumbled backward and collapsed in a heap on the path. Gasping, I struggled upright and looked at the ronin, who lay on the ground, unmoving. His eyes were open and glazed, and he was as white as parchment.

"Okame-san!" I shook the ronin's arm; it flopped beneath my fingers, making my stomach twist. "Okame-san, wake up. Can you hear me?"

No answer from Okame. He was breathing—his chest rose and fell in shallow breaths—but his expression was slack and he stared at nothing. Blinking rapidly, I looked at the noble. "He's not responding. Daisuke-san, what can we do?"

The noble sat up, wincing, and peered down at the still form of the ronin between us. "My master used to say, sometimes a whisper is all that is required to calm a storm, but when words fail, sometimes you need the thunder."

I frowned. "What?"

He turned to the ronin and gave a quick bow. "My apologies," he muttered, and struck him hard across the face. The crack of his palm against the ronin's cheek echoed loudly in the darkness.

"Ow!" Okame jerked upright, put a hand to his face and glared at the noble. Realizing where he was, he slumped back with a groan. "Kuso. Is this Meido? Are we dead?"

Daisuke smiled. His long white hair had fallen into his eyes, and his robes, already torn, had suffered even more abuse. He looked quite disheveled sitting there on the ground, but still somehow managed to uphold his dignity. "Not yet, I'm afraid," he murmured. "Though you did try your best a few seconds ago."

"Damn." Okame scrubbed a hand across his face. "Bastard ghosts. I really thought I saw Yasuo for a few seconds there." He eyed Daisuke, a puzzled frown crossing his face. "Why did you save me, Taiyo?" he demanded in a rough voice. "It's not like I'm a samurai. I'm a filthy ronin dog with no honor left to salvage. There's no shame in letting a worthless ronin get yanked into the realm of the dead by his own stupidity."

A furrow creased the noble's brow. "You must think very little of me, Okame-san," Daisuke said, sounding more hurt than offended. "We have bled together, fought together, battled monsters, demons and oni side by side. I've sworn to protect Yumeko-san, but there is an unspoken oath that I follow. For as long as I am able, my blade will defend those I cherish—my family, my friends, my fellow warriors." He looked the ronin in the eye. "No matter who they are or what they have done in the past."

Silence fell over the path. The two men seemed to have forgotten I was there. Daisuke continued to hold Okame's gaze, unwavering but not accusing or challenging, and it was the ronin who blinked and looked away first.

"Kuso," he muttered again. "This place is twisting my mind and making everyone do weird things. My bastard brother has been dead nearly five years, and we never got along. But when I saw him tonight..." He shook his head. "I felt that me dying was the only way for him to be at peace, the only way to make things right." He snorted a bitter laugh, shaking his head. "It sounds ridiculous now."

"It's not," I told him, and both men looked at me in surprise, as if just remembering I was there. "I felt something similar," I went on. "I saw...Master Isao and the others...calling to me. Telling me I belonged here, with them."

Daisuke nodded grimly. "I had a similar experience," he admitted, letting Okame pull him to his feet. "This place..." He gazed into the fog, where ghostly faces swirled through the mist, their voices sobbing and angry. "It's not the spirits that call to us," he murmured. "It is our own failures and regrets we see. The things we wish we could have changed, the memories that haunt us."

"That is the lure of Meido," said a wheezy voice, as Master Jiro came toward us on the path. Ko walked at his side, her white fur glowing softly against the constant gloom. "Only a few souls are pure enough to go to Tengoku, the Celestial Heavens, when they die," he continued, his staff thumping softly as he came forward. "Those who have lived their lives without regret, who have suffered no uncertainty or hesitation. On the other end of the spectrum are the souls who are corrupt, who indulge in travesty with no regret. They will find that Jigoku awaits them at the end of their lives. For the rest of them, the souls who are neither unblemished enough for heaven nor wicked enough for

Jigoku, they find themselves in Meido, awaiting the time they can be reborn. That is why it is also known as the Realm of Waiting, of reflection. It is a place to ponder your past life, to remember every regret, every failure, all the things you would have done differently. According to the teachings, only when you have come to terms with your past, when you have relinquished your previous life, can you be reborn." His gaze slid to the ghostly figures in the fog, and his brow crinkled with what looked to be pity. "Though for some, it can take centuries, if they cannot let go of their former lives."

"Daisuke-san! Yumeko-chan!"

With Chu bounding along beside her, Reika hurried forward and slid past Master Jiro to peer down at us. "Are you all right?" she panted, looking equally worried and exasperated. "One moment you're right behind me, the next you're nowhere to be found. I blinked, and you were gone. What happened?"

I stared at her in amazement. "Didn't you hear the spirits calling to you, Reika-san?" I asked. "Was there no one from your past, urging you to join them in Meido?"

She made a face. "Of course there was. My spiteful mother, who never wanted me to become a shrine maiden. She was planning to marry me off to a wealthy samurai so she could reap the benefits of my marriage. I had to listen to her call me terrible things all my life—why would it be any different, now that she's dead?"

That made Okame laugh. "I wish I had seen it," he chuckled, as Reika frowned at him. "I wish I had been there to see the spirits of the dead get scolded by our shrine maiden."

"Well, I see you are all taking this as seriously as I expected." Naganori materialized a few yards down the path, watching us with a rather sour look on his face. "And you have all survived the temptations of the path, how...inspiring."

I scowled at him. "You could have warned us what would happen."

One corner of his mouth curled. "Did I not?" he asked in a voice of infuriating calm. "Well, no matter. Come." He turned his back on our glares and raised a withered hand. "The night is waning, and we have wasted enough time chasing shadows. We will be on the path for a while, yet. This time, if you are inclined to wander off, do it quickly so the rest of us don't have to search for you. I would like to make the border of Earth lands before dawn."

Okame glared as the majutsushi strode away. "I suppose it wouldn't be very honorable to accidentally shove him off the path," he muttered as we started following Naganori once more.

Reika snorted. "I would advise against it," she said, "but only because I'm fairly sure it's already been tried."

"I guess you're right." Okame sighed. "A guy like that is probably pretty paranoid. Too bad. Hey, Taiyo-san." He glanced at Daisuke, walking calmly beside him. "I'm curious. So, Yumeko saw her old master, I saw my brother, and Reika was harassed by her mother's ghost. Who did you see, out there in the mist? With all your victories as Oni no Mikoto, I bet the list is pretty long. Was it a rival of the court? The spirit of a warrior Oni no Mikoto defeated on the bridge?"

"No." Daisuke's eyes grew haunted. "I saw the ghost of a maidservant who once served Lady Satomi."

I drew in a sharp breath. When we had followed Lady Satomi to an abandoned castle in search of Master Jiro, there had been a hitodama—a human soul—that had guided Reika and me through the castle to reach the priest. And then, after the battle with Yaburama and the amanjaku, I remembered finding Daisuke, wounded, bleeding and nearly unconscious from his fight with Satomi's demons. The ghost of a girl was beside him, pale and luminescent in the shadows. She had smiled at the noble, and though it had seemed that he couldn't sense her, she had softly brushed his cheek, before reverting to a ball of light drifting away over the wall. I'd wondered who she was, and if she had found the peace to move on.

"A servant girl?" Okame sounded shocked. "You're telling me that, in all your duels and years at court, the death you regret the most is a *servant girl*?"

"The court is court," Daisuke said. "The game is vicious, but the players all understand the rules. Reputations are destroyed. Favor is earned, honor and livelihoods are lost. That is how it is, how it has always been. The same is true for the duels I fought as Oni no Mikoto. The challenge, and the rules surrounding it, was always clear. There was always the option to decline with no loss of face or honor. The warriors who died on those bridges fought Oni no Mikoto with bravery and conviction—to regret killing them would bring dishonor to their memories.

"But that little servant girl…" Daisuke hesitated, gazing away into the mist. "Mura Suki, the daughter of the city's celebrated flute maker. She was not a noble or a warrior, but she knew beauty when she saw it. We met only once at the Imperial palace, and I have not seen her since." He sighed, looking pained. "She was Lady Satomi's maid. I was fairly certain that the woman killed her, but now there can be no doubt. Suki appeared to me here, angry that I did not save her from Satomi-san. That she died because I did nothing."

"That wasn't Suki, Daisuke-san," I said. I was about to add that the real Suki was a ghost hanging around Satomi's castle, but stopped myself. I didn't know if Suki's soul still lingered in the mortal world or had moved on. And it seemed cruel to tell Daisuke that Suki was a ghost, after all, especially since, in all his dealings with the court and duels as Oni no Mikoto, the death of a servant girl was the one that had hit him the hardest.

"I know, Yumeko-san," Daisuke replied, smiling at me.

"When we were at Satomi's castle and I was nearly delirious from my wounds...I saw something. For just a moment...I thought I heard her voice." His brow furrowed. "I hope I'm wrong. I hope that Suki's soul has moved on, that it does not linger in the mortal realm. But if that truly was her that night, it was not the same spirit as the sobbing, hateful thing who called to me a few minutes ago. It looked like her, and it was as if the spirit spoke directly to my guilt, but that was not the girl I met. Suki might have been a servant, but she had the soul of a poet. She would not linger here for long."

"Huh," Okame said. He had a strange look on his face, like he wanted to be scornful but couldn't quite bring himself to do it. "You're a terrible noble, Taiyo-san," he said at last. "Talking to servants? Treating them like they're real people? How have you survived the court all these years without committing seppuku?"

Daisuke smiled. "I am a lover of art and beauty, Okame-san," he said with a shrug. "I have learned that it can be found anywhere, regardless of station or circumstance. True beauty is rare, hidden and often overlooked by others. And it can appear at the strangest times. I try to appreciate it when I see it."

"I think that's a lovely sentiment, Daisuke-san," I said. "It sounds like something Master Isao would say."

"Yes," Okame agreed in a flat tone of voice. "Except that it tells me absolutely nothing."

"You three." Reika turned to glare back at us. At her feet, even Chu looked annoyed. "This is the path through the realm of the dead, not a spring festival," she scolded in a whisper. "Your constant babbling is attracting attention. Can you attempt to be silent until we are clear of angry spirits who want to drag us into Meido?"

"Sorry, Reika-san," I whispered, as the other two made appeasement noises, though Okame couldn't resist making a face at Reika the second her back was turned. The spirits of the dead continued to wail and cry, their sobbing accusations grating in my ears, but their voices seemed distant now, unimportant. Between Okame, Reika and Daisuke, I knew what was real. The dead couldn't tempt me anymore; I had too many important things to accomplish.

Just wait, Tatsumi. I'm still coming. I'll see you again soon, I swear.

We continued down the path in silence.

7

THE CURSED TOMB

HAKAIMONO

*I*t was taking the better part of a week to get over the mountains, and I was not in a good mood.

I had already killed two tsuchigumo, giant mountain spiders who would ambush unwary travelers as they passed by their cave, and now my steps were being hounded by an okuri inu, a monstrous dog yokai black as pitch and larger than a wolf. It lurked behind me on the trail, keeping just out of reach, waiting for me to stumble and fall so it could tear out my throat. If I hadn't been in a hurry, I would've stopped to deal with the nuisance yokai, but the snow-laced wind was getting worse and okuri inu had the uncanny ability to know when you were faking a fall, so they could not be lured in by deception. So I continued walking, my clawed feet crunching over snow and rock, ice pellets stinging my exposed skin.

Tatsumi, I noticed, had withdrawn deep into himself; I'd

hardly felt his presence at all the past few days. Just a flicker of emotion every now and then, reminding me he was still there, still inside. Honestly, it was a little annoying; I'd been expecting the demonslayer to suffer through months, or even years, of despair and helpless rage watching me slaughter his clan before finally giving up. Still, his withdrawal wasn't entirely unexpected. Tatsumi had been trained as a weapon, to feel no emotion or attachments. He was very good at suppressing his feelings.

The wind finally died down, and a faint orange glow crept over the shrouded peaks, driving away the stars and the annoying okuri inu at my back. As the sun rose into the sky, staining the snow pink, I reached the summit of the Dragon Spine Mountains at last and gazed over the land stretched out before me.

Far, far below, the valley was still cloaked in darkness, tiny clusters of light indicating the villages, towns and cities of the Mizu family, the Water Clan. Three huge lakes slept in the shadow of the mountains, with dozens of rivers, streams and smaller ponds laced through the fertile valleys and farmland. The enormous River of Gold spilled from between the Dragon Spine Mountains, snaked through Mizu territory, and continued west toward the coast, where it would eventually empty into Dragon Mouth Bay in Seiryu City, capital of the Water Clan.

Thankfully, I wasn't going that far. As I stared down into the valley, my gaze fell on my next destination. The waters of Seijun Muzumi, the largest of the three great lakes and the biggest in Iwagoto, were dark in the shadow of the mountains. Scatterings of light circled the huge body of water, farms and villages clustered along the edge, with plains and entire forests in between settlements. The lake was so massive, it was a two-day ride from one side of the bank to the other.

With the sun at my back, I started down the mountain. Though my goal was in sight, the path was steep and winding, and it took me the rest of the day to descend the Dragon Spine.

Evening was falling when I finally reached the dense forest and rolling hills at the foot of the mountains, glad to be out of the snow and into the normal muggy temperatures of late summer. Oni could not freeze to death, but we were creatures of fire and heat, and our blood could burn human flesh where it touched. I was not fond of the cold.

The moon was rising when I at last reached the edge of the trees and found myself near a dusty road that meandered toward a lonely little village on the edge of the lake. Thatched huts were built on stilts near the water, and a series of wooden docks lined the lake's edge, with dozens of boats bobbing on the surface. From here, Lake Seijun looked like a small sea, stretching so far into the darkness that you couldn't glimpse the other side.

A breeze rippled through the air, smelling of fish and lake water, and the faint sound of humming reached my ears over the lapping of the waves. Scanning the lake edge, I spotted a lone fishing boat near the shore, the light of a lantern bobbing on a pole at the back. A wiry human hummed as he dragged a net filled with wriggling fish over the side, and I smiled.

Silently stepping out of the trees, I began walking toward the lake.

Preoccupied with his fish and his humming, the old human didn't even see me until I had leaped quietly into his boat. "Pardon me," I said as he dropped his catch to the deck and whirled. His scowl changed to an expression of terror and he opened his mouth to scream, but I clamped a talon over his withered neck and squeezed, crushing the sound from it. "But I need to borrow your boat."

The human thrashed. His hands flew to my wrist and clawed frantically, as his mouth gaped, trying to make a sound. I raised him off the floor, waiting until his struggles ceased and he dangled limply from my grasp, nearly senseless, before loosening my hold just enough for him to suck in a ragged breath.

"Now," I said pleasantly. "As I said before, I need to borrow your boat. And you, my good human, are going to take me to the island in the middle of the lake. You know the one, I'm sure." He gasped, and I tightened my hold again, squeezing the breath from his windpipe before he could protest. "You can either take me to the island," I went on, "or I can dump your guts in the lake for the fishes, your choice. What's it to be?"

The human was as white as parchment, now, his lips tinged with blue and his eyes wide. He scrabbled at the claws around his throat, then pointed frantically to the oars, lying in the bottom of the vessel. I bared my fangs in a grin. "A wise choice."

I dropped him to the floor of the boat, where he landed in a crumpled heap, whimpering like a dog. I waited to see if he would try to hurl himself over the side. If he did, he would find himself with his stomach ripped open and his entrails floating in the water. After struggling to his knees, he threw out his hands and pressed his forehead to the wood, ignoring the water and the fish that flopped and gasped over the planks.

"Please," he whispered. "Please, great lord, I beg you, have mercy! It is forbidden to set foot on the island. The curse…"

"I am well aware of the curse, mortal," I interrupted. "It does not concern me." I stepped forward so that my shadow fell over his cringing form. "If you cannot take me there, then I have no further need of you. Say hello to the fishes when you meet them at the bottom of the lake."

"No!" The human flinched. Straightening, he picked up the oars lying on the floor of the boat and climbed slowly onto the seat. "Kami, forgive me," he whispered. Without looking at me, he pointed the nose of the vessel northwest and started paddling into the darkness.

Several minutes passed, and the shoreline disappeared, followed by the lights. Soon, there was only open water, the moonlight reflecting off the waves and the stars overhead. As the fisherman worked the oars, I kept my gaze on the horizon where the water met the sky.

After a few hours of steady rowing, I finally spotted something new on the surface of the water. A jagged wall of fog rolled toward us, thick and opaque, reaching out like misty talons. Seeing a tendril coiling around the boat, the human let out a whimper, and the rhythm of the oars faltered.

"Merciful Jinkei." The human trembled, eyes wide as he stared at mist creeping into the boat. "The island is already coming for us. The curse will swallow us whole. I...I cannot..."

I smiled at him, showing fangs. "Would you care to take your chances in the water, then?"

"Kami, no!" His face drained of its remaining color, and he grabbed at the oars and started pulling with renewed vigor. "Heichimon protect me," he whispered, making me curl a lip in disgust. Heichimon was the god of strength and courage. He despised demons, the undead and anything "tainted," and was often depicted as a proud human warrior crushing an oni underfoot. His name was a curse among demons, and were it not for the fact that the human was taking me to the island, I might've ripped the tongue out of his head for speaking it.

The boat surged forward, and we pressed on, into the wall of white.

The fog closed around us like the jaws of a great beast, muffling all sound. I could barely see the front of the vessel as it sliced through the water. Near my feet, the human was whispering a continuous chant of protection, calling on Heichimon, Jinkei and the rest of the kami to protect him.

"You're wasting your breath," I told the quivering mortal, and he flinched. "Can't you feel the taint of Jigoku, infusing this place? There are no kami around to hear you. All you're doing is attracting the attention of whatever is lingering on the island."

The human ignored me, continuing to mutter prayers under

his breath. I contemplated breaking his leg; that would certainly give him something else to think about, but he would probably scream and alert everything lurking in the fog, which would get me no closer to my destination.

There was an angry stirring in my mind, reminding me that Tatsumi was still there, still watching everything that was happening. He'd been so quiet that I'd almost forgotten about him.

I smirked. *You know where we're going, don't you, Tatsumi? Well, keep watching, because there's nothing you can do about it. And I have a feeling the island isn't going to let us float right up without some kind of trouble. Not with the amount of corruption in the—*

A pallid white hand latched on to the edge of the boat, rocking it sideways, as something hauled itself out of the lake. It had been human once, but now it was nothing but shrunken flesh and gleaming bones draped in rags. A naked skull, dripping with algae, turned hollow eyes upon the fisherman, who screamed in terror as a bony claw reached out and hooked his collar. Before I could do anything, it yanked him over the edge. The man's shriek was cut off as he hit the water and vanished beneath the surface.

I raised an eyebrow. "Well, I did try to warn you," I said, as the bubbles from where the human had vanished into the water faded away. Voices echoed out of the mist, garbled mutterings and faint whispers; impossible to pinpoint which direction they were coming from. With a sigh, I drew Kamigoroshi, bathing the fog around me in flickering purple light. With the taint of evil infusing the area, it wasn't surprising that the bodies of humans that had died in the lake would rise to hunt the living, but I found slaughtering walking corpses rather pointless. It was no fun killing something that was already dead.

The unmanned boat drifted lazily through the water, but I was not about to sit down and take the oars. Especially when, through the fog, I could hear quiet splashing getting steadily closer.

Another pale arm exploded from the water, and a drowned specter hauled itself up the side. It stank of death and rotten fish, and its clothes were nearly rotted away. A tortured moan escaped the naked skull as bony fingers reached for me, seeking to pull me down to the depths. I smirked at its impudence.

Kamigoroshi flashed, cutting through the spindly neck, sending the skull toppling back into the water. The headless body jerked and fell away to join it, and the water around me started to boil.

More corpses lunged out of the water, rocking the boat as they grabbed the sides and crawled over the edge. I swung Kamigoroshi, severing heads, cutting off arms, splitting corpses in half as they staggered toward me. The boat was small, and there was a seemingly endless amount of bodies rising from the depths, filling the air with tortured moans and the stink of rot. Kamigoroshi flashed, and body parts flew everywhere, splashing into the lake or landing in the bottom of the boat.

"Come on," I growled, slicing through a pair of corpses at once. "This is too easy. At least try to make it somewhat of a challenge."

As if in answer, more bodies climbed into the boat. As I raised my sword to deal with the swarm in front of me, a cold, clammy hand grabbed my ankle from behind. I turned and kicked the corpse in the face, felt its jaw snap under my boot, before the specter slid beneath the lake's surface again.

Something landed on my back, and sharp nails dug into my flesh and soaked my haori jacket with icy lake water. The reek of rotten fish made my eyes burn as the creature hissed in my ear and bent to bite my neck. I reached back, grabbed the rank, slimy skull and crushed it between my fingers, then yanked the corpse off my back and hurled it at the specters still in the boat, sending them all tumbling back into the lake.

Silence fell, the only sound the quiet lapping of water against the sides of the vessel. I waited, Kamigoroshi pulsing in my hand, but no more bodies crawled out of the lake, seeking to drag me down to the bottom. After kicking away the body parts scattered on the floor of the boat, I picked up the oars and continued rowing.

A few minutes later, there was a loud scraping sound as the boat bottom hit a rocky shore, impossible to see in the mist. I stepped into knee-high water and dragged the boat onto land, before straightening and gazing at my surroundings.

Fog still drifted around me, though not as thick as out on the lake, and through the gloom I could make out a few jagged trees, barren of foliage, jutting crookedly toward the sky. The ground was a mix of rock and mud; there was no grass, and only a few withered bushes huddled beneath the tree trunks. The taint of Jigoku was strong here, courtesy of what was buried on this island. The very land was saturated with infection, tendrils of corruption seeping into everything. This was indeed a cursed place, and it made me a little homesick. Jigoku wasn't *all* fire and brimstone. Beyond the demon cities, away from the screaming, the torture and the constant fighting, there were places like this, barren, misty and ominous, with only a few tormented souls hanging from the trees.

I wondered if the realm had changed in the time I'd been gone. If the demons, oni and O-Hakumon, the ruler of Jigoku, remembered me.

With a snort, I shook myself, dissolving the sudden thoughts of my home realm and the memories of several thousand years. I had spent too much time in the heads of these weak-willed humans. Reminiscing about the past was futile. If O-Hakumon and the rest of my kin had forgotten me during the long millennia that I'd been trapped in the mortal realm, then I would remind them who I was and why I had been Jigoku's greatest demon.

Resolved, I began walking farther inland.

The island wasn't large, and even in the fog, I soon found what I'd been looking for. It was impossible to miss, really. A few undead roamed around the base of a jagged, rocky hill, moaning and shambling aimlessly through the trees. After cutting them down, I circled the obsidian outcropping until I reached the narrow mouth of a cave, really just a split in the rock wall, nearly hidden by brush and hanging vines. The dirt around the cave entrance was littered with bones, and one of the withered bushes twisted around as I passed, raking at me with thorny branches. I ignored the corrupted plant and ducked into the narrow crevice, turning sideways to squeeze into the cave.

My eyes adjusted instantly to the pitch-blackness, for which I was glad. I might've had to share this weak mortal body with Tatsumi, but the demonslayer was a creature of shadow, more comfortable in the darkness than the light, and his physical form reflected that. The cave was small, barely bigger than a hole in the rocks, but on the far wall, a flight of stone steps led down into blackness.

When I reached the top step, a voice whispered out of the darkness, creeping up the stairs. *"Intruder. You walk on cursed ground. Leave this place, or suffer the wrath of Jigoku."*

I grinned. "The wrath of Jigoku?" I called back, my voice echoing down the steps. "I am Hakaimono, first general to O-Hakumon and leader of the oni lords. So trust me when I say I know more about the wrath of Jigoku than you ever will."

"Hakaimono?" the voice whispered back. *"Impossible. Hakaimono has been trapped within the Cursed Blade for the past four centuries. You cannot be the First Oni. I say again, leave this place, or I will send your soul to Jigoku to be torn apart by the true demons."*

With a sigh, I started down the stairs. The voice hissed at

me, warning me again to turn back, that I had no business here. I ignored it, following the steps until they ended at a short hall, beyond which lay a massive cavern. Flickering orange light spilled through the opening as I stepped into the chamber, gazing around for the source.

At first, the room appeared empty. Four torches flickered around a small shrine in the center of the floor. Candles had been lit on the altar, guttering purple flames that seemed to suck in the darkness instead of drive it back. The stone pedestal in the center was empty, as if something had been placed there once, but had either been stolen or lost. As I approached the shrine, the torches sputtered and went out, plunging the room into darkness lit only by the dim violet candlelight.

"You were warned not to come here."

I turned, just as three figures melted out of the shadows. They were women, or more accurately, they were female. Their skin was mottled red, blue and green, a different color for each hag. Their white hair was long and tangled, and sharp yellow nails, each over a foot long, curled from their bony fingers. Small horns poked out of matted hair, and their eyes glowed yellow in the darkness as they surrounded me, thin lips pulled back to reveal jagged fangs.

I smiled. "Well, well, look who it is. Good evening, ladies. I didn't know you three were still lurking around the mortal realm."

"H-Hakaimono?" The green hag's face went white with shock. "It *is* you." Backing away, she dropped to her face on the stones, as the other two did the same. "Forgive us, lord, we didn't recognize your voice. The last we heard, you were trapped in Kamigoroshi."

"I escaped only recently. Although, I will say, I was not expecting to run into the Yama sisters here." Ignoring the prone forms of the hag trio, I gazed at the shrine, still lit by ghostly purple flames, and sighed. "Am I to assume, since the three of you are here, that this tomb no longer holds the Master of Demons?"

The hag sisters glanced at each other. "No, Hakaimono-sama," said the red ogress, rising from the ground. "Like you, Lord Genno escaped his prison very recently, no more than six months past. We were among those who helped raise his soul from Jigoku and bind it to a mortal form so that it may walk this realm once more." She blinked yellow eyes at me. "Is...is that why you came, Hakaimono-sama? Because you heard the Master of Demons has been freed, and you wish to join his army?"

"Actually, I was just hoping we could chat," I said. "I was planning to summon his shade and talk to him in Jigoku, but if he's already out and walking the mortal realm again, I guess that saves me the trouble of having to find a suitable sacrifice." Frowning, I glanced at the red hag, whose name had escaped me again—Uragiri or Usamono—I could never remember which sister was which. "So, you say Genno escaped from Jigoku six months ago?"

"Yes, Hakaimono-sama."

"So, why hasn't he already gathered a new army and declared war on the humans? I seem to remember him swearing vengeance upon the entire realm before he died."

The sisters exchanged glances again. "Well, you see, Hakaimono-sama..." the blue hag began. "Lord Genno's return has been kept a secret these past six months. That's why we are here..." She gestured to her sisters. "So that if anyone came looking for Lord Genno's tomb to confirm he is gone, we could silence them before they revealed he has escaped Jigoku. But, because his body was completely destroyed, we had only his skull to draw him back from the pit."

"Ah," I said. Summoning a soul from Jigoku and permanently binding it to the mortal realm again was a complex and dangerous blood magic ritual, one that had to be performed just right to avoid catastrophe. You had to have a physical body to bind the soul to, and it was best if it was the soul's original remains, or all kinds of mishaps could occur. "Something went wrong, I'm guessing," I told the hags. They winced.

"We were able to bring back Genno's soul," said the blue hag. "But..."

"His physical form never materialized," her green sister finished. "The wretched mortals must've purified his body before destroying it. Lord Genno is here, in the mortal realm, but his soul is bound to his skull." She paused. "Only his skull."

My laughter bounced off the cavern walls, as the hag sisters stared at me. "So, you're telling me that the most powerful human blood mage that ever walked the mortal realm, who commanded hordes of yokai, demons and undead, and single-handedly led a demonic revolution that almost brought the entire land to its knees...is now an angry floating head?"

The red hag moaned. "Not even that. His spirit can materialize, and he can walk the realm as a ghost, but he cannot travel far from his skull. He wields a fraction of the power he once had, because he has no physical body."

"I see." Understanding dawned, and I grunted. The timing was too convenient to be chance. "So Genno was hoping to take advantage of the Dragon scroll," I guessed. "That's why he was brought back in this era, when the night of the Wish is almost upon us."

"Yes, Lord Hakaimono," confirmed the green hag. "His original intent was to use the Wish to make himself emperor and kill all the daimyos. However, with the...unforeseen accident, he needs the scroll for another purpose."

"So he can wish himself whole again, back to his full power."

"And resume his plan to conquer Iwagoto," the blue hag finished, nodding. "Because of his condition, he doesn't have the army he once commanded, but he is steadily growing his numbers. Blood mages, yokai and demons join his cause daily. Just the knowledge that the Master of Demons has returned to the mortal realm is enough to draw disciples from every corner of the land."

"Have you come to join us then, Hakaimono-sama?" the red hag asked. "Like you did in the Master's first rebellion? With you on our side, the humans will fall before us like rice before a sickle."

I smirked. I hadn't so much joined Genno's last little uprising as much as I'd taken advantage of the chaos to spread my own bit of bedlam and slaughter. Four hundred years ago, with an army of undead and demons wreaking havoc through the land, a samurai by the name of Kage Saburo tried to prevent the destruction of the Shadow Clan castle, by taking a powerful, cursed sword from its sealed tomb beneath the keep. He was foolish, desperate and thought Kamigoroshi would grant him the power to kill the monsters invading his home.

He was right, but not in the way he expected. Back then, I was admittedly a little insane from the long, long centuries of imprisonment in the sword. Kage Saburo was the first human I'd possessed, but instead of plotting and planning my next move, that first taste of freedom in centuries had caused something inside me to snap, and I'd gone on a killing spree that the Kage still talk about today in hushed voices. In the madness of the final battle, Kage Saburo was slain not long before Genno was struck down and killed by the clan champions, so many believed that the Master of Demons had struck a bargain with the First Oni, and that we were working together to overthrow the empire.

That wasn't entirely true. I'd never made a deal with Genno; it just happened that our goals were similar. I would happily kill humans alongside the blood mage's army, as long as he understood I was not his to command and never would be.

Hakaimono bowed to no mortal, not even the self-proclaimed Master of Demons.

The first time Genno marched on the empire, I had been a frenzied, raging creature of vengeance, existing only to kill as many as I could before being sent back into the sword. Now, I'd had a bit of time to think, to plan, to ponder what I'd do if opportunity presented itself again. This time, I was ready.

"Actually, I *was* hoping to join," I told the hags, whose yellow eyes lit up like candle flames. "I heard rumors of Genno's return and came here to see if they were true. Too bad he's not here. I would've liked to talk to him, see what his strategy is for overthrowing the empire. But if you say he's just a ghost…"

"We'll take you to him, Hakaimono-sama," the blue hag exclaimed. "I'm sure the Master would be pleased to speak with you. We were simply guarding his tomb in case any mortal came wandering in, but rumors of the island keep most away, and the undead take care of the rest. We are not needed here."

"Yes," the red sister agreed. "Now that Hakaimono-sama is free again, this opportunity is too important to ignore. Will you come with us to speak to Master Genno, Hakaimono-sama? It's a lengthy trip, but we can leave straightaway."

I masked a smile. "Where is Genno hiding these days?"

"The cursed castle of Onikage, in the Forest of a Thousand Eyes."

I snorted. The Forest of a Thousand Eyes was the dark, tangled stretch of wilderness that lay between Water and Fire Clan territory. Its original name was the Angetsu Mori, though only scholars of history and those who lived for many hundreds of years would remember that. Long ago, when the empire was still new, the Angetsu Mori was at the heart of a savage war between the Hino and Mizu families, as each clan tried to claim ownership of the forest and its vast resources. After a few decades of fighting and bloodshed, the emperor stepped in and declared the Angetsu Mori the property of the empire, putting an end to the war and the feud between the two families. A shrine was erected at the border of the Water and Fire territories, hunting in the Angetsu Mori was declared illegal, and only a limited number of trees could be harvested from the edges of the forest each month.

Then, four hundred years ago, the Master of Demons began his uprising against the empire. Using blood magic and a horde of demons and undead, he built himself a castle deep in the depths of the forest. As Genno grew in power, and his army of demons, yokai, blood mages and evil spirits swelled in number, the Angetsu Mori changed. It grew darker, more tangled, and began taking on a life of its own. By the time the Master of Demons led his forces against all of Iwagoto, the forest had become a dark, twisted thing, possessed of a malicious sentience and hatred for all living things. Those who ventured into its depths either never returned or stumbled back out again completely mad. And when Genno was killed in the blood-drenched valley of Tani Hitokage, his body broken and his army slain, the forest was no longer known as the Angetsu Mori. It had become the Forest of a Thousand Eyes, a cursed place, and no sane human ventured into its embrace for fear of being haunted, possessed, devoured, or simply vanishing into the dark, never to be seen again.

"That's a rather obvious place for Genno to set up camp," I told the hag sisters. "But I suppose no one is going to bother him there, either." With a shrug, I raised a claw, indicating the exit behind us. "Very well. Take me to the disembodied Master of Demons. Let us see if we cannot find a way to avoid the mistakes of the past."

I could feel Tatsumi's horror as the hag sisters led me out of the tomb, and I turned my thoughts inward. *What's the matter, Tatsumi?* I taunted. *Does meeting with the Master of Demons whose demon army nearly destroyed the empire four hundred years ago not sit well with your demonslayer convictions?* I smiled at the flicker of rage that pulsed through my head. *Don't worry—I have no intention of submitting to any mortal, not even the self-proclaimed Master of Demons. His little uprising means nothing to me. But if he can give me what I want, I'll play nice, for a little while.* I felt Tatsumi's apprehension join the swirl of anger and disgust, and chuckled. *I would think you'd be happy, demonslayer. If all goes as planned, we'll finally be free of each other. That's what you've always wanted, isn't it? The chance to actually* feel *without…well, this happening.*

He tried to hide it, but the tiny swell of hope that came from the demonslayer was almost pathetic. His weariness seeped into me, a soul poison weighing me down. He was tired. Tired of fighting, of constantly struggling for control. His entire existence had been one of darkness and pain, becoming a weapon who killed for the Kage, because that was all he knew how to do. He hadn't known there was anything more…until he met her.

I perked at this, even as Tatsumi forcibly wrenched his thoughts away from me. But it was too late, and I grinned in delight. *Her?* I gloated, feeling the demonslayer's fury at his own weakness. *You mean the girl, don't you? The kitsune half-breed. Oh, Tatsumi, how shameful, how* dishonorable. *What would your clan say if they knew you had developed feelings for a half-breed yokai?*

There was no answer from the soul inside, no glimmer of emotion or feeling; he had closed himself off. But the echo of his longing still lingered, and I chuckled quietly to myself. This information would come in very useful; I was certain we would run into the fox girl and her companions again.

"Did you say something, Hakaimono-sama?" the blue hag inquired as we left the tomb. A cold wind blew into my face, smelling of fish and lake water and the subtle hint of decay. A few coils of red-black taint followed us from the cave entrance and writhed away on the breeze. I inhaled the familiar, choking corruption of my home realm and sighed.

"No, but it's a long way to Onikage castle, and I've wasted enough time here." I turned to the trio of hags and bared my fangs in a smile. "Let us go and speak with the Master of Demons. I am *very* interested to hear his plans for the future."

8

GUESTS OF SHADOW

Yumeko

*W*e walked the Path of Shadows twice more, listening to the spirits of Meido wail and rant at us through the mist, enduring Naganori's glares and subtle insults, before we finally arrived in Kage lands.

"At last," the majutsushi sighed, as we stepped out of the shadows and into the real world again. I shivered as the breeze hit my skin, smelling of wood and smoke and the realm of the living; the Path of Shadows smelled of grief, hopelessness and despair, things I hadn't even known had a scent until now.

I looked around and saw that we were in a dark, bare room, with no windows to let in outside light. The walls and floors were made of stone, though the ceiling had huge wooden beams running across its length. Torches sat at the corners, flickering erratically, and the scent of Shadow magic permeated the room. A circle had been drawn on the floor in what looked like glowing white paint, with runes, kanji and magical sigils etched around it. As I watched, the circle flared once, then faded away, seeming to melt into the floor. I glanced up at Naganori.

"Where are we?" The last time we had left the Path of Shadows, we'd ended up in a tiny hidden temple in a cave, somewhere in Earth Clan territory. This didn't look like a cave, but I was tired of darkness, shadows and everything that lurked within, and was eager to get back into the sun.

Naganori sniffed. "We have arrived at Hakumei-jo," he stated grandly. "The home castle of the Kage family, and the seat of Lady Hanshou herself." He gave us a critical look, lips curling in what seemed to be barely restrained disgust as he eyed our clothes, torn and dirty from the long days of travel. "You'll of course want to make yourselves presentable before you see the daimyo. The servants will see to your every need. Follow them, and do not attempt to wander off on your own. Hakumei castle can be quite...mystifying for the uninitiated. I have matters I must attend. Please excuse me."

And with that, the head majutsushi of the Shadow Clan turned and glided away, vanishing from the dim circle of light and leaving us alone in the darkened room.

"Okay," Okame muttered as a wooden door thumped shut and silence descended, if only for a moment. His eyes had looked haunted ever since we'd first come out of the Path of Shadows. "Don't worry about us, then. We've just spent three days in the realm of the dead, we'll be fine."

"Honored guests."

I jumped as a woman seemed to materialize out of the shadows beside me. She was small and slender, her jet-black hair streaked with silver, and fine lines threaded out from her eyes and lips. She wore a simple robe in the black-and-purple colors of the Kage, and if she hadn't spoken I would never have known she was there. *Is it just a talent all the Kage have?* I wondered, as the woman bowed and told us to please follow her, she would show us to our rooms. *Or do they teach everyone how to sneak up on people like a yurei ghost?*

We followed her down several hallways, lit by swaying lanterns and flickering torchlight. I surmised we were deep underground, probably beneath Hakumei castle, as the floors and some of the walls were made of damp stone. I wondered how anyone could find their way around, as the corridors all looked the same and there were no signs or any way to get your bearings.

"This place is like a maze," I whispered to Reika, walking beside me with Chu and Ko at her heels. "Do you think the Kage get lost down here?"

Reika snorted under her breath. "From what I know of the Kage," she whispered back, "and it's not much, understand, but I'm fairly certain the castle was built this way on purpose. Hakumei-jo is said to be a nightmare to attack, because it's designed to be as confusing as possible."

"Indeed," came Daisuke's voice, behind us. "Every builder and engineer in the country has studied the works of Kage Narumi, the architect of Hakumei castle. She was brilliant and, according to some rumors, a little mad. Her design for the Shadow Clan castle is how the Kage have held on to their territory for so long, though they are the smallest of the clans and the Hino have done their best to drive them out. It is said not even the Kage themselves know all the secrets of Hakumei-jo, and those who wish to attack the clan must defeat the castle itself, which is no small feat. In the past, armies who have invaded Hakumei-jo have been decimated. Survivors speak of hidden doors, false walls, being trapped in hallways that spew fire or spears or arrows. There was a famous incident of a Hino general who lay siege to the castle, intending to starve the Kage out rather than risk assaulting Hakumei-jo itself. For three months, he and his army surrounded the castle, letting no one enter or leave. All demands for the Kage's surrender were rebuffed, though it was obvious no supplies were going to the castle, that they had no way of feeding their people. The Hino general had greater numbers than the army who huddled behind the walls—it was only a matter of time until the Shadow Clan either surrendered, or perished from lack of supplies. He just had to wait them out.

"Until one day," Daisuke went on, "the commander woke to find half his army ill or dying. His food stores had been poisoned, though no one could tell him how this came to be. Furious, the Hino commander gathered his remaining warriors who could still fight and assaulted the castle, intending to overpower the weakened Kage and destroy them. But when the army reached the inner walls of Hakumei-jo, they found a massive force of Kage waiting for them. Not only had the Shadow Clan thrived during the siege, they had somehow brought in reinforcements, though no one had seen even a single Kage enter or leave Hakumei-jo. The Hino general and his army were wiped out nearly to a man, and no one has laid siege to Hakumei castle since."

"So, the moral of that long-winded story?" Okame broke in, a faint smirk crossing his face as he joined us. "Never try to outbluff a Kage. You'll end up with a sword in your back before you realize they've moved."

His voice was harder than normal, his tone cutting. I sensed an invisible coat of prickly armor surrounding the ronin, as if he was using harsh words and language to keep us all at bay. Reika rolled her eyes, and Daisuke gave the ronin an unreadable look. I glanced ahead of us, to the woman walking quietly down the hallway, making turns without hesitation. It wasn't hard to imagine losing my way in this dark, twisty place, taking a single wrong turn and walking in circles forever. "But how do the Kage themselves not get lost down here?" I wondered.

"That I could not tell you," Daisuke said. "Nor do I think the Kage would reveal their secrets to outsiders, so I am afraid we will have to wonder."

"Maybe they all carry a roll of string, just in case."

We finally came to a flight of wooden stairs leading to the overhead floor. The woman didn't pause, but continued up the steps until we reached the interior of the castle, leaving the damp underground behind. The floors were made of polished wood, with thick beams crisscrossing overhead and shoji panels running the length of one wall, separating individual rooms. A pair of Kage samurai guarding the entrance to the stairs ignored us as we followed our guide into the hallway.

Still silent, our escort led us through another series of corridors, this time made of dark wood, shoji screens and decorated fusuma panels. The images depicted on these screens were beautiful—bamboo forests in the moonlight, lonely cliffs with breaking ocean waves, a pine grove hiding a lurking tiger—but they felt slightly ominous, as if purposefully designed for the viewer to feel uncomfortable looking at them. Maybe that was because I felt they were looking back. As we went farther into the castle, I saw more Kage samurai standing guard or walking the halls, and servants scurrying to and fro like silent, efficient mice. A dismal air hung over everything, making me long to be outside, away from the murk. Though the castle was strewn with hanging lanterns and candlelight, it felt dark, quiet and gloomy, with shadows around every corner and hidden eyes in the walls. I missed the sunlight.

As we turned yet another corner, a man suddenly stepped out of an adjoining room into the servant's path, followed by a pair of samurai. The woman instantly bowed and sidestepped, keeping her gaze on the floor as she backed into the wall. The man didn't spare her a second glance. He was dressed in black-and-purple robes patterned with golden crescent moons, and he carried a shimmery golden fan in one hand. His face was pale, with thick lines of black painted beneath his eyes, accenting their sharpness. Stopping in the center of the corridor, the noble raised a thin, painted-on eyebrow at us.

"Ah. So these are Lady Hanshou's 'honored guests.'" His voice was smooth and oily, and somehow reminded me of an eel. "I was not aware she was taking in commoners. Our daimyo is a truly kind and benevolent soul. Do we have proper accommodations for them, I wonder?" He tapped his golden fan against his pale chin, looking thoughtful. "We want our guests to be comfortable, after all. I worry that we do not have an adequate supply of flea-infested straw."

I didn't know much about the fancy way the nobles of the court interacted, but I was *fairly* certain I was being insulted. And by Reika's dark look and the dangerous sneer creeping across Okame's face, they didn't appreciate it, either. "Excuse me," I said, causing the noble to gaze down at me as if I were a bug on the floor, "but who are you?"

"Insolence!" One of the samurai stepped forward, menacing. "How dare you speak to Lord Iesada without being addressed? Were it up to me, I would cut you down for your disrespect." He turned to the noble with a bow. "Iesada-sama, allow me to remove this insect from your presence at once."

"I am certain Lord Iesada does not want to do that," came Daisuke's voice, cool and unruffled, from behind us. The Taiyo noble stepped forward, smiling, though his eyes were razor sharp and cold as he leveled a gaze at the other nobleman. "I am sure Iesada-sama knows that onmyoji Yumeko is an honored guest of Lady Hanshou," he said, his smile never wavering. "That the Lady is expecting her, that she sent Kage Naganori to Sky Clan lands to escort Yumeko-san to Hakumei castle. An informed man like Lord Iesada would surely know that Yumeko-san is also under the protection of the Taiyo family and the Hayate shrine, and they would take great offense if she were to come to harm." His voice became like silken cloth over the edge of a blade. "But I feel foolish even mentioning this, because the Shadow Clan certainly does not wish to insult the Taiyo and risk the wrath of the Imperial family. Forgive me for even voicing such a thought. I am certain that I will return to my homeland with nothing but compliments for the Kage."

The samurai, who had been glaring at Daisuke through this exchange, went slightly pale as he realized who was speaking to him. Lord Iesada's expression didn't change, though he did raise a hand to wave his bodyguard back.

"Of course you are welcome here," he purred, as the samurai gave us a hasty bow and moved aside. "All are welcome in Hakumei castle, let no one say otherwise. Forgive my men and my thoughtlessness, I was not aware that the onmyoji girl was worthy of the protection of the Taiyo." His oily gaze slid to me. "Then again, if Lady Hanshou herself called her here, then her powers must indeed be of note."

"Well." The noble stepped back with a wave of his fan, dismissing us. "I beg your pardon for this interruption. Please continue, and welcome to the Kage lands." His eyes glittered as he smiled at me again. "I am sure you will find your stay very enlightening."

He sauntered down the hall, his samurai marching in step beside him, and disappeared around a corner, leaving the sensation of greasy tendrils over my skin.

Okame gave an exaggerated shudder. "Yep. This was the reason I was never at court. I was just no good at the whole *insult someone by paying them a compliment* game. Call someone a pig to their face, and you get challenged to a duel. Imply that someone is a pig in a pretty poem or turn of phrase, and the nobles titter at the cleverness of it all."

Daisuke chuckled. "It's not that difficult, Okame-san," he said, his voice light. "Would you like me to teach you?"

The ronin snorted. "You can't teach an old dog new tricks, Taiyo-san," he said with a hard grin. "You can bathe them, comb their hair and try to pretty them up all you want, but they'll still roll in mud and pee on the floors the first chance they get."

Chu put back his ears and growled at the ronin, who smirked at him.

"Oh, like you've never rolled in mud."

"Who was that?" Reika asked the servant, who had melted off the wall once the samurai were out of sight. She hesitated, her gaze flitting to the end of the hall, as if worried that the samurai were still lurking about, listening to us.

"Lord Iesada controls the eastern part of the Kage lands and is perhaps the most powerful noble within the Shadow court besides Lady Hanshou herself," the woman answered. "He is not someone you want as an enemy, nor is he someone we should be talking about in the open where anyone can hear. Please, follow me."

"Here we are." The servant paused at a set of door panels, these showing the image of beautiful maple tree branches and a spider's web between the limbs, stretching across the face of the door. The bulbous, gold-and-black weaver could be seen perched prominently in the center, and looked so lifelike I was expecting it to scurry away from the woman's hand as she opened the panel. Another pair of servants were waiting on the other side as the door slid back. One had a kimono draped across her arms, the other carried an array of items on a tray: combs and pins and ivory hairpieces. Both bowed as the panel opened. "Please," the first woman said, gazing at me. "Make yourself comfortable. Mari and Akane will attend you."

"What about my friends?"

"They will have their own quarters not far from here," was the answer. "They will be well taken care of, I assure you. You are all honored guests of the Kage. Your safety and comfort is our prime concern."

I blinked and looked at the two servant girls waiting expectantly beyond the doors. They smiled and politely averted their eyes, but I sensed them watching me even though their gazes were elsewhere. My heart pounded, and I could suddenly feel the scroll, still hidden in my furoshiki, beneath my tattered robes. "Thank you," I said hesitantly, "but I really don't need—"

"It is no trouble," the older woman said. "Lady Hanshou is expecting you—we must make sure you are presentable to the daimyo. Please." She gestured again to the room, relentlessly polite but letting me know refusal was not an option.

I caught Reika's eye as I hesitated, and the shrine maiden gave a tiny nod, though her eyes were dark with warning. We were being watched. No doubt there were hidden eyes on us in every part of the castle, shinobi taking note of our every move. Any behavior that would raise concern or cause them to become suspicious would likely be reported straight to their daimyo. I couldn't let them think I was anything more than a simple peasant girl or even an onmyoji, and I certainly couldn't let Hanshou discover I had one piece of the scroll. If the Shadow Clan daimyo realized I had the very thing she had sent Tatsumi to retrieve, we wouldn't survive the night.

"We'll be fine, Yumeko-chan," Okame broke in, as the shrine maiden gave him a look of disgust. "Just scream if a shinobi pops out of the wall. We'll come running."

The servant girl's eyes widened at this, but the woman remained fiercely unruffled as she gestured to the room again. Reluctantly, I stepped across the threshold, and the panel closed behind me with a snap, leaving me alone with the two girls.

"Um, hello," I offered, not knowing what to do and feeling

uncomfortable. I'd never had servants attend me before. "You'll have to excuse me, I really don't know what I should do."

One of them smiled, though it was a rather forced, practiced smile and didn't quite reach her eyes. "We are here to make you presentable to Lady Hanshou," she told me. "It is a great honor to appear before the Lady of Shadows—few are called into her presence. The Lady has given you the rarest of gifts. We must make certain you are ready to receive it."

"Oh," I said. "That's...very nice."

"Yes." The second girl nodded. "So, if you would, my lady." She gestured in my general direction. I blinked at her, confused, and her eyes tightened. "Please remove your clothes."

"Nani?" I pinned my ears back. The servants waited expectantly, their faces calm. Obviously this was something they did often. I, however, had never disrobed in front of strangers, or anyone, really. "Right now?"

"Please." The servant gestured again with a fixed smile. "We must make you ready to meet Lady Hanshou. Sadly, there is no time for a bath. Your regular...clothes...will be washed and waiting for you upon your return."

I looked at the kimono hanging from the arms of the servant. It was very beautiful; black with red-and-gold leaves swirling up from the bottom as if caught in a whirlwind. The sleeves were long and billowing, nearly touching the floor. A wide, red-and-gold obi-sash completed the outfit.

"Come." The other servant set her tray down and stepped forward, still smiling. "Please disrobe. We are both experienced in aiding the ladies of court in every way possible. It will not be unpleasant, I assure you."

For a moment, I teetered on the edge of panic. What did I do? To refuse would insult the Kage and worse, it might make Lady Hanshou suspicious. I couldn't meet the leader of the Shadow Clan in torn, filthy robes, even if they were onmyoji robes, but the very thing that she wanted more than anything was sitting very conspicuously in my furoshiki. If I handed it over to the servants, they would certainly find it.

Come on, Yumeko! You're a kitsune. If there are no doors or windows out of the room, go under the floorboards.

I smiled shyly at the servant girl, secretly drawing on my magic. "Sumimasen," I told her. "I don't mean to be difficult. It's just I've never had anyone attend me, and this is very strange. I was raised in a temple, and the monks there were very strict. I have...never undressed in front of anyone before, and it is..."

I trailed off, as if too embarrassed to continue. The servants relaxed, though I could sense one of them masking a sigh. "It is understandable," she told me. "The customs of nobles must be strange to you. We will turn our backs while you disrobe— will that make it easier?"

I bobbed my head. "Arigatou gozaimasu."

They nodded and turned their backs to me. Knowing that other eyes could still be watching, I quickly slipped my fingers into my obi and palmed one of the small leaves I'd stuck into the sash before we came to the castle. And I silently thanked Reika for warning me to come prepared.

I drew the furoshiki over my head, feeling the narrow length of the scroll case under my fingers through the cloth. As smoothly and quickly as I could, I slipped the leaf between the folds, brushing it against the lacquered case hidden inside.

A tapping came at the door, making us all jump. "Mari-san? Akane-san? Have you started?" came a woman's voice through the shoji. "Lady Hanshou will be ready for the girl soon."

They spun around, wincing. "Hai, Harumi-san!" one called, while the other turned on me. "We will work as quickly as we can."

"Hurry." The second servant gave an anxious frown as she

stalked up. "I am sorry, but we must do this quickly, now. Please."

She reached for the furoshiki and took it from my hands. As she did, the cloth opened, and something long and thin dropped from the folds, clinking against the wooden floor.

Both servants looked down, as a long bamboo flute rolled slowly over the planks, stopping when it hit one's toe. "What is this?" she asked, bending to pick it up. "A flute?"

I took a furtive breath as her fingers closed around the instrument, forcing myself to speak calmly. "Yes. It was my former master's. He gave it to me the day I left the temple and said I should practice until I could return and play him a perfect song. I've been practicing when I can, but I'm not very good yet. Would you like to hear?"

"I am sure you are better than you think." The servant gave a tight smile. "Perhaps some other time. I will put this with your other clothes."

"If you don't mind," I began as she turned. "I would like to keep it on my person. It's the only thing I have left of my master, you see. Sort of a good luck talisman. If I always carry it, he will always be with me."

Her lips started to purse, before she stopped herself. "As you wish," she said, barely hiding her impatience. "But you must allow us to attend you now. We cannot waste any more time."

"I understand," I told her, and she handed it back with a firm look. I gave a sigh of relief as my fingers closed around the disguised scroll, feeling the fox magic prickle my skin, and kept a tight grip on it as the servants stripped off my clothes. As cold air hit my exposed body, I flattened my ears and tucked my tail tight against my legs so the humans wouldn't step on it as they circled me like wolves. They couldn't see my kitsune self unless they had a mirror or other reflective surface, or were just adept at seeing the spirit world like Reika, but I didn't want them to trip and fall over "nothing." Not to mention my tail would hurt. Thankfully, after misting my skin with a heady, plum-scented perfume that made my eyes water, they draped a white under robe over my body before finally wrapping the elegant kimono around me. The obi was wide and stiff, spanning my waistline to right below my breasts; I carefully tucked the scroll into the fabric while the servants were busy adjusting the bow at my back.

One of the servants had successfully dragged a comb through my hair a few times, untangling the snarls and sparing me no discomfort whatsoever, when another tap came at the door. "Is the girl ready?" the female voice asked, as I blinked back tears of pain and waited for my scalp to stop screaming.

"Hai, Harumi-san!" called the servant, while the other quickly hurried to the door and slid it back. The older woman from earlier peered in, caught sight of me and nodded.

"Yes, good. She looks presentable. My lady." The woman raised a bony hand, beckoning me forward. "Please, come with me. Lady Hanshou has called for you."

I followed the woman down several corridors and up an impossible number of stairs, seeming to ascend to the very top of the castle. Peering through an arrow slit at the top of one staircase, I could see the night sky, blazing with stars, and below us, the tops of trees that stretched on to the distant horizon. It appeared that a great forest, vast and tangled, lay beyond the walls of Hakumei castle. I wondered what types of creatures roamed those woods, if it was anything like the forest outside the Silent Winds temple. A feeling of acute longing and homesickness washed through me, nearly bringing tears to my eyes. So much had happened since the night the demons burned down the temple and Master Isao had entrusted me with the scroll. I was keeping it safe, but just barely. Everywhere I turned, it seemed there was someone else who wanted the scroll, be it a demon, an emperor, a blood mage, or a daimyo. I didn't know how much longer I could keep it hidden, and one mistake or accident could cost everyone their lives. But I would keep trying. I had promised I would deliver this scroll to the Steel Feather temple, and I would keep that promise even if it killed me.

Two fully armed and armored samurai guarded a pair of painted doors at the end of a corridor. The image on the fusuma panels depicted a tranquil-looking forest, but the silhouettes between the trees and shadows were strange and somehow menacing.

A man also waited a few paces from the doors, watching us as we approached. I didn't see him immediately; he had been standing quietly off to the side and appeared to have the Kage talent for blending with the shadows. But as we came to the doors, he stepped forward, like a ghost coming through the walls, and smiled at me.

I tensed. He was a noble like Lord Iesada, poised and elegant, with graceful features and a magnificent, twilight-purple robe scattered with golden petals. Unlike Lord Iesada, the smile he beamed down at me seemed genuine. Or at least, not mocking and cruel. He was also quite handsome, one could almost say beautiful, nearly rivaling Daisuke in how lovely he was to look at. Briefly, I wondered what would happen if you put the two of them in a room together.

"Thank you, Harumi-san," he told the servant woman, who immediately bowed low with her gaze to the floor. "You may go. I will take the girl from here."

"Of course, Masao-sama," the woman almost whispered. She backed away, melting soundlessly into the darkness, and I was alone with the stranger.

I gazed at the noble, who continued to peer down at me with faint amusement. "Hello," I said, making one of his slender brows arch. I was probably supposed to wait for him to address me, but I was tired, on edge and getting rather frustrated with continuously being looked at like I was some very interesting insect. "I'm guessing you're here to warn me of all the things I should not do while speaking to Lady Hanshou?"

He chuckled. "How the lady sees fit to deal with visitors is her own matter," he said easily. "If one does not know enough to be polite in the presence of the land's daimyo, then there was little hope for them anyway." He regarded me with sharp black eyes that seemed to pierce the fabric of my kimono, his smile never faltering. "But I suspect you are clever enough to know that," he went on quietly. "After all, you convinced the Kage demonslayer to escort you to the Steel Feather temple. How does a simple peasant girl accomplish such a feat, I wonder? Had it been anyone else, Tatsumi might have killed them."

Mention of Tatsumi brought a lump to my throat. At the same time, a flutter of alarm went through me. How much did Masao-san know? If he knew that I was a simple peasant and not an onmyoji, why was I here? I felt I was groping in the dark, and that one misstep would send me plunging down a hole I could never crawl out of.

No matter what, protect the scroll, Yumeko. Don't let them know you have it.

"I needed to get to the temple," I told the noble. "Tatsumi needed to find it, too. I promised I would take him there, and he would fight the demons on the way. It was a simple arrangement."

"Nothing surrounding Tatsumi is simple," Kage Masao said softly. "And you are neglecting to mention a very important piece of the story. Why Tatsumi was sent to the Silent Winds temple. Why it was destroyed. Why there are demons chasing you, because demons do not simply appear out of thin air to wreak havoc. Please do not insult me by pretending ignorance—

we both know why Lady Hanshou has called for you." His smile widened. "But you already knew that, didn't you?"

My heart pounded. I could feel the scroll beneath my obi, pressing into my ribs, and deliberately thought about flowers and music and rivers and butterflies, anything but the scroll. I didn't think Kage Masao could read minds, but I had seen Tatsumi create ghostly twins of himself, and Naganori had threatened to tear Okame's shadow away from him, so you could never be too careful.

"Oh, but I've made you uncomfortable, haven't I?" Masao's smooth brow furrowed, and he looked genuinely concerned, before he offered a slight bow. "My apologies. You are an honored guest in Hakumei castle. Please forgive my rudeness—we cannot have anyone thinking the Kage are not polite, even to peasant girls who are more clever than they seem."

His smile looked so sincere and heartfelt that it almost balanced the ominous tone of his previous statement. "I'm afraid I don't know what you mean, Masao-san," I told him. "I'm only a peasant who was raised in a temple of monks. Everything I know, all the skills I possess, I learned from them."

"You needn't worry, Yumeko-san," Masao said, making me start. I didn't remember telling him my name. He smiled again, wry and amused. "I have no grand aspirations to summon a god. I want only what my daimyo wants. Her wishes are my wishes. I exist to serve the Kage, and Lady Hanshou, as best I can."

Again, he sounded completely genuine, but my suspicions prickled all the more. I thought of Tatsumi, remembered his flat, emotionless claim that he was only a weapon for the Kage, and my heart twisted a little. Tatsumi would throw himself off a cliff if his clan ordered it—he truly believed his life was not his own. Kage Masao seemed more like a noble who moved through the court like an eel through water. "Then why are you telling me this?"

His eyes glittered, though his tone remained the same. "Because, Yumeko-san, I wanted to remind you that you are in Shadow Clan territory. Secrets do not exist here. Darkness is our ally, and nothing can hide from us for long. Remember that, when you speak to Lady Hanshou. She has been alive a very, very long time. She knows things about the clans that would cause the emperor himself to never sleep again. So, consider this a friendly warning. Whatever Lady Hanshou asks, it is best to answer truthfully. She already knows everything about you."

I swallowed, resisting the urge to pin back my ears. *Not everything.*

Masao smiled at me, as if he knew what I was thinking and was too polite to say I was wrong. With a quiet, "Please follow me," he turned, swept past the samurai and opened the painted door between them. I stepped through the frame, and the panel snapped shut behind me.

Instantly, I was struck by the heat; the room beyond was dark, smoky and chokingly warm. Incense hung thick in the air, burning my nose and clogging my throat, but beneath the overpowering smell of sandalwood and cloves, the air reeked of alcohol. As my eyes adjusted to the dimness, I could see the walls were painted fusuma panels depicting more beautiful imagery—a pair of cranes at the edge of a pond, a tiger in a bamboo grove—but looking at them made my tail bristle. It seemed as if the paintings were staring back at me, or that shadowy presences lurked behind them, watching as I took in the chamber. The room had no windows; the only light came from a pair of cast-iron braziers, glowing red with heat, and a single lantern overhead, casting an orange circle of light in the middle of the tatami mats.

Just beyond that light, flanked by the two braziers, a figure waited for me, seated on a thick red cushion. At first, it was an indistinguishable lump, wrapped in layers of robes and hidden in shadow. I thought I could make out the silhouette of a head, and a single arm that held a long-handled pipe, the end trailing curls of smoke into the air. But the light was hazy, and the figure seemed almost hunched over, so it was impossible to see it clearly.

"Is this her?" came a low, feminine voice from the lump in the center of the room. The smoothness of the voice startled me; for some reason, it didn't match the silhouette it was attached to. Masao stepped forward and bowed.

"Yes, Hanshou-sama. As requested, this is Yumeko of the Silent Winds temple. The one who accompanied the demon-slayer until his...unfortunate incident."

"Come forward, girl," purred the voice. "Do not lurk at the edge of the shadows, step into the light."

Beside me, Masao gestured at the circle of lantern light, and I edged forward until I was in the center of the soft orange glow. When he gave a nod, I knelt and bowed to the still shadowy form of Lady Hanshou, touching my forehead to the mats, as one did when facing the daimyo of a great clan.

A ripple of power washed over me, the same soft, cool touch of Tatsumi's Shadow magic, coming from the figure in the center of the floor. I rose and squinted past the haze and the smoke, searching for the daimyo of the Kage family, and nearly gasped out loud in surprise.

A beautiful woman met my gaze, full red lips curved up in the faintest of smiles. Her skin was the color of the moon, almost glowing with its own inner light, and her midnight-black hair was so long that it curled around the hem of her robes like a silken tail. One pale, elegant hand held a pipe, tendrils of wispy smoke coiling around a slender arm, and somehow it made her even more beautiful and mysterious. Luminous dark eyes glimmered in the shadows, watching me over the folds of a magnificent, many-layered kimono, far fancier and more elegant than my own. For the first time ever, I was extremely aware of my station, an insignificant peasant in borrowed robes, facing what had to be the most beautiful woman in the empire.

And then, I felt the cold tickle of Shadow magic again, like the flutter of a moth's wing against my ear, and shook my head to clear it. The image of the beautiful woman rippled like the reflection in a pond and for a moment, I saw the face of a hideous crone, wrinkled as rotten persimmons, toothless and half-blind, only a few strands of hair attached to her withered scalp. Only for an instant, and then the face of the beautiful woman solidified again, but though my feelings of awe and inadequacy had dissolved with the illusion, my tail bristled and my heart began a rapid thud against my chest. This version of Lady Hanshou was what she showed the outside world, like the skin on a peach infested with worms and decay. How old *was* she? How could she still be alive?

The illusion of the beautiful Kage daimyo smiled at me, cool and amused, making me tense. Shadow magic and fox magic appeared to share many traits; covering the truth, making people see things that weren't there. I had to be cautious. If Lady Hanshou discovered I wasn't fooled by her magic, she might become angry, much as I would get annoyed the few times Denga-san had seen through one of my pranks. If she became angry, I didn't know what she would do, but it probably wouldn't be pleasant.

I dropped my gaze to the floor. *If she can't see my eyes, she can't see the truth in them. I hope.* There was a soft chuckle, and then the daimyo's voice drifted out of the shadows.

"Welcome, Yumeko of the Silent Winds temple," Lady Hanshou said, the low, smooth tone not quite able to mask the harsh rasp I heard underneath. "Welcome to Hakumei castle. I hope the journey here was a pleasant one?"

"Thank you, Hanshou-sama," I said, remembering the lessons from Reika about addressing daimyos. Tell them only what they wanted to hear; the truth was inconvenient, impolite and could get you killed. "It was quite pleasant, no trouble at all." *Well, except the part through the realm of the dead.* "Your hospitality has been most generous."

"Has it?" Lady Hanshou looked amused. "You are in the Kage lands now, girl," she said in her rasp-purr. "There are no secrets that can hide from us, not from those who live in the shadows, who know the darkness better than any in the empire. I might not look it, but I have lived a few years longer than you, and I have come to find the polite dribble of court wearisome. Say what you mean in my presence, or do not speak at all. I ordered Naganori to find you and bring you here. I know that he took you through the Path of Shadows, which runs alongside the realm of the dead. I cannot imagine that was 'pleasant,' in any way you might look at it. So, please…" She smiled, and for a half second I saw the face of the ancient hag, grinning menacingly in the dark. "Speak true when you address me in my own castle. I will know if you are lying, and I will not be pleased."

A stab of fear went through me, and for a moment I was certain she knew everything, before I paused to think. *No, that can't be right. If that was true, she would already know I'm kitsune. And that I have the scroll. Why would she say something like that?* I mulled it over for a split second, before the truth came to me. *She's trying to throw me off balance, let me think that she already knows everything about me, so I might as well tell her the truth. But she doesn't. She doesn't know me, and I can't let her discover more than she already has.*

"All right," I said, facing the ancient daimyo again. "If you want the truth, then the Path of Shadows was grim and horrifying, we were all nearly dragged into Meido by jealous spirits and Naganori-san was a rude, unfriendly ogre that I wanted to push off a cliff. Also he smells of old mushrooms."

Lady Hanshou laughed. On the surface, it sounded like delicate wind chimes blowing in a gentle breeze, but underneath I could hear the harsh, coughing wheezes of her real self. It went on for a goodly while, so long that Masao stepped forward and knelt by her side in concern. She waved at him dismissively and continued to chortle.

"Ah," she finally gasped, sitting up. "It has been a long time since anyone has spoken so freely in my presence, even when I give them leave to speak their mind. They simper and continue on with pretty phrases and flowery words, and would have me believe nothing ever troubles them, that I am the most gracious of hosts and that my beauty is surpassed only by my generosity." She sniffed. "The same poem, no matter how beautiful, grows stale the more lips you hear it from. Masao-san despairs every time I must interact with the nobles and their court." She tittered daintily, or more accurately, the illusion tittered. The ancient crone cackled loudly. Masao winced.

"But you are not afraid to speak the truth," Lady Hanshou went on, gazing at me. "Even to a daimyo of a minor clan. And yes, Naganori *does* smell of fungus sometimes. I think he spends so much time in his study, mold starts growing beneath his robes." She chuckled again, and the noble beside her gave a defeated sigh. "You see?" Lady Hanshou said, gesturing to her advisor. "He tells me I will make him prematurely gray. It will only make you more distinguished, Masao-san. I *was* going to threaten you with imprisonment and torture if you did not tell me what I needed," she continued, making me start as she focused on me again, "but you've made a tired daimyo laugh today, and that is not an easy thing. Let us speak to each other plain, woman to woman. Masao-san..." She waved a hand at the courtier, still at her side. "Leave us."

"Of course, Hanshou-sama." The handsome noble rose, bowed to his lady, and walked away, his robes brushing softly over the mats. He reached the door, slipped through the frame and closed it behind him with a snap, leaving me alone with the daimyo of the Shadow Clan.

Lady Hanshou regarded me with glittering black eyes. "You are not as simple as you look, are you?" she mused. "When I questioned my informants about the girl traveling with the Kage demonslayer, they all said the same. She is a mere peasant, a commoner, unremarkable and unimportant. But that is not entirely true, is it?" Her gaze sharpened, as if trying to peel back the layers of figment to see the truth beneath. My heart pounded, though I found it ironic that one illusion was trying to see past another illusion. "Kage Tatsumi does not suffer fools," Lady Hanshou went on. "We trained him too well for that. Who are you, that the Kage demonslayer would not only consent to travel with you, but would protect you with his life along the journey?"

"I'm only a peasant," I said. "No one special. Tatsumi only agreed to come with me because…"

I trailed off and saw Lady Hanshou's brow arch. "Because he thought you could take him to the scroll," she finished.

I held my breath. Lady Hanshou smiled, showing a set of perfect white teeth, and a split-second flash of a gaping, toothless mouth. "I won't ask you to take me to the scroll, girl," she said, to my immense surprise. "I could, of course. I could order you to bring me the piece of the Dragon's prayer from the monks at the Steel Feather temple. Oh yes," she added as I straightened in alarm. "I know the name of the temple that protects part of the scroll. Tatsumi told my Shadow mages everything while he was traveling with you. They watched him constantly, you see, to make sure he followed orders, that the demon in Kamigoroshi did not overwhelm him. There is no conversation you had with Tatsumi that did not flow directly to me."

I thought back to the times Tatsumi would disappear, giving no hint of where he was going or what he was doing. I hadn't pressed him about it, because I knew he wouldn't answer me anyway, but my heart sank at the realization. He had been reporting to the Shadow Clan the whole time.

"So yes, I know of the Steel Feather temple, and that they guard two pieces of the Dragon's scroll," Lady Hanshou went on. "I have already dispatched shinobi to find it. But that is not your concern, nor the reason I called you here. Let us speak of Kage Tatsumi, the demonslayer."

I swallowed the dryness in my throat. "What about Tatsumi-san?" I whispered.

"You traveled with him," Hanshou said. "From the Silent Winds temple in the mountains of the Earth Clan, across the Sun plains, to the capital of Kin Heigen Toshi. How you managed to pick up a ronin, a Taiyo noble, a shrine maiden and a monk along the way without Tatsumi killing any of them is a mystery but not the issue at hand. We watched you enter the city with the demonslayer. We watched you carefully at the emperor's Moon Viewing party. A fine bit of trickery, that. Very well-done." The illusion gave a wide, knowing smile. "Someday, you must tell me the secret of the rabbit and the emperor's fortune, because you are certainly no onmyoji."

I bit my tongue, heart pounding, and tried to appear innocent. Lady Hanshou chuckled at my silence, then sobered immediately, her face turning dark. "And then," she continued, "you followed the emperor's concubine into a storehouse at the edge of the lake, and simply...vanished." She opened slender white fingers to reveal an empty palm. "Without a trace. And not just from the Imperial palace. You disappeared from the city entirely.

"You must understand, this caused the Shadow Clan some concern." She folded her hands in her lap, peering at me intently across the mats. "When Tatsumi disappeared, I sent every shinobi in the capital to look for you and the demonslayer, but all I received were reports of strange mirrors and possible blood magic. And then, days later, a report comes back that someone has spotted Tatsumi, far to the north in Sora territory." Her face darkened even more, and beneath the veneer of the beautiful woman, Lady Hanshou's milky eye burned with searing intensity as it met my gaze. "Only, he is alone and is not Kage Tatsumi any longer."

I shivered and closed my eyes, remembering Hakaimono's terrible voice, his dark promises that he was going to kill me and everyone I cared about. The horror when I realized the oni had possessed the demonslayer, and that the real Tatsumi, his soul or spirit or whatever, could hear every word the demon said and knew exactly what was happening but could do nothing.

He was actually starting to trust you, little fox. Tatsumi never trusted anyone in his life—his clan punished any attachments or weaknesses. But he was starting to trust you, *a kitsune who lied to him, who has been deceiving him from the very beginning. And now, he sees exactly what you are, and how you betrayed him.*

Lady Hanshou's voice burned with the smoldering heat of an ember. "What happened to cause Tatsumi to lose control is irrelevant," she said. "I can hazard a few guesses as to what caused Hakaimono to appear, especially with the rumors of oni and blood mages swirling about, but that is not important. The concern now is that Hakaimono is free, and that Tatsumi is no longer in control of Kamigoroshi. Right now, only a select few know that the demon is loose, but this will not remain a secret for long. The course of action is clear." Her lips thinned as she set her jaw. "Because of the enormous threat Hakaimono represents, to both the Kage and the rest of the empire, I must give the order to kill Kage Tatsumi on sight."

"No!" I saw her thin brow arch and realized that the daimyo of the Shadow Clan probably had never had the word *no* spoken to her before. "Please," I pleaded, leaning forward. "Don't kill him yet. Let us find Tatsumi-san."

"Why would I do that? I would only be throwing more lives to Hakaimono's terrible bloodlust. Do not think that he would spare you, girl." Lady Hanshou shook her head. "Hakaimono is as sadistic and cruel as he is powerful. He will make you think you have a chance, that you are winning, before he tears you apart and laughs at your naivety."

"I know." I remembered the demon's mocking voice. "I realize that, but please hear me out. We think...we might have a way to stop Hakaimono and force him back into the sword."

I thought she would be surprised. I thought both brows might shoot up in amazement and disbelief. I wasn't prepared for what actually happened. Lady Hanshou smiled, this time a slow, knowing smile that told me I had stepped right into her web. "Is that so?" she purred, lacing her fingers together. "Please, go on. You do know that the strongest priests and majutsushi have failed to exorcise Hakaimono once he has taken control of a body, do you not? The one time it was attempted, Hakaimono freed himself and slaughtered every soul present in a spectacular bloody massacre. After that, it was decreed that should a demonslayer fall to his influence again, he would be killed immediately, with no attempts at an exorcism." Lady Hanshou's eyes narrowed shrewdly. "Hakaimono is too dangerous and cunning to take alive. I am quite eager to hear your plans for dealing with the First Oni."

"Um." I swallowed. Lady Hanshou raised an extremely skeptical eyebrow, and I winced. The hazy remnants of a dream came back to me, the words of a white fox telling me what I had to do to save the demonslayer. It still made my stomach churn. "We're still working out the details."

"I see." Now the daimyo's voice was flatter than rice paper. "And let us say that, against all odds, you do manage to capture the First Oni, who has been known to slaughter entire armies at a time. What then?"

Then I will attempt to use kitsune-tsuki to enter Tatsumi myself and bring him back. And try not to get my spirit ripped apart by Hakaimono. But I certainly couldn't tell her that.

"Master Jiro and Reika are from the Hayate shrine," I answered. "They've performed exorcisms before. They will drive Hakaimono back into the sword."

"One priest and a shrine maiden," Lady Hanshou said, and now she did sound incredulous. "Against the most powerful oni this realm has ever known." She tapped her fingers against her arm. "And what happens if you are unsuccessful? If Hakaimono proves too strong for you all?"

Then I'll be dead. And Tatsumi will be trapped forever. Or until someone finally kills Hakaimono. But I'm not going to let that happen. I'll save Tatsumi, even if I have to be evil to destroy evil.

"Then we will very likely get eaten by Hakaimono," I told the Shadow daimyo. "But you lose nothing. Except time. None of your own clan will be in danger. If Hakaimono kills one priest, a shrine maiden, a ronin and a peasant girl, what is that to anyone? But if we're successful…if we *can* bring Tatsumi back…"

A chill slid up my spine. My thoughts had been consumed with getting to Tatsumi, coming to terms with having to use kitsune-tsuki to possess him, facing down Hakaimono and somehow driving the demon out. I hadn't thought about what would happen if we did rescue the demonslayer, but if I freed Tatsumi from Hakaimono's influence…he would probably have to return to his clan. And then what? Would they punish him for losing control? Would he be taken and executed anyway, as a threat to the Shadow Clan?

Or would Lady Hanshou order him to kill us all and bring her the Dragon scroll?

"If you can bring Tatsumi back," Lady Hanshou echoed, "you will have done what all others before you could not. But how successful can you possibly be, taking on Hakaimono the

Destroyer? Even in a human body, he is more than a match for anyone."

"We have to try," I said. "Please. Let us find Tatsumi. Let us at least try to drive Hakaimono out. If the demon kills us all, that will be no loss to you."

"I can offer no help," Lady Hanshou warned. "My hands are tied in this matter. The law is clear—if Hakaimono is released, the Kage must do everything in their power to kill the bearer of Kamigoroshi and send the demon back into the sword. Already there are murmurs of anger and discontent, the various lords of the Kage whining in my ear like mosquitoes, demanding I do something. That the honor of the Shadow Clan is at stake. Should Hakaimono attack any of the other territories, the Kage will certainly be held responsible. I cannot risk war with the other clans. I must do everything within my power to destroy Hakaimono before he causes real destruction.

"But," she added before I could protest. "Should a group of outsiders not affiliated with the Kage in any way *happen* to exorcise Hakaimono and return the demonslayer to himself, well, there is nothing I could have done about that, is there?" Her tone made the hairs on my arm stand up. "And if they learned that the demon was last seen heading toward the Forest of a Thousand Eyes between Hino and Mizu lands, they certainly wouldn't tell any members of the Shadow Clan, for fear of risking Kage Tatsumi's life, or their own."

I blinked. Had the daimyo of the Shadow Clan just given me her blessing to save Tatsumi? And Hakaimono's last known destination? "The Forest of a Thousand Eyes?" I repeated. "That sounds...ominous."

Hanshou nodded. "It is where Genno, the Master of Demons, first rose to power," the daimyo said, pitching her voice very low. "It is a cursed place of monsters and corrupted kami, a place where no mortal man dares venture, and if Hakaimono enters the castle at the heart of the forest, he will be nearly impossible to reach." Her eyes narrowed, staring me down, as her voice dropped to a near whisper. "So if you want to save the demon-slayer and bring Tatsumi back, I would make haste."

Behind us, the door slid open, and then the soft shushing of robes over tatami could be heard. I turned my head slightly and watched Kage Masao mince across the floor and bow before his daimyo.

"Forgive this interruption, Hanshou-sama," the courtier said in his low, smooth voice. "Lord Iesada wishes an audience with you."

"Merciful Jinkei." Lady Hanshou rolled her eyes. "This is the third time in as many days. Send Lord Iesada my apologies. Tell him that I am unwell and not fit to see him at the moment."

"Please forgive me, Hanshou-sama," Masao went on, not lifting his head. "But Lord Iesada is insistent. He said he will become very insulted if an outsider is allowed to speak to the daimyo and he is denied."

The Kage daimyo sighed. Regarding me over the mats, her withered lips curled in a smirk. "Be thankful you are a peasant," she told me, "and do not have to deal with the games, machinations and constant struggles of the nobles within the court. Sometimes I wish I could simply shut them out and be done with them all, but sadly, even a daimyo must play the game from time to time." She gave a very inelegant snort, rolling her one good eye, then returned to formality. "Tonight you will stay in the castle as honored guests of the Kage. Tomorrow, I will have Naganori take you and your friends through the Path of Shadows again, to a town called Jujiro, on the edge of Fire Clan territory. It is the closest settlement to the Forest of a Thousand Eyes, and the farthest anyone is willing to travel in that direction. You, of course, will speak of this to no one. What passed between us here never happened. Is this understood?"

123

"Hai," I nodded. "Thank you, Hanshou-sama."

One slender brow rose. "Remember that you walk among the shadows, girl," she told me. "We are the keepers of secrets, but we are also adept at uncovering them. If what we spoke of today does reach the wrong ear, the shadows also hide silent blades that will cut the life from you while you sleep. So I extend this warning with my apologies—trust no one. Even those with a familiar face could betray you, because once you become entangled with the shadows, they will never let you go.

"Masao-san..." Lady Hanshou turned to the courtier, still bowed low on the tatami mats. "If you would remain but for a moment. Yumeko-san, it has been...enlightening, but I fear my attention is required elsewhere. You may go—a servant will be summoned to show you back to your room."

And just like that, I was dismissed. I bowed to the ancient daimyo and left her presence, slipping out the door into the shadowy hall beyond.

"Ah. If it isn't Hanshou-sama's honored guest."

I froze. Lord Iesada was there, surrounded by his two guards. As our gazes met, the noble sauntered forward, giving me a predatory look that made my tail bristle.

"How curious," he mused, approaching with half his face hidden behind his fan. "That one so young is able to command the attention of our good daimyo, while her betters are turned away and left standing in the cold. Do let me guess what you were speaking of. It will be a fun game to pass the time, ne?"

I bit my tongue. I could think of several other games that involved fox magic, a leaf and Lord Iesada trying to avoid an illusionary rat scurrying up his hakama, but that might cause more harm than good. The noble shut his fan with a snap and tapped it against his arm in mock contemplation as he gazed down at me. "What would Hanshou-sama want with an onmyoji?" he mused. "And one not bound by the laws of the Kage? She has mages, diviners and holy men at her beck and call. Why this sudden interest in an outsider?"

"Perhaps Hanshou-sama is simply being polite," I offered, and his lip curled.

"Perhaps," he repeated, with a subtle glint in his eye that told me he was somehow insulted. "Or perhaps she wishes to discuss matters of a more...demonic nature."

My insides chilled, but before I could say anything, the door opened and light footsteps shushed toward us.

"Lord Iesada," came Masao's cheerful voice, as the advisor swept between us. His billowy sleeves rippled as he gestured grandly toward the daimyo's room, shielding me from the other noble. "Please forgive the delay. Hanshou-sama is ready for you."

Lord Iesada gave him a tight smile and stalked away, though his guards remained where they were. Masao bowed as the noble swept through the doors into Hanshou's chamber but as soon as they closed behind him, he straightened and turned to me.

"Come, Yumeko-san," he said serenely. "Harumi-san is waiting to take you back to your room."

"Why is Lord Iesada so interested in Tatsumi?" I asked as the courtier escorted me out of the waiting area.

Masao didn't answer right away. Only when we had stepped into another hall and away from Lord Iesada's two samurai did he stop and turn to me.

"Iesada-sama is a powerful person within the Shadow Clan," the courtier replied, his voice calm but very soft. "He has the ear of many of the nobles, and lately, he has been expressing concern that our good daimyo is...somewhat distracted. He has even gone so far as to suggest that Hanshou-sama has ruled the Shadow Clan long enough, that is it time for her to step down and let another lead. For the good of the Kage, of course."

Masao's tone remained perfectly neutral as he said this, though his dark eyes glittered, hinting that his thoughts regarding Lord

Iesada were not so neutral. "When Hakaimono broke free of Tatsumi's control, Lord Iesada was the first to suggest that it was Lady Hanshou's decision to continue training demonslayers that brought this shame upon the Shadow Clan," he went on. "Hakaimono has overcome his hosts before, but always while they were still in training, where the Kage could deal with them quickly and quietly. But Lord Iesada has long insisted that Kamigoroshi is too dangerous to be in the hands of any one person, and that Hanshou-sama's reliance upon the demonslayers would bring disaster to the Kage in the end." Masao regarded me with a solemn look, his mouth pulled into a grim line. "For years, he has whispered to the Kage that the demonslayer should be killed and Kamigoroshi returned to sealed isolation. Should word of Hakaimono's release become known, many of those nobles will certainly agree with Iesada-sama."

Realization dawned on me. "That's why Lady Hanshou needs us to save Tatsumi," I guessed. "Because if Tatsumi is killed, she will be admitting that Lord Iesada was right. That the demonslayer was too dangerous to let live. But if we can rescue him and drive Hakaimono back..." I had to stop and think a moment, as all these political games were making my head hurt. "Then, Tatsumi won't be a danger anymore, and Iesada-sama can just be quiet."

Masao's lip twitched in a faint smile. "You are clever, for a simple peasant girl," he said, though not in a threatening or menacing way. "Use that to your advantage. Most nobles think that the commoners are beneath their notice. Be warned, however. There are many who will not take kindly to an outsider interfering in Shadow Clan affairs. If your quest becomes known to certain individuals, they may try to stop you." Masao's dark eyes narrowed, and he drew two pale fingers across his throat. "The Kage way."

I swallowed. "I understand."

"Excellent!" Masao became bright and cheerful in an instant. "Well, good luck and thank you for coming, Yumeko-san. Harumi-san will show you back to your room."

I turned and saw that the older servant woman was waiting for me at the end of the hall. When I looked back, Masao was already striding away, his sleeves fluttering behind him as he went. He did not look back, seeming to forget I was there, and slipped through the door without breaking stride, then shut it behind him.

I followed Harumi-san to my room in silence. I couldn't be certain, but I was almost positive we took a different route back than the way we'd come. Though it was difficult to concentrate on anything with my mind preoccupied with Tatsumi, Hakaimono and my meeting with the Kage daimyo.

Now I *had* to get Tatsumi back, and quickly. Not that I wasn't determined before, but the meeting with Lady Hanshou and her advisor showed me how dire the situation really was. If I didn't rescue Tatsumi, the Kage would kill him themselves.

Though the thought of what I would have to do made my skin crawl and my stomach turn. Kitsune-tsuki. I had never attempted fox possession before, and with all that had happened with the Kage, there was no time to see if I could even do it. I didn't dare ask if I could "practice" on any of my friends. Kitsune-tsuki was dangerous and extremely invasive, according to Master Isao, and I had no idea what I was doing. I did not want to slip into Okame or Daisuke only to realize I couldn't get out again.

But if we did manage to capture the demonslayer without being killed by the Kage or the oni himself, and I did manage to possess Tatsumi... I would have to deal with Hakaimono. Alone. The very thought turned my insides to ice and sent my heart racing around my chest. I doubted the oni spirit that had terrorized the country and had the entire Shadow Clan paralyzed with fear would simply leave if I asked him nicely.

But the alternative was to let Hakaimono wreak havoc as he pleased until the Kage caught up and finally brought the demon down. None of them cared about Tatsumi; he was simply a weapon to them, a thing that should be disposed of now that it had grown problematic. Even Lady Hanshou was simply trying to save face and protect her position. I was the only one who cared if Tatsumi lived or died.

I was so distracted by my thoughts, I didn't realize Harumi-san had stopped until I walked past her. Blinking, I turned to see her standing against the wall with her head bowed and her hands clasped in front of her. Confused, I looked up, and saw we were in what seemed to be a deserted part of the castle. The halls were dim, with only a couple lanterns sputtering weakly down the corridor.

A figure stood in the middle of the hall, where nothing had been a moment ago.

My ears pricked at yet another person materializing out of thin air. He wasn't a noble, or at least, he didn't look like one. He was shorter than most, wearing a simple black haori, gray hakama and a warrior's topknot. It was impossible to tell his exact age; his face was lined, his body lean and sinewy. He approached us easily, making absolutely no sound in the shadowy corridor, and though his face remained impassive, I suddenly felt as if I were being stalked by some large, deadly cat.

"Good work, Harumi-san," he told the servant, his voice no louder than a whisper. "Leave us." Harumi immediately bowed and backed away, vanishing down another hall and out of sight. The man observed me for a moment, sharp black eyes seeing all in a single glance.

"Do you know who I am?" he asked in that strangely quiet

voice, like the murmur of the wind in the trees. You knew it was there, but you barely noticed it.

"No," I said.

He nodded. "Good. If you did, then Tatsumi would have shared far more than he should. Not that it matters now, but I wanted to see the girl who charmed the demonslayer into ignoring nearly all my teachings." His eyes narrowed, but I couldn't tell if he was angry, sad, irritated or impassive. "I am Kage Ichiro," the man went on. "Tatsumi is—or rather *was*—my student."

Tatsumi's sensei. The man who had trained him to be a demonslayer, to fight like a monster himself, and to guard his mind and soul against Hakaimono. He probably wasn't happy that his student had turned into a demon. "Why have you brought me here?" I asked.

"Because Hakumei-jo is full of eyes, and I wanted to speak to you in private. Where the only shadows watching are the ones I control." He lifted a hand, indicating the hallway behind me. "This is my territory, my labyrinth, but do not worry—if I wished to kill you, I would not have bothered to have Harumi-san bring you here. You would simply vanish down a corridor, or perhaps fall through a trapdoor, and no one would ever find you."

I took a furtive breath to calm my heart. "What do you want with me, then?"

"I want nothing from you, girl." The sensei's voice was flat. "Except to extend this warning. I know what Hanshou-sama asked you to do. Nothing happens in Hakumei-jo without the echoes of it flowing to me. But you and your companions are not safe here—there are those in the Shadow Clan who do not wish Lady Hanshou to have her demonslayer returned, and will do whatever it takes to stop you from succeeding."

"Lord Iesada," I guessed, seeing no reaction from Tatsumi's

sensei. "But, why? Why is he so against us saving Tatsumi? Why doesn't he want Hakaimono driven back?"

"The Kage demonslayers are trained for absolute obedience," Ichiro replied. "I taught Tatsumi myself, stripped every weakness from his body and mind, forged him in fire and blood, until only a weapon remained. He does not fear death, pain or dishonor. His loyalty to the Kage is unconditional, but even more than that, he is also the blade that Lady Hanshou wields against her enemies. Long ago, after Genno's rebellion, Hanshou-sama made the decision to begin training shinobi to use the Godslayer, rather than seal its power away. She believed the risk would be outweighed by the usefulness of having Hakaimono under her control. Over the years, I have trained several demonslayers to Lady Hanshou's expectations. They cannot be swayed by bribes, threats, power or manipulation. They are her perfect warriors, the blade in the dark that even the Kage fear."

"They're afraid of him," I realized. "Lord Iesada and the other Kage lords. He doesn't just want Tatsumi killed, he wants Kamigoroshi sealed away forever. So Hanshou-sama can't use the demonslayer to threaten the Shadow Clan nobles."

And whomever else she wants.

"They are right to fear him," Ichiro said gravely. "I have seen Hakaimono, I have spoken to the demon through my students. I know what he is capable of." His sharp black eyes narrowed. "I *thought* I had trained Tatsumi well, that he was strong enough to control the demon. But this failure is my fault. Tatsumi has been taught to resist pain, manipulation, seduction, even mind control and blood magic. But I neglected to warn him about the most dangerous emotion of all." A bitter smile curled one corner of his mouth. "After everything we put him through, I honestly thought the boy incapable of it. Apparently, I can still be surprised, after all these years."

The most dangerous emotion of all. I wondered what Ichiro meant.

I had watched Tatsumi; I knew he didn't feel anger, grief or fear like the rest of us. What "dangerous emotion" could be left?

But, while I was curious, I was also certain that the sensei of the Kage shinobi wouldn't tell me what he meant, so I didn't ask. "I'll find him, Ichiro-san," I promised instead. "I'll find Tatsumi, and I'll save him from Hakaimono."

He snorted. "You are no match for Hakaimono," he said bluntly. "I will not hope that a single girl can defeat one who has slaughtered armies and laid waste to cities. But, in the slight chance that you do manage the impossible, I will tell you something about Tatsumi that not even Hanshou or her clever advisor knows.

"The ones who survive to become demonslayers," Ichiro went on, "are not the strongest, or the smartest, or even the most skilled. They are the ones with the purest souls. Because only one whose soul is pure can resist Hakaimono's influence. Remember that, and know that even now, Tatsumi is fighting."

Kage Ichiro stepped away, the blank mask I'd often seen on Tatsumi falling into place. "Now go," he ordered. "Save the demonslayer, if you can. But remember, there are those who will try to destroy you before you even begin your journey. Trust no one, and you might survive."

"Arigatou," I whispered, but Tatsumi's sensei took one step back and threw something to the ground between us. A cloud of smoke erupted from his feet, obscuring my vision, and when it cleared, Tatsumi's sensei was gone.

A soft chuckle echoed behind me. I spun to see yet another shinobi leaning against the wall with its arms crossed, its features hidden in shadow. Though a moment before the hallway had been empty, I had the sudden impression it had been there the whole time.

"He cares for him, you know."

I pricked my ears, both at the statement, and that it had come from a female. The shinobi raised its head, revealing a slender form in black, long dark hair tied behind her. "Tatsumi-kun," she explained. "Master Ichiro's training has to be harsh, and he can't show any emotion when it comes to the demonslayer, but he cares about what happens to him. More than he does any of us." She shook her head. "Tatsumi has always been his favorite."

"I'm...sorry?"

Her mouth twisted in a bitter smile. "I could have been the demonslayer," she said, pushing herself off the wall. "I was faster, more skilled, than Tatsumi. But they chose him. And now he's fallen to Hakaimono." The smirk grew wider, as a black kunai throwing dagger appeared in her hand, balanced on two fingers. "They should have chosen me," she said. "I could have told them he was too softhearted to wield Kamigoroshi. They thought they could train it out of him, but apparently not."

"What do you mean?"

The shinobi gave me a brief look of pure loathing. "He let you live, didn't he?"

She hurled the kunai at me. I flinched, throwing up my hands, but the black knife missed my head by inches, hitting the far wall with a thunk. Heart pounding, I looked up, fox magic surging to my fingertips. But the shinobi, whomever she was, had disappeared.

Harumi-san found me moments later and silently led me back through countless twisting halls until we had reached the guest quarters. I thanked the servant for bringing me to my room and slipped inside, wondering if I would be able to sleep in a castle full of shinobi. Especially after the unexpected meeting with Tatsumi's sensei, and the female shinobi who seemed to hate me.

As I stepped through the frame, I realized I wasn't alone.

Reika was waiting for me, Chu at her side, her expression

dark. "Close the door," she ordered in a low voice. "And come closer. I don't want to be overheard."

Puzzled, I shut the door and crossed the room to where the shrine maiden waited. "What's wrong, Reika-san?" I whispered. She frowned at me, and I hurried on. "You don't have to worry. *It* is safe. Lady Hanshou doesn't know anything about it—"

"That's a relief," the shrine maiden interrupted, "but that's not why I'm here." She glanced in the corners and at the ceiling, as if there could be shinobi nearby, listening even now, and lowered her voice further. "We have a problem. The ronin and the noble have disappeared."

9

THE FOREST OF A THOUSAND EYES

HAKAIMONO

"*F*inally here," said the blue hag, gazing up at the trees. "We just have to make it through the forest to the castle in the center. It shouldn't be long now."

I crossed my arms, gazing at the forest in question. Four hundred years, and the Forest of a Thousand Eyes hadn't changed, except to get bigger and even more sullen-looking. Tree trunks were bent and twisted, warped into unnatural shapes, like creatures writhing in agony. Branches boasted crooked talons clawing at the sky, or sometimes at living things. Vegetation was thick and tangled, despite the fact that every leaf, frond and blade of grass looked withered and sick. A pallid mist hung over everything, coiling from the trees and creeping along the ground, and the air had a sickly sweet stench that reminded me of rotting flowers.

"Ah, it is good to be home," sighed the red hag. "I sent word ahead to the castle, so they should be expecting us. Lord Genno will be very interested in meeting you, Hakaimono-sama."

"I'm sure he is," I said. *The question is, will he see me as an equal partner, or just another demon he can subjugate? That would be unfortunate. I've never been good at being subjugated.*

"Well," I told the hags, gesturing at the forest. "Shall we go, then? If the Master of Demons is expecting us, we shouldn't keep him waiting." I was eager to get to the castle and speak with the human who commanded it, as well as rid myself of my travel companions. It had been a frustratingly slow trek to the Forest of a Thousand Eyes. The hag sisters traveled only at night; they were nocturnal creatures who were uncomfortable in the sun, and they also wanted to avoid being seen by humans. The second reason I could understand: a trio of ogresses and an oni wandering around in broad daylight would cause any humans who saw us to panic. And while the thought of unrestrained slaughter sounded like a lot of fun, I was trying to avoid fevered mobs and armies of grim-faced samurai. It was infuriating, hiding from mortals, but if I'd learned anything over the centuries, it was that if you massacred one town, settlement or army, ever more humans would follow, angry and zealous, determined to bring you down. At least no untainted mortal would venture close to the Forest of a Thousand Eyes, and the sunlight never pierced the cloud of gloom beneath the canopy. We could travel to the castle without fear of encountering humans, although, given the nature of the forest, I doubted the rest of the journey would be uneventful.

Impatient to be off, I started forward, passing the hag sisters, who blinked and gaped after me. "Wait, Lord Hakaimono," one called. "There is no path to Onikage castle. If you wait but a moment, we can summon a tainted kami to guide us."

"No need for that." I gave them a level stare. "I know the way."

We stepped into the forest, and the mist and shadows closed around us instantly, casting everything in shades of gray and black. I could feel the corrupted heartbeat of this place, like the center of a target, pulsing with dark power. There was no trail, but as I passed through the trees, cutting my way through undergrowth, I saw the gleam of bones beneath a few of their branches, accompanied by the faint stench of old blood and rotting meat. Jubokko were plentiful here—corrupted, malevolent trees that feasted on blood. They haunted old battlefields and heavily tainted areas, places of darkness and mass death, and looked like normal trees until it was too late. Many a traveler had gotten close to a jubokko's trunk, only to be snatched up by clawed branches, impaled with hollow thorns and drained of all blood and bodily fluids. Birds, time and insects would eat the unfortunate corpse still stuck in the tree, until only the bones were left to fall to the base of the trunk. That and the slight stench of rot were the only indicators of the tree's deadly nature.

Bones, bleached and white, glimmered in the roots of dozens of trees as we walked by. I glanced up once and noticed the skeleton of an unfortunate horse caught in the boughs of a particularly large jubokko, and this was still just the outskirts of the forest. I kept a careful eye on the branches as we passed beneath them, ready to draw Kamigoroshi at any time. But jubokko trees were twisted and corrupted things, pulsing with the power of Jigoku, and craved the blood of normal creatures. Oni and demons were not on their list of desirable prey, so the hags and I remained unmolested as we passed the thickest parts of the jubokko groves.

"Lord Genno will be most pleased to see you, Hakaimono-sama," the green hag said again, ducking under a thorn-covered branch. A cluster of bloody feathers buzzing with flies was stuck in a cradle of twigs. Sometimes, even the birds weren't safe from the blood-sucking jubokko. "Many of his strongest demons and yokai were slain in the battle four hundred years ago, and his entire cabal of blood mages were hunted down and executed. The army is not as strong as it was back then, but we're growing. Having you on our side this time will increase our odds of victory a thousandfold."

I nodded. "Is Genno's plan the same?" I asked. "March against the capital, kill the emperor and take the throne for himself? Once he makes a wish on the Dragon and is less incorporeal, that is."

"We're not certain," admitted the red ogress. "Lord Genno hasn't spoken of his plans for the empire, but he has said that he is not going to make the same mistakes. I'm sure he will discuss everything with you once you get there, Hakaimono-sama."

That was very unlikely, I mused. Not if Genno was the same angry, arrogant human I'd encountered four hundred years ago. Though he wasn't always all-powerful. The empire knew Genno as a talented, terrifyingly evil blood mage, and the history scrolls were full of the atrocities he'd committed as the Master of Demons. There was not much information about the life of a certain farmer, the headman of a village somewhere on the edge of Earth Clan territory. At that point in time, the clans were all at war, tearing each other apart and, as was the case in most wars, the commoners suffered in the cross fire. According to one small part of a history scroll, the headman of the Earth Clan village became aware of an invading Hino army and sent word to the local samurai lord, imploring him to send help. But rather than heed Genno's request, the Earth lord pulled all his warriors out of the area to fortify his own castle, abandoning the village to the Fire Clan. The Hino army swept through the defenseless village and razed it to the ground, slaughtering nearly everyone there, including Genno's family.

What happened next wasn't hard to imagine. The enraged headman swore vengeance upon the samurai caste and the empire that had failed him, and turned to blood magic to exact his revenge. Unlike the fickle magic of the kami-touched, Jigoku was always happy to bestow its dark power to willing mortals, in exchange for the practitioner's soul. The angry, grieving headman of the Tsuchi village became an extremely powerful blood mage, and the rest of his story became legend.

Four hundred years ago, I thought, swatting away a mosquito the size of my hand that kept buzzing around my face. *Genno has had plenty of time to scheme and plot revenge while he's been in Jigoku; I wonder if his plans to conquer the empire are the same, or if he's going to try something dif—*

My musings were interrupted by a scream somewhere overhead, as something big and black dropped from the branches of a hackberry tree. I leaped back, drawing Kamigoroshi in a heartbeat, as the trio of hags scuttled away and whirled around, raising their claws with menacing hisses.

The bloated, disembodied head of a black horse dangled upside down from the tree branch, mouth gaping to show rotten yellow teeth. There was no body; a sinewy coil of muscle at the base of its neck was all that kept it attached to the tree. Bulging white eyes rolled back to stare at us, as the creature opened its jaws and screamed again, the shrill, wailing sound of a dying animal.

"Wretched sagari!" The blue hag straightened, giving the swinging horse head a disgusted look. "A curse on all your kind, for I cannot think of a more useless creature to exist in the mortal realm."

I rolled my eyes. Sagari were twisted creatures that came from the spirit of a horse whose body was left to rot where it had died. They were grotesque but harmless; the most they could do was drop down from the tree branches and scream, though some humans had been known to die of fright when they saw one. The bigger concern wasn't the sagari itself, but the hair-raising shriek it produced that could be heard for miles. On a lonely road it was merely an annoyance; here in the Forest of a Thousand Eyes, it had just announced our presence to the entire wood, and every demon, ghost and yokai that lived here.

With a flash of steel, I severed the pathetic beast's neck. The head hit the ground with a thump and another ear-piercing wail, before seeming to melt into the dirt and disappear.

Silence descended, and in that heartbeat, I felt the entire forest turn its attention inward and find us in the shadows. I grinned back at it. *Come on, then. I've gone nearly a week without a fight, and Kamigoroshi is thirsty for blood. Whatever murderous horde, vengeful yurei or towering monster you have hiding in this forest, send it at me. I'm dying for a little slaughter.*

I turned to the hag sisters, who were gazing warily into the trees; they knew something would be coming, too. "Hope you're ready for a fight," I told them. "Everything knows where we are now, and things are going to get interesting."

The hags looked nervous. True, they were demons themselves and fairly powerful, even appearing in a few legends throughout the mortal world. But within the Forest of a Thousand Eyes were things even demons were afraid of. Old, angry things, driven mad with corruption, who cared nothing for legends and who would challenge even an oni. A thousand years ago I was the strongest demon general of Jigoku, and nothing dared to stand against me, but right now I was the size of a mortal and very edible-looking.

We continued deeper into the forest, which grew even darker and more tangled the farther we went. The leaves themselves began to drip with malevolence, mist coiled around our legs, and the ground turned spongy and disturbingly warm, as if the blood of thousands was still steeped into the very earth. I curled my claws around Kamigoroshi, aware that something was about to happen.

There was a flash of movement in the branches, as something large and bulbous flew at the back of the blue ogress. A human head, pale, disembodied and glowing with sickly red light, swooped through the trees, its gaping mouth showing serrated, sharklike teeth. It shrieked as it came in, and the hag whirled, throwing up her arm to slash it out of the air. But the head clamped its jaws around her forearm, and a second later there was a wet, tearing sound, the smell of blood, and the hag screamed. Fascinated, I watched the head rise into the air, the hag's spindly arm clutched between fang-filled jaws, streaming blood behind it. Its jaws worked, smacking greedily, and the ogress's limb vanished down its gullet in a crunching of bones and flesh. Gazing down at its victim, the head's colorless lips curved in a wide, bloody grin as it licked its teeth and the hag shrieked in rage.

There were more flashes in the trees, and nearly a dozen heads came swarming from the branches. Jaws gaping, they descended on us, teeth like broken bits of steel aiming for whatever flesh they could reach. A woman's head, trailing a ragged curtain of hair, swooped at me with a howl, and I split the skull down the middle. The head erupted into reddish-black mist and disappeared.

At the first apparition's death, the rest of the swarm paused and gazed at me in what looked like stunned surprise, then baleful fury. I raised Kamigoroshi and stepped forward.

"What's the matter?" I taunted, flourishing the bloody sword. "Bit off more than you could chew?" The heads didn't answer, but the way their lips pulled back to show jagged fangs indicated they understood every word I said.

With earsplitting screeches, the swarm rushed me, sending a jolt of adrenaline through my veins. I snarled a battle cry of my own and leaped forward to meet them. The first monster lunged at my face, jaws unhinged like a serpent, gaping wide to bite off my head. I swept Kamigoroshi between its teeth, splitting the head in two, and immediately turned to slash another darting in from the left. The blade sliced a bloody ribbon down its forehead to its chin, and the apparition reeled away with a scream. Turning, I flung out my empty claw as another head lunged, slamming my palm into the pale forehead and curling my talons into soft, rotting flesh. Dragging it from the air as it growled and shrieked and snapped at my arm, I raised the sword and plunged the blade between the eyes, pinning it to the earth.

As the head wailed and disappeared, the rest of the swarm hesitated again and floated back to glare at me. From the corner of my eye, I could see the hag trio, the red and the green standing protectively over the body of their moaning sister. Their claws were raised, and they appeared to be chanting something.

I glanced at the swarm, which had drawn into a cluster of hovering faces, still glaring at me with sullen hunger and rage. They seemed reluctant to approach Kamigoroshi now, and for a moment, I thought they would turn and flee.

With frenzied hisses and snarls, the swarm rose higher and began to congeal. One head turned and latched on to the side of another's skull, clinging like a leech, as its victim did the same to a third. As I stared in bemused fascination, the roiling cluster of faces each turned and clamped down on their neighbor, and as they did, their features began to blur and melt together. Eyes shifted and ran into one another, mouths began to slither together like eels, individual faces dissolved like ink in water, shifted around and became one. Two enormous eyes opened and stared at me with the malice of a dozen souls, and a single huge mouth gaped like a pit, glittering with hundreds of teeth.

"Neat trick." I smirked, seeing my reflection in its malignant glare as the single gigantic head loomed over me. "*Now* things have gotten interesting."

The head roared and fell toward me like a boulder. I dove aside as it crashed into the earth, mouth snapping and chewing as it thrashed about, turning rocks, dirt and tree branches into mulch. I rolled to my feet and sprinted forward, then drove the point of Kamigoroshi into its huge ear, sinking the blade in to the hilt. The head screamed and jerked away, tearing free of Kamigoroshi. There was a ripping, sucking sound as it rose into the air, leaving a normal-size head impaled on the end of my sword.

I snorted and flung the limp head to the ground, where it melted into the earth. "And the tricks keep coming," I told the giant face, which whirled around to face me. With a smile, I raised Kamigoroshi and prepared for the next attack. "Do you have any more surprises, or is that the last one?"

It lunged with another roar. Planting my feet, I lifted Kamigoroshi over my head and brought it straight down in front of me, splitting the head right down the middle. Blood flew everywhere, as the face tore in half and flew to either side of me.

A pair of smaller heads thumped to the ground near my feet, eyes unseeing, before dissolving into ethereal goop. But the severed halves of the large head turned on me, becoming two separate faces in midair. I had about a second to be surprised, before they both shot forward and clamped their jaws around my arms, sinking jagged fangs into my flesh.

Pain stabbed through my arms. With a snarl, I jerked back, trying to tear my limbs free. But the teeth were hooked like the jaws of a shark and only sank in deeper. One head had its jaws locked around my forearm, preventing me from using my sword. They rose into the air, taking me with them, and began yanking at my arms like a pair of dogs with a bone between them. Fangs ground against bone and sent flares of agony jolting up my arms.

Through the blinding pain and fury, I could sense Tatsumi's sudden, grim hope that this was it; that the heads would rip me apart, rip us both apart, forcing my spirit back into Kamigoroshi and sending his soul to whatever afterlife awaited him.

You'd like that, wouldn't you, Tatsumi? Between yanks by the floating heads, I caught glimpses of the hag sisters on the ground below. The two uninjured ones had their arms raised toward us, a sphere of roiling purple flames forming between them. *Don't get too excited; this is far from over.*

With a snarl, I drove my horned forehead into the face on my right arm, bashing it between the eyes as hard as I could. There was a resounding crack as our foreheads met, and the jaws around my arm loosened. I ripped the limb free, just as a ball of balefire smashed into the dazed head, engulfing it with a roar. The head screamed, this time in pain and terror. It split apart, a half dozen heads scattering in different directions, but none could escape the consuming flames. One by one they dropped, shrieking and burning, to the earth and dissolved to cinders on the wind.

My sword arm was free, but the head chewing on my other wrist refused to let go, even though we had drifted back to the earth. I turned, raising Kamigoroshi, and plunged it repeatedly into the head still clinging to my arm, stabbing it at several different angles, until the jaws finally loosened. Wounded and bleeding, the head finally tried to spit me out and fly away, but I shoved my hand deeper into its mouth and grabbed the back of its throat, sinking my claws into the slimy, disgusting tongue.

"Where do you think you're going?" I growled, and sank Kamigoroshi into one of the huge, staring eyes, ripping it sideways through its skull. Blood sprayed me, and a head dislodged, falling to the earth with a thump.

"You started this fight," I continued, plunging the blade into the other eye, then yanking it down through the chin. The head screamed a choking gurgle, jerking and thrashing wildly, but I kept my grip. "You should've known that to start a fight with me means finishing it. So, let's finish it!"

I raised Kamigoroshi, and slashed it straight through the middle of the bloody face, cleaving the skull in two. With a final shriek, the giant head fell away into four smaller heads, bloody and torn as they scattered around me. By the time they hit the ground, they were nothing but blobs of ethereal muck, melting into the fallen leaves.

I kicked away an oozing head, setting my jaw as pain stabbed up my lacerated muscles. The skin from wrist to elbow on both arms looked as if a pack of frenzied amanjaku had chewed on it. I growled softly, cursing this body's pathetic healing abilities. In my real form, wounds like this would be gone in a few heartbeats; even severed limbs would regrow in an hour or two. Still, this was half my body; now that I was fully free, my spirit suffused every part of this mortal form, granting it half of my considerable power instead of the fraction the demonslayers had used when I was trapped in the sword. Even if Tatsumi's body was small and frail, the gashes would be vanishing scars by the end of the day. They weren't life-threatening, merely annoying, and yet another reason I desperately missed my real form. Humans were so fragile and healed so ridiculously slowly, it was a wonder any of them survived till adulthood.

The blue ogress staggered to her feet, holding the white, jagged nub that had been her other arm. Blood oozed between her talons and her skin had gone rather pale, but her yellow eyes sought mine as she lurched forward with a gasp.

"Lord Hakaimono! You are injured. Are your wounds serious?"

"I'm fine," I told her, as the other two clustered around as well, barely giving their sister a second glance. For them, lost limbs were not a concern; they were demons and would regrow them eventually. "Hardly even scratches. They'll be gone by the end of the day."

"Oh, that's a relief," breathed the red hag. "With how weak

your body is now, we were afraid an injury like that would be debilitating."

"Is that so?" I crooned.

The hag's face went pale. "I didn't mean—" she began, but it was too late. I stepped forward, reached out and slammed my palm into her face, sinking my claws into her skull. Flexing my fingers, I squeezed until I felt the bone under my talons start to give, then stopped. The ogress squeaked, flailing and waving her hands, while the other two looked on in fearful anticipation.

"Do you feel how weak this body is?" I asked conversationally. "Do you feel safe now, knowing that a mere human cannot crush your skull like an overripe plum and let your brains leak out your ears?"

"Forgive... Lord Hakaimono," the hag gritted out, as a stream of blood ran from one nostril down her chin. "I meant...no disrespect. I was simply concerned that—"

"Did you think I was in danger of being eaten?" I went on, letting scorn seep into my words. "Or that I was unaware of what we just faced? I have lived among the Shadow Clan for centuries, listening to their ghost stories and tales of the horrors that roam this land. I have heard many stories of the family that was murdered in this forest, how their heads were chopped off by bandits and left to rot in the dirt. Did you not think I would recognize the most infamous ghost that haunts these woods?" I flexed my claws, and the ogress gasped, sinking to her knees before me. "I am Hakaimono, First Oni of Jigoku," I growled, "and I was feared long before the legend of the Man-eating Head became known throughout the country. I have killed thousands of men to its dozens. Remember that, for next time I might become truly annoyed."

I released the hag, throwing her back, and she and her sisters immediately fell to their knees and pressed their faces to the dirt. "Forgive us, Lord Hakaimono," the blue ogress pleaded, even as the blood from her jagged stump continued to drip to the ground. "It has been so long since you have walked Ningen-kai, we forgot that you are truly the greatest of all demons. Forgive our insolence. It will not happen again."

"This time," I told them, and turned away, feeling strangely irritated with myself. Not for reminding them who I was or putting them in their place; among demons, if you weren't strong, you were prey. Even the hag sisters, though they called me Hakaimono-sama and recognized my superiority, would turn on me in an instant if they thought I was weak. If one of them had spoken to me like that when I was in my real form, I would have done more than threaten; I would have torn the offender into little pieces and made the other two watch.

But I *hadn't,* and that was the problem. There were three ogresses; killing one to prove a point was what should have happened. I should have crushed the hag's skull between my fingers and let her brains leak over the ground, as I had threatened. I should have made certain the survivors knew that Hakaimono was someone to be obeyed, feared and never questioned. And yet, I'd let her live.

I had shown mercy.

Irritation flared into disgust, and I clenched a fist, barely stopping myself from spinning around and driving my claws through the back of the hag's skull, after all. I was not myself, I realized. I'd spent too many years in the sword, in the minds of weak-willed humans with their feeble emotions polluting me like Jigoku's corruption poisoned the souls of men. I had once been the most feared, ruthless oni lord with no concept of human feelings, but for the past four hundred years, I had been continuously exposed to repulsive sentiments like honor, mercy, kindness and love. And now that frailty was seeping into my consciousness.

Resolve settled over me like a grim cloak. There could be

no hint of weakness in Genno's court, no shadow of doubt or hesitation. If I was going to make the self-proclaimed Master of Demons do what I wanted, I would have to be just as ruthless, if not more so, than him.

We continued through the forest, which had grown eerily still after the battle with the Man-eating Heads, as if the rest of the inhabitants were in hiding. Perhaps they had decided that any creature that could slay the most dangerous ghost to haunt the Forest of a Thousand Eyes was something best left alone. But as night fell and the woods grew darker and even more tangled, I began to see movement in the trees; pale figures sliding through the undergrowth. A woman in a bloody white dress, watching me between tree trunks, a samurai walking behind us on the narrow trail, the front of his armor smashed open to reveal a gaping, bloody hole. They floated or flickered around us, a host of yurei and restless spirits; mortals that had fallen in the tainted forest and were now trapped, unable to find their way to Meido, or wherever human souls ended up. Most of them seemed confused, grief stricken, but one ghost—the bloody woman in white—stalked us through the trees, winking in and out of existence, until I finally drew Kamigoroshi in annoyance. The yurei fled as the blade's cold purple light washed into the trees, and did not bother us again.

At last, with dawn about an hour away, we reached a vast chasm that cut through the forest like an old wound. A rotten wooden bridge spanned the gulf, and on the other side, a skeletal castle loomed, tiered pagoda roofs stabbing the night sky. Pallid mist clung to its walls like ragged curtains, pale tendrils writhing up from the chasm and slithering over the ground. The structure itself was falling apart, half covered in choking vines and roots, as it seemed the forest had not taken kindly to the intruder within its boundaries and was trying to pry it apart. But lights flickered within the windows, and a lit torch stood at the other end of the bridge, indicating the ruin was no longer abandoned.

"Here we are," sighed the blue hag sister as we approached the bridge. Her left shoulder had already sprouted a withered blue arm with knobby digits that would soon become talons. "Let us go, quickly. I am eager to see Lord Genno, and he will certainly wish to speak with you right away, Hakaimono-sama."

The bridge groaned under my weight, creaking and protesting every step, but the rotten planks held. An icy wind rushed up from the misty chasm below, smelling of grave dust and old bones. I gazed across the gorge to the castle, taking note of the gate and large, iron-banded doors barring it shut. "No guards," I mused as we reached the center of the bridge. "Your Master of Demons seems certain that no one is going to attack his castle, if he isn't even posting sentries. Though I'm not sure if that's confidence or arrogance. What's to stop an army from marching across the bridge and strolling through the ga—"

A vibrating groan drifted up from the chasm, and the mist below us started to writhe. The hags tensed and gripped the railings of the bridge, gazing nervously into the darkness, as the wind moaned around us and the planks started to tremble.

An enormous pale skull rose out of the sea of mist. Even bigger than the Man-eating Head, it loomed into the air with huge eye sockets the size of wagon wheels. The skull was followed by an equally giant skeletal body, old yellow bones gleaming in the moonlight as it towered over us, one bony hand big enough to snap the bridge like kindling and send us plunging into the void.

"Ah," I said, as the gashadokuro peered down at us, red points of light glimmering in its hollow eye sockets. Supremely powerful, gashadokuro were relatively rare, formed at sites of massive death and destruction—such as battlefields or a plague-ridden city—or summoned by potent blood magic. As strong a blood mage as Genno was, it wasn't surprising that he would summon the infamous gashadokuro to guard the gates of his castle. "I guess that answers that question."

"Lord Genno is expecting us," the red hag called, craning her neck to stare up at the monstrous skeleton, creaking like an ancient ship in the wind. "We have permission to be here, we are part of his inner circle. You will let us pass."

The gashadokuro didn't answer. I wasn't sure it could even speak, but its huge jaws opened and it rattled menacingly. Its arm began to rise, as if to crush us and the bridge we stood on, and I dropped my hand to Kamigoroshi.

"Your sentry doesn't seem to recognize you," I remarked, tensing to leap out of the way once that giant claw came smashing down. "I'd hate to have to destroy such an expensive guard dog, but if it doesn't back off, I'm going to make a lot of scavengers very happy."

"The pass phrase!" the blue hag snapped, whirling on her sister. "Do you remember? You have to speak the pass phrase—it's the only thing it will understand."

The gashadokuro's arm was nearly at its peak. I gripped Kamigoroshi and started drawing it from its sheath, as the green hag's eyes widened, glaring up at the huge skeleton.

"Death to the empire!" she cried, her voice echoing over the chasm. "All hail the great and terrible Master of Demons. Let all men tremble before Lord Genno's magnificent return!"

The gashadokuro's limb trembled, then stopped. With a slow creak, it lowered its arm and became motionless. I snorted and shoved Kamigoroshi back in its sheath.

"You have to shout *that* every time you want to cross the bridge? I can practically hear Genno's ego swelling."

The hags pretended not to hear me. Passing the now unresponsive gashadokuro, we continued to the end of the bridge and stood before the gates of the castle.

Or, where the gates should have been. The archway stood at

the end of the bridge, its once ornate wooden frame now rotting and falling apart, but instead of a pair of wooden doors that opened onto the courtyard, there was a continuous wall of rock and stone.

I glanced at the ogresses, who all sighed as if they couldn't believe they had to put up with this. Scowling, the red hag marched up to the stone wall, raised a clawed foot and gave it a resounding kick.

"Nurikabe! You stupid piece of rock, I know you see us! Let us in."

"Who wishes to enter Lord Genno's domain?"

The voice was deep and gravelly, and a single red eye suddenly blinked open in the center of the wall, rolling up to stare at the hag. I shook my head. A nurikabe was a type of living wall yokai that seemed to exist simply to baffle and infuriate travelers. They would plant themselves in front of an opening—be it a door, a cave entrance, even a mountain or forest path—camouflage themselves to blend seamlessly with their surroundings and obstinately refuse to move. They could not be knocked down, and attempting to go over or through the nurikabe would cause it to react and kill the unfortunate traveler. Thankfully, there weren't many of them in the world anymore. Nurikabe were slow and stupid, but extremely difficult to kill. Sometimes they could be tricked into leaving or moving aside, but once they made up their minds, the only way past the nurikabe was to destroy it.

The red hag made an impatient noise. "You can see that it's us," she hissed. "Move aside. We have important business with Lord Genno."

Another large crimson eye opened, this one near the bottom corner of the wall, and rolled around as it took us in. "I know you," the yokai said to the hag in a slow, ponderous voice. "I know you, and I know them." Both eyes stilled, flicking past the ogress to stare balefully at me. "But I don't know him," it rumbled. "And Lord Genno was insistent that I do not open this gate for anyone I do not recognize."

"Don't *recognize* him?" the green hag exclaimed. "You stupid blind fool, don't you know who this is? This is Hakaimono the Destroyer, commander of the Four Great Demon Generals and the First Oni Lord of Jigoku."

"Hakaimono?" The eyes blinked slowly, and the yokai seemed to settle even farther into the ground. "I do not know anyone of that name."

I exhaled. This was amusing...and ridiculous. I figured I could circumvent the nurikabe entirely and go over the wall, but I was not going to sneak into Genno's castle like a shinobi in the night. The Master of Demons knew I was coming; he should've known better than to put this absurd obstacle in my path.

"Not going to let me pass?" I asked, and the nurikabe glowered, its eyes a sullen red in its stony body. I drew Kamigoroshi, and the blade flared a bright purple in the face of the monster. The three hags skittered aside; they knew better than to get in the way. Three more eyes opened in the nurikabe's featureless wall, and with a rumble of stone and dirt, a pair of thick stone arms emerged from the monster's body, huge fists clenched in front of it. I grinned, flourished Kamigoroshi and sank into a low stance. "Then I guess I'll have to carve a path right through you!"

"Enough!" boomed a voice. A figure shimmered to life overhead, pale and translucent in the moonlight, a broad-shouldered human in a pure white robe, wide sleeves billowing around him. His hair was long, the sides pulled into a topknot, and two tendril-like strands extended from his upper lip nearly to his belt, floating down his chest like dragon whiskers. His eyes were sharp, his brows sharper and his chin was the sharpest of all; a razor blade of a face pulled into a grim frown.

"Lord Genno," said the blue hag, and all three of them bowed. I remained standing, watching as the specter floated closer. It ignored the three ogresses, circling me like a pale shark, leaving trails of wispy light behind it. I didn't move, even when the yurei passed behind me, cold dead eyes on my back, before floating around again.

"Hakaimono," the figure stated, gazing down at me. "So, you really have come, after all."

"Genno," I acknowledged, with a smirk and a very slight nod. "You look exactly the same as you did four hundred years ago. Well, minus a body."

The specter's bloodless mouth thinned. "And you are the same irreverent demon that got in the way of my army four centuries back," it said irritably, and pointed at me with a long, elegant finger. "Let me remind you, Hakaimono—you might be the greatest of the oni lords, but you are still trapped within the body of a mere mortal. This is my domain, and you are a lot easier to kill."

"No need for threats." I smiled, showing fangs. "I didn't come here for a fight, human. I heard you had a bit of trouble with your new body, so I thought I'd offer my assistance."

The specter of the Master of Demons raised a pale eyebrow. "Intriguing," he mused. "The First Oni comes to me with an offer of help. Not for free, of course."

"Of course not." I snorted. "Enlisting the service of an oni lord is never cheap, you should know that better than anyone, Master of Demons." I spread my arms, smiling up at him. "If you want my help, I'm willing to join your little quest to take down the empire, and I'll probably have a great time doing it. But I've got a price, and I think it's one you'll be willing to pay."

"And what makes you think I need your assistance?"

"Because you're not a fool. Because you know I'm far too powerful an ally, and far too dangerous an enemy, to refuse this offer. Besides..." My smile grew wider. "I think you will be *very* interested to hear this offer, especially considering the times."

Genno's brows rose. Very slightly, but it was noticeable. The specter drifted back, his shimmery form becoming even paler. "Come to my tower," he said, folding his hands into his billowy sleeves. "I am uncomfortable speaking in the open. Nurikabe," he said without looking at the wall monster. "Allow them to pass. I will see you shortly, Lord Hakaimono," he continued, as his form faded slowly into nothingness. "The Yama sisters will show you the way."

The Master of Demons vanished on the wind, leaving us alone in front of the castle gates. The nurikabe glared at me with its multiple red eyes, but with a grinding of stone against stone, the heavy slab of wall dragged itself away from the gate entrance, just enough for a body to fit through without having to squeeze.

I turned to the hag sisters. "Shall we?"

Without waiting for an answer, I stepped forward, slipping through the space between the gate and the nurikabe, and into the Master of Demon's domain.

10

NEKO AND LUCKY FROGS

Yumeko

I blinked at Reika. "What do you mean, you can't find them?"

The shrine maiden glared at me and lowered her voice even further, indicating I should do the same. "I mean, they're gone," she said again. "After we were shown our quarters, I kept having this eerie feeling that I was being watched, especially when Chu kept growling at the walls and ceiling. So I decided that I should find the others and discuss this little predicament we've found ourselves in. When the tea was delivered, I asked the servant where the others were staying, and when she left I stepped out to find them."

"No one stopped you, Reika-san?" I asked in a whisper.

"Not a one. Though make no mistake, I'm certain I was being watched. Anyway, when I got to their rooms, both were empty. Taiyo-san and the baka ronin had both disappeared, and I have no idea where they are." The shrine maiden made a frustrated, exasperated gesture. "It's the middle of the night—who knows what trouble the ronin is getting into. We should not be separated now, not when we have something so important to accomplish. And of course, none of the servants were of any help. No one had seen them leave, or knew where they had gone." Reika grimaced. "And they expected me to believe that, in this castle where the walls have eyes and the floors seem to be listening to your every word." She gave me a weary look. "So I figured I'd better come find you, make sure you hadn't up and vanished, either. Especially after talking to the daimyo. Speaking of which, what of the meeting with Lady Hanshou? Can we be certain she knows nothing about *it*?"

It? Oh, the scroll. "Yes, Reika-san," I said, and the shrine maiden relaxed a little. "She doesn't know about...erm...*the thing*. But I did meet Tatsumi's sensei, who warned me that Lord Iesada might try to have us killed."

"Killed?" Reika's brows shot up. "Why?"

"Because...I...um, promised Lady Hanshou that we would find Tatsumi and save him from Hakaimono."

"You did *what*?" The miko's eyes bulged, momentarily forgetting to be quiet. "Merciful Jinkei, why in the name of all the sacred Kami would you promise something like that?" I took a breath to explain, but she held up her hand. "No, I don't want to hear about it now," she said in a whisper. "This is something we all need to be present for, Master Jiro especially. And then you can explain to us all why you made the decision to go chasing after the demonslayer instead of taking *it* to the temple." She glared at me in exasperation, then let out a sigh. "This is bad. If you say Lord Iesada is working against Hanshou-sama's wishes...I need to find Okame and Taiyo-san, before they disappear down a dark hallway and are never seen again."

"Where should we start, Reika-san?" I asked.

She gave me a stern look. "*You* aren't going anywhere. You are going to stay in this room where I don't have to worry about where you are or what trouble you're getting into. It will be safer than having you wander around this maze of a castle. And don't pin your ears at me." She returned my frown. "If we get lost or separated, I don't want to spend even more time trying to find *you* as well as Taiyo-san and the baka ronin. You'll be safer here. A guest being attacked by shinobi in their own quarters would bring eternal shame and dishonor to the clan hosting them. If you're safely in your room, you won't raise any suspicions."

"What about Lord Iesada?" I asked. "He could have shinobi of his own. There could be assassins hiding under the floors or in the wall paintings, waiting to ambush you."

"All the more reason I should go alone. I'm just a humble shrine maiden. I'm not carrying anything important. No one will care if I disappear."

"*I* would care, Reika-san."

She gave me a pointed look, as if that were the end of it. "You're not coming with me, Yumeko. End of story."

She wasn't going to change her mind, so I nodded and sighed. "All right, Reika-san," I told her, "but how will you find the others? This castle is like a maze. Oh, do you need string? I could probably make you a ball of string."

"No. I'll get Chu to follow their trail. He should be able to track them by scent, as odorous as the ronin is." The shrine maiden wrinkled her nose. "He'll be able to find his way back, as well. What I don't want to do is go gallivanting through Ha-kumei castle without knowing where you are." She pointed a finger at the floor. "So you are going to stay right here, in this room, and not leave, understand? If anything strange happens, remember that Master Jiro and Ko are across the hall, and neither of them are defenseless." Her lips thinned. "Still, I need to hurry. I don't like the idea of leaving him alone in this place.

Baka men." She walked to the door, shaking her head, as Chu followed. "What could have come over those two, that they would just up and leave without a word to anyone?"

"Okame-san hasn't been himself since the Path of Shadows," I said as Reika pushed open the shoji and peered into the hallway. A dark, polished floor, flickering lanterns and fusuma panel walls greeted her as she leaned out of the room. "I hope he's all right."

Reika sniffed. "He probably wandered off to get drunk, and dragged Taiyo-san along with him," she muttered, gazing up and down the corridor. "It looks clear," she said, and glanced back into the room. "I'm going. Remember what I said, Yumeko. Stay here. Don't get into trouble. Promise me."

I nodded. "Be careful, Reika-san."

"Chu," the miko said, gazing down at the dog. "Let's go. Find the ronin and Taiyo-san."

The small orange dog immediately put his nose to the floor and trotted into the hallway, his claws clicking over the wood. With one last stern glare at me, the shrine maiden shut the door between us, and I listened to their footsteps pad away down the corridor.

As soon as the sound faded into silence, I rose and walked to the door. I trusted Reika, and I knew she was just trying to protect the scroll, but if Daisuke and Okame were in trouble, I certainly wasn't going to sit by myself and do nothing. The miko would be cross, but I'd never actually *agreed* to stay in my room. As I'd once pointed out to Jin when he had made me promise not to eat the rice cakes he'd left on the counter, I had never spoken the actual words out loud, thus I couldn't be held to it.

However, when I opened my door, I came face-to-face with my maid. Even with a full tea tray in her hands, I hadn't heard her approach; it was like she'd materialized out of thin air, or had learned to hover over the ground like a yurei ghost when she walked.

"Oh," she exclaimed, taking a quick step back as if startled. "I'm sorry, I didn't know you were coming out. Please excuse me, miss." She bobbed her head and slipped past me into the room, averting her eyes as she did, and put the tea on the low table. I watched her suspiciously, looking for any sign that she might've been spying on us, but she acted perfectly normal.

"Is there anything else you need?" she asked, still keeping her gaze demurely on the floor as she straightened. "If I can fetch you anything, you have but to ask."

"Ano," I said after a moment's hesitation. The maid, who had been ready to leave, glanced up at me curiously. "I'm sorry, but I've never been inside a castle before," I went on, looking away as if embarrassed. "I'm not sure... I mean, could you show me... where the toilets are?"

"Oh." The maid smiled and relaxed. "Of course. Please, follow me."

"Thank you."

We slipped from the room, and I followed her down the narrow hallways, passing a few samurai and servants in black. Even though it was quite late, there were still a lot more people up and about than I would have thought. Perhaps they disliked the sunlight. Perhaps the Shadow Clan preferred doing most of their business in the dark like owls or bats. In any case, none of them paid us any attention, though I could still feel eyes on me in the hall and all the way down the stairs to the lower floor. The maid led me to a room with a stone floor and several stalls made of wood. In the center of each, a narrow rectangular pit dropped down into pitch-blackness.

"Shall I stay, miss?" the maid asked, sounding reluctant but trying not to show it. "Do you need to be shown the way back?"

"I don't think that will be necessary," I told her, and watched relief flit over her face. "I should be all right from here. Thank you."

The maid left quickly, and I smiled, mincing my way into

one of the stalls. Here, at least, I was fairly certain no one would be spying on me.

Huddled against the wall with the pit at my feet, I fished into my furoshiki and withdrew two more of the small, slightly crushed leaves I'd picked up before we arrived at the castle.

Sometimes you're very cranky, Reika-san, I thought, placing one leaf on my head. *But I guess I have to thank you for this.*

A puff of white smoke filled the toilet stall. As it cleared, I shook away the tendrils and took a quick glance at myself, seeing a simple robe and a pair of slender hands clutching a tea tray. Nodding once in satisfaction, I exited the stall and strode into the hall.

All right, I thought, gazing around. A samurai rushed past me with a curt grunt, ducking into one of the stalls. I quickly moved away from the toilets before I started hearing things I'd rather not. And also before he could wonder why I was holding a tea tray while going to the toilet. *Where could Daisuke and baka Okame have gotten off to? Maybe I'll check their rooms first, in case they left anything behind.*

Holding the tray, I made my way back to our quarters, taking care not to get lost in the labyrinthine maze of corridors and passageways. More servants and a few samurai passed me in the passages, none of whom gave me a second glance.

I slid open the door to what I was certain was one of our rooms, though I wasn't sure whose yet, and looked around. It was empty, and I turned to leave.

However, as I slipped out the door, I felt a firm grip on my upper arm. With a yelp, I spun and came face-to-face with the older servant, who glared at me with hard black eyes.

"What are you doing?" she demanded, with none of the cool politeness she'd shown me earlier. "You are not supposed to be here now. I sent you to the kitchens for Hanari-san's tea. Why aren't you at your station?"

"I…um…the girl asked me to show her the way to the toilets," I stammered, earning an annoyed huff from the other woman. Before she could say anything, I added, "She also wanted to know where her two missing companions were, and when they would return. What should I tell her if she asks again?"

The woman sighed. "The last I heard, the Taiyo and the yo-jimbo had left the castle and were heading toward the Lucky Frog gambling hall on the east side of town. Our shinobi are tracking them as we speak, but they are not important."

"Oh." I kept the puzzled frown from my face. *But, Reika said that no one had seen Daisuke or Okame leave the castle. Are they deliberately trying to mislead us?*

"Do not let the girl leave." The woman gave me a warning scowl. "The others can come and go as they wish, but Masao-sama was very specific that the peasant girl not be allowed to leave the castle until Lord Iesada returns to his own lands. It could be dangerous if she goes into the city, or anyplace our shinobi cannot keep an eye on her. If she asks where the men are again, tell her they went to visit the Painted Smile geisha house for the evening. That should keep her from venturing after them. Now, go." She gestured firmly down the hall. "Return to your duties. You are wasting time loitering about."

I bobbed a quick bow and hurried away in the direction she pointed, my mind spinning with this new information.

Well, that confirmed what I'd suspected since arriving here. The walls *did* have eyes and ears. There was probably a shinobi lurking by the toilets right now, waiting to see when I would come out. That thought made me snicker, but it did present a problem. I needed to go outside to look for Daisuke and Okame, but the Kage didn't want me to leave the castle. If they saw me leave, they would likely stop me.

If they saw me.

Slipping into an empty room, I made certain I was alone before pulling the third and final leaf from my obi and placing it on my head, letting fox magic engulf me again. When the smoke cleared, I did a quick scan of my white haori and red hakama, making sure everything was in place. Now, if anyone spotted me, they would see a no-nonsense, very determined shrine maiden, and hopefully not get in her way. The only thing missing was Chu, and I hoped the Kage would not notice or care that the miko was without her dog.

All I had to worry about was running into Reika herself.

I shivered. Quickly, I slipped from the room and began striding down the hallway, searching for a way out, while keeping one ear open for the click of dog nails on the hardwood floors.

After a couple inquires using my best Firm Reika Voice, I finally found the front entrance to the castle, where across a vast hall of polished wood and onyx statues, a pair of huge double doors stood half-open. Two samurai guarded either side of the large frame, flickering lantern light gleaming off their black armor and tall yari spears. They eyed me with stoic interest as I approached, but didn't move to block my path, though one gave me a stern look as I walked toward them.

"Going into the city?" he asked.

I nodded.

"You are welcome to leave," the samurai told me, "so long as you do not cause trouble within Ogi Owari Toshi. Be advised, you are under Kage law, and all who break the rules of the Shadow Clan will be dealt with accordingly." He gave a solemn nod of his head. "Have a pleasant evening, and please be safe while in the city."

I smiled at him and escaped into the cool air of the outside.

My sandals crunched against gravel as I made my way across the courtyard, toward the front gates of the high stone wall surrounding the castle. Aside from my footsteps, the night was quiet and still. From the position of the moon overhead, it was very early morning, perhaps a few hours until dawn. I glanced over my shoulder once to see Hakumei castle towering behind me, the main keep standing rigid against the navy sky, tiled pagoda roofs sweeping gracefully upward. Much like its people, the Shadow Clan's home castle was elegant and ominous, beautiful and menacing at the same time. I wondered if that was deliberate, to remind the rest of the world that though the Kage were proud and cultured like the rest of the clans, they were not to be trifled with.

Shaking off my morbid musings, I continued walking, the shadow of Hakumei-jo swallowing me even as I moved away from it. Past the barren but meticulously groomed courtyard, I reached the large front gates, which stood open and were guarded by more samurai, none of whom said anything to me. After passing beneath the huge wooden frame, I paused just outside the gate and gazed down the road in wonder.

Hakumei castle sat on a hill overlooking what I assumed was the city of Ogi Owari. Down the winding road from the front gates and across an arched stone bridge over a wide, sleepy river, the Kage capital glimmered with torch and lantern light. It sprawled in every direction, rows of houses sitting primly along the streets and the banks of the canals that cut through the city. Large trees were interspersed among the buildings, branches draped over roofs and hanging in the streets, as if the city reluctantly shared the space with a forest, and neither were willing to back down.

With an eager smile, I hurried down the road, crossed the bridge and entered the city. Despite the late hour, it was far from empty. People wandered the roads, shop doors stood open against the night, and merchants lurked in doorways or manned wooden stalls, waiting for customers. At first, it reminded me of another, smaller town, Chochin Machi, which also came to life and thrived when the sun went down. But as I continued through the streets, I began to see the differences. Chochin Machi had a bright, almost festive feel to it, encouraging visitors to dance and smile and leave their troubles behind. Though it was lit up and busy, Ogi Owari Toshi was definitely not festive. No one in the streets smiled or laughed; often an individual or small group would stagger down the road, as if they had no control of their limbs. Sometimes, people sang or argued with each other, their voices slurred and unsteady like their legs. A large man, clutching a sake gourd like Okame's, called out to me in a garbled voice and then rumbled a laugh, making my tail bristle. It wasn't a very nice laugh. Much like the city, it held the edge of something ominous beneath the veneer of frivolity, a smiling illusion over a patiently waiting predator.

Pausing at a crossroads marked by a large, twisted maple tree, I glanced up at the moon through the branches, noting its position and that the night was rapidly slipping away from me. *All right, I'm here. Now, I have to find this gambling hall; the Dancing Frog or Lucky Frog or something like that. So, where am I?* A sign, tacked to the trunk beneath the large rope that marked the tree as sacred, read Beware of Bad Fortune, which told me nothing at all.

"What are you doing near my tree, fox?"

With a start, I looked up and saw a pair of green eyes staring at me from a limb. For a second, they appeared to float in the air, but then I saw they were attached to the lean, furry body of a neko—a common cat—lying on a tree branch, its glossy black fur blending perfectly with the shadows. An extremely long, slinky tail lashed its hindquarters as its gaze met mine. As I watched, a second tail rose from behind the neko to twine with the first, making my eyes widen. I didn't know much about cats, but in kitsune lore, the more tails a fox had, the older and more powerful it was. The strongest kitsune in existence were called ninetails, for in the stories, when a fox grew its ninth tail, its fur would turn silver or gold, and it would possess magic to rival the gods themselves.

Of course, a ninetailed fox was a creature of legend, as rare as a dragon or the sacred kirin. To meet a kitsune with even two tails was a great honor, though I wasn't sure the same custom extended to the feline world. Still, it was probably wise to be polite. Cats had never spoken to me; the old black-and-white feline at the Silent Winds temple had merely tolerated my presence, and after all the times I'd used him for a prank, if he could have spoken, he would have told me off numerous times. But neko were strange, fickle creatures, and you never knew what they were thinking. If one day that old cat had started speaking to me, I wouldn't have been shocked at all.

The cat in the tree curled its whiskers and wrinkled its nose. "Ugh, I can smell your stink from here," she remarked. "Leave this place, kitsune. You belong in the fields with the rabbits and bears and the rest of the common forest dwellers. Go back to plaguing farmers and fishermen outside the city walls, and leave the civilized places to us." When I didn't move or reply, she flattened her ears. "Are you simple as well as repulsive?" she asked. "I shall speak slowly so your barbaric forest brain can comprehend. You have no place here, fox. This is my territory, and you are making it unbearable. Go away."

"There's no need to be rude." I frowned at her. "I'm just visiting Kage lands, I'll be gone soon enough. Besides, you're mistaken. I didn't grow up in a field, I grew up in a temple. I can read and write, and even eat with chopsticks. Can you?"

The neko sniffed, twitching her tail. "Giving a monkey chopsticks and dressing it in a fancy kimono does not make it civilized," she said in a bored voice. "So you have learned a few tricks. Congratulations. You are still a fox. Your ancestors chased rabbits and defecated on the floor of their dens, as all wild creatures will."

"And what about you?" I demanded. "Your ancestors probably chased mice and mated under the full moon. You're not any more civilized than I am."

"Is that so?" The cat slitted her eyes, regarding me lazily, and turned her head. "Do you see that fish vendor over there?" she asked, pointing with a flick of one of her tails. "I can walk into his shop, twitch my ears and he throws me his leftover fish guts. If you are so civilized, kitsune, why don't you change forms and do the same? Become a fox, and let us see how he reacts."

For one crazy moment, I considered it, then shook my head. "No, this is ridiculous. I don't have time to be standing under a tree arguing with a cat. I have to find the Lucky Frog."

"The gambling hall?" The neko tilted her head. "Why would you want to go there, fox? Nothing to see but loud, shouting men who reek of sake. Although, they would certainly find your company more pleasant than I."

I looked up at her again, pricking my ears. "You know where it is?"

"This is my territory." She waved her tails in an arrogant manner. "I know where everything is."

"Would you take me there?"

The neko sneezed several times. After a moment I realized she was laughing at me. "Why in the name of the Split-tailed Marauder would I do that?" she finally asked. "Do I look like a fawning, slobbering dog that does everything the humans say?"

"No, you look like a cat," I said, confused. "Why would I mistake you for a dog? You said you knew where everything is in your territory. I thought you could show me the way."

"I *could*," said the cat, and settled more comfortably on the tree branch. "But I won't."

"Nani? Why not?" I scowled, falling silent as a man walked by the tree, giving me a quizzical look. "Are you doing something else?" I whispered after he'd passed. "Something important?"

"Very important." The neko gave one tail a languid wave. "I am sitting in this tree observing all that goes on in my territory. It is an essential part of my night, something a common field fox would not understand." She yawned, showing a flash of long yellow teeth, before closing her eyes. "Now, be gone and leave me in peace. I find everything about you offensive."

I pinned my ears at the arrogant creature. *Stupid neko. How would Okame or Reika-san handle this?*

I thought about it a moment, then stepped back. "I see. Well, thank you for your time, neko-san. It's all right if you don't know where it is. I can find my way there on my own."

"Didn't you hear me, field fox?" The neko opened her eyes and peered down at me. "I said I know where it is, I just have no interest in taking you there." I didn't answer, and her gaze narrowed. "I know what you are doing," she warned, as her tails began an agitated thump-thump against the branch. "Your little kitsune tricks will not work on me. I have no interest in playing tour guide to a common field fox, now begone."

I shrugged. "As you say, neko-san. I'm sure I can find someone who knows the way. Have a good evening."

I stepped away from the trunk, and the cat hissed. "Halt, forest creature," she ordered, making me pause and glance back. Lashing her tails, the neko rose and leaped out of the branch, landing without a sound at the base.

"Do not speak to me," she said, stalking past with both tails held high. "I am not helping you, I am merely proving that I know every inch of my territory and that you are a barbaric forest creature who does not belong here. Follow if you must, but not too close, and try to stay downwind. I do not wish to smell you the entire way to the gambling hall."

I hid a smile and followed my surly guide into the shadowy back alleys of Ogi Owari.

★ ★ ★

The Lucky Frog gambling hall stood on a narrow street next to a textiles warehouse and a dilapidated restaurant. It was a large, two-story building with blue tiled roofs, wooden slats across the windows and a pair of burly looking men guarding the entrance. A faded sign picturing a smiling frog holding up a gold coin hung crookedly over the door.

The neko sniffed. "There," she stated in a tone of bored grandeur. "The Lucky Frog gambling hall, exactly where I said it would be. Now, don't you feel foolish doubting the word of a cat, field fox?"

"This is the Lucky Frog?" I murmured, gazing up at the rooftops, looking for odd shadows or flickers of movement that shouldn't be there. "I hope Daisuke and Okame are all right." Glancing down at the cat, I offered a smile and quick bow. "Thank you for escorting me here, neko-san. I'm in your debt."

She curled her whiskers. "As if I need the favor of a forest creature," she said disdainfully. With a sniff, she raised her chin and turned away. "I am bored now. Do what you like, kitsune. Hopefully I will not see you again in the future. Oh, but a friendly warning. In case your pathetic human instincts could not sense it, we were being followed."

Alarm flickered and I looked around, though the shadows overhead were empty. "Followed? By whom?"

"A human." The cat yawned, waving her tails. "A silly human in black, thinking it is being silent and unseen as it creeps through the darkness. I see their kind often, skulking through the city. Pretending they are cats. Pathetic." She twitched her whiskers. "Farewell, forest creature. Do leave my territory as soon as you are able."

Twin tails in the air, the neko trotted away, slipped into an alley between two buildings and was gone.

Keeping an eye out for lurking shinobi, I hurried across the road and approached the entrance to the Lucky Frog. The two men standing at the doors were both very large. Their haori jackets hung open in the front, showing off their enormous stomachs and swirls of painted skin. I saw a tiger in lethal combat with a white snake etched down one man's body, while his friend was so covered in colorful ink it looked like he was wearing another shirt. They saw me approaching and straightened, puzzled looks crossing their jowly faces, but before I could do or say anything, the door between them slid open and a body came hurtling through. It hit the edge of the street and rolled to a stop in a cloud of dust, as lantern light flickered over a familiar reddish-brown ponytail. I gasped and hurried forward as the body groaned and shifted in the dirt.

"Okame-san!"

"Kuso," growled the ronin, struggling upright. Raising his head, he glared at the door, where another large man dusted his hands off and turned away. "I didn't have anything in my sleeves, you bastards!" he called. "And if you think I was the only one with weighted dice in there, you're dumber than the monkeys tattooed on your ass!"

"Are you all right, Okame-san?" I asked, as the ronin pushed himself to his feet, swaying unsteadily. His clothes were different, I noticed; his brown hakama and unmarked red haori were absent of blood and grime, and he was mostly clean. "What happened to you?" The ronin gave me a dark, slightly sour look and turned away, brushing at his pants.

"What are you doing here, priestess?" he growled, making me blink in confusion, until I remembered that I wasn't Yumeko right now, I was Reika. "Did you come all this way to lecture me on the evils of drinking and gambling halls?"

"No, Okame-san." I shook my head. "You disappeared from

the castle, you and Daisuke-san both. We...erm... Yumeko and I were worried about you."

"I had to clear my head," Okame gruffed. "Sitting around that castle was making me jumpy. Getting drunk and losing a lot of money has always worked in the past." He scowled back at the doors. "Except the nights you hit on an extremely lucky streak and the brutes who run the hall accuse you of cheating. Those were the house dice I was using, you cheap bastards!" he snarled at the two large men, who glowered back stonily. The ronin snorted and nearly fell over, the rancid-sweet smell of sake wafting around him, stronger than usual. "Kuso. Still partly sober. Now I'm going to have to find somewhere else to drink."

"Where's Daisuke-san?"

The noble suddenly ducked through the doors of the gambling hall, looking both embarrassed and apologetic as he strode forward. I blinked. Like Okame, the Taiyo wore a clean but unmarked haori, dark blue with four white diamonds patterned on the shoulder. His long hair had been tied behind him, but even with a wide-brimmed straw hat perched on his head, there was no mistaking his noble bearing.

"My apologies, Okame-san," Daisuke said as he joined us. "You were doing so well. I was unaware that you had been... escorted out." His gaze slid to me, slender brows lifting. "Reika-san. What are you doing here? This is not a place for respectable priestesses."

"Or respectable samurai," Okame muttered.

"Rei...um... *Yumeko* and I were worried about you," I told them. "We couldn't find you in the castle, and thought something might've happened."

Daisuke gave a slight frown. "Odd. I specifically told a servant girl that we were going into the city, and to let our companions know that we would return by the hour of the Rat. No one gave you this message, Reika-san?"

I started to answer, when a shiver ran up my back, and my tail bristled. My kitsune instincts were telling me something wasn't right.

"Above you, fox!" hissed a shrill voice from the shadows. "On the roof!"

My blood chilled. I looked up, and saw a figure in black perched on the roof across the street, arm raised as if to hurl something.

"Daisuke, behind you!" I cried, and the noble whirled around, his sword clearing its sheath in an instant and slashing the air in front of him. There was a clang, and something glinted as it was knocked aside, skittering into the street. At the same time, a flash of cold, dark metal streaked past my head, ruffling a few strands of hair, and thunked into the post behind me.

Heart pounding, I looked up to see the figure on the roof dart back into the shadows, and I immediately sprinted across the road, hearing Daisuke and Okame call after me. Ducking into the alley between buildings, I searched the roof tiles for a figure in black, foxfire tingling against my fingertips, to no avail. The mysterious assailant had disappeared into the night.

"Reika-san!"

Pounding footsteps echoed behind me, and the noble and ronin entered the alley. "Reika-san," Daisuke repeated, as Okame stumbled forward, glaring blearily around. "Did you see who attacked us? Or where they went?"

"No," I said, and he exhaled.

"As I feared." He straightened, gazing up at the rooftops as well, his voice contemplative. "It seems that someone in the Kage has taken offense to our presence here."

"That didn't take long," Okame muttered. "Though I wonder if this was a planned attack by some pompous noble who couldn't be bothered to do it himself, or if some shinobi took offense to my face and decided to use it for target practice."

"It was Lord Iesada," I supplied, making Daisuke's pale brows arch. "He's been at odds with Lady Hanshou over...a thing, and he didn't want us to interfere."

"Iesada-sama." Daisuke didn't look surprised, though he did appear a bit tired. "Even on the other side of the empire," he sighed, "the game of court never changes. We are all but pawns in an endless match of power and favor, until fortune abandons us and we are removed from the board." His brows lowered, his voice taking on a faint edge. "Though it seems that the Kage method of removing problem pieces from the game is much different than that of the Taiyo. The Sun Clan would not stoop to such cowardly attacks in the dark." Daisuke sniffed, then gave me a contemplative look, tilting his head. "How did you come to find this out, Reika-san?" he asked.

"It's...a long story."

"Indeed." He set his jaw, looking grim. "And one best told away from dark alleys where something just tried to assassinate us. We should return to Hakumei castle immediately."

"An excellent idea," said a familiar voice from the mouth of the alley, one that made my stomach drop.

Okame's brows shot up. "R–Reika-san?" he stammered, as the shrine maiden materialized from the darkness, arms crossed, blocking the way out of the alley. Chu stood beside her, gazing at us all with a bored expression on his canine face. "But... you're right here... How... Is this your long-lost twin we didn't know about?"

The priestess gave a very loud, despairing sigh and turned to me. "Are you enjoying yourself?" she asked. "Would you care to show these gullible fools what is going on, or do I have to stand here and explain the obvious?"

"Yumeko-san," Daisuke breathed, just as I reached up and stripped the leaf from my head, dispelling the illusion in a puff of smoke. Okame's eyes bulged.

"Yumeko-chan! Then, it was you the whole time, not the priestess?" He looked back and forth between me and Reika. "Why?"

"So I could leave the castle," I explained, feeling all their gazes on me. "I couldn't just walk out the front gates, not without attracting the attention of the entire Shadow Clan. They were watching me after my meeting with Lady Hanshou. You weren't in your rooms, and no one had seen you in the castle, so we thought you might be in trouble. We agreed to look for you."

"No, we did not," Reika snapped. "We agreed that I would look for them, and you would remain in your room at the castle. What part of that did you not understand?" She lowered her voice to a near whisper, still glaring at me. "You are the bearer of the You-Know-What. We cannot risk the Shadow Clan discovering the truth."

Okame let out a snicker. "Ah, there's the normal uptight priestess we were missing. For a minute there I was afraid you were dying."

"And you." Reika turned her wrath on the ronin. "What made you think it was a good idea to leave the castle and wander down to the city at night in Shadow Clan territory? You know the importance of our mission. Why would you risk everything just for one night of whoring, gambling and getting drunk?"

"It is not like that, Reika-san," Daisuke interjected before the ronin could respond. "Forgive me, I fear I have caused a misunderstanding. You see, it was I who suggested we go into the city."

"Taiyo-san." Reika blinked at him. "You did? Why?"

"I wished to discuss matters concerning what we saw on the Path of Shadows," Daisuke said. "Okame-san was kind enough to listen. We did not want to be overheard at the castle, so we decided to come here."

"Don't take the fall for me, peacock," Okame growled. "I don't need your pity. Might as well tell her the truth, that my goal tonight was to get drunk off my ass and you were afraid I'd end up facedown in a gutter somewhere." His tone turned surly. "Frankly, I don't know why you bothered to come."

Daisuke blinked. "It was never pity, Okame-san," he answered in a quiet voice. "I came with you because I enjoy your company, nothing else. Regardless…" He turned back to Reika. "Perhaps we can discuss our plans back at the castle? We appear to have made a powerful enemy among the Shadow Clan, and remaining in a dark alley when there are assassins about is not the wisest course of action."

"That I can agree with." Reika nodded with a final glower at me. "Let us go quickly, before anything else happens. Hopefully when we return, the Shadow Clan will not question exactly *how* Yumeko snuck out of the castle without being seen, but there is nothing we can do about that now."

As we moved to leave the alley, awareness made me pause. I turned to glance over my shoulder, and saw the black cat sitting atop the fence, watching us depart with glowing green eyes, her twin tails waving behind her. I smiled and offered a short bow, and when I looked up again, the neko was gone.

11

THE CASTLE OF DEMONS

HAKAIMONO

Dozens of eyes watched me as I walked through the court-yard of Onikage castle, whispers following me across the stones.

"Has Lord Genno summoned a new demon?"

"Who is that? It doesn't look like any oni I've seen before."

"Wait. Is that…Hakaimono-sama?"

Yokai and a few minor demons stared at me from nooks and shadows of the courtyard. Amanjaku, lowest of the demon hi-erarchy, scuttled between cracks and into crannies, yellow eyes wide as they peeked out. Of all the creatures here, they at least knew who I was. The rest of them, at least the ones I could see, were all monstrous yokai, from the bloated jorogumo crouched atop the castle roof, eight long legs folded against her thorax, to the kappa peering at me from the rancid pond, to the trio of nezumi ratlings huddled in the wreckage of a smashed cart, watching me with beady rodent eyes. They were wary, curious or hostile, but only a few were openly fearful. I smiled grimly. That would change after I spoke to Genno. When I was done with the blood mage, I would return and remind any who had forgotten who the First Oni was and why he was feared.

I could feel Tatsumi inside as well, watching the demons and yokai warily. Certainly, strolling so casually into a castle full of creatures who wanted to kill him would make even the demon-slayer nervous. Not to mention the Master of Demons, who still awaited us at the top of the keep.

The hags led me across the courtyard and then up a flight of stone steps to the entrance of the castle. A human stood before the double doors, waiting for us, her arrogant posture making me bristle. The human's robes were elegant: black with crimson threads gracing the sleeves like spidersilk, but the woman herself barely filled them. She was tall and thin, almost emaciated, with elongated limbs and a gaunt, narrow face. Pale skin clung tightly to her bones, giving her a skeletal appearance, and her eyes had turned a subtle yellow. A blood mage, both Tatsumi and I saw; one who had been practicing her art for a while, whose soul and energy had been siphoned away by Jigoku, until she was something not quite human. I gave her another year, two at most, before the taint suffusing her body consumed her, and she became just another demon.

"The Master is waiting for the oni," the blood mage rasped, staring at me with hooded yellow eyes. "I am to take him before Lord Genno, once the binding is performed."

I arched a brow. A binding was a human's attempt to control the creature they had summoned, usually a demon, so that it would obey their commands. It also prevented the demon from turning on and harming the caster, which was a valid concern when working with the denizens of Jigoku. However, Genno was smart enough to realize the oni lords were too powerful to be bound, that even suggesting it was an insult.

So, either he was testing me, or this pathetic excuse for a human had no idea what she was dealing with.

The hags, at least, looked equal parts enraged and terrified. "A...a binding?" the green one exclaimed. "Don't be ridiculous, mortal! Do you know who this is?"

"I do not," the blood mage replied. "I see an oni. A very small oni, one that has somehow shrunk down to man-size. Either that, or a human half-breed. Still, the rules are clear. Demons who come into the castle must be bound, regardless of who or what they are. If you do not approve, take it up with Lord Genno. But this creature will submit to the binding before he is allowed into the Master's presence. You needn't bother assisting me," she told the hags. "My blood coven will oversee the ritual."

"Is that so?" I smiled, showing all my fangs. "And who might you be, human?"

"I am Mistress Sunako, the head witch of Lord Genno's blood coven, and the one who will be binding you to his will, demon. It is by the Master's orders that I am here, and by his will that you are allowed to see him." The witch raised her hand, a tanto clutched in bony fingers, and pointed the knife at me. "You will submit to the binding, or you will not set one foot beyond this hall. Resist, and my coven will make you wish you had stayed in Jigoku. Is that clear?"

The hags swelled with fury, bristling and opening their mouths to argue, but I held up a claw. "Perfectly clear," I said, still smiling. "Perform the ritual then, human. You three," I told the sisters, "make sure we are not interrupted. Stand guard at the steps, and do not interfere."

The hags glared at the blood witch, as if contemplating sinking their talons into her pale flesh and ripping it from her bones. But they bowed their heads to me and moved away, hovering at the top of the stairs.

I turned back to the witch and raised my arms. "Well, I am at your mercy, I suppose. Let's get this over with."

She nodded briskly and motioned me inside. I stepped through the doors into a vast, shadowy hall, pillars of black stone marching down the center and lining the walls. Unlike most human castles, the interior of Onikage was stark, unadorned and, after several decades of abandonment, quite filthy. The wooden floor was warped and rotting, vegetation grew through the walls and cobwebs hung from every corner. Despite the filth and the horde of monsters roaming outside, nearly a dozen humans, all females in various stages of corruption, stood in a loose semicircle in the center of the hall. Hollow eyes in gaunt, sallow faces watched me as I stepped into the middle of the room.

"No summoning circle," I noted, glancing at the bare floor at my feet.

The head witch eyed me, suspicion and dislike written across her narrow face. "I see you are no stranger to bindings, oni," she rasped. "True, there is no summoning circle, no words of power to hold you here. Perhaps that would be vital for a novice calling on his first amanjaku, but my coven is no stranger to demons, and I have been dancing with Jigoku for decades. My blood magic is surpassed only by the Master himself."

"Ah. My mistake. Do continue."

Pursing her lips, Mistress Sunako raised an arm and her sleeve fell back, revealing a brittle, sticklike limb covered in scars. "Do not attempt anything foolish, demon," she warned, placing the edge of the knife against her forearm. "I am no fragile lady who swoons and faints at the mere mention of monsters. I have led Lord Genno's blood coven for half a century. I am not one to be trifled with, and you would do well to remember that."

"I wouldn't think of it," I said, and raised both arms. "No trickery from me, mortals. You have my word. I will not move until you are finished."

Her eyes narrowed, but she drew the blade across her fore-arm, carving a gash in her papery flesh. Blood oozed, running down her skin, though far more slowly than a normal cut, as if the witch had already used most of the blood in her body. As it started dripping, the witch lowered the dagger and caught the trickle with the blade. As more blood covered the steel, turn-ing it red and shiny, she and the other witches began chanting in low, gravelly voices, words of dark power, fed by the energy of Jigoku.

Still chanting, Sunako lifted the blade, then flung the blood at me. It arced through the air, flared red and turned into glow-ing chains that wrapped themselves around my arms and chest. For a moment, they burned like molten metal, sizzling against my skin, though there was no smoke and no smell of burning flesh. Then the links seemed to melt into my body, vanishing into skin and muscle, and the chanting came to an end.

I took a deep breath, testing the strength of the witch's spell, and smiled pleasantly. "Are we finished?" I asked. "Do I have leave to move about the castle now?"

Sunako sniffed and stepped back. "You are free to enter," she rasped. "Though be warned, while you are within these walls, that binding will prevent you from harming any mortal, be it blood witch, servant or slave. So behave yourself while you are here, demon. We would not want to have to send you back to Jigoku."

I chuckled and took a single step forward. "You really have no idea who I am, do you?" I asked, and grabbed the witch by the throat.

The chains flared up instantly, searing into my flesh as before, infuriatingly painful as they tried to drag me to the ground, to force me to kneel or prostrate myself at the witch's feet.

I lifted the human off the ground, watching her eyes bulge and her mouth gasp for air as she clawed at my fingers. "What's wrong, mortal?" I asked, as the rest of the coven gaped and stared. "I thought your binding was supposed to prevent this type of thing."

"Release her!" one of the witches cried, raising a bloody hand. I grinned and swung my arm toward her, putting the body of the head witch between us.

"Go ahead and cast one of your spells," I challenged. "But be sure to kill me on the first try, otherwise I'll drag this mortal to Jigoku with me."

"Who...are you?" the head witch choked out. Her other hand, the one not clamped around my own, moved rapidly, bloody fingers twitching as she attempted to cast another spell. I smiled.

"Well, that's something you should have asked before you started this," I told her. "If you had, you would have known that binding Hakaimono the Destroyer is a futile endeavor. Many before you have tried and failed. I bow to no one."

The chains squeezing my arms, chest, legs and neck were quickly becoming intolerable. My whole body felt like it was on fire, and though that sensation was unpleasant given that human flesh did not take burning as well as an oni's, the pressure of the chains was the most annoying. They continued to tighten and pull, trying to force me to the ground, and my temper flared. "If you had asked me who I was," I went on, glancing at the circle around us. "You would have discovered that, while no human can bind me to their will, I find every attempt extremely bothersome, and every human who has tried it has lived only long enough to regret what they've done, before I tore the head from their neck and scattered their entrails over their own summoning circle."

The head witch raised her arm, fingers glowing red with power, before they lengthened into black, obsidian claws. With a desperate shriek, she stabbed them at my face.

I grabbed her wrist before the pointed black talons sank into my eyes. With a snarl, I tore the arm from her body, yanking it out of the socket in a spray of blood and ripping tendons. The witch screamed, a high, agonizing keen, her voice ringing off the rafters and echoing through the entrance hall. I dropped the limb to the wooden floor, drove my claws through her middle to grab her spine and pulled the human apart.

Blood flew everywhere, spattering my face and splashing to the floor in puddles. The witch's scream came to a gurgling stop, and the glowing chains wrapped around my body flared once and vanished, taking the pain with them.

Behind me, something cackled with glee. I turned, still clutching the two halves of the human, to see a dozen or so faces gazing at me through the open chamber doors. The hag sisters stood in the wooden frame, toothy grins stretched ear to ear. A crowd of yokai clustered behind them, obviously attracted by the sounds of violence, the screams and the smell of blood. Their eyes were huge and fearful as they stared at me over the hags, gazes sliding to the eviscerated blood witch in my claws. The rest of the coven seemed to be frozen in stunned horror. I dropped the bloody halves at my feet, letting them thump wetly to the planks, and smiled at my audience over the mangled body of Mistress Sunako.

"My name is Hakaimono," I said, raising a claw that was covered in blood to the elbow. "If any would like to challenge me, please step forward right now. If any would like to attempt another binding," I continued, glancing at the coven, who flinched and cringed away, "you are welcome to try again, but fair warning—this time I will not stand quietly. Any who wants my head is welcome to try to claim it. I care not if you come at me alone or all at once. But know that if you do, I will paint the walls in blood and snap the bones of every living creature in this castle before I am finished. This is your one chance to decide if you are an ally or an enemy." I narrowed my eyes, gazing around the hall. "Choose wisely."

At first, no one moved. The yokai were motionless. The coven didn't even appear to breathe, standing like frozen statues in a circle.

The hag sisters were the first to come forward. "Hakaimono-sama," the red sister said, and sank to her knees, touching her forehead to the floor. The other two followed her example.

One by one, the rest of the yokai followed, sinking to their knees or bowing their heads in silent respect. The jorogumo, nezumi, even the lone kappa, bowing as best it could without spilling the water from the bowl in its head. The humans, of course, were the last to move, standing motionless in their circle, perhaps too proud to bow their heads to a demon, a creature they were used to controlling. I turned and bared my fangs in a grin.

"You know the saying, humans," I said, meeting their flat, stony glazes. "The status between a demon and a mortal can only be one of master and servant. There is no room for compromise. If you wish to be the master, you had best put a binding on me right now, otherwise I might have our association confused. And I don't like being confused. So, which is it, master or servant? You have five seconds to decide. Four. Three. Two…"

The humans paled. Moving stiffly, they bent forward at the waist and as one, silently lowered their heads. I smiled triumphantly and raised my voice.

"Let it be known to all," I said into the dead silence that had fallen over the chamber. "Hakaimono the Destroyer has returned. All who stand with him will live to see glory, but any who stand in his way will be purged so thoroughly from existence, no one will even remember their names."

"Hakaimono!"

A thunderclap went through the chamber, causing the ground to shake and the lights in the hall to flare once and go out.

A ghostly blue light filled the chamber, and the spectral form of Genno himself appeared, hovering over the crowd. His hair and robes billowed behind him, and he did not look pleased. The yokai cringed even further, trying to press themselves into the floor, and the circle of humans instantly prostrated themselves on the ground. The spectral Master of Demons glowered over the cowering mob, then turned burning black eyes on me.

"*Lord Hakaimono,*" the ghost said in a voice of controlled fury. I sensed he was angrier about his army's reaction to my presence than the death of the human witch. *"My apologies for keeping you waiting. Please, come to my quarters. I believe we have much to discuss."*

There were no further interruptions on the way to Genno's tower. I followed a trio of gleeful hag sisters through the dark, shadowy halls of a nearly empty castle, until we reached the flight of wooden stairs spiraling up to the tallest keep.

"We can go no farther unless we are called," the green hag explained. "Lord Genno's personal chambers reside at the top of the steps."

They bowed once more and disappeared, leaving me to make my way to Genno alone.

As I approached the steps to the tallest keep, my instincts bristled. A pair of figures lounged on the steps in the center of the staircase, blocking the way. They were young, pretty, and nearly identical; twin sisters with pale skin and glossy dark hair pulled into a braid. They wore tight black clothing reminiscent of the Kage shinobi's preferred uniforms, and their eyes were shiny black orbs in their pale faces. A spiked chain, lethal and wickedly sharp, was wrapped around each of their waists, but their sneakiest weapons lay behind them, at the end of their long swinging braids, where a barbed scorpion tail lay coiled and hidden in the strands.

The Sasori twins, a pair of infamous scorpion yokai, grinned and waved at me from their spot on the stairs. In the past, the sisters had offered their services to blood mages, monstrous yokai, even ruthless humans, acting as bodyguards and assassins for those who could pay. On occasion, their paths had crossed with the Kage demonslayers, but the sisters were tough, skilled and extremely protective of each other. I had watched them kill one demonslayer, only to be nearly slain by another a few decades later. The blood mage they had been serving at the time was destroyed, but the twins escaped and disappeared for a while. Unsurprising they would find their way here, to Genno's castle. The Sasori twins lived for slaughter and bloodshed, and the Master of Demons would provide that in full.

"Hakaimono-sama!" one of the sisters called in a bright, high-pitched voice. "Is it really you? Have you come to join the Master's fun little uprising?"

I smirked. "Perhaps. Depends on what your master and I can agree on."

"Oh, I do hope you can join us," said the other twin, sounding wistful. "I would love to watch you on the battlefield. We've heard stories of you slaughtering entire armies of humans at a time. It would be an honor to fight and kill beside the First Oni of Jigoku."

"Yes, well, to do that, I will have to meet with Genno first. And the path to his chamber seems to be blocked."

The twins giggled. As one, they hopped up, scorpion braids bobbing behind them, and gave a quick bow. "Welcome to Oni-kage castle, Hakaimono-sama," they recited, as if they had practiced for this moment. "We look forward to working with you."

They leaped off the staircase and hit the floor with a thump then scampered off, laughing, the deadly braids swaying rhythmically at their backs. Their high-pitched voices echoed down the corridor, then faded into silence.

I shook my head. With the way finally clear, I climbed the steps to the top of the keep, and strode in without waiting to be acknowledged.

It was empty. Or, at least, it appeared empty. The chamber itself was small and square, with narrow windows and an opening that led to a balcony outside. Through the open balcony doors, a sickly orange moon peered through the clouds like a malevolent, swollen eye.

In the center of the room, a black stone plinth stood unguarded, a red silk cloth draped over the top. A naked, grinning skull sat atop the plinth, glowing with a subtle power, almost daring someone to snatch it up as soon as they stepped through the door. I snorted and crossed my arms, almost amused with the blatantly obvious temptation.

"Hakaimono."

The empty eye sockets flared to life, and glowing purple flames burst out to engulf the skull, casting the room in dark luminance. A ghostly mist emerged from the mouth of the skull and floated up to solidify into the spectral form of the Master of Demons, who still did not look pleased as he glared at me.

"That display in the main hall was entirely unnecessary, Hakaimono," the blood mage said, crossing incorporeal arms to his chest. "If I were a suspicious man, I would think you were attempting a coup."

"Don't play games with me, human," I scoffed. "You planned that entire scene, just to see how strong I really was. Sending your pet witches to bind an oni lord was a calculated gamble—you knew they would fail, unless I had grown considerably weaker from being trapped in a human body. Whereupon you would simply perform the binding ritual yourself, and make me your servant like all your other demons." I shrugged. "A sadly transparent ploy. Much like this smoke and light show you're putting on now. The skull atop that pedestal isn't yours. No intelligent blood mage would leave something that valuable out in the open. It's a decoy, in case any of your overly ambitious subjects has a sudden desire to betray you. I'm sure the real skull is safely hidden away, far from prying eyes. Probably being guarded by your pet half-demon in the corner over there. Tell him he can relax, I'm not about to steal the candlesticks."

The ghost of the Master of Demons grunted. "Aka," he called, and the creature that had been lurking on the balcony came into the room. Like the Sasori twins, he looked almost human; the only hints that he was something unnatural were the horns, the pointed ears and the wild mane of crimson hair falling down his back.

My instincts bristled, and I felt a strange twinge of familiarity, of recognition. Aka the Red, a half-demon whose name was quickly rising through the ranks of monsters and humans alike, met my gaze with glittering crimson eyes that held no emotion whatsoever. His origins were a mystery, but according to Shadow Clan rumor, ten years ago a child with flaming red hair was spotted in the center of a massacred village, covered in gore and licking blood off his hands. How he'd survived alone no one knew. Some tales claimed he was found and raised by mountain hags, some that he was the unholy abomination of a woman and an oni. In recent years, a demonic figure with red hair began appearing throughout Iwagoto, always at the sites of brutal killings, but no one, not even the Kage, knew much about him.

And now, much like the Sasori twins, he had been drawn here, to Genno's side, probably with promises of blood and destruction. He was, I realized, the most dangerous thing in Genno's army, which was why he was here, in the Master of Demon's personal chambers. A last resort against those foolish enough to challenge him.

It made my claws itch, wanting to tear him in half, just to prove who was the strongest demon in the realm. But slaughtering Genno's favorite pet would not get me the results I wanted here, so I refrained.

"You mortals are so predictable." I shook my head at Genno's flat stare. "But, it's exactly what I would do were the situation reversed, so I can't fault you for trying. However…" I gave him my toothiest smile, fangs and tusks bared. "I do hope you've come to realize that forcing an oni lord into your service will not end well for anyone. I am no one's servant, I bow to no master and no mortal will ever control me. I came here offering an equal partnership, nothing less. If you cannot accept that, I will gladly take my leave, my offer of friendship and a great deal of your armies' heads, before I go."

In the corner, Aka the half-demon didn't move, but I could see a faint smile cross his brutish face, as if he found me amusing. I ignored him, though a part of me was almost hoping he would try something, give me an excuse to paint the walls in blood. I could sense that the half-demon wouldn't go down easily, that a battle with him would be extremely nasty, which just incited me further.

"There is no need for unpleasantness, Hakaimono." Genno drifted lower, hovering only a few inches from the ground. "Certainly, a mutual partnership would benefit us greatly. Though I am not a fool. You did not come here simply to join my cause. The Hakaimono I remember cared nothing for our vision of the empire. He simply reveled in the slaughter of the Shadow Clan. Taking vengeance upon the Kage has always been your desire, so why are you here now? Ah…" The ghost of the Master of Demons nodded slowly, a smile curling his transparent lips. "You want something from me. Something only the greatest blood mage in the empire could grant. You wish to make a deal."

"I want something," I admitted. "I won't deny that. But in return, I'm offering something just as valuable."

"Intriguing." The specter floated back a few steps, giving me an appraising look. His long, spidery fingers folded beneath his pointed chin. "And what makes you think I would agree to this? You know what they say about making bargains with demons."

"About the same as making deals with blood mages." I

shrugged. "In both cases, you stand to lose your soul, but that isn't much of a problem for you, is it?"

"Well put." Genno waved a billowy sleeve. "Very well, then. I am curious. Let us say that I will consider your offer. What would the great Hakaimono the Destroyer, the First Oni of Jigoku, want from me?" He raised his hand. "Bearing in mind that I am not quite the mage I once was. Without a body, my powers are...somewhat limited."

"Yes," I said. "I am well aware. Which is why I think you're going to like what you're about to hear." Grabbing Kamigoroshi by the sheath, I pulled it from my obi and held it up to the ghost. "Do you know what this is?"

"Of course I do," Genno replied. "We have all heard of the Cursed Blade, the Godslayer, the blade that trapped the spirit of an oni lord. The name Kamigoroshi is a curse among gods and yokai alike. That an oni wields it now is likely of much concern to the Shadow Clan." His pale gaze flicked to the blade in my hand, and I bit down a smile. Even Genno, the Master of Demons, feared the sword that could slay ghosts and spirits. What became of the few yurei Kamigoroshi had destroyed in the past no one, not even the Shadow Clan, could say for certain. The notion that a soul could die, that it could cease to exist without any hope of passing on or being reborn, was so horrifying to the mortals that the Kage demonslayers were forbidden from cutting down a ghost unless their own lives were in danger.

I, of course, had no such concern.

"So, yes," Genno finished, his hair rippling behind him as he stared at me. I sensed he was deliberately staying in one place, instead of easing back to put distance between us. Wouldn't want to give me the idea that he was afraid. "I am aware of Kamigoroshi, and what it is capable of. I do hope that was not a subtle threat, Hakaimono. Why bring up the Godslayer if you are not planning to use it?"

"Because," I replied, and slammed the sheath on the pedestal with a crack that echoed off the walls. "I want it destroyed," I growled. "I want the curse removed, so that the next time a stray arrow hits this pathetically weak body in the heart, I won't be sucked back into Kamigoroshi for another four centuries. I don't want to lose my mind again while being stuck in that wretched blade, doing nothing, only watching as some insignificant mortal uses my power to kill yokai. I want to be free of it, so that when I die, I can finally return to Jigoku and be reborn from the pit like the rest of my kin."

Deep inside me, there was a flicker of anger and horror; Tatsumi, reacting to the plan to destroy Kamigoroshi once and for all. He had always known, of course. Sharing a body and a mind made it impossible to keep anything hidden from each other for long; he knew my darkest thoughts just as I knew his. But bargaining with the Master of Demons, ending the curse on Kamigoroshi and setting my spirit free once and for all—that was every Kage's nightmare.

"Destroy Kamigoroshi." Genno didn't sound surprised. "End the curse and set you free. That is what you would ask?"

"Yes." I bared my fangs. "The sword can't be destroyed by normal means. Humans, demons and yokai have all tried. The blade has been snapped, dented, broken and tossed into the sea. It has been plunged into fire, buried in the earth and left in the ice atop the highest peak in Iwagoto. And yet, it always reappears, whole and unscathed, within the sacred shrine of the Kage. The only way to destroy the sword is to break the curse attached to it, the one that binds my spirit to the blade and keeps me imprisoned in the mortal realm."

"And what makes you think I am capable of such a feat?" Genno inquired, and raised his open palms, his sleeves billowing behind him. "Or that I would want to unmake such a powerful curse? I am in the habit of binding demons to my will, not freeing them."

"That is precisely why I think you can," I said. "You know more about binding and sealing demons than anyone in the history of the empire. You studied the forbidden knowledge of curses, seals and dark magic, and you were the most powerful blood mage the empire had ever seen. This is your area of expertise." I crossed my arms. "As for *why* you would agree to help me, you have not heard my end of the bargain yet."

"Oh?" The Master of Demons cocked his head. "Then tell me, demon. What do you have to offer? If you wish to join my army and help us destroy the human empire, I'm afraid that will not be enough. I would gladly welcome you into our ranks, and the great Hakaimono would certainly be a powerful ally, but as you can see, I have an army. One that is growing daily. The aid of a single oni, while a great boon, will not be necessary."

"You're a fool if you think that," I said calmly, making him frown. "Your army already responds to me—they know who I am and what I'm capable of. And if you think that rabble out there does not need a strong general to lead them into battle, you've learned nothing in the past four hundred years. Demons respond to strength, and yokai will fall to chaos if they cannot be controlled. If the majority of your army discovers that you possess only a fraction of the power you once held, how long do you think your hold on them will last?

"Lucky for you," I went on, as the blood mage's scowl darkened, "I have no interest in overthrowing the empire or becoming king. I want only one thing—to be free of this cursed sword so that I may take my vengeance upon the Shadow Clan. And you are going to help me achieve that."

"Again..." Genno crossed his arms. "I fail to see why I should."

I gave him a wide, toothy smile, baring all my fangs. "Because I can give you the one thing you need, human. The one thing standing between you and the empire. The item that will guarantee your glorious return." I paused, just to make him figuratively sweat, before closing the trap. "I can give you the Dragon scroll."

There was a long moment of silence, in which Genno appeared to mull over my words and not appear stunned. I could see the flicker of hunger in the sorcerer's eyes, though he did a fair job of remaining calm. "You?" he asked skeptically. "Can retrieve the Dragon scroll?"

"The pieces, actually," I corrected. "Two of them. You already have the one, I assume."

Genno did not bother to answer that question, which told me everything I needed to know. The blood mage already had a piece of the Dragon scroll in his possession. I'd been guessing, really. The Scroll of a Thousand Prayers had been well hidden by those who decided such power did not belong in the hands of mortals, but Genno was determined and cunning and, from what I had seen in his first rebellion, completely ruthless. If he had decided to summon the Harbinger, he would be searching for the missing pieces tirelessly. Honestly, I was a little surprised he had found only the one piece so far.

"Forgive me, Hakaimono," Genno said slowly. "But I have been attempting to gather the fragments of the Dragon scroll ever since I knew of the Harbinger's coming. I have minions across Iwagoto searching for the missing pieces, for any hint of where they might be. We have scoured the empire from corner to corner and have yet to turn up more than one. I *had* a servant in the capital, who swore she could get another of the pieces, but she failed. And the night of the Wish is rapidly approaching." Genno turned and gazed at the sickly moon visible outside the balcony, his voice turning grim. "Time is running short," he mused darkly. "If the pieces are not brought together by the time the Dragon stars fade over the empire, the Wish will be lost, and the Harbinger will not reappear for another millennium. I cannot allow that to happen. If I have to sacrifice the whole of the empire to Jigoku, I will be the one to summon the Dragon."

Genno turned back, raising his sleeves so that they fluttered in an imaginary wind. "So imagine my surprise," he said, "when the demon Hakaimono strolls into my castle, after centuries of being trapped within Kamigoroshi, and casually announces that he can bring me the very thing the entire empire is seeking. You'll have to excuse me if I find that rather difficult to believe."

"Believe what you want," I replied, knowing he was hanging on my every word now. "But I know where the scroll is. Both pieces, actually. And if you agree to play nice, I'll even go get them for you."

The human's eyes glittered. He wanted the scroll, was desperate to have it. It was, as I had always known, the one thing he couldn't pass up. But Genno wasn't stupid; the Master of Demons knew the dangers of bargaining with Jigoku and was understandably skeptical. "Would you?" he asked, narrowing his gaze. "And the thought of summoning the Dragon yourself doesn't interest you? The final pieces of the prayer to summon the Harbinger are in your grasp, and you would simply turn them over?"

I snorted. "The Harbinger doesn't respond to demons or yokai—his bargain was with the humans. Only a mortal soul can call the Kami from the sea."

"True, but you could always force someone to make the Wish for you," Genno reasoned. "Use it to free yourself from Kamigoroshi. Isn't that your greatest desire, Hakaimono? Would you not seek out the scroll for that alone?"

"No," I said firmly. "I have no interest in the Dragon's Wish, no desire to call upon the Harbinger of Change." Curling a lip, I shook my head. "You humans and your constant quest for power... There is no mortal I would trust who, at the penultimate moment, would not use the Wish for himself. Besides..."

I sneered and glanced at Kamigoroshi, still lying on the pedestal. "Demons and Kami don't exactly get along. I wouldn't trust the Harbinger to undo what he brought about a millennium ago. In fact, if the scaly, wish-granting bastard appeared before me, right now, I'm fairly certain I would take Kamigoroshi and shove it up his dragon hole."

No change in expression from the Master of Demons. "You would bring me the scroll pieces," he repeated, "in exchange for breaking the curse on Kamigoroshi and allowing your spirit to return to Jigoku. That is your bargain?"

I nodded. "Couldn't have said it better myself."

Genno's pale lips thinned. "Very well," he murmured. "If that is what it takes, then you have a deal, Hakaimono. But I'm afraid I will need you to bring me the scroll before I can attempt to break the curse." He raised transparent arms so that the moonlight filtered through his sleeves. "As you can see, I am not at my full power. After the Dragon is summoned and I have my new body, I will gladly honor your request."

"I figured as much." Picking up Kamigoroshi, I tucked it through my obi again. "Don't worry, I'm not some conniving blood witch who has to send minions to do her dirty work for her. You'll have the complete scroll before the night of the Wish, I assure you."

"Out of curiosity," Genno mused as I took a step back. "How do you know where to find the scroll, Hakaimono? My servant, Lady Satomi, informed me that she knew where a piece was, that she was getting close to acquiring it. But now it appears Lady Satomi is dead, and the scroll fragment lost. How is it that you know where the final pieces are located?"

I smiled. "Jigoku is eternal, Master of Demons," I said. "I'm older than you can even fathom, and my memory is very long. The Kage have had a long history with the Dragon scroll—the second Wish was spoken by Kage Hanako, better known today as Lady

Hanshou, who desired immortality and to rule the Shadow Clan forever. She got her wish, though not in the way she expected. As it turns out, eternal life is not the same as eternal youth."

There was a faint rustle from the soul inside, Tatsumi's curiosity stirring at this newest revelation. I chuckled inwardly at his ignorance. If he only knew the truth, the depth of his daimyo's obsession.

"But even before the Kage," I continued, staring at Genno, "I am no stranger to this realm. I was around when the empire was young, when demons and yokai outnumbered men. I remember the places that have been lost to human history. And thanks to a naive little fox girl, I know where to find the last pieces of the scroll."

"The Steel Feather temple," Genno said flatly, revealing that he, too, knew where the scroll was being held. Probably from Lady Satomi. But he didn't know where the temple itself was located, because the crusty guardians who lived there knew how short and fickle human memory was. They didn't even need their magic to hide themselves away; all they had to do was not interact with the mortal world for a few hundred years, and the humans would forget they ever existed.

But Jigoku was eternal. Jigoku did not forget.

I just smiled, and Genno's brow lifted. "You know where the temple is," he stated quietly.

Deep inside, I could feel Tatsumi's anger, his desperation, but especially, his worry and concern for a simple peasant girl who, even as we spoke, was on her way to the temple. Whose path would surely cross with mine once more.

"Yes," I said, savoring Tatsumi's despair as I answered. "I do."

12

Through Yume-no-Sekai

Yumeko

"Lady Hanshou asked you to do what?"

We had returned to Hakumei castle in the darkest hours of the night. As quickly as we could without attracting attention, we slipped through the halls and through the doors of Master Jiro's room. The old priest was sitting against the far wall when we came in, long-handled pipe curling tendrils of smoke into the air, gnarled staff resting on his knees. Ko lay curled up beside him, looking like an oversize dandelion puff, and barely flicked an ear when Reika and Chu herded us through the doors.

"Ah," Master Jiro breathed, taking the end of the pipe from his mouth. "You found them, Reika-chan. Thank the kami."

The shrine maiden hadn't answered right away. After shutting the doors, she'd reached into her haori and pulled out a familiar slip of white paper—an ofuda—one of the talismans that allowed her to work her magic. This one read *silence* in stark black ink, and Reika pressed it firmly to the doorframe between the shoji panels. I felt a ripple of energy emanate from the little strip, spreading over the walls of the room, a barrier that would keep prying ears from listening to our conversation. As the magic settled, I felt a prick of vindictive satisfaction. *Ha, try eavesdropping on us now, nosy Kage.*

"No thanks to these three," Reika growled, turning to glower at me, Daisuke and the ronin. "I'm not even going to mention the stupidity of certain individuals who go wandering around the Shadow Clan capital by themselves. *Or* a certain lying yokai who told me she'd stay in her room and then went gallivanting into the streets of Ogi Owari with no thought for herself or the *very important thing* she is carrying."

"That isn't true," I argued, making her scowl at me. "I *was* thinking of the very important thing, which is why I disguised myself as you. No one even knew I left the castle. I was perfectly safe. Well, until the assassins."

Ko raised her head and growled. Master Jiro blinked.

"Assassins?" he repeated. Taking the pipe from his mouth, he tapped the end on a square of tissue and set it aside. "I fear you are going to have to start from the beginning, Yumeko-chan," he said.

So I had. Beginning with my meeting with Lady Hanshou, and her shocking request to save Tatsumi and free him from Hakaimono. Reika's eyes had nearly bugged out of her face when she heard the daimyo's request, and she was sputtering before I even finished the sentence, leading to her question.

"Save the demonslayer from Hakaimono?" the shrine maiden went on, answering her own inquiry. "When her own majutsushi cannot?" She gestured fiercely. "And what did you tell her?"

"I told her I would try," I said quietly, making the miko groan. "This doesn't change anything, Reika-san. We were going to look for Tatsumi anyway."

"After we took the scroll to the temple, Yumeko! The scroll is more important—"

"I know it's important!" I pinned my ears and glared back at her. "I know I have to take the scroll to the temple and prevent the coming of the Dragon. But...I can't forget about Tatsumi." Thinking of the demonslayer made my stomach tighten, and I took a quick breath to steady myself. "Please," I said, gazing around the room. "We owe him this. Tatsumi fought Satomi's demons alongside us. He faced an oni to allow us to reach Master Jiro. We can't abandon him, and we can't wait. The Shadow Clan is already tracking Hakaimono down. Tatsumi might be killed before we can even get to him."

"We don't even know where he is."

"I do," I said. "Lady Hanshou told me. She said that Hakaimono was seen traveling west, toward a forest beyond the mountains."

Reika snorted. "Can you be a little more specific?" she said, and waved a billowy sleeve. "There are lots of forests in the general direction of west."

"It was the big forest between Hino and Mizu lands," I said, and saw Master Jiro's eyes narrow. "What was its name, again? Lady Hanshou told me, and it sounded very ominous. The Forest..."

"The Forest of a Thousand Eyes," Master Jiro finished, and Reika jerked up as if she'd been stung. "The site where the Master of Demons gathered his army to declare war on the empire."

"That accursed place?" Reika grew pale, and she shook her head fiercely. "Absolutely not. I refuse to let Master Jiro set foot anywhere near that forest. Finding Hakaimono is one thing. Going into the Forest of a Thousand Eyes is like walking into Jigoku itself."

"You don't have to come," I said. "I won't ask any of you to follow me. But...I'm going after Hakaimono. I've already made up my mind. I'll find him myself and—somehow—I'll get Tatsumi back."

"How?" Reika demanded. "You keep saying you're going to save him, but you know nothing of exorcism, binding rituals or the nature of demons. How do you think you're going to defeat Hakaimono, Yumeko?"

"I *will* save Tatsumi. Even…even if I have to possess him myself."

There were a few heartbeats of silence after this statement as, one by one, my companions realized what this meant.

"Kitsune-tsuki," Reika said, her tone disapproving. I waited for her to berate me, to tell me that it was evil, to insist that I find another way. But, for once, Reika was quiet, thoughtful, as if coming to the realization that this might work, even if she didn't like it.

"I know it's not ideal," I said, gazing around the room. Master Jiro looked grave, Reika's jaw was set, even Okame looked uncomfortable with the talk of possession. Beside him, the noble's face was unreadable, but his eyes were dark and troubled. "I would rather not perform kitsune-tsuki if I had the choice. But, if it's the only way to drive out Hakaimono, I feel I have to try."

"But, you're only half-kitsune, Yumeko-chan," Okame pointed out. "Are you sure you can do it?"

"I…think so," I stammered, earning raised brows from Reika and concerned looks from everyone else. "It's not something I've ever tried," I admitted, "but I was told that it came naturally for kitsune. That, when the time arrived, I would know what to do." I did not mention that the someone who had encouraged me to use this particular kitsune talent was a mysterious white fox who'd appeared to me in a dream.

"So, our plan, such as it is," Reika continued in a dubious voice, "is to find Hakaimono, somehow restrain him and then you will possess the demonslayer using an ability you're not

even certain you have. And once you're inside, you're going to…
what? Convince Hakaimono to leave? By asking him nicely?
Or, do you intend to fight the demon while you're both inside
Kage Tatsumi?"

"If that is what I must do," I said. I did not relish the thought
of fighting Hakaimono, but Reika was right; he wouldn't just
leave if I asked him politely. "Whatever it takes, if I have to, I'll
drive Hakaimono out myself."

"And what do you think that will do to the demonslayer's
soul?"

"I…" I faltered, pricking my ears. "What do you mean?"

She shook her head, but there was a sadness in the gesture,
not exasperation. "Kage Tatsumi has been wholly possessed by
Hakaimono," she told me. "A soul, be it human or oni, cannot
be destroyed, only suppressed or driven out. If your kitsune-tsuki
is successful, there will be three presences inside him, three separate wills competing for control of his mind and body. If you
fight Hakaimono inside Kage Tatsumi, the demonslayer might
not come out of this ordeal unscathed."

"What will happen?"

The shrine maiden raised both hands. "I have no idea," she
said. "A fox possessing a mortal to drive an oni spirit back into
a sword has never happened before." She grimaced, and I tried
not to dwell on the absurdity of that last statement. "However,"
she went on, "I do remember a case of tanuki-tsuki that Master
Jiro was called on to exorcise. The tanuki had taken possession
of a young woman, and by the time they brought her to the
shrine, she was very sick, having gorged herself on sake and rice
cakes for three days straight. And yet, she still continued to cry
with hunger, demanding we bring her food and alcohol. The
tanuki spirit was driven out, but sadly, the young woman never
recovered, and died a few days later in her home."

"Why are you telling me this?"

I felt a cold lump settle in my gut, the chill spreading to all parts of my body. Reika continued to watch me, her sympathetic expression still in place. "All I'm saying is that the human soul can be very fragile, Yumeko," she said softly. "I know you think your demonslayer is strong, but we don't know what Hakaimono is doing to him, mentally and physically. I want you to be prepared. Even if we do save him, Kage Tatsumi might be…different than he was before."

"Oh, stop with the doom and gloom already." Okame sat up, giving the shrine maiden a disgusted look. "We'll deal with that problem when we come to it. First, we have to find the oni bastard, and then things will get really interesting. So where was he spotted again? The Forest of Evil Eyes or something like that?"

"The Forest of a Thousand Eyes," Daisuke corrected. "Also called the Wood of One Million Curses. The stories say that any human who enters the forest is never seen again."

"Sounds cheerful." Okame shook his head. "So, I guess we'll be leaving soon."

"Tomorrow," I said. "Lady Hanshou wishes us to do this quickly. Naganori-san will take us through the Path of Shadows to the edge of Fire Clan territory."

No one seemed pleased by that statement. Master Jiro thinned his lips and Reika wrinkled her nose, but Okame went slightly pale, one fist clenching on his leg.

"Right. So, I'm going to need to be really, really drunk," he muttered. "That way, if Yasuo drags me off the Path into Meido, at least it'll be tolerable."

"That will not happen, Okame-san," Daisuke said. "As I said before, I will be right behind you. And should your brother wish to claim you again, I will convince him otherwise. I swear this on my life."

The noble's voice was quietly intense. Okame glanced up, and for a moment, something passed between the two, some flutter of emotion or understanding I couldn't place. But before I could wonder too long on it, Master Jiro cleared his throat.

"We should try to rest," the priest announced. "The night is nearly gone, and I fear we will not get much of a chance afterward. Certainly there will be no sleeping on the Path. But, may I suggest staying together? After tonight's events, I feel that no one should be alone in Hakumei castle."

"Of course, Master Jiro." Reika stood up, waving a hand at me. "Come, Yumeko. We'll stay in my room. Chu," she added, looking at the dog, "you and Ko stay here. Protect Master Jiro, all right?"

The small orange dog wagged his tail in a very solemn manner, then turned to pad over to the priest, joining Ko at his side.

Okame glanced at Daisuke, his lip curled up in a faint smirk. "Guess that leaves us, Taiyo-san," he said. "If it won't stain your honor to share a room with a ronin, that is."

"There is no dishonor in that request, Okame-san," Daisuke replied, rising smoothly to his feet. "I would welcome your company. If you don't mind sharing a room with...what was the phrase? A swaggering court peacock."

"Eh, I'm sure I'll manage somehow."

"Yumeko-san." Daisuke nodded to me. "Master Jiro, Reika-san. Oyasuminasai. I will see you all in a few hours."

"Good night," I echoed, and watched the two men leave the room, Okame giving me a grin as he passed. After following Reika into her room, I watched as she fished a second ofuda out of her sleeve and pressed it to the door, silencing our conversation to any outside ears, as well.

"You're not angry, are you, Reika-san?" I ventured as the miko finally sat down on the other futon in the corner. She shot me a dark glare, then sighed.

"No," she murmured, shaking her head. "I'm...terrified."

Shocked, I sat on the futon facing her, crossing my legs. "Of Hakaimono?"

"Hakaimono, the Forest of a Thousand Eyes, the Dragon scroll, all of this!" She gestured wildly at nothing. "It might come as a surprise, Yumeko, but this is my first time outside Taiyo lands. Before you and the others came to my shrine, my days were peaceful, spent talking to the kami, dancing at festivals, banishing the occasional ghost or yokai. Now I find myself sitting in Hakumei castle surrounded by those who wish to kill us, preparing to track down the most dangerous oni that has ever lived, in the hopes that a kitsune who knows nothing about the world can somehow manage to defeat him. Provided that Hakaimono doesn't slaughter us all the moment he sees us.

"So, yes," she finished, glaring at me again. "I'm terrified. I'm afraid I know how this is going to end, and it isn't good for any of us. And if we fail, what will happen to the Dragon scroll? The best I can hope for is that the piece you carry will be lost, and the Harbinger will not be summoned in this era."

"Why do you care so much about the Dragon scroll, Reika-san?" I asked, genuinely curious. "It was never your duty to protect it, but you seem to hate the fact that it exists at all."

Reika gave a bitter smile. "I've studied the history of the scroll," she answered. "I know what the Wish can bring about. But, even more than that, I know the evil that lurks in the souls of men. You don't have to be a shrine maiden to guess what mortals will do when granted the power of the gods. The Dragon is not called the Harbinger of Change for nothing. I would rather not live in a world created by the whim of a single man."

Her stare turned challenging. "That is my interest in the Dragon scroll, Yumeko," she said. "My reason to never see the Harbinger called upon. What is yours? Do you even have one? Or are you so blinded by love that you've forgotten your first duty is to protect the scroll and prevent the coming of the Dragon?"

"I…" I stared at her, feeling like I'd been hit in the stomach. "I don't… What are you saying, Reika-san?"

She sighed. "You don't even see it, do you? It's plain as day to the rest of us."

"I don't love Tatsumi," I said, still reeling from the implication. "I can't. I just…"

I faltered again, as words failed me. Love was an alien concept, something I'd never even thought about. I'd read about men and women falling in love; the library at the Silent Winds temple had a book tucked away among the scrolls that told the story of a samurai who loved a geisha. But he had a wife and a family, and so he visited her at night, where they fantasized of him someday paying off her debt and running away together. There was a lot of internal agonizing on the samurai's part, for though he loved the geisha, his duty was to his family and his daimyo, and he could not abandon them. The tale ended tragically, with the samurai being called to war and dying in battle, and the geisha throwing herself into the river in grief. The samurai's actions were highly praised, however, both by his comrades and the book itself, for choosing duty over love, though they never mentioned the woman who had died.

It did not paint love in a good light, and in fact seemed a cautionary tale about the dangers of strong emotions, that duty to one's clan, family and daimyo should always come first. I'd found it rather depressing, and had felt sorry for the poor girl who drowned herself, but I didn't understand how she could become so attached to a man that she would rather die than live without him.

That certainly wasn't what I felt toward Tatsumi. I worried for the demonslayer, of course. When I imagined what Hakaimono might be doing to him, I felt physically ill. When we'd first met, Tatsumi had been cold and frightening; a weapon that killed without hesitation or regret. But on our journey, I had come to know Kage Tatsumi, and I had seen glimmers of the soul he kept locked away, small flashes of humor and even kindness. When danger threatened, I'd seen him fight to protect others even though he didn't have to. And I had realized, too late, why he never let down his guard.

You distract him, Hakaimono had whispered to me that night. *Make him feel things. Make him question who he is and what he wants. And that's all the invitation I needed. His last thought tonight, before finally losing himself, was of you.*

So, it was my fault that Hakaimono had been released. My fault that Tatsumi had lost himself to the oni, that he was suffering. That he thought I had betrayed him. I would free Kage Tatsumi from Hakaimono and drive the demon back into Kamigoroshi. I would save the demonslayer, even if it cost me my life. But that wasn't love.

At least, I didn't think it was.

Reika shook her head. "Well, it doesn't matter," she sighed. "Tomorrow we start the hunt for the First Oni, as crazy and suicidal as that sounds." She gestured at the futon. "Get some rest while you can. I don't think I'll be doing much sleeping tonight."

I didn't think I would sleep, either. My mind was filled with swirling thoughts, about Tatsumi, Hakaimono and the Dragon scroll. About Lady Hanshou, Lord Iesada and the attack we'd just survived. I lay there in the darkness, wondering where Hakaimono was now, how we were going to defeat him and how I was going to possess the demonslayer when we did. And I wondered if Tatsumi was thinking of me the way I was thinking of him.

The next thing I knew, I was dreaming.

★ ★ ★

The white fox was waiting for me, sitting on a log beneath the shade of a pine, his magnificent tail curled around his feet. Fireflies drifted around him, blips of green light winking in and out of the darkness. Lazy golden eyes watched me as I padded up, my paws sinking into moss and dirt, making no noise on the forest floor.

"Hello, little dreamer."

"Hello again."

"Have you given any thought to my proposal?"

I nodded. "Yes. I need to know how to drive out Hakaimono. Please…" I hesitated a moment more, then blurted, "Show me how to save Tatsumi-san."

The white fox smiled.

His bushy tail uncurled, rising into the air behind him, swaying to and fro as if it had a mind of its own. "You are no match for Hakaimono in the physical world," he crooned. "Your priest and your shrine maiden will not be strong enough to force him out. If they try, you will all die. The answer lies with you."

His tail, swaying like a serpent behind him, abruptly burst into blue flames at the tip. They flickered and danced over his head, casting him in a ghostly light. "A warning, little dreamer," he went on, as I stared at the kitsune-bi on the end of his tail. "Simply possessing the demonslayer will not be enough. If you want to free your human, you must be prepared to fight Hakaimono inside Kage Tatsumi."

I trembled, tearing my gaze from the mesmerizing sway of his tail. "Yes, but how will I do that?" I asked desperately. "I don't have a sword. I'm not a warrior like Tatsumi-san. I don't have anything that can stand up to a demon."

"On the mortal plane, no." The white fox twitched his long ears. "The physical world has rules that must be followed. On the plane of the soul, however, it is a different story. Much like in Yume-no-Sekai, reality can be shaped, twisted into something that suits your needs, if you know how. For example, in the mortal realm, your foxfire is a distraction at best, a vague annoyance at worst. But here, in the realm of dreams..."

He flicked his tail, and a ball of kitsune-bi flew through the air, striking a tree a few yards away. It instantly burst into flame, flaring a blinding blue-white a moment before it was consumed. Leaves burned to nothing, limbs blackened and withered away, and the trunk turned to ashes that scattered to the wind.

My jaw dropped, and I felt the white fox smile. "It can be as deadly as you wish," he said smugly. "Deadly enough to burn even an oni lord. Now, you try it." He turned, pointing an elegant muzzle at a gnarled oak several yards away in the fog. "Destroy the tree."

I followed his gaze, facing the tree, and took a deep breath. With a wave of my tail, kitsune-bi flared to life, casting me in a circle of ghostly light. Pinning back my ears, I hurled it at the oak.

The sphere of foxfire struck the gnarled trunk and exploded in a burst of light, tongues of blue-white flames flaring up only to dissolve in the air, writhing away to nothing. Disappointed, I looked back at the white fox, who shook his head.

"You still don't believe foxfire can be dangerous," he said in an unruffled voice. "You must know, beyond any doubt, that within the realm of dreams and on the plane of the soul, your kitsune-bi can burn. Sear. Kill. Banish any uncertainty from your mind." His ears twitched, and he waved his plumed tail at the oak. "Try again."

With a growl, I faced the tree once more, curling a lip at the gnarled giant. *This is for Tatsumi,* I told myself, as foxfire burst to life once more, dancing on my tail tip. *If you want to save him from Hakaimono, you must do this. Burn!*

I gave a defiant snarl, and threw the ball of foxfire at the tree again. This time, when the flames struck the oak, there was a roar, and a blue inferno sprang up to engulf the tree. It blazed like a tiny sun, blinding and intense, and the huge oak vanished in the glare, turning to ashes in a heartbeat.

The hairs on my back stood up, and I heard the white fox chuckle behind me. "Good," he said, padding gracefully to my side. "Within a mortal soul, pure emotion is a powerful thing. The stronger the conviction, the brighter the magic becomes. Just be certain it does not burn so bright it consumes everything around you." He gave me a solemn, golden-eyed stare. "But learn quickly, little fox. And heed this warning. Hakaimono will be a challenging opponent. Even if you master your power, he will be the hardest enemy you will ever encounter. Driving him back into Kamigoroshi will not be as simple as throwing foxfire in his face."

"But it's a start," I whispered. "It will give me a fighting chance."

"It will," the white fox agreed. "Unfortunately," he continued in a warning voice, "there is still one small problem, and that is the demonslayer himself. The human spirit is a fragile thing, and will not take an invasion into its essence well at all. If you use kitsune-tsuki to possess Kage Tatsumi, you will very likely damage his soul."

I blinked, remembering what Reika had said earlier that night. "How?"

"It is already under a lot of duress with Hakaimono," the kitsune went on. "Another forced intrusion could very well cause the host's mind to snap—it is not uncommon with mortals who have been possessed. Worse, if you start flinging kitsune-bi around, and the demonslayer gets caught in the battle between you and Hakaimono, who knows what it will do to his soul? He might come back different, or mad…or not at all."

I swallowed the frustration rising to my throat. "Then, how

206

am I supposed to help him?" I demanded. "If possessing Tatsumi will just cause him to go mad, I'm no better than Hakaimono."

"I did not say it would be easy," the white fox said, still insufferably calm. "I said I would give you the means to drive out the demon. However, there is a way to ease the shock of yet another presence forcing its way into his soul. You must let the demonslayer know you are coming. If he recognizes you as a friend and not another enemy, he might be more accepting of your presence." The white fox waved his plumed tail. "Of course, you will still have to be careful that you do not damage his soul while battling Hakaimono, but that is a problem for when and if your kitsune-tsuki is successful."

"Let Tatsumi know I'm coming?" I stared at the white fox. "How? I can't send him a message. Anything he knows Hakaimono knows, too."

"That would be true, were we in the physical world," the kitsune said. "However, this is Yume-no-Sekai, the realm of dreams. And even Hakaimono must sleep sometimes.

"Come." He rose before I could ask what he meant, his bushy tail rippling languidly behind him. "Follow me. Stay close. And remember, nothing you see here is real except the native baku— the dream eaters—and the souls of those who slumber."

"Where are we going?"

"I am taking you into another dream. But we must hurry— our target is a very light sleeper. Once he wakes, his presence will vanish from Yume-no-Sekai, and you will not have a second chance to speak with him. Quickly now."

I bounded after the white fox, and suddenly, the cool, misty forest surrounding us changed. One moment, we were trotting down a shadowed game trail through the tangled undergrowth, the next, we were at the edge of an arched wooden bridge over a river, a full silver moon shining down directly overhead.

"Where...?"

"Don't be alarmed." The white fox looked back at me, eyes glowing like candles in the moonlight. "Remember, nothing here is real. We've simply left your dream and have entered another's."

"Whose?"

"Draw your weapon."

The calm, quiet voice drifted over the bridge, causing the hairs on the back of my neck to rise. I recognized that low, elegant manner of speech. Looking up, I saw a lone figure in the middle of the bridge, bare-chested and white hair unbound, the moonlight glimmering off the pale oni mask covering his face.

I blinked. "Daisuke-san?"

Oni no Mikoto, the demon of the bridge, ignored me, his gaze focused on something behind us. At my back, a quiet chuckle drifted over the breeze.

"I think you've made a mistake, Oni-san," said another familiar voice. I turned to see Okame standing at the edge of the bridge, facing the demon prince. His bow was missing, though a short blade hung from his obi, and he made no move to draw it as he stepped forward. The white fox and I skittered aside, and neither of the two men seemed to notice us. "I thought you only challenged honorable warriors to duels. Not filthy ronin dogs."

"Whose dream is this?" I whispered to the white fox, entranced by what was happening before me. "Is this Okame's dream, or Daisuke's?"

He gave me a slightly irritated look. "Does it matter? It has nothing to do with us, or our objective. Let us continue."

"There has been no mistake," replied the other, and when I glanced back, it was no longer Oni no Mikoto with the demon mask and cold eyes, only Daisuke. His long hair still rippled and flowed around him, the moonlight shining down the length of the sword in his hand. "And I see no disgraced warrior before me. Only a man who has lost much, and is struggling to find his way."

A smirk pulled at one corner of the ronin's mouth. "It doesn't matter how you put it, Taiyo-san," he said, and though his expression was mocking, his voice was sad. "I'm no samurai. I'm still ronin, still a wild, honorless cur, and nothing will change that."

Daisuke stepped forward, closing the distance between himself and the ronin. "That is true," he said quietly. "I have known many samurai. In the court, the capital and on bridges throughout the country, I have seen my share of honorable men. Their loyalty to the empire is irrefutable, they follow the tenets of Bushido religiously, their honor cannot be questioned. Like the petals of a sakura tree, they are flawless, perfect, irreproachable. And like the sakura petals...exactly the same. One can compose only so many poems about cherry blossoms before one grows tired of their flawlessness."

Okame glanced up, a wary, almost hopeful frown crossing his face. Daisuke smiled and stepped closer; now only a couple feet separated the two men. I couldn't breathe, couldn't move or look away, despite the growing impatience from the fox beside me.

"Of late," Daisuke murmured, "I find myself fascinated by the violent storms at sea, by the passion, the unpredictability and danger of it all. And by the eagles that soar over the mountaintops, wild and free, beholden to no one." He paused, a slightly pained look crossing his face, before continuing. "It is...a dangerous thing, this curiosity," he said in a low tone. "I am afraid that if I reach out to the eagle, it will savage me and fly away. But I cannot seem to stop myself." He closed the last few feet between them, trapping Okame against the railing, his gaze intense. "If I am left with scars, then so be it."

"Are you...sure about this, peacock?" Okame's voice was husky. His lean body was frozen against the rails, as if fearing that any movement would shatter the dream around them. "I wouldn't want to ruffle your family's tail feathers, or bring dishonor to your entire house."

In answer, Daisuke's long fingers rose, tracing the side of the ronin's face. Okame's breath hitched, and he closed his eyes. For a moment, the noble hovered there, torn between leaning in and drawing away, as the dream itself seemed to hold its breath.

There was an impatient growl behind me, the feeling of being yanked back, though my body didn't move. The bridge with the two men vanished, whipped away from me like a cloth covering a painting, replaced with another scene entirely. I let out a dismayed bark and turned on the white fox.

"Hey! What happened? Go back, I want to see how this ends."

"That dreamer is not the reason we are here," said the white fox calmly, though his tail lashed his flanks in irritation. "The night grows short, little fox, as does our time in Yume-no-Sekai. Do you wish to see your demonslayer before he wakes, or not?"

I pinned back my ears. *Tatsumi,* I thought guiltily. *I'm coming. Don't disappear on me yet.* "I'm sorry," I told the white fox. "Yes, I'm ready now. Take me to him."

He nodded and turned away, and we slipped into the everchanging shadows of the dreamworld.

PART 2

13

PROPHECY FOR A GHOST

Suki

Suki was restless. And not just because she was a ghost.

Lord Seigetsu was meditating again, sitting on his cushion between identical torch stands, next to the pond beneath the sakura trees. Same perfect picture, though Suki had no idea where they were or what was real anymore. Everything surrounding this mysterious, silver-haired man seemed dreamlike and surreal; just this morning, she had been riding in a beautiful carriage that, from what she could tell, flew on the wind. There had been no horses or servants carrying it, and neither Taka nor Lord Seigetsu appeared troubled by the fact that they were soaring among the clouds hundreds of feet in the air, but Suki had been so disturbed she could not hold on to her ghostly human form and spent the majority of the ride as a trembling ball of light in the corner.

When the carriage finally touched down, it was in the same

perfectly groomed courtyard as before, though Suki had been too relieved to be on solid ground again to pay much attention to their surroundings. Lord Seigetsu immediately excused himself to meditate, with instructions not to disturb him, and Taka had wandered off to prepare a meal, leaving Suki floating there by herself.

She watched Seigetsu-sama for a few quiet minutes, but he was so very still, like a beautiful statue, or a painting that had been captured not on canvas but in the air itself. Not a breath of wind ruffled his clothes or tossed his long silver hair, as if even the air kami were obeying his wish not to be disturbed. Only his eyes flickered and moved beneath his closed lids, as if he was dreaming or in the throes of a nightmare. Briefly, Suki wondered what a man like Seigetsu-sama dreamed of. If he was a man at all.

"Suki-chan!"

Taka's voice drew her attention, and she turned to see the little yokai waving to her beneath the trunk of a twisted pine. Drifting over, she saw that Taka had rolled out a bamboo mat and arranged a full tea set and several plates of food atop it. Fried tofu, red azuki beans and a platter of colorful mochi-rice cakes surrounded the lacquered tea tray, filling Suki with a sense of longing. She remembered the sweetness of a mochi ball, the simple pleasure of sipping tea on a cold winter night, feeling warmth seep into her fingers. Things she would never experience again.

"There you are, Suki-chan," Taka said as she joined him under the pine tree. "I didn't know if you still ate food, so I made extra just in case. Can you...?" He gave her an expectant look, but Suki smiled sadly and shook her head, making him blink. "Oh, that's too bad," he murmured. "Forgive me, Suki-chan. I don't think I would like being a ghost." He raised his chopsticks, then selected a pink mochi ball from the platter and stuck it in his mouth, chewing thoughtfully before swallowing.

"Well, please enjoy yourself anyway, Suki-chan. Lord Seigetsu will be joining us soon. He is always hungry after meditating."

Suki looked back toward Seigetsu, noting the faint glow surrounding the man, before drifting down to sit beside Taka. Unease gnawed at her, like the feeling of being lost in a dream, the sensation that the world around her wasn't quite normal. Of course, she was a yurei, so perhaps this odd nightmare world of yokai and flying carriages was something only ghosts experienced.

Why am I here? Suki wondered in a rippling burst of clarity. *Am I doing something wrong? Why haven't I moved on?*

"Brr." Taka suddenly shivered and rubbed his arms. "That's strange, it got cold all of a sudden," he muttered. "Suki-chan, did you feel...?"

She turned to face him, and Taka jerked, then went as rigid as a steel pole. His huge eye widened, glazing over, the pupil expanding until nothing was left but darkness. That terrifyingly blank gaze fixed on Suki, as his mouth gaped open and a hissing voice emerged.

"Lost soul," he rasped, and Suki shrank back from him, nearly losing her human form as she did. "The chains of longing cannot be undone, the flute snaps in the shadow of a god and the world grows red with blood. The white-haired prince seeks a battle he cannot win. He will break upon the demon's sword, and his dog will follow him unto death."

Terrified, Suki floated back and felt a shadow fall over her from behind. Shivering, she turned to gaze into Seigetsu-sama's amused golden eyes.

"And she comes into the story at last." His voice was a caress, gentle but triumphant at the same time. "I was wondering if it was you," he continued, as Suki floated there in abject fear and confusion. "If you were indeed the 'lost soul' Taka had glimpsed from time to time." One corner of his mouth curled in subtle amusement. "Deciphering his visions is an art in itself, one that has taken me many years to perfect, and even then, I must work within the bounds of metaphor and vagueness. They are usually not quite so literal."

Suki trembled. Part of her wanted to fly away from this man and his frightening, terrible predictions of the future. Claims that she was part of something much greater, something she didn't understand, terrified her. She was a simple maid, and the ghost of a maid at that. She was too insignificant to play a part in his grand story, whatever it was.

At the same time, a tiny voice of curiosity rose to the back of her mind, breaking through the fear and confusion. Could she, a simple maid, be important in death as she never was in life? Was this why she had lingered?

"You needn't fear this, hitodama." Abruptly, Lord Seigetsu stepped around her and lowered himself to one knee on the blanket. Startled, Suki watched as he eased the limp, shivering Taka onto his back and placed a hand on his forehead. "All souls have a destiny. Some are simply brighter than others. It is very difficult to change one's fate, even if one knows about it. Sleep, Taka."

A tremor went through the yokai's body, before he relaxed. His mouth fell open, and a raspy snore emerged between sharp fangs. Seigetsu watched the slumbering yokai a moment, before rising with the fluidity of water and turning to Suki again.

"The future is a very fickle mistress," he said. "Think of it as millions of streams, running into each other, crisscrossing, forming an endless network of rivers. If you dam one stream, it does not simply stop. It changes course and runs into another, which might also overflow its banks, thus disrupting yet another stream. Sometimes the results are negligible. Sometimes they are catastrophic. For many years, I have tended those streams, carefully nudged them in the direction they needed to go. I have

guided the souls that required my help, and removed the ones
that would hinder them. And now, we are nearing the end of a
very long shogi match, and all the pieces are finally in place."
His golden eyes seemed to bore into her, brilliant and mesmerizing. "I would prefer to have all the pieces in my hand, but I
realize I cannot force you to stay. So I will offer this instead. I
know why you linger, hitodama. Why you cannot move on."

Suki jerked up, eyes widening. Thinking, of course, of Lady
Satomi, and the death that had started everything. Seigetsu simply smiled.

"It has nothing to do with vengeance," he continued, as if
reading Suki's thoughts. "Or justice, or any emotion regarding
your own demise. Were that the case, you would have disappeared as soon as Lady Satomi left the world. The answer to why
you linger can be found in the prophecy Taka gave you tonight."

Frowning, Suki thought back, trying to remember. Truthfully, she had been so startled when Taka turned that blank-eyed
stare on her that she had barely heard the words he'd spoken.
Something about chains and darkness, and a god staining the
land in blood...

The flute snaps in the shadow of a god.

Everything inside her went very still. The swirling thoughts
ceased, the flickering emotions calmed. One memory came to
her, as clear and distinct as blood against the snow: the high,
sweet sound of a flute, and the most beautiful, pale-haired man
turning to smile at her.

The white-haired prince seeks a battle he cannot win.

"Yes," Seigetsu murmured, his voice seeming to come from
a great distance away. "Now you understand. Your tie to this
world had nothing to do with vengeance, or anger, or justice.
It is not revenge that keeps you here, but longing. Love." He
shook his head. "The most dangerous of human emotions."

Suki was too dazed to even try to answer. Thinking back to

that terrible night, she suddenly remembered that, right before the demon tore her apart, she had cried out to Daisuke-sama. Knowing he wouldn't save her, that he was so far above her station she would never even have crossed his mind, she had called his name, his face the last thing she'd envisioned before she left the world of the living.

"I do not envy you, little hitodama." Seigetsu stepped back, giving her a look of sympathy. "Vengeance is easily rectified. Unrequited love is far more difficult. Now we know why your destiny is tangled with his, with all of them. The half-fox and the demonslayer move ever closer to the end, and the fate of millions of souls follow in their wake. Including the Taiyo noble, who has sworn to protect the half-fox with his life. Though it appears that his destiny will catch up to him very soon."

Suki raised her head, and Seigetsu smiled grimly. "Did you not hear what was foretold? *He will break upon the demon's sword, and his dog will follow him unto death.*" His voice softened, unbearably gentle in its finality. "Taiyo Daisuke is fated to die in battle, Suki. *When* it happens is not certain, but the time is not far. Perhaps when he dies, you can finally move on, continue your journey to Meido or wherever it is your soul is destined." He shrugged one lean, elegant shoulder. "Or perhaps you will linger in this realm for all time, a restless, wandering soul unable to find peace. As I said before, vengeance is easy. One can never be certain with an emotion as dangerous and unpredictable as love."

"*No.*"

Seigetsu raised a brow at the strangled whisper that came from Suki's mouth. She stared up at him, anguish a burning, twisting knife below her breast, forcing the words to spill from her lips. "Can…it be…changed?" she whispered. Her voice was breathy, broken with disuse, but she forced herself to continue. "Can we…warn him…somehow?"

Seigetsu gave her a long, level stare, making ghostly snakes writhe and coil in the pit of her stomach, before one corner of his mouth curled. "Fate is a fickle mistress," he said again. His voice was soft, as if he feared Destiny itself might be listening. "It has a way of protecting itself, and the outcomes, of those caught in its stream. One must know just how far to push, how much to change, to divert the flow of the future. However, as I said before, I am too heavily invested in this game to make mistakes, and I would rather have all the pieces in my sight, rather than wandering the winds." He held out a hand, and his smile was like the promise of the sun. "Fox, demon, dog, priestess, blade. If one falls now, the game is lost. Let us see if we cannot change the fate of your white-haired prince."

14

CASTLE OF NIGHTMARES

The Demonslayer

I was lost.

The halls of the castle surrounded me, dark and abandoned. Shadows clustered along the walls and polished floors, thrown back by the occasional lantern and stream of moonlight through the windows. A heavy silence hung in the air, broken only by my own whispering footsteps, as if I was the only living soul here. How long had I been wandering this place? I was supposed to be hunting…something, but I couldn't remember what. Still, I had to complete my mission. I could not return to the Shadow Clan without finishing my objective, whatever it was.

Turning a corner, I stared in dismay at the statue of the demon at the end of the hall, its fanged maw open in a grin. I had come upon this same statue numerous times. No matter where

I turned or which direction I went, I always seemed to find myself back here.

A sense of weariness crept over me. I was going in circles, with no objective and no sense of direction. How long would I be here, wandering this endless castle, aimlessly drifting down empty corridors like a shadow, only to end where I had started?

Angrily, I shook myself, dissolving the hopelessness and the numbing fatigue that had settled deep in my bones. I could not give up. I was the Kage demonslayer, and this was my job. No matter the obstacles and difficulties in my path, even if they proved impossible, I was expected to complete my mission. Failure was never an option.

As I drew back, ready to turn down another hallway once more, a whisper of sound shushed behind me, the faintest hiss of footsteps over polished wood. I spun, my blade clearing its sheath in an instant, ready to cut through whatever monster had crept up on me.

A girl stood at the end of the hall, staring at me with wide dark eyes. And for a moment, for perhaps the first time in my life, my muscles froze and my mind went blank with shock.

Yu...Yumeko?

The sword in my hand trembled. I lowered my arm, hardly believing she was there. I had the fleeting thought that this was a trick, an illusion conjured by the seemingly malicious castle to show me what I desperately wanted to see. But...it *was* Yumeko. She glowed in the darkness of the corridor, dressed in a white robe trimmed in red, her shining hair falling around her shoulders. Despite the impossibility of it all, something inside me leaped up, as if recognizing what it had been searching for all along.

"Tatsumi." Her voice was a whisper, soft with relief. She stepped forward, and the dark hallway seemed to ripple as she passed, like the surface of a pond that had been disturbed. As if the castle was merely a shadow, a reflection, and she was the one that was real. I couldn't move, could only watch as the girl drew close, seeing my own reflection in her dark eyes.

"I found you."

One hand rose, and a shiver went through me as her fingers gently brushed my cheek, her gaze searching, as if making certain I, too, was real. Almost against my will, my eyes closed and my body relaxed, submitting to her touch.

"Yokatta," she whispered, expressing her relief. "Tatsumi, you're all right. I'm so glad. I thought Hakaimono might have…"

Hakaimono?

A flicker of apprehension went through me at the name, a memory just out of reach. Why would she bring up Hakaimono? Did she know about the demon in the sword? Had I…told her of my link with Kamigoroshi? I tried to think, to remember what had passed between us, but my thoughts were scattered, like moths flitting around a light, and I couldn't settle on any of them.

"Yumeko." Reaching up, I took her hand, curling my fingers around hers. Her skin was smooth, her hand light and delicate beneath my palm, and my stomach tightened. For a moment, I had to catch my breath. "You need to leave," I told her softly. "You can't be here now. There's a…" I paused, still unable to remember why I had come, what I was supposed to be hunting. "There's something dangerous roaming this castle," I finished. "I have to find it. I can't have you following me."

She shook her head. "No, Tatsumi, listen to me. This is a dream." Dropping her arm, she took my hands, gazing up at me. "You're dreaming right now. None of this is real."

A dream? I frowned. No, that couldn't be right. Master Ichiro sent me here to…

I faltered. I couldn't remember why I was here. I didn't recall a conversation with Master Ichiro, or any details regarding this mission. And the more I thought about it, the more unlikely it seemed. I was the Kage demonslayer. I did not forget.

"This is a dream," Yumeko insisted. "Think back, Tatsumi. Do you remember Lady Satomi's castle? The five of us went there to find Master Jiro. Do you remember what happened?"

Master Jiro. The name was familiar, as was Lady Satomi. I closed my eyes, trying to still the memories that flitted around my head. "Lady Satomi...was a blood witch," I said slowly. "We met her at the emperor's party and followed her through a mirror to a castle on the other side." Yumeko squeezed my hands, assuring me that I was right, encouraging me to go on. "There was...an oni," I continued, frowning as more pieces of the night came back to me. "Yaburama. I fought him, and then..."

And then...

The bottom dropped out of my stomach. My hands shook, and I staggered back as memory rushed in, drenching me in an icy wave. The moment I lost control, the demon's howl of triumph as he rushed into my mind. "Hakaimono," I whispered, feeling Yumeko's gaze on me. "I'm still..."

Numb, I leaned against the wall, as everything came flooding back. Hakaimono was free. I had failed to keep him contained, and now he was threatening not only the Shadow Clan, but the whole empire. My blood chilled as I remembered his threats against the Kage, the slaughter he had caused already and the mass carnage that would happen if he couldn't be stopped.

I felt Yumeko draw close again, a bright, solid presence against the hanging darkness. "Tatsumi, listen," she said, as I looked up and again saw my reflection, bleak and anguished, in her eyes. "We're coming for you," she went on. "I won't let Hakaimono win. We're going to find you, trap Hakaimono and force him back into Kamigoroshi."

"No." My voice sounded strangled in my ears. Stepping forward, I gripped her forearms, making her blink. "Yumeko, if you face Hakaimono alone, you're going to die. Everyone who challenges him is going to die. You have to kill him."

"Tatsumi—"

"Please." The intensity in my voice sounded strange, like it belonged to someone else. "There's not much time," I continued. "Take this message to the Shadow Clan, the emperor and any who will listen. Hakaimono is free, and he has formed an alliance with Genno, the Master of Demons."

"Genno?" Her eyes widened, indicating that she recognized the name. I didn't doubt she'd heard of him; the Master of Demons was the most famous and feared blood mage in the history of Iwagoto. Even Yumeko, with her sheltered upbringing, would have learned of the man who nearly destroyed the empire.

"But...Genno is dead," Yumeko argued. "That all happened four hundred years ago, didn't it?"

"He has returned," I said. "His soul has been summoned from Jigoku and bound to the mortal realm. He has an army of demons and yokai waiting in the ruins of his old castle. The only reason he hasn't attacked the empire is because he has no body, so he is not at his full strength. Hakaimono intends to fix that... by giving him the Dragon scroll."

The blood drained from her face. She slumped in my grip, and I suspected she might have fallen if I hadn't been holding on to her. "Hakaimono," she whispered, "is going after the Dragon scroll?"

I nodded. "He knows where the Steel Feather temple is," I said, and she went even paler. "He's on his way there now. If you don't stop him, he's going to slaughter everyone and take the pieces of the scroll back to the Master of Demons. Genno already has one fragment of the prayer. If he acquires the others and summons the Dragon, the empire will be thrown into chaos. You have to stop him."

"How..." Yumeko still seemed a bit dazed. Carefully, I released her arms, letting her stand on her own, and waited until she met my eyes again.

"Kill me," I told her softly. "It's the only way. Before Hakaimono reaches the scroll. End my life, and send Hakaimono back into the sword."

She jerked back, a look of dismay crossing her face. "No," she whispered. "I won't kill you. Tatsumi, please don't ask this of me." She stepped forward, her gaze beseeching, and my heart clenched painfully in my chest. "We can save you," she insisted. "Just give us a chance."

"You can't exorcise him." I made a hopeless gesture, shaking my head. "The Shadow Clan has tried. Our best priests and most powerful majutsushi have attempted to exorcise Hakaimono in the past. He's too strong. No one has ever succeeded—the last time they attempted it, Hakaimono freed himself and slaughtered everyone present. I can't...watch that happen to you."

Yumeko set her jaw, her gaze defiant. I knew she was going to refuse again, thinking she could save me from Hakaimono, and desperation rose to curl with the despair. Hakaimono had already slaughtered several members of my clan, and I could do nothing to stop it. I knew his ultimate plan was to wipe the Kage from existence, and I would have to watch, helpless, as he destroyed them all. And if Genno summoned the Dragon and rose to power, I would be responsible for the fall of the entire empire. My honor was gone, my soul tainted beyond all redemption. But the thought of her dying, of facing the sadistic First Oni only to be killed by my own hand, was too much. He wouldn't just kill her; he would torture her, make her suffer, because he knew it would affect me. And he would never let me forget.

I hesitated, then sank to my knees before her and bowed my head, hearing her sharp intake of breath. "Please," I said softly. "I will beg if I must. I cannot be the instrument that allows Genno to rise again. I cannot be the catalyst that brings about the destruction of the Shadow Clan. And I…" My voice faltered; I had to pause, swallowing the tightness in my throat before continuing on, "I cannot watch him kill you, Yumeko," I whispered. "Hakaimono knows…how important you are. He would take great pleasure in making you suffer. Of all the atrocities he has committed, if you died by my hand…" I shuddered. "I would rather cut open my stomach than live with that."

Yumeko remained silent. I could feel the weight of her gaze on me, solemn and helpless, perhaps realizing the truth of my words. "My life is worth nothing," I went on, still staring at the ground between us. "If my death means ending the threat of the First Oni and the second coming of the Master of Demons, I offer it gladly. But I can't do it myself." I lowered myself even farther, the fingertips of one hand touching the ground. "Kill me, Yumeko," I whispered. "End my life, and drive Hakaimono back into the sword for good."

For a few heartbeats, there was silence. Then a soft rustle as Yumeko knelt in front of me, and a moment later her cool palm pressed against my cheek.

"I won't let him have you," she whispered in a fierce voice. "Your life *is* worth something—to me." Her other hand touched my face, making me shiver. "Look at me, Tatsumi. Really look at me, and tell me what you see."

I dragged my gaze to hers and met a pair of glimmering golden eyes. Startled, I drew back slightly, and Yumeko's outline seemed to blur for a moment, like I was seeing her through water or heavy smoke. The haziness faded, and I was staring into the golden eyes of a fox, black-tipped ears and bushy tail standing out in my peripheral vision.

Kitsune. Yumeko was kitsune. Somehow, I had forgotten. Her posture was stiff, as if she was waiting for me to recoil, and I remembered the night Hakaimono had taken over, he had gleefully taunted the fox girl, telling her that I could see exactly what she was now, and that I despised her for it.

I didn't. I had been surprised of course, stunned that I had been traveling with a fox, a yokai, since the night I'd saved her from the demons. But even that paled to the consuming horror and rage I'd felt toward myself for allowing Hakaimono to break free. The identity of the fox girl was far less concerning than the demon possessing my body. And Yumeko being kitsune... It wasn't all that surprising, really. I remembered the times she'd spoken to the kami, all the instances where she could see spirits and yurei as easily as the mortal world. Many small things, seemingly insignificant at the time, had fallen into place. The fact that she was a fox, a yokai, should have angered and disgusted me, but Yumeko was...Yumeko. Kitsune or human, she was still the same.

Yumeko smiled, though it was a slightly sad smile, as if she knew something between us had shattered, and could never be put back together. "I'm asking you to trust me," she said in a soft voice. "Not as Yumeko the peasant girl, but as a kitsune who swore she wouldn't let the demon win. Hakaimono is strong, but strength does not automatically win battles, and there are a few tricks he hasn't seen. I'm not giving up. I just need you to wait for me a little longer."

"What are you planning to do?" I whispered.

For a moment, she looked troubled, almost embarrassed. Her gaze dropped, and the tip of her tail beat an agitated rhythm against the floor. "I need your permission, Tatsumi," she said, to my confusion. "Everyone has told me that a normal exorcism won't work on the First Oni, that he's too strong for anything to work from the outside. So, when we reach Hakaimono, I plan to face him...from within."

It took only a moment to realize what she was saying. "Kitsune-tsuki," I murmured, and she nodded, wincing.

"Yumeko," I said gently, "Hakaimono won't be any easier to defeat inside me. If anything, his soul will be even more powerful."

"I know," she whispered, and her ears flattened in open fear. "But I'm going to do it. I just...want you to know that I'm coming, Tatsumi. And that I'll fight for you, as hard as I can. I'll free your soul from Hakaimono, one way or another."

My chest felt tight. No one in my seventeen years of existence had cared so much to try to save me. I was nothing; a weapon of the Kage, trained to kill and to obey. If I died on a mission, the only loss to the Shadow Clan was that they would have to find a new demonslayer. No one would remember me. No one would mourn my passing. To give my life in service to the clan was an honor, and the price of failure was death. That was how it had always been.

Looking into Yumeko's fierce, determined face, seeing the promise burning in her eyes, made my stomach churn with emotions I couldn't even place. That this girl would face a demon lord, the strongest oni in Jigoku, to save the worthless, tainted soul of an assassin... "And if you can't drive him out?" I asked. "If Hakaimono is in danger of stealing the scroll and killing everyone who stands between it and him?"

Her eyes closed. "If there is no other way," she whispered, and her voice was a little choked. "If I cannot stop him, then I...I will honor your request, Tatsumi. If I must...I will end your life, and Hakaimono's. The First Oni will not reach the scroll, I promise."

I bowed my head, fisting my hands on my knees. "Arigatou," I murmured. "If this is what you've decided, Yumeko, then I'll wait for you. And...I'm sorry."

"Sorry?"

"For what you're going to have to face to reach me."

"I'm not afraid." She shifted closer, placing her hands over mine. I looked up and found her face a breath away, golden eyes shining as they met my own. "If it means I'll see you again, I'll fight a dozen Hakaimonos." She blinked, and atop her head, her ears twitched nervously. "There's only one, right?"

My heart pounded, and I drew in a slow breath to calm it. "As far as I know."

"Oh, good," Yumeko whispered, and slumped a bit in relief. "Because more would be terrifying, now that I think about it."

A tremor went through me. Unbidden, my hand rose and brushed the hair from her cheek, my fingers trailing across her skin. Yumeko didn't move, holding my gaze, and the trust I saw in those golden fox eyes made my breath catch. She smiled at me, just the smallest curve of her lips, answering my unspoken question, and the last of my resolve crumbled to dust. Almost without thinking, I leaned forward.

But as soon as I moved, the girl flickered, like a candle caught in a strong breeze. Frowning, I drew back, seeing her sputter again, her presence gone and reappearing in a blink. "Yumeko? What's happening?"

Yumeko looked equal parts stricken and apologetic. "Gomen, Tatsumi," she said, grimacing as she flickered once more. "I told you we were in the dream world, right? I'm sorry, but I think I'm about to wake—"

And she was gone.

I knelt, alone, in the halls of an abandoned castle, staring at the spot where a kitsune girl had been moments before. I could feel myself fading, as well, the reality around me fraying as my consciousness began to stir. Already, the world seemed darker, colder, without the presence of a cheerful fox girl. I wondered if I would truly see her again, if she would hunt me down as she promised, before I grew angry at my own weakness. It would be better for everyone if she stayed away, far from me and the demon possessing my body. Yumeko was brave, resourceful and had many kitsune tricks she could call upon, but she had never faced a foe as terrible as Hakaimono. I would rather the Kage track us down and kill us both than watch Hakaimono tear the kitsune girl in half and laugh at me for daring to hope.

Around me, the castle was growing less substantial, less real, by the second. I knew I could open my eyes anytime I wished, but for several heartbeats, I didn't move, wanting the dream to last as long as it could.

For me, the nightmare would continue as soon as I woke up.

15

TEA WITH MY ENEMY

Yumeko

"Hakaimono is going after the Dragon scroll."

Silence followed my announcement, four pairs of eyes staring at me in alarm and disbelief. At my insistence, we had all gathered in Master Jiro's room, with Reika's ofuda firmly across the doors to prevent eavesdropping. It was still very early morning; the castle was still dark, and Okame had frozen with his mouth open midyawn, Daisuke looked grim and Reika's cheeks had gone deathly pale. Master Jiro sat motionless in the corner, flanked by Chu and Ko. I saw his withered fingers tighten around his staff.

"Are you certain of this?" Reika was the first to speak, her voice matching the expression of horrified disbelief on her face. "How do you know the First Oni is going after the Dragon scroll?"

"I...had a dream." At their incredulous looks, I hurried on.

"I went to Yume-no-Sekai, the realm of dreams, and I saw…" My face heated, remembering the other incidents that happened while I was with the white kitsune in the dream realm. "Well, Tatsumi was there, too," I went on. "He told me that Hakaimono intended to seek out the Dragon scroll, and that we had to stop him before he could reach it."

"The demonslayer met you…in a dream?" Daisuke said slowly. He and Okame sat side by side, I suddenly noticed, their knees almost touching. Neither seemed to notice the proximity, but perhaps I was seeing too much in it. "You spoke to Tatsumi-san directly?"

I nodded. "I know it sounds ridiculous, but I really did speak to him."

"But…demons have no use for the Dragon scroll," Reika argued. "They can't summon the Harbinger or use the Wish. Only a mortal soul can do that. Why would Hakaimono suddenly want the Dragon scroll?"

"It's not for him," I told her. "It's for Genno, the Master of Demons."

Okame choked on his sake jug. Coughing, he bent over, gasping for breath, while the rest of us looked on in mild alarm. "Sorry," he gasped, sitting up again. Tears streamed down his cheeks as his red, bleary gaze met mine. "Very clever, Yumeko-chan," he told me. "You almost had me fooled. At least now we know it was just a dream."

"I'm serious, Okame-san." I frowned at the ronin, pinning back my ears. "The Master of Demons has returned, and he sent Hakaimono for the Dragon scroll. He's on his way to the Steel Feather temple right now."

"Genno." Okame put down the sake jug and gave me a dubious look. "The guy from the history scrolls who raised an army of demons and undead horrors to overthrow the empire? Whose exploits were so heinous they inspired the Oni's Night festival with a parade of 'monsters' fleeing the city? That Genno?"

"There is only one Master of Demons, ronin," Reika snapped. "Unless you can think of a different blood mage with an undead army who nearly destroyed the empire, I believe we are talking about the same person."

"The same person in books, poems and Kabuki theater." Okame frowned at the shrine maiden. "Myth and legends tend to get bigger and more exaggerated the longer they endure. Didn't the real Master of Demons die over half a century ago?"

"Four hundred years ago." This from Master Jiro, his pipe held thoughtfully to his chin, Chu and Ko at his side. "And unfortunately, the legend of the Master of Demons is a pale comparison to the real thing. The stories all focus more on the exploits of the heroes who opposed him, rather than the man himself. The empire loves tales of honor and sacrifice, brave warriors fighting against the impossible and triumphing in the end, usually by giving their lives for the cause. Like the story of General Katsutomo's final stand at the Valley of Spirits."

"A moving and riveting tale," Daisuke broke in. "The battle of Tani Hitokage is a legend, an exciting and bloody tale for Kabuki theater, of which the Silken Dance troop in Seiryu City gave an exemplary performance last summer." He gave a tiny sigh, sounding wistful for a moment. "Ah, Mizu Subato, your portrayal of Katsutomo's noble death could make even a stone weep."

"Yes," Master Jiro said, sounding less impressed. "As you can see, the empire loves a tragic hero's story, and the tales surrounding the Master of Demons are full of them. However, the truth of Genno's rise and final defeat is far more grim. The empire nearly fell. The Master of Demons and his army marched straight through the capital to the Imperial palace virtually unopposed, slaughtering and burning everything on their way."

"Where was everyone else?" I wondered. "The rest of the clans, I mean? I would think a huge demon army attacking the capital would be cause for concern."

"They were all fighting among themselves," Reika answered. "No one can even remember how it started, but the Hino had declared war against the Mizu for some imagined slight, the Earth Clan was fighting the Shadow and Wind clans, and the Moon Clan was off doing their own thing on their islands per normal, and not getting involved. No one realized the danger Genno represented until it was too late."

"Yes," Daisuke added solemnly. "The day that the Master of Demons marched upon the capital, the Taiyo stood alone, a single oak before the tsunami."

"Four hundred years ago," Okame repeated. "And the empire *almost* fell, but it rallied. The other clans pulled their heads out of their asses, banded together and marched on the capital to take it back. The way the stories tell it, Genno was defeated, executed and his remains are buried in some secret, remote tomb. Hard to threaten the empire when you're a pile of bones."

"Unless," Reika put in, "someone is trying to revive him using an ancient and powerful artifact that will grant a single wish."

"Merciful Kami," breathed Master Jiro. "I have heard of cults, cabals, of blood mages, who worship the Master of Demons as a fallen god. Whose minds have been corrupted by Jigoku's power so they are no longer human. Who despise the empire and every honorable soul within it, and would see Genno rise again to bring chaos and darkness to the land. If they got their hands on the Dragon scroll, if they used the Wish to bring Genno back to life…"

"They don't have to," I said. "The Master of Demons is already here."

Everyone stopped and stared at me again. "Hakaimono isn't

retrieving the scroll for a cult of blood mages," I said. "He already made a deal with the Master of Demons, or his ghost, I suppose—if he went to the Steel Feather temple and retrieved the pieces of the scroll, Genno would break the curse that binds him to Kamigoroshi."

"Jinkei preserve us," whispered Reika, going very pale. "This gets worse and worse. A freed Hakaimono and a returned Master of Demons? The land will not survive." Her gaze sharpened, cutting into me. "How do you know this?" she demanded, suddenly dubious again.

"Tatsumi told me."

"In your dream."

"Yes."

"Yumeko..." The shrine maiden paused a moment, then sighed. "Dreams are important, I fully understand that," she began. "They can be visions, warnings, portents of the future. But sometimes, they can just be dreams. I know you're desperate to help Kage Tatsumi, but your vision might not be what you think. The souls that can consciously journey though Yume-no-Sekai are few and far between. Are you certain this isn't your worry and...other feelings for the demonslayer coming to the surface?"

"I am very certain," I told her, deliberately ignoring the last question. "I walked through Yume-no-Sekai and found Tatsumi, who told me that Hakaimono and the Master of Demons had struck a bargain. Tatsumi said that Hakaimono was going to the Steel Feather temple to get the scroll for the Master of Demons, and that we had to stop him." *No matter the cost, even if we have to kill him to stop Hakaimono.* My stomach clenched, remembering the look in Tatsumi's eyes, the quiet despair as he pleaded for me to end his life. I set my jaw. *No, I won't let that happen,* I promised. *I won't lose Tatsumi to Hakaimono, and I won't let the First Oni win. Whatever it takes, I'm going to bring him back.*

Reika sighed, clearly uncertain, then glanced at the older priest in the corner. "Master Jiro? What should we do?"

The priest was silent for several heartbeats.

"This changes nothing," he said at last. "If anything, it confirms the importance of our mission. We must reach the Steel Feather temple before Hakaimono does. We must defeat the demon, and either drive him back into Kamigoroshi or, failing that, destroy him and his host completely. And we must protect the pieces of the scroll at all costs. Under no circumstances can we allow Hakaimono to deliver them to the Master of Demons."

"So we have to get to the Steel Feather temple," Okame said, frowning. "The one supposedly hidden and lost to the ages for hundreds of years. Sounds easy. Um…where was it again?"

"The northern part of the Dragon Spine Mountains," Master Jiro said, sounding like he was quoting the passage from a history scroll. *"Seek the place where the mountain kami gather, and look to the crows that will point the way."* He paused, brow furrowed slightly, before shaking his head. "Not the clearest of directions, I grant you, but it is what we must go on."

"Gonna be a long walk," Okame sighed. "The Dragon Spine separates the Tsuchi and Mizu families, and the northern part of the range extends all the way up into Wind Clan territory. Which, conversely, is on the other side of the empire. Unless Hakaimono has a broken leg, or is on this side of Iwagoto with us, I don't see how we're going to beat him there."

"The Path of Shadows," I said, making him wince. "It's the fastest way, and Lady Hanshou already gave us leave to use it. We should find Naganori-san, and get him to open the Path for us."

Through all this, Daisuke had been unusually quiet. Now, as we prepared to leave the room, he set his jaw and rose gracefully from the mats.

"Forgive me," the noble said, his voice apologetic but firm. "But I am afraid I cannot come with you this time."

I blinked at him in shock. "Why, Daisuke-san?"

"I am a Taiyo." He gazed around at all of us, solemn and proud. "My duty is to the emperor, my family and my clan. Anything that puts them in danger is an affront to me, as well. The Master of Demons is a serious threat to the empire. Honor demands I return and inform His Highness of what I know."

"The Kage have messengers, Taiyo-san," Okame said immediately. "Send a missive with one of them. Apparently they're very adept at traveling across the country in the blink of an eye."

But Daisuke shook his head. "I am sorry, Okame-san. But I would not trust something this important with a clan who have very recently attempted to have us killed. Any message or note I might send could be seen by the wrong eyes, and I am not willing to risk that. Besides, the Shadow Clan have garnered a reputation for being...untrustworthy, within the Sun lands. Better that I deliver this message in person. My family will listen to me."

"You would leave us," Reika demanded, glaring angrily at the noble. "Knowing what is at stake. Knowing we must reach Hakaimono before he gets the scroll."

"I am sorry," Daisuke repeated, sounding repentant but firm. "But I've made my decision. I must return to the Imperial city to warn the emperor. Yumeko-san." He bowed in my direction. "It has been an honor. I wish you luck on your journey, and I truly hope you can save Tatsumi-san." He turned away, sliding back the door to the hall. "Sayonara. Hopefully someday our paths will cross again."

"Never took you for a coward, Taiyo-san."

Okame's voice was mocking, and the brittle silence that followed was a tangible thing, making the hairs rise on the back of my arm. Daisuke had gone very still, his back to us, but I saw his hand come to rest on his sword hilt. Reika exchanged a glance with me, and then slowly scooted back against the wall, drawing Master Jiro and the two dogs with her. Okame seemed oblivious to the tension, standing in the center of the room with his arms crossed, a furious look on his face.

"Okame-san." Daisuke's voice trembled, but whether from anger or something else, it was hard to say. "I would ask you to take that back."

The ronin's glare morphed into a smirk. "Why should I?"

"Because honor demands that I challenge you to a duel for such an insult, or that I cut you down right here. And I have no desire to do either. So please…" Daisuke still didn't turn, but his eyes fluttered shut. "Retract your statement. Apologize, so that we can forget this and move on."

"Oh? Am I not duel-worthy, then?" Okame stepped forward, his sneer defiant. "I'm not the Kage demonslayer, I wouldn't be much of a challenge. Or is it because I'm ronin? Don't want to waste your skills on the unworthy, is that it?"

"I don't want to kill you, Okame-san!" Daisuke finally spun, glaring at the ronin, though his expression was conflicted. "How many times must I say it before you believe me—I care not that you are ronin, that you are no longer samurai. You are a brave warrior. I have watched you stand with us against monsters, demons, assassins and vengeful ghosts. You have become a brother in arms, and I consider you a worthy friend. I do not wish to challenge you, because I far prefer you alive, but…" He sighed, briefly closing his eyes, as if pained. "I will not deny you a duel. I will give you an honorable death, if that is what you desire."

"You once challenged Kage-san to a duel," Okame said, making Daisuke frown in confusion. Reika, too, furrowed her brow, uncertain where the ronin was going with this. "Remember that? It was to be your greatest duel ever, the one that would test your skills to the limit."

"Yes," Daisuke said slowly. "I remember. But, even before my own desires, my duty to the empire comes first. I truly regret that I might never cross blades with Kage Tatsumi."

"So, answer me this, noble, and answer truthfully." Okame took a step forward, staring the noble down. "Do you think *I* would have any chance against Kage Tatsumi if I challenged him on that bridge?"

Startled, Daisuke frowned at the ronin, pure puzzlement crossing his features. "If...you were to duel Kage-san?" he repeated.

"Yeah." Okame crossed his arms. "If I stood in Kage Tatsumi's way and demanded he fight me on the bridge, what do you think would happen?"

"Okame-san..." Daisuke paused, as if gathering his thoughts. "You are...a passionate warrior," he began. "And your skill with a bow is such that I have never seen before."

"Oh, stop with the mincing around, peacock." Okame snorted, shaking his head. "We both know the answer. He would destroy me. If I challenged Kage Tatsumi on that bridge, I wouldn't even have time to blink before my head would be in the river."

Daisuke frowned, but he didn't deny it. Striding forward, Okame came within a few feet of the Taiyo noble and leaned in, his gaze intense. His voice was low as he growled, "So what makes you think I'll be able to protect Yumeko-chan when we face Hakaimono?"

Daisuke stepped back, eyes widening. Okame didn't move, continuing to glare at the noble with hard black eyes. "You've seen the demonslayer fight," he went on, his voice grim. "I wouldn't stand a chance. Without Tatsumi, you're our sword, Taiyo-san. You are the only one who can maybe go toe-to-toe with the Kage demonslayer and not be sliced to pieces in the first pass. I can stand a hundred yards away and annoy him with arrows for a little while, but once he closes the distance...I'm dead. And then Yumeko-chan, Reika and the priest will be left to face Hakaimono…alone."

"Do not dismiss us so casually, ronin," Reika broke in, sounding annoyed. "We are not entirely defenseless. Chu and Ko will fight to the death, and Master Jiro and I have the power of the kami at our fingertips. Even against a demon like Hakaimono, we would give him a fight to remember."

"I know," Okame said without glancing at her. His gaze was still riveted to Daisuke, who hadn't looked away, either. "I know we would all fight very hard, and that we're all ready to give our lives to stop the demonslayer. But from what I've heard of Hakaimono, it's going to take each and every one of us working together to have any hope of bringing him down. Taiyo-san, if you leave now…" Okame paused, thinking, then shook his head. "I can't see us winning. I'm not the type of warrior who can stand against an oni of that power. If you return to the Imperial city, Hakaimono will kill us. And then he will take the pieces of the scroll to the Master of Demons, who will then be free to summon the Dragon. And the empire will fall."

Daisuke was silent, his features expressionless. Okame held his gaze, unrelenting. "I know I'm an honorless ronin dog," he said quietly. "I know I've lost all concept of duty, obligation and sacrifice. The emperor must be warned that Hakaimono is free and the Master of Demons has returned, I realize that, but… right now, we need you more, Taiyo-san. If you return to the Imperial city and we fail to stop Hakaimono, you might not have an empire to protect much longer. So, I'm asking you, as a friend and a brother in arms, will you help us save Kage Tatsumi?" One corner of his mouth twitched, the hint of a smirk crossing his face. "Or do you still need me to drop to my knees and humbly beg your forgiveness for implying that you're a coward? I don't normally beg, for anything, but I'll prostrate myself right now, if that's what it takes."

"Okame-san..." Daisuke closed his eyes. "You..."

"Excuse me." A soft tap came from the door, a moment before the servant slid it open, peering in at us on her knees. "Pardon the interruption," she said, with a wide-eyed glance at Daisuke and the ronin, facing off a few feet away, "but I have an important message from Lord Iesada. Before you depart, he wishes the Lady Yumeko and the rest of her companions to join him for tea in the autumn wing of the castle. If you follow me, I will take you there."

"Give us a moment," Reika said shortly. The maid blinked, either in surprise or offense, but slid the door shut once more, leaving us alone. I wrinkled my nose as Reika immediately rose, walked to the door and pressed another ofuda to the frame, silencing the room again.

"Why does Lord Iesada want to see us?" I wondered. "He's been horribly rude, not to mention his shinobi tried to kill us in the city. Do you think he wishes to apologize? Is this an 'I'm sorry I tried to assassinate you' tea ceremony?"

Reika snorted so loudly that the dogs raised their heads and pricked their ears at her. "Most assuredly not," she said, rolling her eyes.

"Well, we don't have to attend, do we?" I asked. "We can sneak out of Kage lands through the Path, and Lord Iesada would be none the wiser."

Daisuke turned then, his expression faintly horrified as he faced me. "That would be an enormous insult, Yumeko-san," he said. "Iesada-sama is a lord of the Kage and does us a great honor. To ignore him would be unforgivably rude. The Shadow Clan itself might take offense to such a slight."

"What do you care about it, Taiyo?" Okame demanded roughly. "I thought you were going back to Sun lands. Don't worry about the rest of us—I'm sure we can muddle through somehow."

Daisuke's shoulders slumped, and he bowed his head with a sigh.

"You shame me, Okame-san." The noble's voice was soft. "I know of no samurai who would admit an opponent was too strong for him, but you, a ronin, put aside your own honor, your own pride, to make me see the truth. You are absolutely correct—warning the emperor will accomplish nothing should the Master of Demons succeed in summoning the Dragon. My place is here, with those I have sworn to aid.

"Yumeko-san," he continued, rising to face me, his expression intent. "I must beg your pardon, as well. If you would still have me, let me swear a new oath. I vow to protect you and the Dragon scroll, to be the blade that stands between you and your enemies, for as long as I have the breath to keep fighting, or until the Harbinger has passed on from the world once more. Let me accompany you to the Steel Feather temple, and I will face Hakaimono unflinchingly. On my honor, he will not touch you as long as I still breathe. That is my new vow. If you will accept it."

I nodded. "Arigatou, Daisuke-san."

"Good," Reika snapped. "So, if we're finished making vows and being honorably dramatic, perhaps we can leave? Hakaimono isn't getting any farther from the Steel Feather temple. And now, we have to decide if we're going to attend Lord Iesada's tea ceremony. Though I might be getting slightly ill, because I think I agree with Yumeko's plan. What do we care if we insult the Kage, if it prevents the coming of the Master of Demons and the Dragon?"

"Forgive me, Reika-san," Daisuke said, stepping farther into the room. "But insulting Lord Iesada is not the only issue at hand. Sometimes, sitting across from your enemy is the quickest way to discern their secrets." He lowered his voice, even though Reika's ofuda still clung to the door, keeping our conversations secret. "Once we leave Kage lands, we must reach the

Steel Feather temple as quickly as we can to warn them about Hakaimono, and to prepare for the demon's arrival. If any in the Shadow Clan intend to stop us, we must be ready for them. The wise tactician keeps his intentions close, speaks softly and pries his enemy open without the other even realizing it. I believe we should attend Lord Iesada's ceremony. Perhaps we will learn something that we did not know before."

"I have to agree," Master Jiro put in, surprising us. "Someone in the Shadow Clan wishes to stop us. We must discover all we can so that we are not taken off guard. However," he continued, and put a fist over his mouth as his voice grew husky. "I believe I will let you young people attend the ceremony. Please tell Lord Iesada that I am unwell, and send my apologies. I will remain here with Chu and Ko, make sure they do not wander into trouble."

Reika gave her master a suspicious, amused look. "How can you be a priest and not like tea?" she asked. Master Jiro sniffed, drawing a pipe from his robes.

"When you are old, Reika-chan, you are allowed certain eccentrics. Not liking tea, or anything to do with it, is one of them."

Okame groaned. "Ugh, I hate tea ceremonies. They're so unbelievably boring." He sighed. "You chatty types can do the talking. I'll just sit back and try to remember all the steps I have to take before I can actually drink the tea. Blink twice if I'm about to do something offensive. I wouldn't want to hold the teacup wrong and bring so much dishonor to our flawless noble, he'll have to fall on his own sword in shame."

"I would certainly not fall on my sword," Daisuke said, giving the ronin a wry look. "That implies that I tripped and tumbled down the stairs, impaling myself at the bottom like a graceless water buffalo. I would kneel on a pillow and perform the ritual with honor and precision, like all noble samurai."

"I've never been to a tea ceremony," I mused as we all stood to leave the room. "Jin and Master Isao used to have them occasionally, but Denga said I was forbidden from attending until he was certain I would not sneak all the sweets for later or make the teapot dance around the room." I sniffed. "I only did the teapot thing twice. Denga-san never let me forget anything."

Reika winced and gave both me and Okame a resigned look. "Why do I have the feeling this isn't going to go well at all?"

Okame was right. The tea ceremony was incredibly dull. And long. I had thought we would attend Lord Iesada's gathering, have a cup of tea and then politely excuse ourselves. But the actual ceremony started in the morning and continued into early afternoon. We were escorted to a designated tea room, where Lord Iesada waited for us, and knelt on pillows while we watched the tea-master first bring the utensils into the room one by one. It was then a lot of greeting and bowing, watching the utensils cleaned, and waiting for the tea-master to prepare the tea, carefully spooning in the bright green tea powder and adding spoonfuls of hot water, before whisking it into a froth. I nibbled on a plate of sweet rice cakes that had been set before us and tried hard not to fidget. When the tea was finally ready, a single bowl was used to serve the tea to guests: one person took their time admiring the bowl and the tea itself, before turning the bowl to the left and taking one contemplative sip. He then wiped the rim with a special cloth and passed it to the next guest, who did the same. It was a terribly bitter tea; I held my breath as I swallowed, choked out a comment about the delightful flavor and hurriedly passed the tea to Okame. Then we had to watch the tea-master clean the bowl and the utensils again, slowly and with the utmost care, before the entire process could start once more.

"I am curious," Lord Iesada said, in the space between waiting for the next round of tea to be served. "You all traveled with the Kage demonslayer for a time. Tell me, how is it he did not kill you to a man?"

I jerked, causing Reika to give me a sharp look over the tatami mats. Fortunately, Daisuke sat closest to Lord Iesada, and gave him a serene smile.

"An interesting topic, Iesada-sama," he said in a voice of cool politeness. "I myself am curious as to why one would bring up the subject of your clan's demonslayer. Please forgive my ignorance— in the Sun lands, the topic of demons is considered unfit for polite conversation."

I reached for another sweet, a bright pink rice cake wrapped in a leaf, and let the flavor melt away the bitter taste in my mouth. Okame caught my gaze and rolled his eyes, and I bit back a grin.

"Ah, forgive me," continued Lord Iesada, his own voice unruffled. "I forget that in the Sun lands, everything is far brighter and safer than in our humble lands of Shadow. The people there do not have to fear the dark, nor the creatures that lurk within. Often I wish our own samurai knew such peace and frivolity, but alas, such danger is part of our everyday lives. I meant no offense, of course."

"Of course," Daisuke replied, still smiling. "Certainly, it is understandable that the Kage can sometimes struggle with the concepts of etiquette and social graces. Being so far from Sun lands and the Imperial capital must be a terrible burden for your clan. Lady Hanshou must be commended for doing so much with so little."

I shifted my weight on the pillow, absently twirling the discarded leaf between my fingers. Beside me, I heard Okame's bored, barely audible sigh. Without looking at me, he pointed to the black iron teapot sitting on the brazier, then waggled two fingers in a strange, dancing motion. Reika, unfortunately, caught the gesture, and very slightly turned her head, pinning me with a tight-lipped, wide-eyed look that very clearly said *do not dare.*

"Taiyo-san is too kind." Lord Iesada's voice held a bit of an edge now, before his cold black gaze shifted to me. "But what does our esteemed guest have to say regarding the demonslayer?" he purred. "I understand she traveled all the way to the capital with him. Did he do anything to put you in danger? Did you know he had a demon lurking inside his sword, waiting to be unleashed?"

I lightly cupped the leaf in my fingers, hiding it in my palm as a flutter of fox magic went through the air. "He saved my life," I told the Kage lord. "The road was very dangerous, yes, but I wouldn't have survived if not for Tatsumi-san."

"Tatsumi-san, is it?" Lord Iesada looked amused. "I had not realized you and the demonslayer had grown so close. Perhaps you think you owe him a debt of gratitude, then?" He chuckled, shaking his head. "Do not bother. The demonslayer is naught but a weapon. A tool that the Shadow Clan uses to slay dangerous monsters and yokai, because he is as much a monster as the creatures he hunts. He has no feelings, no emotion, no personal honor. He is barely human. You might as well owe a debt of gratitude to an ox cart for carrying you to the next town."

"I'm sorry, Lord Iesada, but you're wrong."

Lord Iesada raised both pencil-thin eyebrows in either shock or outrage. "Excuse me?" he exclaimed.

"Tatsumi isn't just a weapon," I said. "He's not an unfeeling monster. He was brave and honorable, and was constantly worried about Hakaimono. And he was worried about Hakaimono because he didn't want to hurt me, or bring shame to the Shadow Clan. That isn't the mind-set of a creature who is barely human."

Lord Iesada stared at me, eyes glittering. "You are quite bold for a woman, and a peasant," he said at last, managing a tight smile. "Consider yourself lucky that you are Hanshou-sama's honored guest, for in my estate such audacity would not be tolerated. I shall tell you a simple truth about Lady Hanshou's demonslayers. They are monsters, because we train them to be monsters."

I frowned. "What do you mean?"

"Do you wish to know how the Kage demonslayer is created? When one demonslayer dies, a boy is chosen from the ranks of our kami-touched to become the next bearer of the Cursed Blade. He goes through intense training to purge all weaknesses from his mind and body, and to prepare his soul for the intrusion of Hakaimono. The demands on his body are harsh—some say too harsh—but it is nothing compared to what his mind must endure every single day. Some boys do not survive. Some go mad, trying to resist the constant presence of Hakaimono. Some die from the rigors of training, torn apart by yokai, or succumbing to wounds inflicted by their own sensei. In fact, I believe that only one in four boys lives through the initial few months. The rest die in agony, or are killed because they could not resist Hakaimono. Talented, kami-touched boys who could have become honorable samurai instead waste their lives to feed that cursed sword and the demon that inhabits it. And those who do make it through the process have been irrevocably changed. They are no longer human. They are simply vessels for Hakaimono's power, a hand that wields Kamigoroshi in the name of the Kage."

Lord Iesada paused a moment to pluck a colorful rice ball from the plate with his chopsticks, admire the color and fragrance, and pop it into his mouth. "So," he said, dabbing his lips with a silk napkin. "Now you understand. The demon Hakaimono is a monster that must be stopped, and it is the duty of the Kage to bring him down. That the oni has been freed and is rampaging through the country has already brought shame and dishonor upon the Shadow Clan. Hanshou-sama knows this—to suggest that she would seek aid from those outside the Kage is an absurd notion. Why, if any were to meddle in our affairs, we would have to respond to such an insult in force." He smiled coldly across the tatami mats. "But my apologies, I speak of clouds that have not yet formed, and rain that has not yet fallen. I am certain Lady Hanshou has the matter of Hakaimono in hand. Let us return to more pleasant subjects, yes?"

I was still getting used to the flowery idioms and roundabout phrases of the nobles of court, but I was fairly sure Lord Iesada had just threatened us. Or at least, warned us not to go after Tatsumi. Anger flickered. They could say what they liked; I *was* going to save Tatsumi, even if I had to dodge Shadow Clan shinobi the entire way to the Steel Feather temple.

"Taiyo-san," Lord Iesada continued, reaching for a rice cake with his chopsticks. "Have you tasted Noriko-san's mochi balls yet? I simply insist that you try them—they have the most delicate fragrance..."

He plucked a pink rice ball from the plate, and a furry brown head poked up, whiskers twitching as the sweet was removed. Lord Iesada let out a yelp, jerking his hand back, as the tiny rodent darted from the plate, zipped up to the lord and vanished into the folds of his hakama.

"Nezumi!" The Kage lord leaped to his feet, flapping his arms so that his sleeves whipped about like sails in the wind. Wide-eyed, we watched the noble flail wildly, shaking his legs and slapping at his hakama with his fan. The mouse didn't reappear, though a tattered rice ball leaf came loose and fluttered to the ground near Lord Iesada's feet. No one seemed to notice it.

Finally, when the mouse didn't appear to be hiding in his hakama, Lord Iesada straightened and with great dignity turned to bow at us. "Please forgive my outburst," he said in a calm, unruffled voice. "I fear, for obvious reasons, we must end the ceremony early." His jaw tightened, nostrils flaring as he continued. "Rest assured, we will find whomever is responsible for this atrocity, but for now, I must bid you farewell."

I snuck a glance at my companions. Daisuke looked stunned and slightly amused but, like Lord Iesada, he was doing a remarkable job of hiding his reaction. However, Okame's face was red from holding in his laughter, and Reika's hard black gaze was fixed on me, her mouth drawn into a tight line. Not fooled in the slightest.

"Of course, Iesada-sama," Daisuke said with a small bow of his own. "We will show ourselves out. Thank you for inviting us. Your hospitality is truly inspiring."

Okame and I managed to keep a straight face until we had left the tea room and were a goodly ways down the corridor. But the second we made eye contact, the ronin gasped and doubled over, hands on his knees, and I leaned against a shoji screen, bracing myself on the bamboo frame, as laughter echoed up and down the hall.

"Did...you...see him flap?" Okame wheezed. "He looked like a rooster trying to Kabuki dance."

"Baka!" Reika stepped forward and smacked the ronin upside the head, then turned to glare at me. "I hope you two enjoyed that," she said. "Because now we've made a terrible enemy of a very powerful person in the Shadow Clan. Lord Iesada won't forgive this embarrassment, even if he never suspects who's responsible."

"Ite." Okame straightened, rubbing his skull, to face the miko. "That's assuming he wasn't planning to kill us, anyway," he retorted. "I haven't been a samurai in a while, Reika-san, but I know when I'm being threatened."

Daisuke, watching this whole scene with a bemused smile on his face, shook his head. "Amusing, and disturbing, as this is, I'm afraid the ronin is right, Reika-san. Lord Iesada was our enemy long before he invited us to tea. Should we continue our search for the demonslayer, it is certain we will run into his servants, who will attempt to keep us from our objective."

"Let them try," I said, making them all look at me. "Hakaimono is going after the Dragon scroll," I reminded them. "We can't let anything stop us. We have to get to the Steel Feather temple before he does."

"And hope that, once we do, the First Oni doesn't laugh in our faces, rip us to bloody shreds and take the scroll back to the Master of Demons," Reika added. "I'm still uncertain as to how we're going to avoid that, but it seems our path has been decided." A shadow of uncertainty crossed her face, and she shook her head. "In the past, Hakaimono and the Master of Demons have slaughtered armies and leveled entire cities. We are but five—seven, if you count two shrine guardians—who stand between the First Oni and the most powerful blood mage the country has ever known."

"Yes," Daisuke added, and there was a current of excitement beneath his steely resolve. "A small group who stand against insurmountable odds, who give their lives for the glory of the empire? It is what Bushido is built on." He raised his head, a smile crossing his face as he gazed out a window at the evening sky, his white hair rippling in the breeze. "I for one, welcome the chance to test my skills, to face my enemies with honor and to die with a sword in my hand. Think of the poems they will compose about our noble sacrifice."

Okame winced. "I'd rather they compose poems about our noble victory."

"I've never been in a poem," I mused. "Does it have to be very sad? All the poems I've read seem to be quite sad. Well, except for a haiku about a tanuki and a farmer's daughter. I never quite understood that one, and Denga refused to explain it to me."

"Miss Yumeko?"

I turned to find the older servant woman standing a few yards away, again appearing as silently as a ghost.

"I come with a message from Kage Masao," she informed us, as formal as ever. "Masao-san and Naganori-san await you all on the last floor of the castle. The Path of Shadows is ready."

16

THE FROZEN GARDEN

Suki

*T*here were days when Suki missed being alive. Days that a memory would creep, unbidden, into her heart—a cool spring breeze, the sweetness of a favorite food, the warmth of the sun on her skin—and she would wish, just for a moment, that she was not an intangible ghost.

Today was not one of those days.

"I'm freezing," Taka complained, hunching his shoulders against the driving snow. The little yokai's lips had turned a subtle blue, and his teeth chattered as he trailed miserably after Lord Seigetsu, stepping in his master's footsteps. Ice clung to his sleeves, and the wide-brimmed hat atop his head was covered in snow. "Are we n-nearly there, master?"

"Yes," Seigetsu replied without looking back. "And the ruler of this wood is listening. If you do not wish to have your lips frozen shut forever, I would be silent."

Taka immediately snapped his jaw and hunched even further into his straw cloak, making himself very small. And even though Suki couldn't feel the cold, she shivered anyway. Around them, the shadowy forest stood frozen, tall shaggy pines drooping under the weight of snow and ice. It was an oppressive weight, Suki thought, drifting closer to Taka. Cold and domineering, as if the snow was a cruel master, demanding silence and respect from everything it touched.

As they stepped into a small, peaceful clearing, the snow falling from the sky abruptly ceased, and the forest around them grew still. Not a breath of wind stirred the branches, though Suki could almost see the cold in the icicles that hung from the trees, in the billowing clouds writhing from Taka's lips. Lord Seigetsu didn't stop; he strode across the flat ground, Taka and Suki following in his wake. The snow was quite deep here, and it crunched under Taka's feet, as if he was walking across branches or a bed of pebbles.

"Ite!" Taka suddenly stopped, hopping on one foot, as if he had stubbed his toe. "Ow, ow ow, sharp! What is that?" Lord Seigetsu paused, looking mildly annoyed as he turned around.

"Taka." His voice was a warning.

"Sumimasen!" Taka whispered, wincing as he reached into the snow. "Forgive me, master. I think I stepped on a broken branch…"

He stammered to a halt, his eye going huge, as he pulled a shattered half of a skull out of the snow. With a yelp, he dropped the grinning jawbone; it hit the ground with a muffled crack and rolled away, revealing yet another skull hidden beneath the blanket of white.

A soft, feminine chuckle rippled along the edge of the clearing, carried on the wind and stirring snow into the air. *Welcome to my garden*, it whispered, as Suki gazed around wildly and Taka darted behind Seigetsu's hakama. *I don't get many visitors, not anymore. Would you care to stay for a spell? Perhaps you would like to plant something here yourself?*

The wind gusted, tossing snow into the air, whipping at Seigetsu's hair and tugging at his sleeves. It blew away the top portion of white, revealing the carpet of gleaming bones beneath. Skulls, rotting armor and weapons, skeletons both human and animal, all lying half-buried in the frozen ground. Taka gasped, and Suki felt herself lose form, changing into the glowing ball of light. The strange voice giggled at their reactions. Seigetsu sighed.

"I have already seen your garden, Yukiko," he called to the empty air. "It is not the reason I am here."

Oh, Seigetsu-sama, you're no fun. The voice almost sounded pouty, and snow continued to swirl around the clearing. As Suki watched, lacy fingers of windblown snow brushed Seigetsu's sleeve, then curled around Taka, tugging at his hat. *Are you sure you don't want to leave me a present? I don't have a one-eyed skull in my collection yet.*

Taka cringed and whimpered, clutching at his master's hakama. Seigetsu's golden eyes narrowed.

"No, and don't think you need any more 'decorations,'" he said firmly. He raised a hand and waved it through the snow threads coiling around him. "I have come to collect on my favor, nothing more."

The windblown flurries drifted back. *That was years ago, Seigetsu-sama,* the voice almost whined. *Centuries, and you never came to visit me since then. I had almost forgotten about it.*

"But I have not." Seigetsu's tone was unyielding. "Are you going to honor the promise you made to me that day, Yukiko, or should I become offended that I was misled?"

A long, dramatic sigh caused the snow to swirl frantically around the clearing. *No, Seigetsu-sama,* the voice said, sounding put-upon. *I will honor my word. Let no one say Yukiko of the North does not keep her promises. What is it you need me to do?*

Lord Seigetsu smiled.

"There is an oni by the name of Hakaimono on his way to the Steel Feather temple as we speak," he replied. "I need you to stop him from getting there."

17

THE PRICE OF ILLUSION

Yumeko

*N*aganori waited for us in the bowels of Hakumei castle, standing with his arms crossed in the center of the stone-walled room, but he wasn't the only one.

"Yumeko-san." Kage Masao smiled at me from just inside the door, the flickering torchlight casting his pale face in shadow. He was dressed in blue hakama trousers and midnight-black robes, with pink-and-indigo petals drifting across the fabric like rain. A black silk fan rested between his fingers as he nodded in my direction. "And the rest of our honored guests." He gave a slight bow as the rest of the party entered the room. "Forgive me, I did not have a chance to introduce myself before. I am Kage Masao, chief advisor to Lady Hanshou. I hope your stay in Hakumei castle has been a pleasant one."

Okame snorted, which turned into a grunt as Reika kicked him in the ankle. Masao politely refused to notice. "I have taken it upon myself to oversee your final travel preparations," the courtier went on, and gestured to a servant, who came out of the corner with a handful of papers in one hand and a large, rectangular pack dangling from the other. The pack was made of woven bamboo, with a pair of leather straps that allowed one to carry it on their shoulders. "Here are your travel documents, signed and sealed by Lady Hanshou herself, that will allow you to journey between territories without harassment. And a few supplies to get you to your final destination. Master Naganori has been kind enough to open the Path of Shadows once more, so I fear your time with us has come to a close." As Master Jiro took the documents and Okame took the pack, his sharp black eyes fixed on me. "Do remember, Yumeko-san, once you leave Kage lands, you will be outside the range of Lady Hanshou's influence. I would advise caution. Others might attempt to stop your journey, and we will not be able to help should you find yourself surrounded by dishonorable assassins."

I nodded. "We understand. Thank you, Masao-san."

The courtier smiled and gave me the barest of nods, then turned to the glowering Kage Naganori in the center of the room. "Naganori-san? Are you prepared?"

The majutsushi gave me a stiff, flinty smile that did not reach his eyes. "Whenever they are ready, Masao-san."

"Naganori-san will use the Path of Shadows to take you to Jujiro, a merchant town that sits on the border between the Fire and the Water Clan territories," the courtier went on, turning back to me. "From there, if you travel due north, you will reach the Forest of a Thousand Eyes in two days' time. We cannot bring you any closer than this." Masao spread his fan and regarded me over the black silk. "I do wish to warn you, Yumeko-san—when we realized Hakaimono had gone into the forest, we sent a unit of samurai and shinobi to guard the perimeter, in case he emerged again." He paused, then went on grimly, "Those men were never heard from again."

I swallowed the dryness in my throat. "What happened?"

"We don't know." The noble shrugged an elegant shoulder. "Overnight, it seems the entire unit disappeared. Even the shinobi vanished without a trace. As if something tracked them down and silenced them all.

"We can only assume Hakaimono wearied of being hunted," Masao went on, "and decided to slaughter his pursuers, both to end the threat they represented and to blind us to whatever he is doing in the forest. Which means there is something in the Forest of a Thousand Eyes that he does not wish us to see. Unfortunately, that could be any number of things—an evil place of power, a cabal of demons left over from the last war." His voice grew softer, chilling the blood in my veins. "And of course, there are the ruins of Genno's castle, at the very heart of it all. Were I to hazard a wild guess, I would say that Hakaimono is probably headed there. For what reasons, I can only presume the worst."

A cold lump settled in the pit of my stomach, and I could feel the weight of the scroll, heavy and terrible, beneath my robes. Masao watched me over the edge of his fan, sharp black eyes assessing. As if he knew I wasn't telling him something.

Fortunately, at that moment Naganori stepped forward, radiating impatience. "With your leave, Masao-san," he said with a stiff bow, and gestured us all toward the torii gate. "The night wanes quickly, and it is dangerous to leave the Path of Shadows standing open."

"Ah, of course. Please excuse me." Masao smiled and stepped away, fluttering his fan. "I wish you and your companions luck, Yumeko-san," he said cheerfully, as the majutsushi turned us toward the gate. "Remember, let us know the moment you have completed your mission. If you succeed, you will have done what the most gifted priests and majutsushi failed to accomplish.

Lady Hanshou will be most pleased, and you will have earned the favor of a daimyo."

I didn't care much about the favor of the Kage daimyo; it seemed to me she wanted Tatsumi as her own personal living weapon. But saying so seemed awfully rude, so I merely smiled and bowed to the courtier, then followed Naganori to the torii gate in the center of the room.

"I have opened the path for you," the majutsushi told us, as I shivered in the cold air wafting from the space between the posts. "You will not need me to guide you this time. You must simply walk it until you reach your destination. There will be another majutsushi waiting to open the path on the other side. If nothing happens and you do not go careening off the path into Meido, you will find yourself in the basement of one of the merchants in Jujiro. They will be expecting you, but do not linger, and do not attempt to converse with the owners of the house. Depart the property as quickly as possible and search for the north gate out of the town. Your travel papers will get you past the guards with little to no trouble, but it is still advisable to be cautious, to keep your heads down and avoid attracting attention."

He glanced at Okame as he said this, making the ronin grin. "Oh, don't worry, Naganori-san," Okame said. "An onmyoji, a ronin, a priest and a shrine maiden, two dogs and an Imperial noble walking around together? We're sure to fit right in."

Naganori's mouth thinned, but he turned back to me. "When you do find the north gate," he continued, "all you have to do is follow the road. It eventually ends at the abandoned village of Takemura near the edge of the Forest of a Thousand Eyes. When you reach an empty, overgrown village likely haunted by yurei and demons, you'll know you're close. Do you have any questions before we send you off?"

I shook my head, and the majutsushi gave a brisk nod. "Then

there is nothing else to be done here," he said, and gestured to the torii gate. Between the posts, the air darkened, like a shadow creeping over the floor. I could feel the icy tendrils of the space between reaching out to me, clawing at my skin, and shivered. "Sayonara," Naganori said, and stepped away, as if already dismissing us. "Good luck on the path."

I looked at the inky blackness through the torii gate and took a deep breath. *Hold on, Tatsumi. I'm coming.*

Flanked by Daisuke and Okame, and with Reika, Master Jiro and the two dogs at my back, I stepped forward onto the Path of Shadows. As soon as we were through, the light behind us faded, the tear between realms sealed and we were alone in the land of the dead.

I could already feel their eyes on us and, for a moment, could only stand there shivering.

"Come." Master Jiro stepped forward, Chu and Ko at his side. The two dogs seemed to glow softly in the inky shadows of the path, twin balls of luminance in the gloom. "Let us not repeat our mistakes the first time we came through," the old priest said, his voice sounding weak and rough in the black. "Our faith in each other must be stronger than the calls of the dead. Reika-chan, if you would…"

"Hai, Master Jiro." The shrine maiden reached into her sleeve and withdrew an ofuda, the kanji for *path* written down the strip of paper in black ink. "If you feel yourself slipping," Master Jiro said, as Reika stepped to the front, "look to your companions. They will not let you fall to the darkness."

Raising her hand, the miko released the ofuda, which spiraled into the air like an eel through water. It circled us once, then fluttered down the path, casting a faint glow against the shadows. Reika smiled.

"It's found the path," she said, watching the slip of light flicker and dance against the darkness. "If you ever start to lose your way, just look for the light."

"Then let us go," said the priest. "Before the voices of the dead call to us."

Something whispered my name in the dark, low and anguished. Tatsumi's voice. A shadow appeared, familiar and heartbreaking, in the corner of my vision. Pinning back my ears, I closed my eyes and turned away, refusing to look at it. *It's not him,* I reminded myself, swallowing the lump that rose to my throat. Tatsumi wasn't dead. He waited for me at the end of the road, at the Steel Feather temple, where the fate of the Dragon scroll would be decided. I would see the demonslayer again, and I would free him from Hakaimono. Or the First Oni would kill us all, and the Master of Demons would rise again. Simple as that.

"Yumeko-chan?" Something touched my arm. I jumped and opened my eyes to see Okame gazing down at me, his eyes concerned. "Are you all right?"

"Hai, Okame-san." I nodded. "I'm just…thinking about the mission, and what I have to do when we find Hakaimono."

He grinned. "Don't worry about it, Yumeko-chan," he said brightly. "We just have to save the empire from the First Oni and the Master of Demons. Easy stuff, right?"

I frowned at him. "I don't think it will be easy, Okame-san. Do you?"

"Nope." The ronin shrugged. "Not at all. But I can't take this too seriously, considering we're all probably going to die. Just think of the ballads they'll compose in our honor."

"You two," came Reika's impatient voice from up ahead. "Whatever you are talking about, can it not wait until we are off the Path of Shadows and out of the realm of the dead?"

"Gomen, Reika-chan," Okame called, his voice still obstinately cheerful in the darkness. "Yumeko and I were discussing what kind of ballads they'll write of our tragically honorable deaths while fighting Hakaimono. Personally, I would like mine to be done in haiku."

"Baka," Reika muttered, rolling her eyes as she turned away. "Don't compose our fates before we even get there. Besides, who would write a poem about your idiocy?"

"The archer unbowed," Daisuke murmured as we started down the path. "The demon could not break him. He laughed as he died."

"Ooh," I said, pricking my ears forward. "That was impressive, Daisuke-san."

The noble chuckled. "I am a man of many talents, Yumeko-san. I believe that if one takes an interest in something, one must strive to perfect it, and himself."

"That," Okame said, glaring at Daisuke with a half-gleeful, half-annoyed expression, "was entirely too easy, Taiyo. I would expect you would spend at least a week agonizing over the words of my death." He struck a dramatic pose on the path, making us pause. "My death must be poignant and tragically noble, like the endings of all the Kabuki plays."

"Okame-san." Daisuke gave the ronin a faint, almost sad smile. "Should you perish on this mission while I somehow live, I swear I will compose a ballad in your honor that will make even the kami weep. However, you must promise to do the same for me, for I do not intend to sit idly by. When the time comes, I plan on meeting that glorious death right alongside you."

My stomach twisted. "Has anyone ever composed a ballad where the heroes win, the enemy is defeated and no one else dies?" I asked. "Perhaps where, at the end of the tale, they go home with their friends, marry their love and live a peaceful life until the end of their days?"

Daisuke laughed, a strange, light sound in the gloom and darkness with the voices of the dead moaning all around us.

"That would make for a very anticlimactic tale, Yumeko-san," he chuckled. Raising a hand, he motioned us forward again, and we trailed the priest and the shrine maiden into the dark, following a sliver of light that fluttered and danced up ahead. "In the best stories, the heroes always give their lives, for honor, duty, sacrifice and the glory of the empire. Anything less and it is not much of a story at all."

The journey back through Meido and the Path of Shadows wasn't as bleak and horrifying as the first time; we knew what to expect and were prepared to close our ears to the calls of the dead. But it still wasn't pleasant. I glimpsed Denga and Nitoru again, scowling at me, their faces dark as they glared through the mist that lined the trail. I knew it wasn't really them, but my stomach twisted and a lump caught in my throat all the same. My friends were beside me this time, and I knew we wouldn't let each other step off the path. Daisuke's face was serenely blank as he strode forward, looking neither left nor right. Behind him, Okame stalked down the path with his arms crossed and his lips twisted in a smirk. Every so often, he would glance into the swirling mist and sneer, as if he was daring the spirits of the dead to do their worst. Once, I saw a spirit reach out for Reika, moaning, but there was a dart of orange in the gloom, as Chu rushed the ghost with a tiny but fierce yap, and the yurei recoiled, drawing back into the mist.

Ahead of us, the ofuda strip glowed like a miniature dragon as it fluttered and darted about, always moving forward but always visible, even if it was just a thread of light against the darkness. But, just as I was wondering when this morbid journey would end, the strip of paper winked out and vanished into the black.

I jerked up. "Um, Reika-chan?" I called, seeing the miko glance at me over her shoulder. "Your ofuda," I pointed. "It disappeared. Do you think a yurei got it?"

"No." The shrine maiden shook her head, her shoulders sagging with visible relief. "It must have found the end of the path. Which means we're nearly there."

As she spoke, the blackness dropped away, like we had stepped through the mouth of a cave, and I blinked in the sudden glow of orange lantern light. Squinting through the haze, I found myself standing in a small room, with rough wooden floors, windowless walls and a high ceiling. When I glanced over my shoulder, I saw a small red torii gate standing against what looked to be a solid wall. A few wisps of fog curling around our feet soon dissolved in the shadows, but there was no sign of the path or the entrance into the realm of the dead.

We were in some kind of storeroom. The rest of the chamber had shelves running the length of the walls that were stocked with all manner of crates, boxes and full sacks of what I guessed was rice. Barrels were stacked in three corners of the room, and rolls of cloth stood upright against the fourth.

I turned to Reika. "Where did Naganori say we would end up?"

"In the basement of one of the merchant houses in Jujiro," the shrine maiden replied, also gazing around. "From the looks of things, I'd say we made it."

"You have arrived."

We turned at the quiet voice. A young woman wearing long robes of black and purple stood at the base of the steps leading up. White makeup and black lips marked her as a majutsushi of the Shadow Clan. "Please follow me," she said simply, and turned away. "I will escort you out."

Not long after, we stood on the corner of a cobbled road, shivering in the predawn stillness, as the town of Jujiro slowly woke up. Across the street, past a row of warehouses guarded by rough-looking men, I could see a structured web of wooden docks and dozens of brightly colored sails, drifting or bobbing lazily on the water. A constant breeze blew in from the harbor, smelling of fish and river water, or maybe that was from the rows of fish being gutted and sliced open at the market across the street.

"I've never heard of Jujiro," I said, marveling at all the sights and sounds of the harbor. "How close are we to the Dragon Spine Mountains?"

"I'm not really sure," Reika said. "I've never been to Jujiro myself."

"If you'll allow me," Daisuke said, and took the lead as we started down the road. "I have traveled through this area a few times in the past. Let me share what I can remember. The town of Jujiro is also known as the Crossroads," Daisuke continued, oblivious or uncaring of Okame rolling his eyes at his back, "and it is the only town in the empire that isn't controlled by any one family or clan. Because it sits at a juncture where two rivers meet it has become an important hub for trade and economic growth. In the past, wars were fought to see who would control Jujiro, but in the end, the emperor decided that it would belong to no clan and every clan." He nodded to a warehouse on one of the many docks, flying the banner of a familiar moon engulfed by an eclipse. "That's why the Kage have a presence here—all the clans do. I believe this is the River of Gold, which, if you followed it east, would eventually lead you to Kin Heigen Toshi." His voice grew somber as he pointed in another direction. "If you travel north, in two days' time you will see the edge of Angetsu Mori, known today as the Forest of a Thousand Eyes. Which is likely the reason Lady Hanshou sent us here. Jujiro is the closest major town to that cursed forest.

"However," he continued, as I shivered in the cool night air, "if we ignore Lady Hanshou's wishes and follow the River of Gold east…"

"We hit the Dragon Spine Mountains," Okame finished, and Daisuke nodded.

"Then that is our destination," Master Jiro wheezed. He tottered down the road, leaning heavily on his staff, Chu and Ko staying close at his heels. "We must find the eastern gate, if such a thing exists." He coughed, bringing one fist to his mouth, his thin shoulders trembling, until the fit passed. At his feet, Ko gave a concerned whine.

"Forgive me, Master Jiro," Daisuke said, his brows furrowed. "With all due respect, are you feeling well? Enough for a long trek up the harshest of mountain terrains?"

"I am well." The old priest waved off Daisuke's concern. "My lungs are not used to these rapidly changing temperatures, but I will adapt."

"Are you sure?" Okame asked, looking dubious over his crossed arms. "You're old, and I don't want to have to carry you all the way up the mountain."

"I will be fine, ronin." Master Jiro's voice was a bit sharper now. "If I can walk the Pious Pilgrimage from Shimizu in Water Clan territory all the way to Heichimon's Shrine in Hino lands, I can endure a hike up the Dragon Spine." He sniffed. "Besides, how were the lot of you planning to bind Hakaimono on your own, even enough to slow him down? You are going to need a priest of my…ahem…*experience*, if we are going to trap an oni lord."

"That's assuming we can find the Steel Feather temple," Reika muttered. "And that whoever lives there, be it monks or priests or hungry ghosts, will believe us when we say we're not their enemies and that we've come to stop the First Oni from barging in and stealing their piece of the Dragon scroll. By *not* exterminating him." She sighed, shaking her head. "I hope whoever lives there is the understanding type and doesn't decide to kill us all."

We left the Shadow Clan district of the docks, moving away

from the river and warehouses and entering what was apparently the center of town, judging from the converging crossroads and the signpost in the middle proclaiming it such. Despite the early hours, Jujiro bustled with activity. All manner of shops lined the roads, their doors already open, vendors busy setting up booths and wooden stalls. A young woman in a beautifully colored kimono strolled past, a parasol balanced on one shoulder. Her face was painted white, her lips and eyes touched with crimson, but unlike the makeup of the majutsushi, it made her look elegant and doll-like instead of stark. Her hair, pinned with flowers and ivory combs, was styled so that not a strand was out of place. She smiled at us as she passed, her gaze lingering on Daisuke, before continuing on.

As we made our way toward the eastern side of the city, the first rays of dawn finally peeked over the horizon, touching the very tops of the rooftops with soft orange light. I took a deep breath, relieved to be out of the oppressive darkness of Shadow Clan territory. Away from the Kage and their prying eyes and ears, where I didn't have to worry that my every move, my every word, was being watched, recorded and judged. Where my secrets weren't in constant danger of being discovered and stripped away, and my friends weren't being threatened or in danger of being killed should any one of those secrets come to light.

No wonder you were always so paranoid, Tatsumi. I closed my eyes, smiling faintly, as the sunlight touched my face. I knew we hadn't been with the Shadow Clan long, and the instance we'd ventured outside the castle had been at night. But within the walls of Hakumei-jo, it had felt as if the sun didn't exist and the entire land was cloaked in eternal darkness and shadow. *If I had to live with the Kage for even a month or two, I might go crazy.*

My stomach fluttered as the demonslayer invaded my thoughts again. *Tatsumi...I hope you're all right. We're coming, for you and Hakaimono both. Wait for me just a little longer.*

Master Jiro began coughing again, a harsh sound that caused all of us to stop in the middle of the road and gaze at him in concern.

Reika frowned. "Master Jiro…"

"I…am fine," the old priest insisted, holding up a hand. "Do not worry about me. Look." He gestured down the road between buildings, where the sweeping corners of a huge arched gate could be seen over the roofs. "The eastern gate is straight ahead. We cannot stop."

"Master Jiro, please." Reika put herself in front of him, her expression one of concern and stubborn resolve. The two dogs stood at her ankles facing the old priest, seeming to echo her words. "The last time your cough appeared and you pushed yourself, you couldn't get out of bed for a week."

"Hakaimono could already be closing on the Steel Feather temple," Master Jiro argued, his voice thin and raspy. "We cannot allow the Master of Demons to acquire even one piece of the scroll. There is no time to delay." He straightened, gripping his staff tightly. "I will endure. I can do no less—the fate of all depends on us."

"That might be true," Okame said, as a horse-drawn cart rolled by us, wheels creaking against the dirt. "But that doesn't mean we should kill ourselves trying to get there." He gave the cart a quick glance as it continued down the road, heading toward the gate, then smirked. "Wait here. I'll be right back."

"Where are you going, ronin?" the shrine maiden demanded, but Okame was already jogging away. We watched as he caught up with the cart, brought it to a halt, then held a quick conversation with the driver. The man, perhaps a merchant or a farmer, judging from the number of empty crates in his cart, peered back at me as Okame pointed a finger in our direction, and his eyes widened beneath his conical straw hat.

"All right," he announced, striding back to us with a rather

SOUL of the SWORD

smug look on his face. "It's settled. Roshi there has agreed to take us east until he reaches his home town of Mada Ike. From there, it's a half day's walk to the Dragon Spine."

Reika crossed her arms. "And what did you tell the poor man to get him to agree to that?" she asked dubiously.

"Simple. I told him that Yumeko is a distinguished onmyoji who is on a secret but important mission for the emperor himself—that's why Taiyo-san is here—and that it was his duty to assist her in whatever way he could. He, of course, was all too happy to comply."

"So you lied."

"Is it really a lie if the emperor himself believes it?" Okame's grin was defiant in the face of the shrine maiden's scowl. "According to the Imperial palace, Yumeko is an onmyoji of great renown, who recently performed so well for Taiyo no Genjiro that she was offered a position in the emperor's court. I'm sure that, if our wise emperor knew what was happening with Hakaimono and the Master of Demons, he would want us to accomplish our mission." His grin became sharp. "You certainly had no qualms about marching into the palace under less than honest pretenses. Taiyo-san is exempt because he didn't know at the time, but *you* certainly were well aware that our good onmyoji is really a clever kitsune in disguise. And, last I checked, lying to the emperor of Iwagoto is punishable by death."

"That was necessary." Reika didn't back down. "We had to find Lady Satomi and free Master Jiro from her evil blood magic. You're using an innocent bystander and pulling him into our affairs. What we're attempting to do is dangerous. This man's life will be at risk just being around us."

"Do you want to get to the Dragon Spine quickly or not?" the ronin asked. "We could walk, of course, and waste both time and Master Jiro's health marching across the plains. Or we could accept Roshi's generous offer and save ourselves at least half a day getting to the base of the mountain."

Reika took another breath to argue, but was interrupted by Master Jiro's raised hand.

"If this man truly wishes to help, Reika-chan, then I see no reason to refuse." The old priest glanced at the waiting cart with what could almost be relief. "We mustn't bring shame to his household by refusing such generosity. For the good of the empire, of course."

The miko sighed, ignoring the ronin's triumphant grin. "As you wish, master."

Moments later, with the exception of Master Jiro, who had taken the seat beside the cart driver, we had all crowded into the back of a creaky wooden cart and pressed ourselves between stacks of empty crates and barrels, feeling every bounce and jolt through the wagon as it rumbled down the road.

"Well," Okame muttered, wincing as the cart hit a dip in the path with a jolt that clicked my teeth together. "It's no kago, but at least we're finally on the road and moving faster than if we were on foot. That's something at least." He eyed the noble, sitting across from him with his back straight and his hands in his lap, and a faint grin quirked his mouth. "Don't worry, Taiyo-san. If we spot any samurai coming down the road, I'll be sure to yell so you can hide in one of the barrels. Wouldn't want them to see a noble Taiyo traveling in a vegetable cart with a bunch of dirty peasants."

Daisuke only smiled.

"Let them see," he said calmly. "I travel with the most interesting and honorable of companions, and I am not ashamed. If they cannot see beyond the outward appearance, that is a stain on their honor, not mine." One eyebrow rose, and he regarded Okame in an almost challenging manner. "Unless you simply want to see me dive into one of the sake barrels, Okame-san."

The ronin smirked. "Would you?"

"No." Daisuke shook his head, though his own smile widened. "At least...not alone."

Beside me, Reika made a strange gagging noise in the back of her throat. I blinked at her, while Chu and Ko, sitting in a stack of empty crates, poked their heads out to look at us. "Are you all right, Reika-san? Do you need some water?"

"Maybe some sake," she muttered, rubbing her eyes. "Merciful Jinkei, I hope it's not going to be like this all the way to the Steel Feather temple. You and the demonslayer, and now these two baka. It appears Master Jiro and I are the only ones with our heads not in the clouds."

I looked up at the wisps of clouds streaking the otherwise empty sky and frowned. "I don't understand, Reika-san."

She rolled her eyes, but did not explain.

The cart rattled on, weaving a jostling but steady pace through the lands of the Mizu, the Water Clan. After we left Jujiro, the land flattened out, becoming rolling plains with shreds of clouds drifting above them. We passed many small lakes and rivers, where flocks of white-and-black cranes clustered along the banks and in the shallow water. Sometimes, a pair of them would face off in a strange, leaping dance, wings spread and necks craned to the sky, almost seeming to float in the air. Daisuke appeared to share my fascination, for he murmured a poem about rippling water, a summer moon and two dancing male cranes. It sounded very pretty, but there must have been a hidden meaning that I didn't catch, for Okame went extremely red and stared at the side of the cart for a long time after that.

Sometime in the afternoon, a dark ridge appeared against the horizon, looming and ominous, making my insides curl.

The Dragon Spine Mountains.

The sun climbed higher into the sky, sliding in and out of the clouds, and the rolling plains went on. We dozed in the back of the cart, Reika slumped against the crates, Daisuke with his hands in his lap and his head on his chest. Okame snored quietly, echoing Master Jiro's shallow, wheezing breaths and occasional cough from the front. My eyes fluttered closed, and in that strange place between consciousness and dreams, I thought I heard Tatsumi's voice. Calling to me.

A tiny growl cut through the silence.

I opened my eyes, just as Chu climbed out of the box he shared with Ko and hopped onto a stack of crates, facing the wind. Raising my head, I squinted in the bright sunlight and gazed around. We were on a wide dirt road that cut through open plains, a sea of waving grass surrounding us in every direction. Wind whispered through the stalks, and the sun beat down on us relentlessly, scouring faces and reddening skin. But except for the buzz of the cicadas and the hypnotic sway of the grass, nothing moved in the silver-green ocean surrounding us.

Chu growled again, and the hairs on my arms rose. I looked at the others and saw Daisuke's eyes snap open, his gaze hard and frightening. His fingers tightened around the hilt of the sword across his lap.

"Daisuke," I whispered, "what—"

I heard it then, a sudden hissing all around us, like a swarm of insects flying through the air. I looked up just in time to see a hail of arrows strike the horse and driver's seat from two directions, catching Roshi and Master Jiro in a deadly cross fire. As arrows tore into them, both men jerked and toppled sideways off the seat.

For a moment, the world seemed to stop, crystallizing into a strange, surreal moment where nothing was real. Then the horse gave a strangled whinny and collapsed, black shafts peppering its side and neck, and Reika screamed.

Around us, the grass exploded, as several black shapes hurled themselves into the air. I froze, but Daisuke spun, already on his feet, his blade slashing in a vicious arc before him. There was a chilling screech of metal, as he knocked several things out of the air, and they flashed in the sun as they were deflected away. At the same time, three shiny black daggers struck the pile of crates I sat next to, embedding themselves in the wood with sharp *thunks*. Chu leaped off the crate stack just in time to avoid being impaled, and the blood froze in my veins.

"Ambush!" cried Daisuke, as a pair of black-clad figures in masks leaped toward the cart. His sword flashed, cutting one figure in half as it tried to leap into the cart bed, and the assassin gurgled as it fell back, leaving a streak of blood across the wood. The other sprang to the edge of the cart, raising his sword, and was struck in the chest by an arrow before toppling to the ground. Grimacing, Okame pulled another dart from his quiver and ducked behind a sake barrel.

Another arrow struck the crate, barely missing my arm, and I winced. I could see Okame, firing arrows into the long grass, hearing muffled thumps and falling bodies with every dart loosed. From the corner of my eye, I saw Daisuke smack an arrow from the air, spin gracefully with his white hair flowing behind him and impale an assassin leaping into the cart.

"Reika!" I gasped, seeing the shrine maiden huddled behind another stack of crates, face white and her eyes staring. "Where are Chu and Ko? Can you order them to help?" A couple komainu stomping around would certainly give the assassins something to think about.

She shot me a frantic look, then shook her head. "They're not dogs, kitsune," she spat. "They're holy shrine guardians, meant to drive away demons, yokai and evil spirits. They cannot attack normal humans, only those corrupted by blood magic."

A shadow fell over us. Heart lurching, I spun to see an assassin perched on the edge of the cart, kama sickle raised, before he sliced it down toward me.

I snarled. Reacting on instinct, I threw up my hand, releasing a gout of kitsune-bi into his face. He yelped, twisting aside to avoid it, but was momentarily blinded by the sudden flare. As he staggered, Reika snatched one of the black throwing knives sticking out of the crate, rose and stabbed him through the neck with the inky blade, then pushed him back out of the cart.

Instantly, she dropped back behind the crates to avoid the sudden hail of arrows that zipped overhead. Breathing hard, she stared at the bloody knife in her hand, trembling. "Oh, kami," I heard her whisper, her face going as pale as the grains of rice scattered between the floor planks. "What have I done?"

"Reika." Alarmed, I bent close, grabbing her sleeve. "Are you all right?"

Her eyes flashed as she stared up at me. "Do something!" she hissed, making me fall back. "You're kitsune! You have magic."

"Fox magic," I argued. "Illusions and shadows. None of what I do is real."

"That doesn't matter! Not to them." She pointed fiercely to the battle raging behind us. "They don't know you're kitsune, or that your magic is just illusion. Use that to your advantage— make them believe that what they see is real. If you don't do something, we're *all* going to be killed! Don't let Master Jiro's death be for nothing!"

A chill shot through me. Turning, I snatched a pair of twigs lying on the bottom of the cart, took a deep breath and reached for my magic.

All right, Kage. Arrows still flew through the air, striking the cart, as Okame and Daisuke continued to fend off the attackers. An unfamiliar fire kindled to life, fed by anger and fear, and I felt a snarl rising in my throat. *You're so good at shadow play and*

*covering up the truth with illusions. Let's see how good you are at see-
ing through them yourselves!*

I stood and hurled the sticks into the air. With a flash and a
crack of lightning, two enormous fiery dragons appeared, spiraling up into the cloudless sky. Trailing blue-and-white flames,
they curled around with twin roars and dove at the assassins
lurking in the grass.

Shouts of alarm filled the air. The hail of arrows ceased as
the assassins switched targets, firing at the two enormous beasts
that had appeared out of nowhere. They certainly didn't think
the dragons were illusions. Perhaps they knew something was
wrong, but it was difficult to ignore two howling serpents de-
scending like vengeful gods.

A sudden, savage glee flooded my veins. Snatching a handful of rice from the floor, I grinned and let my magic infuse the
grains in my hand. *Murdering humans! You should have all stayed
home, spying on visitors and assassinating people in dark allies. Now
you're dealing with a kitsune!* I hurled the rice over the cart, and
a dozen floating heads appeared, laughing and gnashing their
teeth, as they flew into the grass. Standing straight, I flung out
a hand, and the grass erupted in a circle of foxfire, blazing blue
and white as it surrounded us.

Shouts became screams. The assassins scattered like ants, slashing wildly at the darting heads, firing at the dragons swooping
down on them. In the corner of my gaze, I saw Okame duck behind a barrel, his face pale in the flare of kitsune-bi, as a dragon
soared overhead. Daisuke stood at the edge of the cart, his eyes
hard as he raised his sword and slashed a flying head out of the
air. It vanished with a pop and a small cloud of smoke. The
fact that my own companions believed the insanity happening
around them struck me as hilarious, though none but Reika had
seen me use fox magic before.

You haven't seen anything yet. With a grin, I snatched up another handful of rice and threw it into the air. With small pops of smoke, identical masked assassins appeared, dropping into the grass. With chilling battle cries, they raised their swords and started attacking their real counterparts, who responded with surprise, then panic. Standing atop the crates, I watched the chaos: the swooping, roaring dragons, the shrieking heads, the roaring flames and the masked men attacking each other with wild abandon, and laughed in delight.

"Yumeko!"

Something grabbed my sleeve, snapping me out of my revelry. I blinked and glanced down into Reika's grim, pale face.

"Enough," she whispered in a shaky voice. "Yumeko, that's enough. They're all dead."

Dead?

Blinking, I waved my hand, dismissing the magic. Heads popped into small clouds of smoke, the masked figures disappeared, and the blue-white flames flickered out. The two dragons circling overhead shivered into coils of mist and dissolved in the wind, as a pair of twigs dropped from the air and vanished into the tall grass.

The cart under my feet swayed, and a sudden bout of dizziness made my head spin. The next thing I knew, I was slumped against the corner, the blurry faces of Reika, Daisuke and Okame standing over me.

"Yumeko." Reika's voice seemed to come from a great distance away. I blinked, and her worried expression swam into focus. "Are you all right?"

"I...yes." I hadn't realized how much magic my body had used, and how much it took out of me, until now. I would have to be careful about that in the future; fainting in the middle of a battle or a fight for our lives was probably a very bad strategy.

I pulled myself upright and froze, gazing around at a scene of slaughter. The bodies of the assassins lay scattered around us in the grass. Some of them had a single arrow jutting from their chest, lodged in their throat, or shot through their head. Courtesy of Okame, I suspected; in the short time I had known him, the ronin had never missed what he shot at. And there were a few lying in the grass right beneath the cart, headless or sliced open with a single precise stroke. Their reward for attempting to cross blades with Oni no Mikoto.

But the rest of them, scattered through the grass with their faces frozen in panic, were free of arrows, and too far away for Daisuke to have slain. Many of them lay in pairs, their swords drawn and bloody, with gaping wounds that turned the grass around them red. A few had been peppered with those black throwing knives, the dark iron blades sunk deep into their flesh. One assassin lay facedown a few yards away, pinned to the earth by a sword, the curved weapon sticking up from the center of his back.

"What…happened?" I whispered, turning in a slow circle, feeling a bit ill as I took in the carnage. This couldn't be right; I hadn't struck a single one of them. "My magic…none of it was real. My illusions couldn't have killed anyone."

Reika sighed.

"No," she agreed. "It wasn't real, but they *believed* it was real. They were terrified, and when their own started attacking them, they responded in kind. Your illusions didn't kill them, Yumeko-chan—they killed each other."

Biting my lip, I looked to the others. Now that the rush of fox magic had faded, I felt almost frightened by what I had done. What my power could really do. This hadn't been a simple prank. I hadn't merely annoyed anyone by making a teapot dance, or changed my appearance to look like someone else. People had *died*. Of course, they were trying to kill us first, so I wasn't going to shed any tears for them. But that still didn't change what I was responsible for: pure, mindless chaos. Madness, confusion and death.

"Yumeko-san." Daisuke's voice was grim, his expression caught between horror and awe as he watched me. "The dragons, those monsters. That was…you?"

"Gomen," I whispered, not knowing who I was apologizing to, or why. "I didn't…"

A low groan drifted up from behind the cart, making us straighten. We hurried around the crumpled body of the dead horse to where Master Jiro lay in the long grass, a whining Ko beside him. A few yards away, Roshi, our driver, also sprawled motionless in the road, his eyes blank as they stared up at the sky, a trio of arrows jutting from his chest.

"Master Jiro." Reika knelt at the priest's side, her face tight with grief and rage. Arrow shafts pierced his stomach and shoulder, and a trickle of red crawled down his chin. There was nothing we could do for him, and everyone knew it. "Damn Lord Iesada," Reika hissed, baring her teeth. "These were his shinobi, I'm certain of it. Another cowardly attack to keep us from reaching the demonslayer. Curse the courts and their endless politics to the bowels of Jigoku." She trembled with fury, then took a deep, shuddering breath to compose herself. "I'm sorry, Master Jiro," she whispered. "This wasn't your fight. I wish we never dragged you into this mess."

The priest coughed. "Do not regret, Reika-chan," he breathed. "Regret solves nothing. We both knew the risks…when we agreed to this mission. But now, you must make certain Yumeko and the scroll…reach the temple. You cannot allow… Hakaimono to retrieve the prayer for the Master of Demons. Genno cannot summon the Dragon. It would mean ruin for the entire world." His withered hand gripped her sleeve with fading strength, and he glanced at me now, as well. "Stop Hakaimono," he wheezed.

"Whatever the cost. Promise me you will not let the Master of Demons win."

"Master Jiro." Reika's voice was numb with despair, and she gazed down at the dying priest in desperation. "Please. We need you. I can't... I'm not strong enough to bind Hakaimono on my own."

"I am sorry, Reika-chan," murmured the priest, his voice barely audible. "I am afraid...that we must part ways for now. You must make sure the scroll reaches the temple, and that Hakaimono is stopped. Nothing else matters. But I hear Meido calling, and I must go." His lips curved in the faintest of smiles, as the light in his eyes flickered and started to fade. "You have always been...so talented," he breathed, as his whole shriveled body relaxed in the grass. "I am...proud."

He didn't move again.

Reika sniffled, clearly trying not to cry, as she fisted her hands on the priest's lifeless chest. "I'll avenge you," she whispered, a steely glint in her dark eyes. "If Lord Iesada *is* responsible for this, I'll find him again and make him pay. And I won't let Hakaimono anywhere near the scroll. You have my word."

Behind us, Ko threw back her head and howled, making us all jump. The white dog's tiny body started to glow, growing brighter and brighter until, with a blinding flash, it exploded into motes of light and disappeared. Sitting alone on the ground, Chu raised his muzzle to the sky and howled as well, long and mournful, as the sun hovered over the empty plains and the Dragon Spine Mountains loomed on the horizon.

18

YUKI ONNA

HAKAIMONO

*T*atsumi was being silent again.

In the two days since we'd left Genno's castle, I hadn't felt him at all. No flicker of emotion, no hint of thought or feeling that wasn't my own. He had retreated deep inside himself, shutting me out completely, and nothing I did seemed to penetrate the wall he'd erected between our consciousnesses. If I wasn't so preoccupied with traveling to the Steel Feather temple, I might've been concerned, or at least curious; why this sudden change? What could have happened to make him hide his thoughts from me completely? As it was, however, I had other issues to worry about.

Like finding a hidden temple somewhere deep in the Dragon Spine Mountains.

At least it had been an easy two days of travel, journeying across the forested rolling plains of the Water Clan. I traveled at night, avoiding the sprawling towns, farms and villages spread across the plains, like someone had flung a handful of rice and let it fall where it would. There were a *lot* of towns. Save for the Imperial family, the Mizu were possibly the wealthiest of the great clans simply by virtue of location; their lands were lush and fertile, protected by ocean on the west and the Dragon Spine Mountains in the east. And the Forest of a Thousand Eyes separated their lands from their hotheaded neighbors to the south. Add the fact that the Mizu were well-known for their pacifism, and that they boasted the finest healers in the empire, and the Water Clan rarely had scuffles with the rest of the empire. Or at least, they had fewer scuffles than the Hino, the Fire Clan, who, it seemed, declared war against the other clans every other year.

On the third night, I finally reached the foothills of the Dragon Spine Mountains. The longest mountain range in Iwa goto began far to the south in Earth Clan territory, curved up past Fire and Sun lands, and ended near Dragon Mouth Bay in Water Clan territory, essentially cutting the empire in half. It was a harsh, endless stretch of icy peaks and soaring cliffs, and I was already mildly annoyed that I was going to have to cross it a second time. There was one pass that cut through the Dragon Spine, but it was farther south and also heavily guarded, and I wasn't going to waste another two days of travel going around the mountains.

Leaning against a pine at the base of the hills, I looked up. The Dragon Spine soared above me, bristling and dark except for where snow touched its highest peaks. Somewhere among those crags and ice-covered cliffs was the temple that held the final pieces of the scroll.

I felt a flash of irritation that bordered closely on rage. I was Hakaimono the Destroyer, Jigoku's strongest oni, being sent to fetch an item like a dog. The fact that Genno had promised to break the curse on Kamigoroshi didn't help. Maybe when I had completed this task and Genno had upheld his end of the deal, I would remind the Master of Demons why it was always a risky business to bargain with Jigoku. One thing was certain—when I was free of the sword and at my full power, the Shadow Clan would pay for the centuries of imprisonment, madness and torture I'd endured since the day Kage Hirotaka made his wish to the Dragon a thousand years ago. They would die in droves, man, woman and child, and I wouldn't stop until I had made my way to their immortal daimyo herself, ripped the head from her withered neck and torn the heart from her chest to eat it in front of her.

I paused in my thoughts of revenge and turned my consciousness inward. *Nothing, Tatsumi?* I thought to the emptiness inside. *I know you're still in there. Not even a flicker of remorse for the complete destruction of your clan? Have you given up so easily?* I pondered that, then smiled. *Or, is it something else—someone else— that you're worried about?*

There was the faintest stirring, like a spider drawing even farther into a crack to escape a predator. I chuckled. *Oh, Tatsumi. You can't hide what you feel for that girl from me. But don't worry; I have something special planned for her. She is going to die slow, screaming in agony, and you are going to be forced to watch. Before she dies, I'll make certain she knows that you can see everything and cannot save her. What do you think about that?*

Nothing. No flicker of emotion from the soul inside; he had closed off his mind tightly. But I knew I had touched a nerve; his concern for this fox girl was blatantly obvious, though the demonslayer himself didn't understand what he was feeling. Humans were pathetically weak when it came to emotions; that a kitsune, a yokai who had deceived him from the beginning, who had lied to him, played him for a fool and put him in danger countless times, had somehow wriggled her way into his affections, was proof of that. He should have killed her when they first met on the road to the Silent Winds temple. He should have struck her down without mercy, and saved himself the torment that would come later.

But it was too late. I knew his secret. And when the time came and the fox girl was at my mercy, I would savor Tatsumi's rage, grief and helpless despair for many years to come.

I started into the foothills, following a narrow game trail as it snaked its way through trees and rocks. The air grew colder the farther I traveled, until I saw tiny flurries dancing on the wind.

I blinked. *The hell? What is this?* It was too late in the year for snow; even this close to the Dragon Spine Mountains, I shouldn't have been seeing white until I got past the tree line.

The snow, however, worsened, flakes turning large and heavy as I pushed my way into the foothills. Soon everything—ground, trees, rocks, branches—was covered in a thick layer of white.

And still, the storm intensified.

Sleet began to fall, pelting the trees and branches, covering the fresh blanket of snow with a layer of ice. It stung like tiny needles as it hit my skin, soaking my clothes and coating my horns with ice. Visibility disappeared, along with all sense of direction. It was impossible to see where I was going through the snow, ice and driving wind.

All right, this is ridiculous. Reaching up, I scraped a half inch of ice from my horns and shook my head to dislodge the snow. Icicles hung from my tusks, and my hakama trousers were frozen stiff. *Whoever is behind this, you're about as subtle as a demon in a teahouse, and I'm starting to get annoyed.*

Shielding my face, I stumbled around a bend and the snow... ceased. I lowered my arm and found myself at the edge of an abandoned village completely encased in ice. Thatched huts were scattered throughout the tiny clearing, each one perfectly preserved in a layer of crystal. As I walked cautiously forward, all senses alert and ready for a fight, I quickly discovered it wasn't abandoned at all.

An old woman, frozen in ice, stood motionless near the bamboo fence that surrounded the village. She held a bucket, and her face was upturned, eyes wide and frozen in terror. A frozen dog lay on its side a few yards away, legs outstretched as if it had been running back to the village. Behind the old woman, a child crouched in the snow, one arm flung toward the dog, icicles dangling from brittle fingers. Curling a lip, I drew Kamigoroshi and walked through the gate into the frozen village.

More dead, ice-covered humans and animals greeted my gaze as I ventured farther in: a mother carrying her infant, an old man pushing a cart, a goat curled up with its nose tucked into its side, sleeping for all time. An unnatural stillness hung in the air, broken only by my breath and the crinkling sound of icicles in the breeze. The snow began falling again, drifting from the sky to settle over the rooftops and the frozen corpses. Except for the light crunch of my feet, the village was dead silent.

Near the well in the center of the village, I stopped. Lowering Kamigoroshi, I gazed around the silent, ice-shrouded clearing, took a deep breath and raised my voice.

"I know you're here," I called into the stillness. "And I'm pretty sure you've been waiting for me. Stop playing games, and let's get on with it."

A giggle echoed around me, impossible to tell from which direction. I gripped Kamigoroshi and waited, scanning the spaces between huts, the confusing play of light over the surface of ice and snow.

The giggle came again, behind me this time. I spun, but there was nothing there, just a cloud of flurries being swirled away by the wind.

I know who you are, whispered a voice, a woman's, on the breeze. *Why don't you stay awhile, Hakaimono, and keep me company?*

I smirked. "Like these villagers are keeping you company?" I returned. "I'd rather not, thanks. No offense, but I hate the cold."

A disdainful sniff. *Mortals are such boring creatures.* The voice swept over the frozen ground like a breeze, never staying in one place, though I still could see nothing except little whirlwinds of snow skipping over the ice. *One touch, one kiss, and their skin turns blue, their insides freezing solid. I wonder if an oni from Jigoku would be more resilient?*

There was a pale shimmer in the corner of my eye, and I turned.

A woman stood at the edge of the clearing where nothing had been before, swirls of snow and ice sparkling around her. Her billowing robes were spotless white with swirls of icy blue, the sleeves trailing to the frozen ground. Long, jet-black hair fluttered in the wind, the ends seeming to writhe away into mist, as did the hem of her robe and sleeves. Her skin was whiter than the snow falling around us, her lips the pale blue of a frozen corpse.

The yuki onna smiled at me over the icy clearing, cold blue eyes glittering like frost, and raised a hand. "Let us find out, shall we?"

I dove away as a blast of frigid air shrieked toward me, leaving a jagged trail of ice spears in its wake. Rolling to my feet, I saw the snow woman had appeared just a few feet away, hair and sleeves billowing around her as she smiled at me. I raised Kamigoroshi and lunged with a growl, aiming for that pale, skinny neck, as the yuki onna's lips parted and she blew in my direction.

Wind shrieked around me, howling in my ears, ripping at my mane and clothes. Ice coated my skin and spread rapidly across my body. My muscles stiffened and froze from the bone-numbing chill. The cold flooded my nose and mouth, turning solid, cutting off the air to my lungs and making my vision blur.

The yuki onna stopped and drifted back, a serene smile on her face. I couldn't move, frozen midlunge with Kamigoroshi outstretched before me. Through my blurry vision, I could see my arms and the sword covered in ice several inches thick, hanging in spears from my skin and the edge of the blade.

The yuki onna laughed, her voice sounding muffled in my ice-filled ears. "There now, Hakaimono, you can keep me company, after all," she said, floating around me like a sculptor admiring his work of art. "I think you are possibly the finest of my statues. Fitting that you should be here, in the center of the village, where everyone will be able to see you."

All right, now I was angry. I couldn't breathe, couldn't speak, and as I'd stated before, I despised being cold. The yuki onna tittered and swirled in place, smiling at me through the prison of ice, and my blood boiled.

With a roar and the sound of breaking porcelain, the ice prison shattered, frozen shards flying in every direction. The yuki onna whirled around, eyes going wide, as I shook myself and stepped forward, bringing Kamigoroshi into the light.

"Is that your best attempt?" I sneered, baring my fangs and stalking toward her. The snow woman floated backward, her white face blank. "You thought you could stop an oni with cold and ice?" I laughed, the sound echoing over the frozen village. "The fires of Jigoku flow through my veins. You might as well expect a snowball to survive being thrown in a volcano."

"Insolent demon." The yuki onna's face contorted with rage, and she raised her arm. Frost swirled around her fingers, and with a flash of ice, a gleaming yari spear appeared in her hand. Lowering the weapon, she pointed the glittering head at me. "I am Yukiko of the North," she announced, as wind began to whip at her hair and sleeves, billowing them into mist. "The ghost of the Frostfang Mountains. I have frozen armies of men in their tracks. You will go no farther, Hakaimono."

I flourished Kamigoroshi and sank into a crouch. "I'd like to see you stop me."

The yuki onna narrowed glittering blue eyes…and vanished in a swirl of snow. I counted three heartbeats before I spun, bringing up my sword, as the snow woman appeared behind me with a blast of wind, stabbing her yari at my chest. The icy weapon was knocked away with a screech, and I slashed Kamigoroshi at my opponent's pale little head, hoping to sever it from her neck. She darted back like a puppet attached to strings, then flew at me again with a flurry of blindingly quick thrusts. I fell back before the onslaught, swinging with Kamigoroshi and knocking the spearheads away as the yuki onna pursued me across the yard. She was very fast, I had to admit, grinning as I was driven back through the village. Much faster than a human could ever hope to be, and quite skilled with that ice yari. This would be a good fight; I was thoroughly enjoying myself, though something nagged at the back of my mind.

Knocking away a spear thrust, I spun with the movement, circling inside the snow maiden's reach, and lashed out with Kamigoroshi, aiming for that slender white neck. The yuki onna's eyes widened, but the moment before the edge would've cut the head from her body, she dissolved into a swirl of snow and mist. The blade passed harmlessly through, tossing flurries in its wake, and I growled, shaking my head.

Lowering my arm, I gazed around the village, carefully watching snow eddies as they swirled and danced over the ground.

"Yukiko of the North," I repeated, turning in a slow circle, knowing the snow maiden could hear me. "Ghost of the Frostfang Mountains. The Kage tell stories about you, did you know that? Do you know why they never bothered to send their demonslayer after you? Because they didn't care about the armies invading Sora territory, or the wars between the Sky and Wind Clans. Because the ghost of the North stayed in the North, and as long as you don't meddle in Kage affairs, they have no reason to come after you. Even a yuki onna whose territory is filled with an army's worth of bones and weapons, hidden under the snow."

There was no answer from the frozen village, just the wind howling through the rocks and surrounding peaks. I continued to scan the surroundings carefully, all senses primed to respond if needed. "So, my only question is what is the Ghost of the Frostfang Mountains doing way out here in the Dragon Spine, so far from home? This isn't your territory. You have no claim to these mountains, no reason to be here. Unless…" I paused, smiling as the obvious reason came to light. "The sole reason you're here, at this exact spot, in this exact time, is because you knew I would be coming through," I said. "You're here for me."

There was a blast of frigid air at my back. I spun, knocking away the ice spear stabbing at my chest. Immediately, the yuki onna vanished again, dissolving into snow swirls, then came at me once more from another direction. I barely avoided being skewered a second time, but didn't have time to respond before I found myself fending off lightning-quick attacks from all sides. The snow maiden would lunge, stabbing at my chest or face; I would parry and she would vanish in a billow of white, only to repeat the attack from another direction. Staggering under the relentless assault, I slashed viciously at the snow maiden in front of me, only to have her vanish like before. At the same time, something finally struck the back of my shoulder, sending a jolt of pain up my spine.

Annoyance flared. The snow maiden appeared before me in a swirl of white, but this time, instead of parrying the yari thrust at my chest, I ignored the weapon and slashed at the yuki onna instead. The icy spear tip hit me in the ribs, lodging between bone, but Kamigoroshi bit into the snow maiden's arm, severing it at the elbow. With a shriek, the yuki onna jerked back, clutching at the pale stump, and disappeared.

Wincing, I reached down and yanked a shard of ice from my

ribs, the pointed tip covered in steaming blood. As I watched, the whole thing melted in my hand, running between my claws and dripping to the snow.

"Monster."

The snow maiden appeared once more, glaring at me with glowing blue eyes. Her empty sleeve billowed and flapped in the wind, but as I watched, snow swirled around her, and a pale new arm emerged from the storm of white, clutching another ice yari that crinkled as it came into being. Brandishing the weapon, she gave me a chilling, triumphant smile.

"You cannot defeat me, Hakaimono," the yuki onna said, drifting forward again. "I am as formless as the falling snow, as eternal as winter." She twirled the yari, floating toward me with a grim, murderous expression on her face. I recognized that look. She had finally wearied of toying with her prey and was coming in for the kill. "Fighting me," the yuki onna continued in a soft, lethal voice, "is as futile as trying to cut down a blizzard. I am not flesh and blood—I am cold given life. And I am everywhere."

White flakes swirled around her, a whirlwind whipping through the air. As she spoke, it split apart, becoming two, four, eight separate whirlwinds that surrounded me. Abruptly, the winds died, fading away, leaving me surrounded by eight identical snow maidens, each pointing a lethal ice yari in my direction.

"It is time for you to die, Hakaimono," the yuki onnas said, eight identical voices chiming as one, "like all the mortals before you. They thought they could survive the storm, and the cold, and the ice, and their frozen bodies lie beneath the snow, preserved for all time." The snow maidens twirled their spears, and the wind around us whipped into a gale. "And now, you can join them!"

They flew at me all at once, blinding flashes of white against the snow. I lashed out with Kamigoroshi, cutting two from the air at once, then whipping the blade around to slice down another pair. With piercing cries, they dissolved into flurries and vanished.

Unfortunately, I couldn't kill them all.

Screaming pain ripped through my body, as four ice spears slammed into me, grating against bone and slicing through flesh as they plunged deep. I felt the razor points pierce my ribs, my shoulder, my thigh and back, skewering me like a straw doll, and clenched my jaw to keep from howling.

I slumped against the spears and heard the yuki onnas' high-pitched laughter. "You see?" they mocked, and three of them vanished into swirling white powder. The last yuki onna bared her teeth in a savage grin, the blade of the yari sunk deep in my shoulder. "You cannot win against cold itself, Hakaimono. Your blood and flesh will freeze, and you will die, frozen on my spear, for all time."

Raising my head, I met her gaze and smiled.

"I think you're forgetting something," I told her, making her brows drop sharply into a frown. "Winter is *not* eternal. It fades to spring, then dies to summer, every year. Your cold can kill, freeze flesh and turn things to ice, but fire and heat will drive it back, and melt you into a puddle that evaporates on the wind."

I took a breath, feeling the ice spears dissolve, as my blood welled and began streaming to the ground, hissing and leaving holes where it struck. Putting my free hand to my stomach, I grinned at the scowling yuki onna.

"Winter is not forever," I told her. "Nothing in this realm endures. But Jigoku… Jigoku is eternal. And the fires that burn through my homeland would melt this place in a heartbeat. I carry the fires of Jigoku in my veins, and it's more than hot enough to deal with your ice!"

I flung out my hand, and a spray of dark, steaming blood hit the yuki onna in the face. It sizzled where it touched, melting holes in the pale, delicate skin, burning through her robe like fire on paper. The snow maiden screamed, a high-pitched keen that caused icicles to surge out of the ground at my feet. She released the spear and brought both hands to her face, snow swirling around her, trying to heal the gaping burn marks. I raised Kamigoroshi, as purple fire erupted along the sword edge, and brought it slashing down through the yuki onna, splitting her in two. This time, she didn't explode or vanish in a puff of snow. The edges where I cut her in half caught fire, indigo flames consuming her from the bottom up as she shrieked and writhed in the conflagration, hair and sleeves flailing wildly, and finally dissolved into ash.

Gritting my teeth, I slumped and knelt in the snow as the last of the ice spears melted away and my blood leaked in rivers to the ground. Dammit, I didn't have time for such distractions. This wouldn't kill me, but even I had to recover a bit from being run through with giant icicles. The confrontation had reminded me again how very fragile mortal bodies really were. The Ghost of the North was an ancient yuki onna who had killed hundreds of humans, freezing entire armies in place and leaving the floor of her territory covered in stiff white corpses, but I shouldn't have had to rely on shedding my own blood to destroy an enemy, even a powerful one.

Around me, the snow was melting into the earth with the death of the yuki onna. The frozen humans scattered throughout the village were slowly uncovered as the ice melted, their bodies slumping or collapsing to the ground, losing the morbid beauty of a pristine ice statue and reverting to ordinary corpses.

Setting my jaw, I pushed myself upright and walked toward one of the defrosting houses, leaving spatters of red behind me in the slush. Being run through with several spears, while not quite fatal, would definitely take some time to heal. Which was probably the intent of whomever had sent the yuki onna. The Ghost of the North hadn't decided to stalk this exact path on a whim, not when her mountain range was clear across the empire in Sky Clan territory. She was sent here to either slow me down or stop me in my tracks. Which meant someone knew I was looking for the Steel Feather temple and didn't want me to get there.

Genno.

I shook my head. No, that didn't make sense. The Master of Demons needed me to reach the temple and the scroll; attempting to halt my progress was counterproductive to his plans. Though I wouldn't put a betrayal past him once he got the scroll, he wouldn't try to stop me from getting to it unless he was very stupid.

Yumeko?

With a snort, I dismissed that thought, as well. The kitsune girl wasn't old or powerful enough to deal with something like the yuki onna. And even if she was, her obvious concern for Kage Tatsumi would keep her from sending such a powerful spirit to block his path and possibly kill him. She cared for the demonslayer too much to cause him harm.

I smirked, ducking into the hut. Water dripped from the thatched roof, pooling on the dirt floor, but one corner was fairly dry, as the snow had stayed mostly outside. *Foolish little half-fox,* I mused, pulling Kamigoroshi's sheath from my obi and easing into a sit. *So transparent, you and Tatsumi both. Your feelings for the demonslayer are going to get you and all your friends killed. Don't expect me to show any mercy when we finally meet.*

Clenching my jaw, I slowly leaned against the wall, putting Kamigoroshi against a shoulder as I settled back. The yuki onna had been left here for me, that was certain. So, if it wasn't Yumeko or the Master of Demons who'd sent her, that meant there was someone else, some*thing* else, trying to keep me from the Dragon scroll. Another player in this game.

All right, then. Tilting my head back, I closed my eyes with a smile. The yuki onna had inconvenienced me, but my wounds were slowly healing. I figured I'd be fine by tomorrow. *Things are getting interesting. Whoever you are, I hope you're ready to take me on once I reach the temple. Because nothing will stop me from getting to the scroll, even if I have to carve my way through an army to get to it.*

19

THE SOUND OF A FLUTE

Yumeko

*W*e buried Master Jiro atop a small hill on the rippling plains of the Water Clan. Leaving his body to the crows and scavengers was unthinkable, as his ghost could linger at the spot of his death, unable to pass on, if his body was not properly taken care of. We had no tools to dig a grave, so we spent the afternoon searching for rocks, slowly building up a mound to cover the wise old priest. And, because Okame insisted, we also built a small grave for Roshi, our driver, the man who had been killed simply because he agreed to help us. When we were finished, a pair of stony graves sat atop the rise, Master Jiro's staff thrust upright in the center of the larger one. And we all stood solemnly while Reika, her eyes glassy but determined, performed the death ritual to help a soul move on to the next world. Her chanting voice echoed over the plains, carried by the winds, a haunting litany that droned in my head and entwined with my thoughts.

This is my fault.

I clenched a fist under my sleeve, feeling my hands tremble. *They died because of me, protecting me. How many more?* I glanced at my friends, at Okame and Daisuke, standing side by side. Daisuke's expression, as always, was composed, expressing the perfect mix of serene remorse. Okame, standing with his arms crossed and his jaw set, looked like he would either snarl at anyone who touched him or burst into tears. Reika chanted, her voice shaking only slightly, her hair and sleeves billowing in the wind, and Chu sat primly in the grass, the tops of his ears barely visible. *How many more will die before this is over? When I'm facing Hakaimono and Tatsumi, will I be strong enough to do what has to be done?*

I reached up a hand and touched the furoshiki beneath my robes, feeling the thin case of the scroll within. The thing Master Jiro, and so many others, had given their life to protect. Master Jiro, Master Isao and all the monks at the Silent Winds temple. The list of names of the dead was growing long indeed. I feared that, by the end of this adventure, it would be even longer. And it was still a lengthy journey to our destination.

One step at a time, I told myself. *Find the Steel Feather temple. Face Hakaimono, drive him back into the sword and free Tatsumi. Hand the scroll over to whatever guardians are waiting for it. Then you'll be done. You will have upheld your promise to Master Isao. After that...*

I faltered. Then what? What was next for me after I had delivered the scroll? I had no home, nothing to go back to. Perhaps, whoever lived at the Steel Feather temple would let me join their order? But that thought made my nose wrinkle. I had seen so much. I had been to the great golden capital and the shadow-shrouded lands of the Kage. I had talked to monsters, yokai, yurei and demons. I had fought great evil, seen wonders and magic, and had performed for the emperor of Iwagoto himself. And yet, I knew there was more out there. More to see, to experience. Now that I was outside the temple walls, I didn't want to go back. How could I, when I finally knew what lay beyond?

Don't be naive, Yumeko. Do you really think it will be over once you deliver the scroll to the temple? What about Lady Hanshou, and the Master of Demons? What about Tatsumi?

My stomach twisted. *Tatsumi.* What would happen to the demonslayer if I managed to free him and drive Hakaimono back into the sword? His mission, before the First Oni had taken over, had been to retrieve the pieces of the Dragon scroll. Would he continue his mission, even if it meant fighting the guardians of the Steel Feather temple? And…the rest of us? Reika, I knew, would never allow him to take the scroll back to Lady Hanshou, and Daisuke would protect his family, his clan and his emperor at all cost. The only question mark was Okame, but I had the feeling he wouldn't want the Shadow Clan to get their hands on the Dragon's Wish, either. Would Tatsumi attack them all to acquire the scroll? If he did, if it came down to choosing between Kage Tatsumi and protecting the scroll, what would I do? Who would I stand with?

Was I making a terrible mistake, trying to save him?

"Yumeko."

Reika's voice jerked me out of my dark musings. The shrine maiden stood before me, looking tired. Bags crouched under her eyes and her skin was pale and wan, but her eyes were dry. "We're done here," she said in a quiet voice. "It's time to move on."

Silently, we continued down the road on foot, away from the crows and scavenger birds already gathering, and the site of the ambush soon faded behind us.

That evening, we made camp in a nearly dry creek bed very close to the road. According to Okame, who had talked to Roshi before the driver's unfortunate death, we would reach his village by tomorrow afternoon, and then it was just a short walk to the base of the Dragon Spine.

"We should be able to replenish supplies at the village," he said, using a twig to poke at the flames of the fire he'd started. A tiny black pot sat on stilts above it, bubbling cheerfully; part of the supply pack Masao had sent along with us. It contained barely enough rice to make each of us a rice ball, but we couldn't be picky. "We're going to want more rice, and I'm going to need about a quart of sake in my system before I tackle the Dragon Spine." He stirred the boiling pot with the twig, then leaned back and sighed. "And I'll need to find Roshi's wife and family, let them know he's not coming home."

"Is there time for that?" Reika asked, not unkindly. But Okame's mouth thinned, and his voice was steely as he answered.

"We'll make time."

Surprisingly, the shrine maiden didn't argue.

The next evening, we came to the village, tucked in the foothills of the Dragon Spine Mountains. As villages went, it seemed typical, with simple thatched-roof huts spread in a haphazard pattern around the center square and a series of tiered rice paddies set into the grassy hills. I did notice several horses in fenced pastures or tethered to various points in the village, something I'd never seen before.

We were also getting stared at. Villagers stopped what they were doing to watch us as we passed, their gazes a mix of surprise and wary curiosity. No one seemed openly fearful, though I figured a shrine maiden, a ronin, a Taiyo noble and a girl in onmyoji robes didn't come through this village often, if ever. I smiled and waved at a little girl watching us from the side of the path, and was rewarded with a shy grin before she darted off.

"This village seems to be doing well," Daisuke remarked as we made our way toward the center square, which was a large dusty area with a single well in the middle. "I wonder, perhaps, if we can acquire the supplies we will need to scale the Dragon Spine." He gazed toward the distant jagged peaks, silhouetted against the setting sun, and his brow furrowed. "It's going to be quite cold in the mountains. Some blankets or heavier clothes would not be remiss."

"Some horses would also be nice," Okame added, glancing at the scattered mounts milling about the village. "Wonder if we can convince someone to part with a couple?"

"Excuse me."

A woman stood beside the path, watching us approach. She was a younger woman, wearing simple but sturdy peasant clothes, her hair tied back and a wide-brimmed hat perched atop her head, tied under her chin with a strip of cloth. Below the brim, her dark eyes were both hopeful and apprehensive.

"Forgive me," she said, dropping into a deep bow as we stopped before her. "I don't mean to pry, but I must ask—have you, by chance, come from Jujiro? And if you have, I wonder if you have seen a wagon on the road?"

I closed my eyes, as a somber air descended on us all and guilt gnawed the pit of my stomach. "My husband was supposed to have returned last night," the woman continued, "but he has not yet arrived, and I fear something might have happened to him. Please, if you have any information, I will be in your debt. His name is Roshi, and he drives a one-horse cart from here to Jujiro and back."

For a moment, there was silence, as each of us wondered who was going to break the news, then Reika stepped forward.

"I am sorry," she began, and Roshi's wife's face crumpled, already guessing the news. "Your husband is dead."

The woman's hand rose to her mouth, trembling, before she took a deep breath and lowered it again. "I…I feared as much," she whispered. "I knew I should have made the journey to pray at the mountain shrine. The kami were merciful when my daughter became sick last season. I should have made the pilgrimage up the Dragon Spine once more. Oh, Roshi." Her voice broke, and she covered her face with both hands.

"I'm so sorry," I told her. "It was my fault. Roshi was kind enough to offer us a ride to his village. But we were ambushed by shinobi on our way here."

"Shinobi?" The woman dropped her arms, her face going pale. "I thought that shinobi were myths," she whispered. "Stories that court nobles told their children. I didn't know they were real. Oh, Roshi, what did you get yourself involved in?"

Reika shot me an exasperated look, as if I had said something I shouldn't have. I didn't understand. If I was Roshi's wife, I would want to know how he had died, and who was responsible.

Roshi's wife took a deep breath, composing herself, then faced us again. "If...if you would be so kind as to tell me where his body is," she said. "I must go and fetch it before the scavengers take too much."

"We've already buried him," Reika said gently. "And performed the proper death rites. Your husband's soul should not linger in this world. But if you want to see for yourself, he is buried about a day's walk east of here. Just look for the hill with two graves on the side of the road."

The woman gave a watery smile. "Thank you," she whispered, looking at both Reika and me. "Thank you for not leaving him, for giving him the proper rites to pass on. And I know my Roshi. He wouldn't have offered his cart to just anyone." She eyed my onmyoji robes, then glanced at Daisuke, taking in his clothes and hair. Even if he wasn't wearing his family mon, his noble bearing was obvious. "I know you must have important matters to attend," she said, turning back to me. "Please excuse my forwardness, but are you traveling to the shrine of the mountain kami near the top of the Dragon Spine?"

I pricked my ears. "Mountain kami?"

"Yes." Roshi's wife nodded. "Forgive me, but I thought that was your destination." She turned, gesturing to the distant silhouettes against the sky. "Every few years, a pilgrim will pass through our village to pray at the shrine of the mountain kami. It is an arduous journey, but it is said that if your heart is pure and your prayers fervent enough, the mountain kami will grant you a bit of their secret knowledge. This is the last village before you reach the path that leads up the Dragon Spine. I simply assumed that was where you were going, as well."

"Where is this shrine, if you don't mind telling us?" Daisuke asked.

Roshi's wife nodded at the road that cut through the final houses. "Just past the village, you'll find a path that heads due east," she said. "If you follow it for half a day, it will take you into the Dragon Spine Mountains, to a peak that overlooks the valley. The shrine sits at the very top."

"Thank you," I said, and bowed to her. "You've been most kind. We won't trouble you any longer."

"Wait." Roshi's wife glanced at me, then at my companions. "If you mean to journey up the Dragon Spine, you shouldn't go tonight," she warned. "The path is narrow, and treacherous in the dark. One slip, and you could tumble all the way down the mountain—it has happened to even the most sure-footed of travelers. And the Dragon Spine is home to all manner of spirits and yokai. Most are indifferent to humans, but no yokai is predictable, and a few are very dangerous. If you are to attempt the pilgrimage to the shrine of the mountain kami, it is best to do so in the light."

I glanced at the sun setting behind the mountain peaks and nodded. "That is probably a wise idea. Is there a place we could stay in the village, a ryokan or inn of sorts?"

She shook her head. "We are a small village. Even with the shrine to the mountain kami, not enough travelers come through to warrant a ryokan. The headman often lets pilgrims stay at his home for the night, provided they pay a small fee, or perform a favor for the village if they have no coin."

"Well, that sounds like us," Okame said with a sardonic grin at Daisuke. "We left Kin Heigen Toshi in such a hurry, our noble Taiyo didn't have time to grab his coin pouch. Now he's just as poor as us peasants and ronin."

"Indeed." Daisuke's voice was wry. "Though I will point out that I usually have no need of coin, and to even discuss matters of money is seen as exceedingly poor taste. It is within my right, as a samurai and of Imperial lineage, to expect that all amenities are offered without compensation, in service to the empire. Most of my kin would agree that it is a privilege for those of lesser stations to serve the emperor's finest warriors, and they should be honored to provide whatever the samurai requests. There are those in my family who do not even know the values of the different types of coin."

Okame snorted, letting everyone know what he thought of *that*, and Daisuke smiled. "However," he went on, "if you have not noticed, Okame-san, I myself sometimes harbor…unpopular opinions among my clan. Many have forgotten, but 'samurai' means *one who serves*. The Code of Bushido states that compassion and humility are just as important as honor and courage, and if I cannot show those virtues to those of lesser status, can I even call myself samurai?"

"Oh?" With his arms still crossed, Okame raised an eyebrow, a mischievous smile on his lips. "Well, if that's the case, what are your thoughts on chopping wood or thatching a roof, peacock? Hard, hot, peasant work, best done in a loincloth—wouldn't want to get your fine clothes all sweaty, would we?"

"It would not be the first thing I have done in a loincloth, Okame-san," Daisuke said easily, and while I was wondering why Reika's face had gone red, he turned to Roshi's wife, still watching us from the side of the road. "Wife of the honorable Roshi," he began, "please excuse this intrusion into your life. If you would kindly point us to the headman's abode, we would be in your debt."

"Honored guests." The woman clasped her hands together. "It is no trouble. You have done me a favor today, and I know my Roshi. Were he here, he would insist that you stay at our home tonight. It is small, but we do have an extra room at the back of the house that would suit your needs. Please, stay with us tonight, in honor of his memory."

I looked to my companions. Reika, still a curious shade of pink, gave a short nod, and I turned back to Roshi's wife. "Thank you," I said. "If it's truly no trouble, we would be grateful."

She nodded. "Tonight I will cook a feast in honor of my husband," she announced shakily. "And tomorrow, when you visit the shrine of the mountain kami, would you mention his name when you say your prayer? That is all the thanks I require."

I gave a solemn nod. "Of course."

I awoke to the sound of a flute.

Yawning, I raised my head from the pillow and gazed around. The room was still dim, illuminated by only the embers in the brazier and the moonlight coming through the window. A few feet away, Reika slept soundly, her hair spilling over her pillow in a shiny black curtain.

Chu sat in the open doorway, triangular ears pricked, the moonlight casting his shadow over the floorboards.

I started to lay back down, when the faint melody came again, making me pause. I had half thought I'd dreamed it, but I heard it now, a low, mournful refrain drifting over the breeze.

Careful not to disturb Reika, I rose and padded silently to the door. Chu twitched an ear at me but didn't move as I crouched down next to him. For a moment, I bristled at being so close to the dog, my kitsune nature reacting instinctively to the inu. But I reminded myself that Chu was not really an inu; he was a shrine guardian, part of the spirit world, and honestly more like myself than any normal dog.

"Konbanwa, Chu-san," I greeted in a whisper. "Do you hear it as well?"

I received a slightly disdainful glance from the dog, before he trotted away from me into the room. Claiming a corner of Reika's blanket, he curled up and lay his head on his paws, though he kept his gaze on the door, ever watchful and alert. Still, if Chu didn't think there was danger, we were probably safe and whomever was playing the flute wasn't a threat.

Which made me even more curious.

"I'll be right back," I whispered to the dog, thankful that it was Chu that was awake and not Reika. The miko would not approve of me sneaking outside by myself late at night. "I won't be long, but if you hear me scream, be sure to wake Reika up, ne?"

The inu yawned. Not knowing if he would follow my requests, but knowing he understood my words full well, I slipped out the door onto the veranda and escaped into the moonlight.

I followed the haunting sound of the flute through the field, feeling the cool night air on my skin. Fireflies blinked in and out of the darkness, rising in swarms as I moved through the grass. The faint, melodic notes rose and fell with the breeze and rustling grass stalks, growing steadily more distinct as I approached an old cedar tree in the middle of the field.

I paused, suddenly feeling like an intruder. The song was so beautiful, pulling me forward and tugging at my emotions, but I feared going any closer would cause it to stop, and whomever was playing to flee. My clumsy human body wasn't made for creeping through the grass unseen.

My fox self, on the other hand...

I closed my eyes and called on my magic. It flared to the surface a moment before there was a silent explosion of smoke. Opening my eyes, I found myself much closer to the ground, the tops of the grass hiding me completely. The night was suddenly far clearer, the shadows not so dark, the air full of life and sound. My fox ears could hear everything around me: the hum of crickets in the grass, the trill of a nightbird in the trees, the buzz of firefly wings in the air. A flood of smells filled my nostrils, mysterious and tantalizing, and I was struck by the desire to leave everything behind and go bounding through the tall grass, to chase mice and insects, to breathe globes of kitsune-bi into the air and dance under the moonlight.

However, a glimmer of a dark, lacquered scroll case lying naked in the grass brought all those desires to a crashing halt. Pinning back my ears, I swiftly pounced on the case and seized it firmly in my jaws. The wood was hard, unyielding, the outer shell clacking against my teeth. I rolled it around in my jaws, trying to find a comfortable position, resisting the urge to spit it out and leave it lying in the dirt.

Well, this isn't ideal. I hope no one spots me and wonders why a fox is carrying around a scroll case.

Finally, I shoved the case to the front of my mouth, holding it as a dog would a bone. Mildly annoyed with my burden, I flattened my ears and slipped through the grass, continuing toward the great cedar in the center of the field.

The music continued, growing clearer the closer I drew to the tree. As I eased under a bush, I caught a glimmer of white in the branches of the tree and froze as I looked up. A figure sat in the V of the trunk, leaning back against the tree with one foot planted for balance, his sleeves and pale hair reflected in the waters beneath. He held a thin length of dark wood to his lips, and the sweet, haunting notes filled the air around him.

Daisuke?

Lowering my head, I crept closer, sliding through the long grass toward the tree. Taiyo Daisuke's eyes were closed, his hair and sleeves billowing softly in the breeze as fireflies drifted around him, as if drawn to the music themselves.

I heard another set of footsteps shushing through the grass behind me, and quickly darted to the side just as a pair of long legs strode past. A scent came to me, earthy and familiar, before a rough, amused voice broke the spell of the flute.

"Here you are. I thought this might be you." Okame walked beneath the trunk and paused, crossing his arms as he peered up at the noble. "So, did you have a wistful samurai moment?" he wondered. "Did the moonlight speak to you so much that you had to compose a song to the night, or couldn't you sleep, either?"

Daisuke lowered his flute and gazed down calmly, a small, slightly smug smile crossing his face. "I will admit to feeling rather wistful tonight," he said. "And the moonlight was very beautiful. It would be easy to get lost in it, but my true purpose for playing has already been fulfilled. It drew you here."

Okame raised a brow. "You could've just asked me to join you, peacock, rather than drag me out of bed by mysterious flute playing in the middle of the night."

"But then, I would not have known what I needed." Daisuke raised his arm, the instrument held easily between long fingers. "I would not be so forward as to presume. The song asked the questions. That you came, that you responded, is the answer I was hoping for."

"Taiyo-san." Okame rubbed his eyes. "I've not been a samurai for a while, and even then, I barely understood the language you nobles use. Pretend you're speaking to a peasant, or perhaps a tamed monkey. I can't keep up with all the metaphors and hidden meanings."

"Very well." The Taiyo noble tucked his flute into his obi

and dropped from the trunk, landing gracefully beside the pond. "Why don't you ever call me Daisuke, Okame-san?"

"Because you're a Taiyo," growled Okame. "And I'm a dishonorable ronin dog. Even I know that's about as far apart in status as you can get. I might as well be speaking to the emperor of Iwagoto. And don't tell me rank means nothing to you, Taiyo. It's easy enough to say when you're part of the Imperial bloodline, but if I spoke so casually to you in a court setting, I'd likely have my head cut off for the insult to your family name."

"Do you despise me then, Okame-san?" Daisuke's voice was soft. "Because I am a Taiyo, the noble class you hate so much? Does my bloodline make me a villain in your eyes?"

Okame snorted. "What are you talking about?" he said, sounding uncomfortable. "I have nothing but respect for you, even though a year ago I would've spit in your direction for being such a court monkey. There, I said it. Does that make you happy?"

Unexpectedly, Daisuke smiled, his eyes shining as he faced the ronin. "Arigatou," he murmured. "I'm glad. Your opinion means a lot to me, Okame-san."

Okame shook his head. "It shouldn't," he muttered, looking into the shadows.

"Why?" Daisuke eased closer, his expression serious. "I admire you, Okame-san. I'd hoped…" He paused, then said in a soft, earnest voice, "I thought I'd made my feelings for you abundantly clear."

"Stop it." Okame's voice was a whisper. The ronin closed his eyes, turning his head from the noble a few feet away. "Now you're just toying with me. There is no situation, in the entire empire of Iwagoto, where a Sun Clan noble being with a ronin dog would be socially acceptable. The dishonor would be so great that entire families would commit seppuku in shame, and the stain would be passed down to your children, your children's children and their children, forevermore. Every generation after would know the story of the golden Taiyo's greatest downfall. Even I'm not that profane."

"If I wasn't a Taiyo, then." Daisuke hadn't moved any closer; he stood quietly by the trunk, long hair rippling in the breeze. "If you could ignore my name, my family and my bloodline for only a moment. Would you be able to look at me that way? Would these emotions be reciprocated at all?"

"Damn you." Okame opened his eyes to glare at the noble, baring his teeth. "How could they not?" he almost snarled. "From the moment I saw you on that bridge, I've had nothing but forbidden thoughts swirling through my head. It's grown rather tiresome—I don't normally think this much." He sighed and stabbed his fingers through his hair, raking it back. "I wanted to hate you," he said, though his voice was tired now. "It would've been so much easier. If I could've despised you like all the pompous, swaggering nobles that came before. Because it doesn't matter what I think. It doesn't matter that being around you is painful, that I have to pretend I feel nothing, that your teasing and pointed comments don't affect me at all." He sighed again, giving Daisuke a look of bitter amusement. "I'm not blind, Taiyo-san. I've gotten the hints. I just... I know my place. And I'm not going to drag you into the mud with me."

Daisuke was silent a moment. Then, shockingly, a quiet chuckle drifted over the grass, making Okame scowl. "Am I that amusing then, noble?"

"Forgive me." Daisuke glanced up, a faint smile still on his face. "I just find it ironic," he mused, "that a ronin, who claims to despise samurai and makes a mockery of the Code whenever he can, would be so concerned about staining my honor."

"Don't read too much into it." Okame scuffed a foot. "I'm just protecting my own head. I'd prefer for it to stay on my neck, if at all possible. Being around the royal bloodline has caused many a samurai to lose their head in the past."

Daisuke straightened and took two steps forward, causing Okame to flinch and eye him warily. "My family isn't here, Okame-san," he said in a quiet voice. He raised a billowing sleeve toward the distant mountains. "The Imperial court is many miles away. No one is watching. No one will judge. What happens here tonight, the world need never know."

I needed to leave. What was happening between Daisuke and Okame was their business alone. I was the intruder, privy to something that should not be seen, the hidden eyes in the grass. But I couldn't turn away. My heart pounded, and I found myself unable to move. I crouched motionless in the grass, my tail wrapped around my legs and my ears swiveled forward as far as they would go, loath to miss a word.

"You're playing with fire, noble," Okame husked out. "Are you sure you want this? I don't..." He hesitated again, then sighed. "I don't want to wake up tomorrow morning and find you've committed seppuku to absolve your shame."

"No," Daisuke said with one of his small, rueful smiles. "Have no fear of that, Okame-san. I've already promised Yumeko that I would accompany her up the Dragon Spine, and to protect her from any that would try to stop us. I cannot die yet, not when my greatest battle still lies ahead. And the end of this road is the Steel Feather temple...and Hakaimono." His eyes shone with anticipation and excitement. "I am ready. It will be a most glorious battle. And if I fall, it will be in service to the empire, fighting to stop the rise of the Master of Demons. I will die on my feet with my sword in hand, facing my enemies, as all samurai should. What is one night, compared to an eternity of glory?"

"One night, huh?" Okame shook his head, a bright, slightly feral look entering his eyes. "Ah, the hell with it. When you put it that way..."

He took three long strides, grabbed the collar of the other's robe in both hands and yanked him close, pressing their lips together.

My eyes widened, and I would've gasped had I been human. Daisuke himself drew in a sharp breath, his body stiffening, but after only a moment he relaxed, his hands coming up to grip Okame's arms. For several heartbeats, they stood like that beneath the giant cedar, the moonlight blazing down on the two bodies locked together, and for a moment, the world seemed to stop.

At last, Okame drew back, his eyes still bright and intense, gazing down at the noble. "Is this…what you wanted, Daisuke-san?" I heard him ask, his voice husky and slightly strained. Daisuke gave a faint smile, his own gaze fevered as he stared back.

"It's definitely a start."

Okame's lips curled in a smirk, and he lowered his head once more.

Leave, Yumeko, I thought, as guilt finally overrode curiosity. *You need to leave, right now!*

With an effort, I wrenched my gaze from the figures below the cedar tree. Keeping the scroll clamped firmly in my jaws, I turned and slipped into the tall grass, leaving them truly alone.

I changed back into a human at the gate, then tiptoed inside the house. As I came through the bedroom door, Reika was still asleep in the corner, snoring softly, but Chu raised his head and gave me a disapproving look. Ignoring the dog, I slid under the blankets again and pulled the quilt over my head. The night beyond the door was quiet; no haunting music stirred the breeze, no sounds of a flute on the wind. A strange sense of longing filled me, twisting my stomach and making my heart ache. I remembered the fierceness in Okame's eyes when he kissed Daisuke, the look on the noble's face as he returned it.

And I wondered if Kage Tatsumi would ever look at me that way.

20

GUARDIANS OF STONE

Yumeko

A tiny shrine, weathered and gray, sat within an alcove in the side of the mountain. It was easy to miss; being the same color as the rocks and the mottled sky, it nearly blended into the background. The shrine itself barely reached the top of my head, and was littered with dead flowers, scattered coins and empty sake bottles; offerings to the mountain kami. At one point, the wood might've been brightly painted, perhaps in the vermillion, teal and white of its larger brothers. But weather and time had scoured the wooden planks, and now it seemed just another part of the mountain, as much as the rocks and the few scraggly bushes poking through the stones.

"Well," Okame said, gazing at the tiny structure with his arms crossed. He looked cold, hunching his shoulders against the wind, but trying not to show it. It had been a long, chilly hike up the Dragon Spine Mountains, following a narrow, winding path that was barely more than a goat trail. The higher we went, the colder and more unwelcoming the weather became; snow flurries now danced on the air, and the sky overhead was as gray as the rest of the mountain. "We found the shrine to the mountain kami," the ronin muttered. "Now what?"

I gazed around, hoping to see a temple, or any hint that could point to a temple. But there was nothing but rock and snow-shrouded peaks as far as the eye could see. "Reika-chan?" I asked, turning to the shrine maiden. "What did Master Jiro say about finding the way to the temple?"

"Seek the place where the mountain kami gather," Reika answered, "and look to the crows that will point the way."

I looked up at the mottled gray sky. "I don't see any crows." Or any birds, for that matter. Not even the hawks and falcons soared this high.

She sighed. "Well, we'd better find some quickly, before night falls and it gets really cold."

We searched the area, looking for statues, signs, drawings scratched into the rock, anything that could resemble a crow or any type of feathered creature. But after a couple hours, we had turned up nothing. The shrine remained the only piece of the mountain that was different from everything around it. And beyond the distant peaks, the sun was beginning to set.

I shivered in the rapidly dropping temperature, huddled against the alcove wall to escape the wind. *Kami,* I thought, as a breeze blew a cloud of snow flurries into the space with me, *if you would like to give us a hint right now, we would appreciate it.*

"Perhaps," Daisuke mused, gazing at the shrine with a furrowed brow, "we are looking at this the wrong way. We have been searching for a physical crow, a sign of sorts, to point us to the Steel Feather temple. What if the crow Master Jiro spoke of was metaphorical in nature?"

Okame frowned. "I'm not sure I follow, Daisuke-san."

I saw Reika's brow arch at Okame's statement, a reaction to the ronin calling the noble by his first name, which he had never done before. My face heated and my heartbeat sped up. Fortunately, the attention was on Daisuke as he pondered the situation and the shrine.

"You have heard the expression 'as the crow flies,' yes?" the noble asked. "It refers to the straightest line between two points, the fastest route that can be accomplished without swerving or changing direction." He gestured to the shrine. "We already have one point. What if our 'crow' was to fly straight to the Steel Feather temple? Which direction would he take?"

We looked around. "Well, he wouldn't be able to go north," Reika said, gazing at the alcove where the shrine sat. "And he couldn't fly south, either, not with that ridge in the way."

"East?" Okame suggested. "Personally, I hope not, because that's an awfully long plunge straight down the mountain. I guess it wouldn't be a problem if you were a crow."

"Yes, but look at the peaks," Daisuke said, nodding to the distant mountaintops. He moved directly in front of the shrine, raising his arm straight out in front of him and closing one eye. "From here, there is no direct path between any of them. You would have to go over or around. So, that leaves…"

I turned. "West," I said. "Right up that ridge, straight on between those two peaks where the sun is going down. It's the only path you can take without running into anything."

"If Taiyo-san is correct," Reika said. "We are going on theory, after all, but at this point, I fear we have little choice." She sighed, glancing down at Chu, who stared back solemnly. "Very well. Then let us walk the path the crow flies, and see where it takes us."

The sun set, and the temperature dropped sharply as we continued up the mountain, following the trail of an invisible crow as it flew overhead. As the light faded, flecks of snow began drifting from the cloudy sky, swirling around us and dancing on the breeze. I huddled into the mino and straw hat Roshi's wife had provided and found myself longing for a cup of hot tea to wrap my fingers around.

At last, when we had lost the light completely and were all shivering under our mino, the path ended at the bottom of a massive cliff. It rose straight into the air, the snow-shrouded peak hidden by clouds, the base dark in the shadow of the mountain.

"Well," sighed Okame, gazing up at the obstacle before us. His breath writhed into the air before coiling away into nothing, and his teeth chattered slightly as he spoke. "I'd say this path has come to an end. I never thought I'd see the day, but it looks like you were mistaken, Daisuke-san. Unless the crow flew straight into the side of the mountain."

Straight into the side of the mountain. I wonder... On impulse, as Reika and Okame began arguing about what to do next, I started walking toward the cliff. The massive wall of rock and stone loomed before me, ancient and unyielding, but I didn't stop. I heard Okame call after me, wanting to know what I was doing, but I kept walking until I was a mere two paces away from the side of the mountain.

I blinked in surprise. I'd been bracing myself, expecting to run straight into the wall, but now that I was this close, I could see I stood in the mouth of a fissure, a narrow crack in the side of the mountain. It had been so well hidden that, had I not literally walked into it, I would have never known it was there.

"Minna," I called, addressing the group over my shoulder. With a flick of my hand, a ball of kitsune-bi sprang to life, illuminating the walls and floor of a narrow tunnel that snaked away into the darkness. "I think I found something."

The rest of them crowded behind me, gazing down the passageway. "That doesn't look like the entrance to an ancient temple to me," Okame mused, as a centipede scuttled away from the sudden glow of foxfire, vanishing into a crevice. "But I guess it's better than standing out here in the cold." He peered dubiously into the tunnel, then shivered as a sharp gust of wind at our backs tossed his ponytail and nearly blew the hat off his head. "*Brrr.* Right, into the dark we go."

We stepped into the tunnel, following the ball of kitsune-bi as it floated and bobbed ahead of us, throwing back the darkness. The passage was narrow, and sometimes so low we had to crouch down to keep going. I envied Chu, trotting down the tunnel without a care, and though it was tempting to change into my fox form, transforming so blatantly in front of other people made me uneasy. They knew I was kitsune, yes, but there was a difference between knowing someone was yokai and walking down a dark tunnel with said yokai beside you. While I was Yumeko, my kitsune nature could almost be forgotten. Not so if I became a fox.

After many long, cramped minutes in the dark, the only light coming from the hovering ball of foxfire, the tunnel opened up, and we stepped into an enormous cavern. The walls soared overhead into darkness, so high you couldn't see the roof of the cave. But the ground below us was of worked stone, not rough cavern floor. I sent my kitsune-bi farther into the room, and in the ghostly blue light, we could see crumbled steps, broken walls and shattered pillars scattered over the ground, indicating at one point, this chamber had been inhabited.

"What is this place?" I wondered, as we ventured warily into the cavern. My voice echoed into the vastness around me, and I suddenly felt very small. "Is this...the Steel Feather temple?"

Behind me, I heard Okame sneeze in the dust cloud that wafted from our footsteps. "If it is," he muttered, "we might have a problem. This place looks like it's been abandoned for decades."

"This cannot be the temple," Reika said, gazing around in

dismay. "There must be a mistake. Master Jiro would not send us to the Steel Feather temple if it had been abandoned."

"Unless he didn't know," mused Okame, his voice drifting between columns and stirring centuries of dust and cobwebs. "I mean, it's been a thousand years since the night of the last Wish, right? Perhaps the guardians have all died, or moved to another temple."

"No," Reika said firmly, and a half dozen *no*s echoed all around us. "That cannot be true," she insisted, but her voice was quietly desperate. "The guardians are here, they must be. What are we missing?"

As I rounded a pillar, a figure suddenly appeared, looming above me in the darkness. I let out a squeak and jumped back, as the foxfire washed over the stern visage and fixed gaze of a stone samurai, fully armored and wearing a magnificent horned helmet. He carried a sword in each hand. One of the helmet's stone antlers had been snapped off, and time had eroded the samurai's features, but he still stood proud and stern on his pedestal, frozen in a stance of eternal readiness.

"Magnificent," Daisuke said at my back, making me jump again. The noble stepped forward, gazing up at the statue in open fascination. "I believe this is Kaze Yoshitsune," he said in a voice of quiet awe. "A daimyo of the Kaze family, and one of the most famed duelists of the Wind Clan. His swordsmanship was unique in that he fought with two blades, using the katana and the wakizashi at the same time. The Kaze family have always claimed their double-sword techniques are descended from Yoshitsune himself, and refuse to teach their swordsmanship to any other clan."

"Why is there a statue of him here?" I asked, and Daisuke shook his head.

"I do not know. Perhaps the guardians of the Steel Feather temple are part of the Wind Clan. Although..." Daisuke tapped his chin thoughtfully, as Reika, Okame and Chu came around the pillar. "There is a legend of Kaze Yoshitsune, one that is told even today, especially among schools of the blade. Of how, when Yoshitsune was a young man, he disappeared from the empire for a time. And when he returned, it was as a skilled swordsman, unbeatable in duels, who possessed the hidden knowledge of the gods. While no one knows for certain, the legends claim Yoshitsune traveled to the home of the mountain kami and lived with them for several years, that the mountain king himself taught the Kaze prince swordsmanship and the path of the double blades." A smile crossed the noble's face. "The legend of Yoshitsune is one every swordsman knows," he said in a quietly awed voice. "How many of us have hoped that the kami would find us worthy to gift us with their knowledge? Kaze Yoshitsune was one of the rare few that were."

"Huh." Okame stepped forward, arms folded as he gazed up at the statue, then at Daisuke. A sour expression crossed his features, and he curled a lip. "He doesn't look like anything special to me."

Reika gave a barely audible chuckle. "Jealousy is not an admirable virtue, Okame-san," she told him. "Especially if it is of a stone statue."

"What?" Okame exclaimed, an indignant look crossing his face. "What are you talking about?" But the miko only smiled and walked past him. "Oi, don't pretend you didn't hear me. What did you mean? Hey!"

The miko and the ronin vanished around a crumbled wall, and the rest of us hurried to catch up.

As we pressed farther into the chamber, more statues appeared in the flickering light of the kitsune-bi. There were armored samurai with stern, unsmiling faces, whose stony eyes seemed to follow us as we passed. But there were also several women, monks, ronin, peasants, even a few children. Sometimes they were missing limbs, or even heads. Sometimes they carried swords, raised above their heads or standing at the ready. One statue was of an enormous, bare-chested man wearing an amused smirk and a circle of huge prayer beads around his neck. Instead of a sword, he carried a spear with a massive, crescent-shaped blade on his shoulders, both thick arms draped over the shaft.

"These are all heroes of the empire," Daisuke remarked quietly, after gazing at the statue of the large man for several heartbeats. "Some of them I don't recognize, but many of them... I have seen their pictures in the history scrolls. I have heard their legends and read about their deeds. That is Tsuchi Benkei, who held a bridge against an army of three hundred warriors to protect his lord. And over there is Hino Misaka, who held up a wall of fire for seven straight days to protect a village from attacking yokai. Wherever we are," he continued, gazing around, "this is a sacred place. A hall of remembering. I wonder who is here, who made these statues?"

"That's a fascinating thought and all, Daisuke-san," Okame said. "But, we're not looking for a hall of heroes. Unless one of them is going to give us directions to the Steel Feather temple, I'd say we've got bigger problems to think about."

As he was saying this, I rounded the statue of a young man wielding a staff, and stopped.

Across the cavern floor, seemingly carved out of the stone itself, a wide staircase ascended into the darkness. The path to it was flanked on either side by stone samurai, standing at rigid attention, and more statues stood on pedestals lining the stairs. At the top of the steps, beyond a landing circled by even more statues, I could just make out a small opening in the cave wall, a doorway into the unknown.

"Minna," I called excitedly, hearing my voice echo into the vast emptiness around us. "I think I've found the way out."

Excited that the end of the journey might be near at last, I started across the dusty stone floor. But, as I approached the stairs, a tremor went through the ground, making me stumble and causing the hair on the back of my neck to rise. I froze, gazing up the steps, feeling a gathering in the air around me, a swirl of ancient energy snapping with power, like the air before a lightning storm.

Magic, I thought, as the invisible storm faded and, for a moment, the chamber seemed to hold its breath. *Very old magic. Something is going to happen...*

Another tremor went through the ground. With a rumble and a grinding of stone against stone, two of the statues lining the stairs stepped off their pedestals and landed on the steps with a crash. They walked down the steps, moving far quicker than a few tons of stone had a right to, each footstep crunching and scraping against the rocks, until they reached the bottom.

I swallowed hard. It was another pair of the statues we'd seen earlier, the young warrior in armor with the double swords, and the large man with the giant spear. What had Daisuke called them? Yoshitsune and Benkei? For a moment, they stood motionless in front of the stairs, blocking the path, their empty, hollow gaze fixed on us. Then, Yoshitsune's stony lips parted, and a raspy voice emerged, like sand sliding over a gravel pit.

"It reveals the way. Prove you are worthy to pass. Or die upon stone."

I blinked. *Did...did it just give us that warning in haiku?*

For a heartbeat, not one of us moved. Then, Daisuke stepped forward, drawing his sword with a screech, making Okame start. "Oi, Daisuke-san," the ronin growled. "What are you doing, peacock? You're not going to fight Boulder one and Boulder two, are you?"

"Of course, Okame-san." Daisuke glanced back, that strangely eager smile on his face. "Didn't you hear it? *Prove your worth to pass.* Yoshitsune was one of the greatest swordsmen who ever lived. If we want to prove ourselves worthy, we must defeat him in battle. Besides..." His gaze flicked to me. "I promised to escort Yumeko-san to the Steel Feather temple, and to protect both her and the Dragon scroll from any who wish to acquire it. If I cannot defeat these guardians, here and now, how can I hope to stand against Hakaimono when the time comes?"

"That is not what the spirits said, Daisuke-san," Reika broke in, stepping forward, as well. "It is not just you who wishes passage to the Steel Feather temple. We all must prove our worth if we wish to pass." She reached into her sleeve and withdrew an ofuda, holding the slip of paper up between two fingers. "This test must be completed together."

I frowned. For some reason, this situation didn't seem right. "Are you sure we have to fight them?" I asked.

Okame snickered. "Well, they're blocking the only way up the steps, and the haiku didn't say 'sit down and have tea.' I don't think they're going to let us pass if we just ask nicely, Yumeko-chan."

"Correct," Reika agreed, and turned to point at me. "You should stand back, Yumeko," she ordered. "Let your guardians take care of this."

I scowled at the shrine maiden. "I'm not afraid."

"I did not say you were." Reika shot me an exasperated glare. "But you must reach the Steel Feather temple, Yumeko. We are close, just one more challenge remains, and the rest of us are here only as your shields. If we fall, that is not as important as you delivering the scroll to the temple and warning them of Hakaimono." Her eyes narrowed. "So for once, listen to your protectors, kitsune, and let us do what we came to do. We don't need you getting your stubborn head bashed in on the temple steps. Go." She pointed, and only when I had retreated off to the side and had stepped behind a pillar did she turn to the men. The noble waited calmly with one hand on his sword hilt, and

Okame had an arrow nocked to his bow. "Taiyo-san, Okame-san? Are we ready?"

Daisuke nodded. Turning to the statues, still watching rigid and unmoving in front of the steps, he bowed. "Guardian spirits," he announced in a solemn voice, "we will not turn back. We will be honored to accept your challenge."

The statues' expressions didn't change. Without warning, the large man swung his great stone spear before him in a savage arc, cutting at the whole party. Okame yelped, jerking back as it missed him by inches, and Reika dove out of the way. Daisuke leaped straight into the air, drawing his sword as he did, and cut at the statue as he came down. But Yoshitsune stepped in front of the large man, raising one of his swords, and Daisuke's blade screeched off the stone weapon instead. Almost at the same time, the second sword lashed out, cutting at the noble, and Daisuke twisted aside, sleeves billowing, to avoid it. He spun to face the other swordsman, and had to leap aside to avoid the giant stone spear smashing to the earth. The smaller statue pressed forward, both blades moving in a spinning, deadly dance, and the noble retreated, his own sword whirling to block and parry.

An arrow ricocheted off the large statue's head, leaving a white gash in the stone but little else. "Um, we might be in trouble, Daisuke-san," Okame called, taking aim from atop an empty statue plinth. He fired again, but the dart struck the large man in the neck and went flying off into the darkness. "Any ideas on how to pierce solid granite?"

"I am still working on it," came Daisuke's breathless, somewhat wry voice. He evaded a flurry of blows, then turned, vaulted off the head of a statue and landed atop a row of broken pillars that stood upright like broken fangs. The swordsman statue didn't hesitate but leaped after him, and Daisuke retreated to the next shattered column. The clang of their weapons rang overhead, as the two master swordsmen continued their duel several feet off the ground.

With a roar, the large statue swung his spear at the ronin, and Okame dove away as the weapon smashed right through the pedestal, turning it into a crumbling pile of pebbles and dust. Okame hit the ground and rolled to his feet, but a fist-size rock struck the back of his head and he staggered, dropping to his hands and knees. The large statue didn't make a sound as it turned, raising its spear to crush him into the stones.

I gasped and, without thinking, stepped from behind the pillar and threw a ball of kitsune-bi toward the statue about to crush Okame. The flaming globe soared over the ronin and exploded in the statue's face, flaring a brilliant blue-white and banishing the darkness like a flash of lightning. The statue paused and staggered back, waving a hand before its eyes.

A booming howl rang through the chamber, as with a streak of glowing red and gold, an enormous komainu leaped over a broken wall and landed beside the ronin. Reika was on his back, sitting between his massive shoulders and golden mane, as Chu's guardian form roared at the statue still looming over Okame. Reika held an ofuda before her, the strip of paper fluttering wildly, and drew her arm back as the statue turned, raising its spear.

"Shatter," Reika cried, flinging the ofuda toward the living statue, as Chu dodged the spear blade crashing into the earth. The tiny slip of paper struck the statue's chest and clung there for a moment, as the kanji on the surface started to glow.

With a sharp crack, a portion of the statue's chest exploded outward, filling the air with dust and rock shards and knocking the giant back a few feet. It made no sound, but flailed as it staggered, lashing out wildly with its spear. The blow was fast and unexpected, and Chu wasn't able to react quickly enough. The haft of the weapon struck him across a meaty shoulder, lifting him off his feet and sending him and Reika flying through the air. They hit the ground, rolled into a statue base and lay there a moment before struggling weakly to get up.

Heart pounding, I looked at the giant. There was a gaping hole in the statue's chest, big enough for a samurai's helmet to fit, but the stone warrior was still on its feet. And though it was nearly impossible to catch any type of expression on its stony features, I thought it looked angry now.

The clang of stone on steel echoed somewhere overhead. Daisuke and the other statue were still dueling on the pillars rising from the ground, running up broken columns and leaping from pillar to pillar, and an idea flitted through my head like a butterfly.

I bent down, snatched up a pebble and stepped away from the column toward the large statue, which was turning its terrifying gaze on Reika and Chu. As it took a thunderous step toward them, I took a deep breath and darted into the open.

"Excuse me!" I called, and the statue turned its stony gaze around, hollow eyes finding me across a shattered column. I raised one hand, a sphere of kitsune-bi igniting in my palm. "You haven't forgotten about me, have you?" I taunted, and flung the globe of foxfire at the looming statue.

The flaming ball hit the giant square in the gaping chest hole and exploded in a flash of brilliant light, but the statue didn't move or even flinch. Raising its spear, it turned and began to stalk toward me, its ponderous footsteps booming over the ground and making the air tremble. I flattened my ears and darted behind a trio of pillars as the tremors drew closer. Closing my eyes, I squeezed the pebble in my hand and felt my power stir to life.

Let's hope these things can't see through magic.

I stepped out from behind the pillars and hurled a ball of kitsune-bi at the approaching statue, causing it to explode in its face. With an angry rumble, it lunged, swinging its huge spear through the air at my head. I ducked, and the blade smashed into the pillar behind me, crushing stone and shearing through in a terrifying display of strength. Pebbles and dust flew everywhere as I scrambled backward and hit another pillar behind me, just as the statue swung his giant blade again. I dodged and managed to put another pair of columns between me and the statue, as his blade smashed another pillar to rubble.

"Yumeko!" I heard Reika shout as I frantically ducked behind yet another column. The clang of metal echoed somewhere close, and then it was drowned out as the giant's spear smashed through the barrier like it was made of salt.

A massive tremor went through the ground, as pillars, statues and columns that had been holding each other up collapsed with the roar of a landslide. The granite columns smashed to the ground, crushing the large statue and everything around him, including the illusion of a kitsune he had been trying to smash into the rock. Overhead, the statue of the swordsman, who had been pursuing Daisuke across the pillars, halted as the stone beneath him gave way. Both swordsmen tried to leap to safety; Daisuke sprang atop a falling pillar, ran along the edge as it fell and flung himself onto the Jade Prophet's enormous head. The living statue tried to follow him, lost its balance and plummeted like a bag of stones to the ground. It struck the rocks and cracked into several pieces where it landed, its head rolling several yards away and vanishing behind a ruined pedestal.

The rumbles faded, and the dust began to settle. I exhaled and stepped out from the column I'd been hiding behind while the stone warrior chased my double around the room. The swordsmaster, Yoshitsune, lay shattered against the pillars, and his enormous friend was nowhere to be seen, buried as he was under several tons of granite. I doubted either of them would come after us again.

"Yumeko!"

Okame's frantic voice rang out behind me, a moment before the ronin skidded into view a few yards away. He was panting, staring furiously at the mountain of rubble, the dust clouds still billowing into the air. Reika was right behind him, she, too, gazing at the pile of stone in utter dismay.

"No," she whispered, and put a hand to her mouth. "Great Kami, please no."

Confused, I stepped forward. "Reika-san, Okame-san," I called, and they both spun on me, wide-eyed. "Are you all right? The statues are destroyed." I blinked at the sudden fury on Reika's face and took a step back. "Ano…is something wrong?"

My ears flattened, for the shrine maiden was stalking toward me with a hard, almost manic look in her eyes. Her fingers dug into my skin as she seized me by the shoulders, her face almost white.

"You're alive," she whispered, giving me a little shake. "You're not an illusion. Thank the kami." She let out her breath in a puff, then glared furiously. "I have half a mind to kill you, fox."

"Ite," I complained, wincing as thin, shockingly strong fingers squeezed my flesh like a vise. "I'm confused, Reika-san. Are you happy that I'm alive, or not?"

Thankfully, she let me go, still glaring at me with eyes like onyx daggers. "I suppose I should be grateful that it was an illusion I watched get crushed beneath all that rock and stone," she snapped, almost sounding embarrassed. "I suppose I should be thankful that you never listen when we tell you something. That you will, in fact, do the exact opposite, because you are a kitsune and chaos flows through your veins as surely as evil through an oni."

I blinked at her. "I'm still confused, Reika-san."

"Yumeko." Okame sighed, and I felt a hand on my head, resting between my ears, as he came up behind me. "Don't scare us like that. We've got to figure out some sort of signal when you're about to do your kitsune thing, so the rest of us don't blunder off a cliff or dive under a collapsing roof trying to save an illusion."

"Indeed," said a new, slightly strained voice, as Daisuke stepped around the rubble pile. He moved smoothly across the rocky ground toward us, but I suspected he was doing his best not to limp. Okame stiffened and stepped around me, brow furrowed, as the noble joined us.

"That was quite the impressive display, Yumeko-san," Daisuke told me, though his smile was pained. "I am correct in assuming you are the one responsible for the sudden collapse of everything, yes? My attention was somewhat diverted when the pillars began to fall."

I winced. Everything had happened so fast. With the giant statue looming over Okame and Reika, I'd made a split-second decision. Only now did I realize it had put Daisuke in danger, too. "Gomennasai, Daisuke-san."

"No." He shook his head. "No need for apologies. Your course of action was possibly the best. Although I admit I would have rather finished that fight myself, steel blades can do precious little against solid stone." He gazed down at his sword, eyes narrowed, before glancing over the rubble pile. "In any case, we completed the challenge. The way up the stairs should be clear."

Picking our way over fallen pillars and broken statues, we made our way back to the staircase. However, as soon as we approached the bottom step, there was another loud grinding of stone, and four more statues stepped off their plinths to crash to the steps, blocking our way.

"What?" Okame stumbled back, staring at the new guardians who had stepped forward. "More of them? How many of these things are we going to have to fight?"

"As many as we must." Daisuke stepped forward and, even though he was bloody, bruised and exhausted, raised his chin and put one hand on his sword hilt. "The entire room, if it means we must get through this challenge."

Okame cast a nervous glance at the dozens, perhaps hundreds, of statues lining the steps and scattered throughout the cavern. "There's an awful lot of statues in here, peacock. If they all come to life and attack us, we're not going to have a good day."

Daisuke only smiled. "A true warrior welcomes battle," he stated quietly. "If he must stand against an army, he knows his death will be with honor."

"Daisuke-san," I said, with a sudden flash of insight, "wait."

Stepping beside the noble, I grabbed his sleeve, making him turn with a puzzled frown. "The haiku in the beginning," I said. "How did it go, again?"

"It reveals the way," Daisuke supplied, still keeping an eye on the statues. "Prove you are worthy to pass. Or die upon stone."

"What if it wasn't a challenge or a test?" I mused, staring at the line of guardians. "What if it was a warning? We tried fighting them, and that didn't work. What are we missing?"

It reveals the way.

"Yumeko!" Reika called, as Daisuke drew his blade in a flash of steel. "Watch out!" The stone statues had started down the few steps separating us, raising their weapons to strike.

Oh!

"Wait!" I cried, and reached into my robes, shoving my hand between layers of cloth to find what I needed. Taking one step forward even as the statues loomed overhead, I pulled out the scroll and held it up before me. "Stop!"

The statues froze. I glanced up and with a chill, saw that their huge stone blades had come to a halt midswing, and had all been aimed at me. "This is what you wanted, isn't it?" I whispered, somehow managing words around the throbbing of my pulse. "This was the key, the *it* that revealed the way. You just needed to make sure we had the scroll."

The statues didn't move. They stood clustered on the steps, silent and motionless, like they had been standing there, motionless, for hundreds of years. I reached out and prodded a stony knuckle, and a bit of dust flaked off to drift to the ground.

Very carefully, still holding the scroll out like a torch, I stepped forward, ready to leap away if any of them twitched. Nothing happened as I eased between granite arms and stony elbows, slipping through the mass until I stood above the statues on the other side. "I think it's safe now," I said, glancing back at my companions. "They know we're not intruders. That we have a piece of the Dragon scroll."

Reika let out her breath in a rush. "One of these days, your luck is going to run out, fox," she warned as the rest of them started up the staircase. "And then what are you going to do?"

"I don't know, Reika-san, but I'm sure I'll think of something."

Two gigantic statues guarded the gates at the top of the stairs, twin figures that dwarfed even the large statue with the spear. They looked more like ancient kami or yokai than mortal men. Their bodies and faces were human, but great feathered wings sprouted from their backs, and their eyes were slitted like a bird's. I wondered if these were the final guardians, the last defense against intruders if all the other statues had failed. Looking into their stern, fierce features, I was glad we'd never have to find out.

The great iron doors through the gateway weren't barred, but it took all of us pushing together to get them to budge. They finally gave way with a reluctant groan, and a cloud of centuries-old dust billowed from the opening. Another stone staircase lay beyond the threshold, this time leading up to a rectangle of navy sky and stars.

Warily, we climbed the final staircase. The air drifting into the passage was shockingly cold and crisp, instead of the dusty, stale air we had left behind in the cavern. Overhead, the stars and a brilliant orange moon blazed down on us, seemingly closer than they had ever been before.

We reached the top step and came out of the passage. A blast of icy wind hit my face, tossing my hair and making my cheeks tingle, and the air tasted of frost.

"Sugoi," I whispered, staring up at what lay before us.

A massive mountain peak rose straight into the air, jagged and unbowed. The very top, scraping the sky and raking the clouds, was tipped with snow. Built into the very side of the cliffs, looking like it was carved from the mountain itself, an enormous temple loomed against the stars. Ancient pagoda roofs swept the sky, curled up at the corners like wings, so weathered and windscoured they looked more stone than tile. The walls of the temple might have been any color once, but were now the same uniform gray as the cliff face. From what I could see, there were no roads, stairs, even a treacherous mountain goat path winding up the peaks. Either there was a secret way into the temple that I wasn't seeing, or we were going to have to learn to fly.

"You've finally come, scroll bearer."

We turned. A pair of figures stood behind us, perched gracefully atop two piles of stones that flanked the passage we'd just exited. They were tall and stern-looking, dressed in black robes, their wooden geta making them even taller. The one on the right was younger, with midnight-black hair flowing loose around his shoulders and framing his face. For some reason, it reminded me of a mane of feathers. The second man was older, his eyes sharp and black and his nose very long.

Behind each of them, flaring to either side and gleaming black in the moonlight, a pair of giant wings rippled and fluttered in the wind.

"Welcome, scroll bearer." The older winged man smiled at me and raised a hand, the nails on his fingertips sharp and curved like a bird's. "Welcome to the Steel Feather temple, and the home of the tengu."

21

THE STEEL FEATHER TEMPLE

Yumeko

I had been right. There was no easy way into the temple.

The two tengu directed us to the base of the cliff, where a large basket had been lowered on creaky ropes, and we'd ascended the mountain two at a time. Reika and me, with the shrine maiden holding Chu in her arms, then Okame and Daisuke, with the ronin looking slightly green as he staggered out of the basket onto solid ground. From there, we followed our tengu guides through a pair of large wooden gates, across a courtyard lined with statues and a painstakingly raked rock garden, and up the steps of the Steel Feather temple. Past the doors, the tengu set a brisk pace through long corridors and narrow hallways, and I hurried to keep up, watching the feathers on their magnificent wings flutter and ripple with every step.

Tengu. My heart beat faster at the word. According to legend, tengu were powerful yokai who possessed great knowledge and stayed far from the affairs of mortals. There were stories of men who sought the wisdom of the tengu, who faced great danger and hardship to find them and prove themselves worthy. Most did not succeed, and of the few who did, even fewer earned the tengu's respect.

At least, that was what the stories claimed. But, if that was true, if they were so aloof, why were they the protectors of a piece of the Dragon scroll? Master Isao never really told me how the prayer came to be separated, or who had decided its fate. I hadn't expected the Steel Feather temple to be full of an ancient race of yokai, but on reflection, I guessed that the tengu had just as much cause not to see the Dragon summoned as the humans did. After all, it was their world, too.

So, these were the keepers of the second piece of the Dragon scroll. The thought that we'd made it, that we'd finally found the Steel Feather temple, only made me sick with worry and a little regret. In another situation, another life, this would be the end of the quest. I could hand over my fragment of the scroll and be done. I would have kept my promise to Master Isao, the pieces would be safe with its real protectors and I would be free.

But...these weren't normal times. And the quest was far from finished. Hakaimono was coming; who knew how close he was even now? My stomach roiled like a nest of snakes. Would I be ready to face the First Oni when he arrived, intent on taking the Dragon scroll? Would any of us?

"Through here, please," said one of our tengu guides, the younger one with the feathery mane of hair, who had introduced himself as Tsume. He slid back a door and gave me a wry smile. "Do watch your step."

A blast of cold wind hit us as the panel was opened, and my heart gave a violent lurch. Through the doors, there was no room, no hallway, or even a floor. The panels opened to the sky and a sheer, heart-stopping plunge down the side of the Dragon

Spine. The moon shone in the frame, seeming to laugh at us, and the tops of the snowcapped peaks rose into the air like jagged teeth.

I could feel the amusement radiating from the tengu beside me, particularly the younger one. Forcing myself not to step away from that sheer drop, I turned to look at him.

"Ano...where exactly are we going? Foxes don't fly very well, though we are good at falling."

The tengu chuckled. "Our daitengu is waiting to speak to you on that peak over there," the older one explained, and stuck a long finger through the doorway, pointing to the left. Making sure my feet stayed on solid ground, I peeked around the frame. A narrow stone staircase hugged the outer wall, winding up a ledge, where a seated figure could just be seen at the top.

"Oh, this will be fun," Okame sighed. "Humans are great at flying. Straight down, at high speeds. Not so good on the landing, though."

The older tengu frowned at the ronin. "Only the scroll bearer may proceed from here," he said. "The daitengu called for her alone. The rest of you must wait until they are finished."

I glanced back at them, wide-eyed. Daisuke gave me an encouraging smile. "This is a great honor, Yumeko," he said softly. "I am sure you will be fine."

"Just don't look down," Okame added unhelpfully, and let out a yelp when Reika kicked his ankle.

"Be polite when you speak to the daitengu, Yumeko," she told me, a warning look in her eyes. "Answer all his questions. And whatever you do, don't stare at his..." She trailed off, pointing a furtive finger at her face. I frowned in confusion, but she didn't elaborate.

Swallowing hard, I turned back to the tiny, narrow path. Keeping my body pressed as close to the wall as I could, I started up the steps.

Wind tore at me, tugging at my clothes and making my eyes water. My sleeves billowed out like sails, seeking to catch the breeze and toss me right off the mountainside. Briefly, I wondered, if I were to fall, would either of the tengu catch me before I hit the bottom? Would Tsume swoop in and rescue me on his great black wings? Somehow, that didn't seem likely. Hugging the stones, I crept up the staircase on all fours, until I finally reached the top.

Carefully, I rose, bracing myself against the wind, and walked along the ridge to the man sitting cross-legged at the very edge. His back was to me, and great feathered wings jutted out from his shoulders, black as night and fluttering in the wind. Feeling like it was the right thing to do, I sat, mimicking his pose on the ground, and waited.

"Scroll bearer." His voice was a raspy whisper, yet I could easily hear him over the howl of the wind in my ears. "You have finally arrived."

I swallowed. "How did you know I was coming?"

"I commune with the wind kami every morning and every night, little fox. They bring me tidings of the world below. We had heard whispers of the destruction of the Silent Winds temple, and knew that the piece of the scroll was on its way here."

"If you knew, why didn't you help?"

"Because that is not our way."

He turned so that he was facing me across the stones, the moon at his back. His ancient black eyes seemed to bore into mine. I blinked. An old man with wild white hair and a long beard gazed back at me, withered claws cupped in his lap. His skin was a bright, vivid crimson, the color of blood on the snow. He wore billowing gray robes and wooden geta clogs, and a tiny black cap was perched atop his head, tied with a string below his chin. A thin, enormous red nose, probably over a foot long, protruded from his face like the handle of a broom.

"Kitsune," the daitengu said, and the huge digit bobbed in the wind as he cocked his head. "Pray tell me what is so interesting."

Too late, I remembered Reika's warning about not staring, and immediately dropped my gaze. "Sumimasen," I apologized. "I wasn't staring at your...ah... I'm sorry. Thank you for seeing me."

He sighed. "For centuries, the tengu have remained here, isolated and far removed from the affairs of the mortal world," he told me. "We watch, and sometimes we offer guidance to exceptional souls, but we have no desire to entangle ourselves in the short, chaotic lives of humans." His bushy eyebrows lowered, his raspy voice turning dark. "However, one thousand years ago, a mortal made a wish to the Dragon that threw the very land into such turmoil, we knew we could not stand by any longer. As the humans' war raged on and the world became soaked in blood, a secret council of yokai, kami and humans was formed for the first time. Together, we decided that the Scroll of a Thousand Prayers was too dangerous to be used again. The scroll was torn into pieces, and each group took one of the fragments, promising to keep it hidden so that the Harbinger's shadow could never threaten the world again."

His enormous nose angled toward me. "Your temple was the human order that swore to keep their fragment safe," he said, not accusingly. "Another piece resides here, at the top of the Dragon Spine Mountains, watched over by the tengu who call this place their home."

"And the third?" I asked.

His mouth curved in a grim frown. "The third piece of the scroll was taken away by the kodama of the Angetsu Mori and hidden deep within the forest. Those kodama don't exist anymore. The Angetsu Mori, or the Forest of a Thousand Eyes as it is known today, has been thoroughly corrupted by Genno and the taint of his blood magic, and the kami who lived there have either fled or have been corrupted themselves. We can only assume the final piece of the scroll is lost, or in the hands of the Master of Demons."

I shivered, remembering Tatsumi's warning that Genno already had one piece of the scroll. The daitengu sighed, and the end of his nose trembled. "In any case," he went on, "you are here, and you have done remarkably well for one so young. The journey could not have been easy. The winds relay to us the goings-on in the mortal world, how dark things are rising with the coming of the Harbinger. It has been this way since the Dragon was first summoned. But you survived, and you have protected the scroll. It is all we could have asked, and for that, you have earned the gratitude of the Steel Feather temple."

"Arigatou gozaimasu," I whispered. "I am grateful, and I know Master Isao would be pleased that our piece of the scroll made it to the temple, that it can be protected. But..." I hesitated, not knowing how to tell him.

"But...the fight is not yet over, is it?" the daitengu finished softly.

I glanced up in surprise, and he offered a grim smile.

"*He* comes," the old tengu said in a voice that sent shivers up my spine. "For the scroll. For you, and your companions. We have felt his approach on the wind, we smell his taint in the snow flurrying around us. We can sense him on the mountainside, the shadow that stalks the peaks, his footsteps getting ever closer. You know of whom I speak."

Numbly, I nodded. "Hakaimono."

"He comes for the scroll," the daitengu said again, sounding grimly amused. "But he will not take it. We will not let it fall into the hands of whomever sends Hakaimono against us. Even if our foe is the First Oni himself, the warriors of this temple will fight, and we will defend the last pieces of the scroll to our dying breaths. We will perish before we let that monster take the Dragon's prayer."

"Ano…" I stammered, making him eye me with a beady black gaze. "Actually, I was hoping that the Steel Feather temple would help us with something…regarding Hakaimono."

The daitengu raised a very bushy eyebrow. "Help you with the First Oni?" he repeated, and his tone became cautious. "What is it you want to do, fox?"

I took a deep breath.

"Save the demonslayer," I said, and the other brow shot up to join the first. "Kage Tatsumi has been possessed by Hakaimono," I went on. "I want to save him, and drive the demon back into Kamigoroshi."

"Impossible," the daitengu said, his voice flat. "Do you know how strong Hakaimono is, kitsune? Even now, we know we are going to lose a great many souls when that monster breaches our gates. He is weaker in a human body, but if we do anything less than destroy him, our clan will be slaughtered down to the youngest fledgling. There is no one who can exorcise that demon from the mortal he possesses. You would likely do more harm to the soul itself."

"We're not attempting an exorcism," I told the ancient tengu. "Not in the traditional sense. *I'm* going to possess Tatsumi myself, and force the spirit of Hakaimono back into the sword from the inside."

"Kitsune-tsuki?" The daitengu blinked. "That has never been done before," he mused. "No fox would ever possess a mortal with the spirit of an oni inside him. Especially if that oni is Hakaimono."

"I would," I said firmly. "I mean… I will. I'm going to. Possess Tatsumi, and face Hakaimono myself."

He gave me a long, level stare. I could sense him sizing me up, taking in my stature, and I set my jaw, staring him down.

Finally, he shook his head. "Do you know how dangerous it will be?" he asked. "Taking on Hakaimono the Destroyer, at his full strength, inside a mortal soul?"

"I know," I said, and shivered. "But I have to do it. I have to try. I promised Tatsumi that I would free his soul from Hakaimono, one way or another. He's waiting for me, and I won't break my promise. But, to even have a chance, I'll need your help—everyone's help. To possess Tatsumi, I'll need some sort of opening, a distraction, so that Hakaimono won't kill me as soon as I come in."

The daitengu was still watching me, his face unreadable. I swallowed hard. "I know I'm asking for a lot..." I began.

"You are," agreed the other.

"And I know that trying to take Hakaimono alive will be far more dangerous than trying to kill him outright..."

"And result in many more deaths," added the daitengu.

"But I have to do this," I said, feeling a lump rise to my throat. "Tatsumi saved my life, and I swore I would free him from Hakaimono. You didn't see him. He..." I remembered Tatsumi in the dream world, the utter bleakness in his eyes, and words failed me. "I have to help him," I finished. "I promised I would. And I will face Hakaimono, with or without your aid. And if you can't help me, I ask only that you not try to kill Hakaimono until you're certain that I have failed to save the soul inside him."

The daitengu stared at me for a long moment, then sighed. "Foolish girl," he rasped, shaking his head. "You are going to die, and your stubbornness will likely get all your friends killed, as well. But, I can see that you will not be persuaded." He closed his eyes a moment, then nodded. "If this is what you wish to do, then the Steel Feather temple will aid you however we can. But," he added, holding up a withered claw, "we will not abandon our sacred duty to protect the scroll. If it seems that Hakaimono is in danger of acquiring what he seeks, we will have no choice but to destroy him."

"I understand," I said, and bowed low to the ancient tengu. "Arigatou gozaimasu."

He rose, his great wings flaring behind him. "You and your friends are welcome in the temple," he told me. "But I fear we do not have a lot of time." He glanced at the sky, where a mass of clouds could be seen over the distant peaks, and frowned. "There is a storm coming. Eat, rest and pray to the kami, for now we plan for what we must do when the First Oni arrives on our doorstep."

"Thank you," I said again. "Truly. Oh, and what about...?"

I reached into my furoshiki and withdrew the scroll, holding it out to him. The daitengu regarded it solemnly, as if he could hear the thoughts of the scroll itself, then shook his head.

"For now, hold on to your burden, little fox," he said. "You have brought it far, and have protected it from many evils. In all your journeys, the demonslayer never realized the very thing he was after was right under his nose, which means the First Oni does not know your secret, either. Keep it safe awhile longer. At least until the fight with Hakaimono is done."

I swallowed and returned the scroll to my furoshiki, tucking it safely into the folds again. I didn't know what he saw, if he saw anything, but I was surprisingly relieved not to have to give up my burden just yet. I had carried it for so long, kept it hidden and safe; it almost seemed a part of me now.

The daitengu gave me a scrutinizing look, his eyes grim in the light of the moon. "Hakaimono will be the hardest opponent you have ever faced, little fox," he warned. "If we make a single mistake, the smallest error of judgment, the First Oni will show us no mercy. It will take every ounce of bravery, determination, strength and fox trickery we can muster to defeat him. If there was ever a time to see exactly what your magic can do, it is now."

22

QUESTIONS OF YUREI

Suki

Lord Seigetsu was meditating again.

Within the red and dark wood interior of the flying carriage, everything was quiet. Taka, exhausted from his frigid march through the territory of the snow woman, had curled up beneath several blankets in the corner and was dead to the world. Occasional snorts and snores came from the quilted lump, breaking the silence, but it didn't seem to disturb Seigetsu, who sat motionless with his back to the wall and his hands in his lap. His ball was missing, Suki noticed. Which was odd, because she was certain she'd seen it when he first began meditating, balanced on his thumbs as usual. But it wasn't there now, so she must have imagined it.

Suki drifted aimlessly around the carriage, floating from one side to the other, wondering when they would reach their destination. For a moment, she envied Taka, snoring obliviously in the corner. When the little yokai was awake, his cheerful, constant chatter was a good distraction. In the silence, she was left with her own thoughts, which terrified her and which she could do nothing about.

"It must be wearying, never to sleep."

Suki looked up. Lord Seigetsu's eyes were open now, shining gold in the darkness of the carriage, watching her. Suki ducked her head, thinking her aimless drifting had disturbed him, but he offered a small smile, indicating he wasn't angry, and tucked his hands into his sleeves. He looked...tired, Suki realized. His shoulders sagged a bit, and his poised, elegant face looked faintly haggard. Seigetsu must have noticed her staring, for one brow arched in her direction, and he raised his head.

"You must think this all very strange," he said. "I forget sometimes how new you are to all of this. That only a short while ago, you were a simple human, with a simple human life. And now, you have been thrust into this world of yokai and magic, demons and prophecies. It must be overwhelming."

Uncomfortable, Suki raised her hands in a helpless manner, but Seigetsu frowned.

"No," he said, making her stiffen. "*Talk* to me, hitodama. Speak your words out loud, otherwise you might lose the ability to make noise entirely. You have questions. Ask them, and I will do my best to answer."

Suki shrank back, withering with the thought of having to speak, then gathered herself in determination. Talk to him, Lord Seigetsu had said. Ask questions. She *did* have questions, she realized. Too many. Why had she died? What was the scroll Lady Satomi wanted so badly? Who was the Master of Demons? Why was Daisuke-sama traveling with a kitsune, and why did Lord Seigetsu seem so interested in this fox girl? For that matter, Suki thought, why did *everyone* seem so interested in this fox girl? From Lady Satomi, to the Master of Demons, to the terrible Hakaimono, to Seigetsu-sama himself. Everyone was after this kitsune, and the scroll she possessed. Why?

So many questions, it made her head ache. She felt as if she had only a few tiny pieces of a massive puzzle, that the rest of the pieces had been scattered to the winds, and that only Lord Seigetsu knew what the completed version looked like.

Lord Seigetsu.

She looked up, meeting the luminous golden eyes. She knew, suddenly, what question she wanted to ask.

"Who...who are you?"

Seigetsu-sama chuckled. "I am a simple shogi master," he answered. "One who has been moving the pieces around the board for a long, long time. Every play has been deliberate. Every piece has been placed and taken with the utmost care." He glanced at Taka, still sleeping in the corner. "Of course, it helps when one knows his opponent's moves before they do, but even so, it has been a long, exhausting game. But the final play is in sight, if I can only make it to the end with no mistakes."

"And...what *is* the end, Seigetsu-sama?" Suki whispered. "What happens...when the game...is finished?"

Seigetsu's eyes gleamed, and a slow smile crossed his face. In that moment, Suki saw a flash of raw ambition in his yellow eyes, a hunger that sent a chill through her whole body. But he only said, his voice low and controlled, "I cannot ruin the ending, Suki-chan. That would just spoil the surprise, for everyone."

Suki paused, gathering her thoughts and her courage to ask more questions. It was as if a dam had been opened inside her; suddenly she wanted to know *everything*. But before she could say another word, the lump in the corner suddenly quivered and gasped. Taka sat bolt upright, shedding blankets, to gaze wildly around the room, his single eye huge with fear.

"Master!"

Immediately, Seigetsu rose and crossed the room to kneel before him, grabbing the yokai by the shoulder as he jerked and panted in short, panicked breaths. "I'm here," he said, his deep voice firm and soothing at the same time. "It's me. Calm yourself, Taka."

Taka shivered, gasping and whimpering, but obediently went still in the grip of his master. Suki floated up, hovering anxiously beside the pair, as Seigetsu's eyes narrowed. "A nightmare?" he asked quietly, and the yokai nodded, biting his lip. "What did you see?"

"An army of demons," Taka whispered. "Marching into the mountains. They attacked a temple and killed everyone there. There was so much blood. Nobody survived, not even the fox girl."

PART 3

23

THE DESTROYER COMES

HAKAIMONO

*T*he temple gates flew open with a crash, and the tremors vibrated from where I was standing, all the way up the mountain. Silhouetted in the frame of the ruined gates, the moonlight casting a long, horned shadow over the stones, I grinned.

Hello, protectors of the Dragon scroll. I'm here. Hope you're ready for me.

Silence. An empty courtyard, windswept and perfectly maintained, was my greeting as the doors bounced and swayed on their hinges, the boom still reverberating through the air. To my immediate left, a pristine rock garden glimmered in the moonlight, thousands of raked white pebbles forming a rocky sea around a few larger islands. To the right, statues of human warriors led the way to the main hall, making me curl a lip in amusement. I was still covered in dust, my body aching and bruised from that last little challenge. I hoped the sculptor who had created all those guardian statues was dead, because his heart would probably burst from shock when he found nothing remained of his creations but gravel and dust.

At my back, the icy wind howled up the sheer drop down the mountainside, a mountain I had to climb to reach the temple at the top of the cliff. I noticed a pulley system with a large basket sitting near the gate; they had obviously pulled the basket up in the hopes that it would stop me. Too bad for them, this wasn't the first mountain I had scaled. I hoped that a cavern full of living statues and a slightly challenging climb up the side of a cliff weren't the only defenses these protectors had, or I was going to be disappointed.

With Kamigoroshi glowing a baleful purple in my hand, I stepped through the gates into the Steel Feather temple.

Nothing happened. I had been bracing myself for arrows, traps, for a burst of magic as the temple defenses went off. A cold wind howled over the rooftops, but other than a dry leaf skipping across the courtyard, there was no movement or sign of life anywhere.

Which meant that they knew I was here, and I was walking into an ambush.

I sighed. "Well, isn't this an obvious setup? You know I'm only going to get mad when you spring whatever it is you're planning," I called, walking steadily across the courtyard toward the temple steps. Kamigoroshi flickered and pulsed in my hand, casting eerie shadows over the stones. "You could save me some trouble and attack me now, or keep hiding and force me to hunt you down. The outcome will be the same either way."

No answer. The courtyard was dark and still as I made my way up the stairs and stepped through the doors into the main hall. The floor of this shadowy chamber was polished onyx and jade, with lines of gold threaded through the tile. Large jade pillars marched down either side of the room, and even more statues of humans and tengu lined the walls. If this was a normal temple, the back of the room would be reserved for the gigantic statue of the humans' Jade Prophet, who was neither kami nor god but simply a mortal who had apparently reached enlightenment. But, as I had guessed earlier, the guardians of the Steel Feather temple were tengu, who believed themselves above mortal enlightenment. Instead of a huge green statue of a meditating woman, a great serpentine dragon had been carved into the wall, head and coils seeming to emerge from the stone. The roaring head hovered over an altar crafted of dark wood and gold, where a long, lacquered case rested on a stand in the very center. But the dais that held it wasn't empty.

A single human with long white hair stood calmly in front of the altar, a shining length of steel held loosely at his side. His face was covered with a pale oni mask, a grotesque parody of my kin, with a grinning red mouth bristling with fangs and a pair of horns curling from the brow.

I smiled, recognizing the noble from Tatsumi's memories, realizing that if he was here, *she* would be, as well.

"Oni no Mikoto," I drawled, walking forward. "Or should I say Taiyo Daisuke of the Sun Clan? Where are your friends, the ronin archer and that annoying shrine maiden? And the little half-fox?" He didn't answer, and I chuckled. "Just you, then? Do the tengu here really believe a single human can keep me from taking the Dragon scroll? Or are you trying to recreate our first meeting on the bridge?"

"You will not touch the Dragon scroll, demon." The human's voice was cool, unruffled. He took one step forward to meet me and raised his sword in a protective manner. "On my honor, I will protect it, and this temple, with my life."

I shook my head. "One human warrior cannot stop me, and the guardians here know that." With a smirk, I stepped farther into the room, raising Kamigoroshi and my voice. "But very well, I'll go along with this little farce, if only to get things moving. I do not believe for a moment that we are alone, but if you want your final duel, mortal, then I will happily give you an honorable death when I carve the head from your body."

Oni no Mikoto hesitated a moment, then calmly stepped off the dais and sank into a high stance, his blade held parallel over his head, the tip pointed toward me. "Then let us dance."

He lunged, a streak of motion across the wooden floor, coming in very fast for a human. I dodged the first blow, letting the sword miss my head by inches, then lashed out in kind, aiming to split the lean body in half. He spun with impressive grace, avoiding the counterstrike, and came at me again.

We danced like this across the floor for a few minutes, dodging, parrying, avoiding our opponent's blade and responding in turn. Oni no Mikoto was quite skilled, I could admit that. I had encountered several master swordsmen in my long years in the mortal realm, and this Taiyo was among the best.

However, he was still only human. And I never agreed to play by the rules.

The Taiyo slashed at me again, a precise, rather vicious blow meant to sever the head from my body. I twisted to dodge it while bringing Kamigoroshi up to parry, and the screech of metal on metal raced up my arm. At the same time, I released my grip on the sword with one hand, clenched it into a fist and swung it at the human's head. It struck him in the temple, lifting him off his feet and hurling him into a pillar with a muffled crack. The human collapsed to the base of the column, leaving a smear of blood on the wood, and struggled weakly to right himself.

Smiling, I strolled forward, stopping a few feet away to watch the human push himself to his knees. Blood covered the side of his face, staining his white hair, and a pointed shard of bone peeked through his right sleeve, indicating a broken arm.

"Oh, sorry, mortal," I mocked, grinning as he raised his head and glared up at me. "Was that not allowed? I forgot to mention I don't play by your human rules."

"Demon." The Taiyo gritted his teeth…and pushed himself to his feet, clutching the sword in his one good hand. His broken limb dangled awkwardly, but he raised the blade and braced himself, glaring at me in defiance. "At least give me the honor of dying on my feet."

I smiled. "As you wish."

Kamigoroshi flashed, a glint of steel in the darkness, and the human's head toppled from his shoulders, hitting the floor with a thump and rolling behind a pillar. The headless corpse swayed in place for the briefest of moments, before it, too, collapsed and leaked blood all over the wooden planks.

I yawned. "Well, that was slightly amusing. Predictable, but amusing. Is that the only obstacle you're going to throw at me, then? One human with a sword?" No answer from the seemingly empty shadows around me, and I sighed. "All right," I muttered, turning and walking toward the now unguarded altar. "Then I'll be taking the scroll and leaving now. Feel free to stop me if you—"

As soon as I set foot on the dais, there was an eruption of smoke at my feet, and the floor tiles under my feet changed. I looked down to see a glowing ring of power, surrounded by sigils and runes that I recognized instantly.

A binding circle.

With multiple eruptions of smoke throughout the room, the statues disappeared, writhing into nothingness as the illusions dissolved. Solemn, scowling tengu emerged from the dissolving mist, their expressions grimly determined as they surrounded me outside the circle. Multiple voices rose into the air, as they began chanting the words to bind a demon and send it back to Jigoku.

Despite the trap, I felt a savage grin cross my face. *She* was close. I didn't see her, but the telltale signs of kitsune illusion magic couldn't be more obvious. The statues and the floor all had the stink of fox magic, though I had to admit, she was getting more powerful with her illusions, to be able to control so many at once.

Your little fox girl is here, Tatsumi. I hope you'll enjoy the show when I find her.

"Hakaimono!"

The shrine maiden stepped forward, a snarling komainu beside her, and brandished an ofuda at me. On her other side, red-faced and with a nose like a broom handle, stood the daitengu of the temple, both claws wrapped around a staff, holding it before him like a shield. He started chanting, as did the circle of tengu around me, their voices rising in unison to echo off the pillars. At my feet, the binding circle flared red.

"You are not welcome here, demon," the shrine maiden called, as the strip of paper in her hand began to glow, illuminating the holy words scrawled across it. "And you will never take the scroll fragment from this sacred place—even if we must seal you away for a thousand years, you will never get your evil claws on the Dragon's prayer."

She hurled the ofuda at me, where it flew straight as an arrow, crackling with spiritual energy. The chanting of the tengu grew louder, and the strip of paper blazed white as it sped toward me.

I slashed the ofuda from the air, Kamigoroshi flaring with power as the blade struck the paper and sliced it in two. As the strips fluttered harmlessly to the ground, I raised my head and smiled at the miko, showing all my fangs.

"You're going to have to do better than that, amateur," I growled, seeing the color drain from her face. "I'm not some weak amanjaku you can seal away with a wave of your ofuda. Dozens of priests and blood mages before you have tried to bind me, and I've decorated the binding circles with their insides."

I glanced around me, at the ring of chanting tengu and raised my sword. "I've always wondered if crow tastes like chicken. Guess it's my lucky night."

Unexpectedly, the shrine maiden gave a grim smile. "Not this night, Hakaimono," she said. "You will not take one step farther. Your rampage ends here, and you will never lay eyes upon the scroll."

She raised a billowy sleeve, as if giving a signal. I felt the danger behind me and spun, just as an arrow streaked from the rafters overhead and hit me in the chest.

Snarling, I staggered back, seeing the shaft buried below my collarbone, and reached up to tear it away. The archer, whomever he was, had missed my heart, and that mistake would cost him greatly.

But then, I saw the familiar slip of paper shoved halfway down the shaft, flaring to life as soon as the arrow touched my skin, and growled a curse.

The ofuda burst into streams of light, rising up and spinning around me like a frantic swarm of eels. With a flash, they became glowing chains that wrapped around my arms and legs, anchoring me to the stones. I roared, my voice booming through the rafters, as I sank to my knees, feeling the chains tighten around me. The chanting of the tengu rose, filling the air with power, feeding the magic of the circle and pouring strength into the seal.

I struggled a moment, then gazed up at the shrine maiden, forcing a smirk. "Oh, well-done, human," I mocked. "I stand corrected. But your seal will hold only for as long as you and your bird friends concentrate. You won't be able to keep this up forever."

Her gaze hardened. "It doesn't have to be forever. Only long enough for this."

There was a ripple of movement beside me, and *she* stepped into the open with a billow of red and white. Her ears and tail were clearly visible, and her eyes glowed a subtle gold in the shadows of the hall. She looked different than the terrified kit-sune we had left at Satomi's castle. This Yumeko seemed... harder, older, clearly not the naive little half-yokai who smiled at ghosts and was innocent to the ways of evil. Her golden eyes held a sadness that hadn't been there before.

Deep inside, I felt a flutter of emotion as the fox girl stepped into the light, a stirring of both fear and cautious relief from the soul within. And I smiled, savoring those tentative feelings of hope, both from Tatsumi, and in the eyes of the kitsune in front of me. They thought they had a chance.

"Hakaimono," the fox girl said, stopping just outside the bind-ing circle. She appeared calm, but her tail twitched a nervous, agitated rhythm behind her robes. "I will ask this of you only once. Release Tatsumi and return to the sword. We don't want to have to kill you."

Meeting the girl's luminous gaze, I started to laugh.

"Oh, naive little half-fox," I chuckled, as the tengu around me stiffened, even as they continued to chant. "You have no idea what you're asking. Or what you're attempting to do." I shook my head and smiled at the kitsune, furtively testing the strength of the chains as I met her gaze. "You see, I knew you were here somewhere. This cunning little trap had the stench of fox magic all over it. I've been wanting to see you again, Yumeko-chan. So has Tatsumi." I chuckled, even as the soul inside me surged up, stronger than I had ever felt before. "I wanted you to come out and play, little fox," I continued, as Tatsumi raged at me, desperate and furious. "I didn't want you skulking back in the shadows, looking on while the rest of your friends screamed and died. Foxes aren't the only ones who can play tricks. And now that you've finally come out of hiding, the real fun can begin."

She paled, her black-tipped ears flattening against her skull. Behind her, the shrine maiden pulled out another ofuda, and the chanting of the tengu grew louder, more insistent. I could feel the chains tightening around me, burning as they dug into my skin, and bared my fangs.

Watch carefully, Tatsumi. Take a good look at your precious kitsune's face, for this is the last time you'll see her alive.

With a roar, I surged up, shattering the chains that held me, and the binding scattered to the wind.

Instantly, the komainu lunged at me with a snarl, jaws gaping wide to tear off my face. I stepped back, raised Kamigoroshi and impaled the lunging dog through the throat. With a ringing howl, the komainu dissolved into a swirl of crimson-and-gold mist and disappeared.

Raising Kamigoroshi, I lunged through the cloud of red, sweeping the blade down at my targets. Yumeko leaped backward with a yelp, but the shrine maiden stepped forward, raising her ofuda, in a foolish bid to intercept me. The blade sliced down, cutting into flesh, and the miko screamed as her arm dropped to the ground, severed at the elbow, bloody fingers still clutching the strip of paper.

An arrow hit me in the back, making me stagger. I turned with a growl and caught sight of the figure standing outside the ring, already nocking another arrow to his bow. He darted behind a pillar, as the tengu who had been chanting at the edge of the circle now drew swords and spears and set upon me with furious cries.

Roaring, I lunged into the midst of the warrior yokai, sword flashing. They split apart like bags of rice, blood and feathers flying through the air. As I stabbed one tengu in the throat, I reached out and snatched his spear as he fell away, tearing it from his grip. Whirling, I cut down another crow warrior and as the yokai fell, hefted the spear and hurled it through the space the falling body had left. The weapon slammed into the annoying ronin archer as he was drawing his bow, hurling him back and pinning him to the column. His mouth gaped, hands clutching at the spear through his middle, before he slumped lifelessly against the wood.

Two down. I grinned, thoroughly enjoying myself now. Spinning back, I whirled and slashed through the final ranks of tengu, carving them into pieces, until only the old daitengu was left. He did not attempt to fight or protect himself as I came in, covered in the blood of his slaughtered clan. He simply stared at me, chin raised, as I brought Kamigoroshi down and split the ancient yokai in half.

Now for the finale.

Straightening, I turned and walked back to the altar, taking a casual swipe at the softly moaning shrine maiden kneeling on the floor as I passed. The blade passed easily through the slender neck, and her head toppled forward, landing with a thump behind her. Headless, the miko slumped to the floor. I looked up, over the field of death and carnage, and met the glazed, terrified eyes of the kitsune, sitting with her back against the altar that held the scroll.

Inside, Tatsumi had gone very still. Perhaps he was gathering his strength for a final, desperate attempt to intervene. Or perhaps he realized there was nothing he could do, and was bracing himself for the inevitable. The kitsune stared at me as I approached, trembling as I stepped over the bodies of her former friends to stand before her. Her eyes were huge, glassy with horror and disbelief. But she still met my gaze steadily, as if searching for the soul trapped within. It was almost endearing, that desperate hope that somehow, even now, she could reach Tatsumi.

Shaking my head, I crouched down so that we were at eye level, seeing my reflection in her yellow fox gaze. "Did you really think this would work?" I asked with a conversational smile. "I've slaughtered armies who've stood in my way, little fox. I've killed entire temples' worth of priests and holy men who have attempted to exorcise and seal me back in the sword. One half-grown kitsune and her motley collection of misfits isn't much of a challenge." Smiling, I leaned in, lowering my voice. "I told you this day would come, didn't I?" I crooned. "I promised I would kill everyone you cared about, that everyone close to you was going to die, and I always keep my promises. Now, it's your turn, little fox. I'm afraid you've lost this game. I'm going to take the scroll fragments, the Master of Demons is going to summon the Dragon and I will finally be free of this pathetic mortal shell. But this was entertaining, and I'm not completely heartless. Before you die, I'll let you talk to Tatsumi one last time, if there is anything you want to say to him." I sat back on my heels, giving her a little room. "So, go ahead. I know he's listening. Do know that anything you say will haunt him forever, and I will take great pleasure in continuously reminding him of this moment, but this is the last time you'll ever talk to him, so I wouldn't waste it."

The kitsune closed her eyes. "Gomennasai, Tatsumi," she whispered. "Forgive me. I tried. I'm sorry we weren't strong enough to free you." Her eyes opened, golden and defiant, gazing up at me. "But whatever Hakaimono tells you, this isn't your fault. I don't regret meeting you, and if we met again under the same circumstances, I wouldn't change anything."

"Very touching," I remarked. "Are you done?"

She trembled, then took a deep breath, bracing herself. "Yes."

"Good," I said, and drove my claws through her chest, feeling bones shatter and snap, to grab her heart. "Then I'll be taking what's mine," I told both stunned onlookers, and yanked my arm back.

Blood erupted from her chest, arcing through the air in a hot stream. The fox girl gave a strangled gasp and fell sideways, striking the temple floor with a thump and a splash of crimson. Her mouth gaped, fingers twitching, before her body stilled and her golden eyes became glazed and unseeing. Blood ran down the steps from the gaping hole in her middle, coating the dais red.

From somewhere inside, there was a soundless cry of rage and horror, of hate stabbing through me like an arrow. One brief moment of pure, beautiful despair before Tatsumi's will collapsed and he slumped in numb resignation.

Silence fell over the hall. I stood, crushing the organ in my fist, then tossed it casually to the floor. Around me, the tengu and human remains lay on the wooden planks, blood and feathers scattered everywhere. At my feet, the corpse of the kitsune girl bled out on the dais, golden eyes staring at nothing. There was a hollowness in the pit of my stomach that wasn't mine, a mire of despair and self-loathing, as Tatsumi raged at his own helplessness and mourned his naive little fox girl. The first soul who had ever seen him as more than a weapon. The first person he had allowed himself to care for. His anguish was as beautiful as I had hoped. The demonslayer's spirit had been truly broken. I had won.

And yet, something didn't feel right.

Stepping over the corpse of the fox girl, I walked to the altar and snatched the Dragon scroll from its stand. The lacquered case came away easily, no final traps or hidden surprises, and I gazed at the item in my hand, curling a lip.

Such a small thing, that this entire realm loses its mind over. I shook my head. *Foolish mortals. You're never satisfied, and after all this time, you have yet to figure out that the Harbinger's wish is never granted in the way you expect.*

With a snort, I turned away from the altar, clutching my prize in a claw. *That's one piece of the Dragon scroll. Now, to find the last fragment. Where would these old birds be hiding it?*

Raising my head, I surveyed the carnage-strewn chamber one more time, brow furrowing as I gazed around at the slaughter. Something still nagged at me, a sense of disquiet I couldn't shake. What was wrong with this picture?

I breathed in slowly, and suddenly I knew. There was no smell. No scent of death, no sweet aroma of blood on the air, no reek of offal spilling from the bodies. I touched a tongue to the blood staining my claws and tasted nothing but my own sweat and skin. Amusement flickered, but beneath that, I felt the faintest ripple of unease.

Another illusion.

I clenched a fist and felt the Dragon scroll crinkle in my hand. *Like paper?* Frowning, I glanced down at it.

It was no longer a scroll.

Opening my claws, I stared in disbelief at the bundle of ofuda in my hand, dozens of them, resting in my palm. And each one of the slips of paper bore the words of a binding ritual in stark black ink. As I gaped in shock, the words flared red with power.

"Kuso!" I dropped the bundle like it was on fire, but it was too late. Like a swarm of moths, the ofuda spiraled upward, becoming streamers of light that swarmed around me. I felt the bite of chains once again, what felt like hundreds of links wrapping around me, anchoring me to the ground.

At my feet, the body of the kitsune vanished, fading to nothing in a puff of white smoke. With similar pops, the bodies of the tengu and slaughtered humans disappeared, as well. Beneath my boots, the wooden floor exploded into smoke, the walls, pillars, altar, ceiling, all turning to mist around me as I stared in shock.

The entire temple *was an illusion?*

Stunned, I gazed down at the massive binding circle surrounding me, seals upon seals, with me in the very center. As the smoke cleared, I looked up to see the dozen tengu standing around the edge, their voices rising in one unified chant.

Enraged, furious at the elaborate trick, I tried lunging forward, straining against the bonds holding me down. But this circle was huge and enormously powerful, drawing strength from the earth and the chanting of the tengu surrounding it. The longer I had stood inside its borders, the weaker I'd become. This entire ruse was created to keep me within the ring, to distract me as I wasted my time murdering illusions, as the real binding circle sapped my strength and grew more powerful by the second.

The chains around me grew even heavier, tightening around my limbs and squeezing the breath from my lungs. Clenching my jaw, I planted my feet and braced myself, determined not to kneel, not to be forced to the ground. I would not submit. The tengu could chant until their throats shriveled and the voices left their bodies, but I would not be beaten. And I would kill any who got close enough to try to end my life.

As the last of the smoke faded away, the ring parted, and a familiar face appeared at the edge of the circle. Alive. Unharmed. Minus a gaping hole where her heart should be. Her gaze met mine over the binding circle, and she stepped forward.

I smiled as she drew closer. "That…was an inspiring ruse, fox girl," I said, gathering my strength to lunge when the time was right. "I'm almost impressed. I didn't think you had the power for that sort of elaborate deception, but you *are* kitsune, after all. So, now the question becomes…are you cold-blooded enough to kill me?"

Her jaw clenched as she drew close, a shadow of both fury and anguish crossing her face, and I chuckled. "Can you do it?" I murmured. "Drive your knife into my heart and send me back into the sword, knowing your precious Tatsumi will die and his soul will go to whatever afterlife awaits?"

The kitsune shook her head, and her eyes gleamed as she looked up. "No, Hakaimono," she whispered, stopping just a lunge away. "I'm not going to kill Tatsumi, but I *am* going to send you back into the sword. On my life, you will return to Kamigoroshi, even if I must destroy my own soul in the process."

I snarled and lashed out, fighting the chains to sink one claw into the loose fabric of her robes. At the same time, the kitsune lunged *forward*, startling me, and grabbed my face with both hands. Her lips parted, mouth gaping wide, as a glowing mist shaped vaguely like a fox emerged between her teeth and hovered before me. With a jolt, I realized what she was doing and tried shoving her body away, but the fox-shaped mist dove forward, filling my vision, and the last thing I remembered was falling.

24

CHANGING FATE

Suki

From the edge of the snow-covered peak, Suki watched the huge army crawl slowly up the mountains and felt sick with terror.

"Well," Lord Seigetsu mused in a somber voice. He stood at the edge of the cliff, arms crossed, observing the dark mass of demons, monstrous yokai and other horrors scaling the peaks of the Dragon Spine. "It seems Genno has decided not to wait for Hakaimono, after all."

At his feet, Taka shivered, his single eye huge and round as he watched the demons ascend. "That's the army from my dream," he whispered. "The one that killed everyone at the temple."

"Yes," Seigetsu murmured. "Genno is no fool. His army is following the trail Hakaimono has set. At the rate they are marching, they will reach the Steel Feather temple in a few hours." He did not appear distressed or surprised, watching the demons like one would a particularly interesting *go* game. "A sound strategy. With everyone at the temple distracted by the First Oni, no one will be expecting an army to come pouring through the gates. They'll be taken by surprise and likely slaughtered in the first wave."

"No," Suki whispered. She could just make out the sweeping roof of the temple, nearly invisible against a distant mountain peak. The kitsune girl was there, as was Daisuke-sama. "Can… can we not warn them, Seigetsu-sama?" she pleaded, looking up at the silver-haired man, who raised a brow at her. "We could… fly there, and…let them know the army is coming. They could flee…before the demons arrive."

Lord Seigetsu shook his head. "I cannot," he told her quietly, making her heart sink. "I am…rather well-known at the temple, Suki-chan. They would not trust anything I had to say. Taka is a yokai—he would be attacked, perhaps killed, before he could give them any warning. The guardians there are rather fanatic about what they protect." One corner of his lip curled humorlessly, before he sobered again. "I'm afraid our hands are tied in this matter. It is likely everyone in the temple will be killed, just as Taka dreamed."

"*I* can warn them, Seigetsu-sama."

Seigetsu blinked, gazing at Suki in mild surprise. "You, Suki-chan?" he asked, and she nodded vigorously.

"They…they don't know me," she went on, stammering a bit as she tried to force the words out, to keep talking. "I'm just a wandering spirit. I can find Daisuke-sama…tell him the demons are coming. They could…flee before the army gets there. They would have a chance then, right?"

Seigetsu tilted his head, regarding her with intense golden eyes. "Perhaps," he almost whispered. "Certainly, if they had warning, they could be ready for the assault. But are you willing to face an army of monsters and the Master of Demons to save your noble, Suki-chan? Are you not afraid?"

Suki trembled, remembering the night of her own death, the demons, the terrible Yaburama, and the blood witch who had sacrificed her to the monsters. "I am afraid," she admitted. "But...I want to save Daisuke-sama. And everyone else. I don't want the demons to kill them all. Please...Lord Seigetsu. I can... warn them. Let me try."

Seigetsu smiled. "I cannot stop you, Suki-chan," he said quietly, and raised a billowy sleeve toward the distant temple. "Go, with my blessing." His eyes glimmered, and the faintest note of triumph entered his voice. "Perhaps it will take a ghost to turn the course of fate this night."

For some reason, that caused a tremor to run up Suki's spine, but she didn't pause to dwell on it. Abandoning her human image, she shivered into a formless ball of luminance, casting Seigetsu and Taka in an eerie, flickering light. For a moment, she hovered there, gathering her courage, watching the mass of demons and yokai swarm against the snow. Then, with a flare of determination, she spiraled upward, above the cliffs, and streaked in the direction of the temple.

25

The Plane of the Soul

Yumeko

The night we'd arrived at the Steel Feather temple, the white fox had been waiting for me in my dreams once more.

"You have no idea what to do against Hakaimono, do you?" he'd asked by way of greeting.

I'd bristled, then slumped. "No," I'd admitted. "Not really." We—myself, Daisuke, Okame and Reika—had spent several hours with the tengu and the daitengu, trying to come up with a plan to defeat Hakaimono without any of us getting killed. The tengu were skilled mystics and had some amount of magic power that they drew from the mountain itself, but not enough to hold Hakaimono for any length of time.

The white fox sighed. "To be young and naive again," he said, shaking his pale muzzle. "You have what you need to defeat Hakaimono, little fox. You are just not thinking like a kitsune. We are not humans, charging our enemies head-on like angry bulls. Doing battle with a fox is like trying to catch a reflection in a pond. We are shadows upon shadows, weaving our own worlds, our own realities. Entangling our enemies so thoroughly, they have no idea what is real and what is not. Nothing we present or reveal is the truth." He waved his tail thoughtfully. "But you cannot underestimate this opponent," he warned. "Hakaimono will not be fooled by simple pranks. It will take all your talent, all your fox magic, and every ounce of cunning and trickery you have, to defeat him."

"I'm not that strong," I whispered. "My illusions are simple things. I have no idea what I can do against Hakaimono."

"Do you really believe that, after all you have done? After you fooled an emperor, and drove the assassins of the Shadow Clan mad with fear?"

"Men," I agreed with a nod. "Not oni. Not demonslayers. I'll be facing Hakaimono *and* Tatsumi. Neither of them is going to be afraid of anything I can do."

"I see." The white fox gave his tail an irritated twitch. "If that is what you truly believe, then I will give you the strength you need to emerge victorious."

His mouth opened, muzzle gaping wide, and a glowing sphere of blue-white luminance emerged from his throat and floated toward me. As it drew close, I could see the ghostly flames flickering around a small white ball about the size of a human fist. It circled over my head, glowing softly from within, then drifted down until it touched the very tip of my muzzle. Cool flames tickled my nose, and I sneezed. As I did, I felt something small and round fly into my jaws and shoot down my throat, burning my tongue where it passed. I coughed and gagged, feeling like I was choking on a peach pit, but the foreign object ignored my attempts to retch it up and settled in my stomach, lighting my insides with what felt like icy flames.

I coughed once more and looked up. The white fox was watching me with an unamused look on his narrow face.

"That is my hoshi no tama," he told me. "My star ball. It contains a small amount of my power. With it, you will have the magical prowess of a dozen kitsune, perhaps more." He gave a grim smile as I gaped at him, stunned and reeling. Who was he, to have so much power? "It is very dear to me," the white fox went on, "and I would like it back when you are done. But for now, you will have the strength you need to challenge even Hakaimono, if you can stop thinking like a human and start scheming like a fox."

"Who are you?" I asked, gazing up at him. The question had been asked before, but it seemed even more important now. "Why are you helping me?"

He only gave that mysterious smile and lifted his face to the moon overhead, as if sensing something on the wind. "Hakaimono is close," he stated, making my stomach writhe in fear and anticipation. "You will have perhaps a day before he arrives, so plan wisely. Remember, Hakaimono will be expecting a trap. He knows that he cannot simply take the Dragon scroll without resistance, that the guardians here will defend the pieces of the scroll with their lives. Hakaimono assumes that he is strong enough to withstand whatever is thrown at him, and he is right. He is too powerful a foe to face head-on. So do what we do best. Dance around him. Make him think he's won. If you are very clever, you might beat Hakaimono at his own game. If you are not..." The white fox flicked his tail and began to disappear, the moonlight shining through his body as he faded from sight. "You and your friends will die, Genno will use the power of the Dragon's Wish to plunge Iwagoto into darkness and Kage Tatsumi's soul will be lost forever. Something to remember, when you face Hakaimono for the final time."

* * *

Silence throbbed in my ears, and I opened my eyes.

A shiver crept up my spine. I stood in a small forest clearing surrounded by ancient trees, great twisted branches woven together to cloak the ground in shadow. Through the canopy, the sky was an eerie bloodred, crimson light filtering through the leaves to mottle the ground.

Something rustled behind me. I turned and saw a trio of children kneeling on the ground, a stern-faced man standing beside them with his arms crossed. Two boys and a girl, no more than six or seven winters old, dressed in identical black haori and hakama trousers. Their heads were bowed, gazes fixed to the ground in front of them, but my heart twisted as I recognized the boy on the end, his small shoulders set in determination.

Tatsumi. I stepped forward, ready to call to the young demon-slayer, but paused. None of the humans looked at me or acknowledged my presence. I stood there, in plain sight of everyone, and no mention was made of the strange girl who had showed up out of nowhere.

This isn't real, I realized, staring around the glen. *It has to be a memory. One of Tatsumi's memories.* Gazing down at the younger version of Tatsumi, I felt my stomach tighten. Even at this age, he still wore the same intense, solemn expression, staring fixedly at the ground, as if trying to be unseen and invisible. Before the man and the children stood a pair of tall, gaunt figures with painted white faces and black lips. Twin gazes swept over each of them in turn. "And these are your best students?" one majutsushi asked the man standing beside the group. His voice was flat and cold, and I saw the other boy's shoulders tremble. "The most promising kami-touched children from the school?"

"Yes," replied the man, nodding to the trio at his feet. "Kage Ayame, Makoto and Tatsumi. Each has demonstrated a remarkable understanding of Shadow magic. They are the best in their class, they have mastered basic shinobi techniques and they pick up new skills almost immediately. Any one of them would serve the daimyo splendidly."

The majutsushi considered this. "And of these three," one mage asked, gazing down at the trio, "who would you consider the most worthy to serve our great lady? To bear the honor, and burden, of the next Kage demonslayer? If you had to choose, right now, which child would you send back with us?"

The man's eyes crinkled with distaste, but he answered calmly. "Ayame is the fastest," he said, a tiny hint of pride in his tone. I looked at the girl and saw the faintest of smiles cross her face, but it was gone in the next blink. "She can run circles around these two, but she's also stubborn. Has a temper. We're working on that. Makoto is a naturally gifted student, and his Shadow magic is the strongest of them all, but he lacks the ambition and drive to truly be the best." The man sighed. "Honestly, if I were to choose the next demonslayer, it would be that one," he said, and pointed to the third child, the boy on the end, who hadn't moved a muscle the entire time. "Kage Tatsumi."

"And why him?" asked the majutsushi in a raspy whisper. "What makes him so special?"

"Why Tatsumi?" Instead of answering the question, the man offered a rather mysterious smile. "Last summer," he began, "one of the village dogs had puppies. The dam was weak, and the birthing was too much for her, so she died. All the puppies died as well, except one, the smallest of the litter. This one," he continued, nodding at Tatsumi, "asked me if he could try to save it. I told him yes, he could try. So he stayed up with that puppy for several nights on end, nursing it back to health. Much to everyone's surprise, the runt lived. Soon, it began following him everywhere, lying outside the door of his classes, waiting for him. The other students called it Kagekage, the shadow's shadow, because you couldn't find one without the other. After a time, they were inseparable." The man gave a grim smile. "Until the day I put a knife in Tatsumi's hand and told him to kill it in the name of the Kage."

The man glanced down at the boy, who still hadn't moved or raised his head, though the set of his shoulders was stiff. "I ordered him to do it quickly, and to bring me proof of its death. He said nothing, but that evening he came to me, tears streaming down his face, with his puppy's head in a little lacquered box, and we buried it in the fields that night."

I felt a lump rise to my throat and blinked back tears, even as one of the majutsushi let out a long, hissing sound of satisfaction. "Excellent," he whispered. "Most encouraging." He pressed two fingers to his blackened lips, looking thoughtful. "There will be trials, of course. Tests to see which of these candidates will be chosen. But I believe we might have found our next demonslayer. Tell me, boy..." He strode forward until he was looming over Tatsumi, casting the small form in his shadow. "Do you know why you had to do what you did? Why you had to kill your dog? Answer me."

For the first time, a tremor went through Tatsumi's shoulders, small hands fisting on his knees. "I killed Kagekage," the young Tatsumi said, his soft, quiet voice making my heart ache for him, "because the Shadow Clan told me to. Because I was given a direct order. That is all I need to know to obey."

I could see the majutsushi's eyes gleam, the smile curling his lips as he straightened. "That will be all," he rasped, as the pair drew back. "You have done your job admirably, and the lady will be pleased. Students," he continued, his voice growing harsh. "You will follow us."

A distant roar echoed over the trees, making the hairs on the back of my neck stand up. No one else seemed to hear it; Tatsumi and the other two children rose obediently to their feet and began following the mages out of the clearing. But, through the trees, I could see something moving. Something huge. Limbs groaned, and branches snapped like kindling, as the massive dark shape plowed toward me through the forest.

Hakaimono, I realized, as a chill unlike anything I'd felt before slithered up my back. The First Oni in his real, terrible form, was coming for me. *I have to find Tatsumi,* I thought, backing away and looking around the clearing. *The real Tatsumi. His soul has to be here, somewhere. I have to go deeper. This is just a surface memory. I have to find Tatsumi's soul before I can face Hakaimono.*

The massive shape in the trees turned toward me, eyes like hot coals glowing through the black, and my insides twisted in fear.

"*Kitsune!*" rumbled a deep, terrible voice, making the very ground tremble. "*I know you're here, little fox! I can feel you. Show yourself, if you think you can drive me out!*"

The memory around me rippled, like a dragonfly landing on the surface of a pond. Flattening my ears, I turned and fled into the trees, away from Hakaimono, and the forest clearing faded into blackness.

I stumbled from the darkness into a small room and immediately had to leap back to avoid the robed figure rushing across the floor. When my gaze followed him across the room, my stomach twisted, and my hands flew to my mouth in horror.

Tatsumi lay on a table near the back wall, face turned toward the ceiling, staring fixedly upward. His shirt was off, and the upper half of his chest was covered in blood, spattered across his skin and dripping to the floor. Two men in ash-gray robes bustled around him, wiping away blood and pressing cloth to torn flesh. They were not being particularly gentle, I noticed, cringing as one of them poured a clear liquid from a vial onto a strip of blackened skin along Tatsumi's arm, making it bubble and smoke. Tatsumi's jaw clenched, and his fingers gripped the edge of the table until his knuckles turned white, but he didn't make a sound.

The door opened with a snap, and a man stepped into the room. Short and stocky, with sharp black eyes and strangely forgettable features, he marched up to the side of the table and glared down at the wounded demonslayer. It took me a moment to recognize him as the man I'd met in the halls of the Shadow Clan castle. Tatsumi's sensei. After a heartbeat of glowering, the man snorted and shook his head in disgust.

"Where was he found?" he muttered, sounding more irritated than relieved.

"Just inside the gate," one of the robed figures answered, not looking up from his task of bandaging the demonslayer's ravaged arm. "Taro spotted him coming just before dawn. He likely dragged himself back from wherever he was sent before collapsing from blood loss."

"How badly is he damaged? Will he live?"

"Most likely. The surface injuries will heal quickly, but the burns on his chest and arm are quite severe and will take time. Thankfully, there doesn't seem to be any nerve damage, but he is going to be in a great deal of pain until they heal."

The man snorted again. "Yes, well, maybe next time he'll remember not to stab a nue with a steel sword when it's getting ready to discharge lightning." Uncrossing his arms, he glared down at Tatsumi again. "Demonslayer," he said, bending closer to the demonslayer's face. "Can you hear me, boy?"

"I…hear you, sensei."

My throat closed up. His voice was tight with pain, but he still tried to speak calmly. The man straightened, gazing down at him without a shred of compassion. "What went wrong?" he asked in a hard voice. "I warned you about the nue's lightning shroud. This shouldn't have happened, Tatsumi."

"Forgive me, sensei," Tatsumi gritted out. "There were…"

He paused, closing his eyes, as one of the robed men splashed that clear liquid onto his chest, causing white bubbles to froth up where it landed. "There were two of them," Tatsumi went on after a moment. "The nue must've had a mate. When the first was killed, the second...ambushed me."

"Two of them." Tatsumi's sensei sounded dubious, but grim. "Well, that explains the amount of disappearances around the area. Nue are bad-tempered and territorial at the best of times. Thank the kami they're relatively rare. Did you kill the second one?"

"Yes...sensei," Tatsumi answered.

"Good. That means you don't have to go hunting it again when you're back on your feet." The man straightened and looked up at the robed figures. "Keep me updated on his condition. If he worsens or looks like he's going to die, inform me at once."

"Yes, sir."

The man stepped back, but I saw him pause, just a moment, gazing down at the suffering demonslayer. A flicker of what might have been sympathy went through his eyes, though it was gone between one blink and the next. Without another word to the severely wounded Tatsumi, the man turned and left the room. As the healers went back to work on the demonslayer, Tatsumi set his jaw and cast his gaze to the ceiling, staring again at nothing.

I bit my lip to keep my eyes from blurring. My heart ached, wishing I could go to him and take his hand, just to let him know he wasn't alone. That someone in his harsh, lonely existence cared if he lived or died. But this was just another memory; the two healers continued their work without looking at me, and on the table, the demonslayer lay silent and long-suffering. Waiting for it to be over.

Deeper, I thought. *Tatsumi's soul isn't here. I have to go deeper.*

371

Turning from the grisly scene, I walked away, following Tatsumi's sensei out the door, and the world faded around me.

Hakaimono followed me. I couldn't always see or hear him, but I could feel him; a terrifying dark presence looming ever closer. Chasing me through the layers of Tatsumi's consciousness. Sometimes I would flee a memory knowing he was right on my heels, that if I waited another moment, he would reach out and snatch me. It didn't help that I had no idea where I was going. I was lost in the labyrinth of Tatsumi's mind, where each memory was darker, bloodier and more depressing than the last. All I knew was that I had to reach his soul, that it was here somewhere, in this bleak landscape tainted by Hakaimono's presence, and I had to keep looking until I found it.

Once more, I found myself in a forest clearing, the sky a mottled red and black through the trees. An old stone well sat in the center of the clearing, outlined in the crimson light of the moon and sky. It cast a long, menacing shadow over the grass, and made my skin crawl just looking at it.

A shiver went through the clearing, and Tatsumi materialized out of the trees like a shadow becoming real. In one hand, Kamigoroshi was unsheathed and glowed a subtle purple against the eerie crimson light.

The demonslayer walked steadily across the clearing until he stood a few feet from the well. Overhead, the full moon emerged from behind a cloud, casting sickly red beams over the lone figure standing motionless in the grass.

A pale hand rose from the darkness of the well, grasping the edge of the stones. Another followed, as something white and ragged clawed its way out of the hole; a woman in a dripping white burial gown, long hair covering her face. Her hands were twisted claws, curved nails glinting in the light, and her skin was a pallid bluish-gray. As I shrank back in horror, the yurei turned its head toward Tatsumi, who stood his ground as the specter crawled off the edge of the well and staggered toward him.

"Am I…pretty?" it whispered, its voice turning my blood to ice. Both arms reached toward Tatsumi, water dripping from its gray skin to vanish into the grass. "Am I…beautiful?" It raised its head, and I saw the streaks of crimson running down its robe from its slit throat, the dead white eyes peering through the curtain of hair. "Will you love me?"

"No, Mizu Tadako." Tatsumi's voice surprised me. Calm and almost gentle. "The bones of a dozen priests and holy men lie at the bottom of your well. The time for exorcism is past." He raised his sword, and the cold purple glow of Kamigoroshi washed over his face, which looked solemn and determined in the flickering light. "Wherever Kamigoroshi sends you, may your spirit find peace."

The specter's face contorted with rage, and she lunged at Tatsumi with a bone-numbing scream.

"Found you, little fox."

My blood went cold for a different reason, and my stomach turned inside out with fear, as *his* presence materialized behind me. Without thinking, I leaped forward, feeling something catch the ends of my hair as I darted away. Heart pounding, I ran for the center of the clearing, where Tatsumi and the ghost woman were swirling around each other, her furious shrieks echoing over the trees. Without looking back, I vaulted onto the edge of the well and, before I lost my nerve, dropped into the yawning blackness, hearing Hakaimono's snarl of frustration follow me into the dark.

I hit the ground hard but managed to turn the fall into a roll and tumbled to a painful stop at the base of a wall. Wincing, I pushed myself upright and looked around, wondering where I'd ended up this time.

I shivered. A massive castle loomed before me, silhouetted

black against the eerie red sky. Lightning flashed through the clouds, unnatural strands glowing purple-black, and in the flickering nonlight, I recognized this place. Hakumei-jo, the castle of the Shadow Clan, sat before me like a great, patient beast. But it was somehow darker and more twisted than its counterpart in the real world. Fat red vines slithered over its walls and coiled around corners, pulsing like they were alive. Small, misshapen things crawled along the tiered roofs, staring down at me with eyes like hot coals. The darkness here seemed a living thing; shadows moved and crawled along the ground and walls, attached to nothing but still reaching out for me.

And suddenly, I knew.

He's here. Tatsumi's soul…is somewhere inside the castle.

Somewhere overhead, nearly drowned by the moaning of the wind through the courtyard, there was a muffled roar that made my stomach drop. Hakaimono was still coming.

I raced up the steps to the castle, making sure not to step on the fat red vines that pulsed angrily as I approached, and pulled open the heavy wooden doors at the top. They groaned, reluctantly swinging back, and I slipped through the opening into the blackness beyond.

Inside, the halls and corridors were dark, the walls and polished floors covered with more heaving crimson vines that slithered in from the windows and pushed through cracks in the wood. The castle itself seemed to be breathing, the walls expanding and contracting, though I couldn't tell if that was my imagination.

Tatsumi, I thought, gazing around in dismay. *Where are you?*

From somewhere deep below, I got an answer. The faintest pulse of a heartbeat, barely noticeable, vibrating through the castle. I took a deep breath and darted forward, and the shadows closed around me.

26

BATTLE FOR THE
STEEL FEATHER TEMPLE

Suki

She barely made it in time.

Daisuke-sama, Suki thought, flying over the walls of the temple. Behind her, frighteningly close, she could hear the panting of demons, the scrape of claws and talons against rock. The sounds terrified her, but she forced herself into her human image, gazing around wildly. *Where are you?*

She saw him then, in the center of the stone courtyard, his white hair and bright haori standing out against the dark. Figures surrounded him, robed creatures with claws and great black wings growing from their shoulders. *More monsters,* Suki thought, balking in fear. The birdlike creatures stood in a large circle, two fingers held out before each of them, chanting words that made the air shiver like heat waves.

Suki looked down, catching sight of what the ring of bird

monsters had surrounded, and would have gasped if she'd had the breath.

A terrible demon lay in the center of the circle, an oni with skin as black as ink and a wild white mane framing his face. His eyes were closed, though his lids twitched and his clawed fingers spasmed, as if he was caught in the throes of a nightmare. Glowing chains, seeming to have emerged from the stones themselves, wrapped around the oni's limbs and chest, pinning him to the ground and throbbing as if they were alive.

Beside the demon, lying on her back with her hands folded across her stomach in the death pose, was the kitsune. The same kitsune that Suki had guided through Lady Satomi's castle the night she had come to rescue the priest. The fox girl's skin was as pale as parchment, her face slack and her body limp. A shrine maiden, her lips pressed into a tight line, knelt at her side, one slender hand on the kitsune's forehead. *Dead,* Suki thought in terror and a sudden, surprising grief. *The fox girl is dead. The demon must have killed her.*

But as she drifted closer, the shrine maiden let out a breath that almost sounded like she was fighting back a sob. "Hang in there, Yumeko," Suki heard the miko whisper. "If anyone can bring back Kage-san, it will be you. You're too damn stubborn to let Hakaimono win."

Suki was almost to the edge of the circle now. She could see Daisuke's face, grim and solemn as he stared at the two figures on the ground, as if expecting something to happen. Everyone, from the humans to the bird monsters to even the small orange dog sitting beside the miko, seemed focused on the two bodies in the center of the ring. But as she drew close, her light falling over the hunched shoulders of the figures surrounding the pair, Taiyo Daisuke raised his head and spotted her.

"S-Suki-san?"

Suki froze at hearing her name on his lips. Everyone glanced up at her, and she suddenly found herself pinned by a dozen wide, startled gazes.

Taiyo Daisuke blinked, gave his head a tiny shake as if to clear it, then stared at her again, eyes wide. "It…it is you, isn't it?" he breathed. "Just like that night in Satomi's castle. I thought…I heard your voice. It was you, after all." His brow furrowed, as the beady eyes of the crow monsters seemed to bore into her from all sides. "Why have you come, Suki-san?" he asked in a faintly sad voice. "Do you desire vengeance? Are you here to haunt me for my failure?"

No! Suki shook her head violently. *Never, Daisuke-sama,* she wanted to say. *I would never do anything to make you unhappy.* But the words stuck in her throat, refusing to emerge past her lips, and she could only shake her head in mute denial.

"Hitodama." The shrine maiden rose, her eyes hard, and stepped away from the motionless bodies of the demon and kitsune. "You have helped us before, so I can only assume you have come for the same reason. But our time is short, and we are in the middle of a very dangerous procedure. We cannot spare much time or attention, so be brief. Why are you here?"

"Demons."

Suki's voice was still a whisper, but it rose into the air, causing everyone to straighten immediately. "Genno's army…is coming," Suki continued into the horrified silence that followed. "They have…followed Hakaimono…to this place. They intend to kill everyone!" Her gaze met Daisuke's, pleading. "You must flee…before they arrive!"

No sooner had the words left her mouth than a booming howl echoed from the direction of the gates, causing everyone to spin around. Suki could suddenly hear them, dozens of claws and boots and feet, scraping against stone, climbing the steps, and despair squeezed her throat. It was too late. She was too late. The army had arrived.

"They're already here." One of the bird monsters stepped forward. Unlike the others, his skin was bright red, a huge crimson nose stabbing the air before him. "They've come for the scroll fragment. I must protect it at all costs!" He spun on the other bird monsters, eyes narrowed and teeth bared as he pointed toward the temple. "Do not let them into the sacred hall. Whatever it takes, we cannot let the scroll pieces fall to the Master of Demons!"

A shriek rang across the stones. Suki looked up and felt terror swallow her in an immobilizing wave. Creatures were spilling into the courtyard, a horde of demons, yokai and other beings straight out of nightmares. Tiny creatures with tattered ears and a mouthful of pointed teeth swarmed over the rocks, cackling and waving crude weapons. A centipede the size of a horse scuttled over the wall, its segmented black carapace glinting in the moonlight. An enormous bloated creature with eight spindly limbs and the pale face of a woman crawled up to perch on a tower, smiling as she observed the chaos below.

Suki trembled, watching the demons approach, waiting for the moment the small group around her would scatter. But instead of fleeing, the winged bird monsters raised their spears and surged forward with defiant battle cries. They met the army in the center of the courtyard, and pandemonium erupted.

A familiar laugh jerked Suki out of her daze. Stunned, she looked up to see Daisuke draw his weapon, a fierce, defiant smile on his face as he took a step toward the approaching horde.

"Come, Okame-san!" he said, raising his sword in front of him. "Our glorious death approaches. Let us meet it with honor."

The other man cursed and sent an arrow streaking into the chaos. "What about Yumeko?" he panted, putting a second dart through the throat of a giant, bipedal rat racing toward them. "We can't leave her unprotected, she'll get torn to pieces. Reika-san?"

With a howl, the tiny dog at the miko's feet reared up, becoming a huge red creature with a golden mane and massive paws. The shrine maiden pulled an ofuda from her sleeves and brandished it before her. "We still don't know what's happening to her inside Kage-san," she snapped, hurling the slip of paper at the raging battle, where it exploded in a burst of fire. "She won't wake unless her spirit returns to her body—she must still be looking for the demonslayer's soul, or fighting Hakaimono. They probably don't know what's happening."

The archer yelped, ducking as a spear hurtled toward him, then put an arrow into the demon that had thrown it. "Well, if we don't retreat, she won't have a body to return to!" he snarled. "We're too exposed out here—we need to fall back."

More monsters swarmed the courtyard. The miko's guardian roared as it reared up and crushed a giant centipede beneath its paws. The shrine maiden grimaced and fell back a step, looking desperate, then her gaze snapped to Suki.

"You..." she breathed, but at that moment a booming howl shook the air, and an enormous flying head, teeth bared and trailing orange flames, fell toward them like a boulder.

27

FINDING THE LOST

Yumeko

*T*he shadows were stalking me.

How long I had been here, in the darkest recesses of Tatsumi's soul, I wasn't certain. Dark, featureless things haunted my steps, trailing me down the narrow corridors and through empty rooms. I didn't know what they were; their inky black forms resembled men, samurai or shinobi following me through the halls of the castle, living shadows come to life. Perhaps they were part of Hakaimono's influence, perhaps they were Tatsumi's fears and regrets, pieces of himself he had lost. I just knew I didn't want to run into them.

The shadows weren't the only things chasing me. Somewhere in the vine-choked castle, Hakaimono's dark presence stalked the corridors, getting ever closer. I could feel his cold amusement through the very walls, patiently searching for me, knowing our paths would eventually cross. I couldn't hide from him forever. Once or twice, I knew he was close, perhaps just another corridor away, a few thin paper walls separating us. I could feel his footsteps through the floor, making the air shiver. Grimly, I pressed on, hopelessly lost, following a faint heartbeat that called to me like a beacon.

Deeper.

Finally, after a few minutes or a lifetime of searching, the hallways came to an end, and I knew I couldn't turn back. Before me, at the end of the corridor, a wooden stairwell led down into utter blackness. Standing at the edge, I closed my eyes and listened, feeling a weak pulse of life somewhere far below.

Calling a tiny ball of foxfire to my hand, I descended into the dark.

I seemed to venture into the depths of the earth itself. Or perhaps the darkest parts of the soul. When the steps finally ended, I stepped into a large chamber, the floors and walls made of worked stone, with heavy wooden beams holding up the ceiling. Torches with sickly purple flames flickered in brackets along the walls and pillars, casting eerie shadows over the rows of cells lining the room. Thick iron bars, rusty and ancient-looking, were set deep into the stone, with no doors or keyhole visible.

A quiet moan drifted out from one of the cells, and my heart clenched.

Tatsumi? Are you here?

Still holding the globe of kitsune-bi, I padded up to the first set of bars and peeked inside.

I gasped. A child sat against the back corner of the cell, his knees drawn to his chest and his arms wrapped around them. I extended my hands through the bars, and the foxfire washed over the face of a young boy with glimmering purple eyes, his dark hair falling into his face.

"Tatsumi?" I called, and the boy raised his head. His tear-ful, wide-eyed gaze met mine, though he seemed to stare right through me.

"I can't do it, sensei," the young Tatsumi whispered. "I'm scared. That voice…it's always in my head now, always whispering. I can't shut it out. Master Ichiro, please let me go home."

Master Ichiro? Tatsumi's sensei? I thought back to the man with the cold, impassive eyes, imagined him standing motionless over this boy, stone-faced as Tatsumi pleaded and cried, and clenched my jaw. *Ichiro-san did care about you, Tatsumi. He could just never show it.*

"Stop it," the young Tatsumi whispered, curling in on himself. "Please, make it go away. I'm scared. I can't do this anymore."

And, before my shocked gaze, he flickered and faded away, and I was staring into an empty cell.

Not Tatsumi, I thought in a daze, backing away from the bars. *Not the real him, anyway.* Perhaps that was a memory he had locked away, an emotion he had suppressed. I remembered something Hakaimono told me, so long ago it seemed, when he had first taken over the demonslayer.

You distract him, make him feel things. Made him question who he is and what he wants, and that's all the invitation I needed.

And then the final, terrible blow. *His last thought tonight, before finally losing himself, was of you.*

I shivered. I realized now why Tatsumi had been so cold, why he never spoke much and kept himself apart, aloof from everyone. Why he suppressed all pain, fear, anger and grief. Not because he was a soulless killer, but to keep the oni in his mind at bay. If Hakaimono spoke the truth, and I was the one responsible for the demon's release from the sword, then I would have to be the one who shoved him back and slammed the door in his face so that he couldn't ever return to torture us.

But first, before I had to face Hakaimono, I would find Tatsumi and tell him how sorry I was, that I never meant for this to happen. If I failed, and the First Oni was too much for me, after all, then at least Tatsumi would know I had kept my promise. He would know that someone cared enough to try to save him, and not because he was a weapon or a pawn in an endless game. Because I had seen a glimpse of the boy beneath the demonslayer's icy mask, and *that* was whom I was trying to rescue.

And then, I had a sudden, sobering realization. If I succeeded here, if I managed to drive Hakaimono back into Kamigoroshi, I would never see that boy again. Not with a thwarted, enraged oni lord poised to seize control of the demonslayer's heart and soul at the slightest moment of weakness. No doubt Tatsumi would have to be doubly vigilant against the demon's influence in his mind, which meant he could never let down his guard, with Hakaimono…or with me.

I shook my head, angry with my selfish thoughts. My personal feelings for the Kage demonslayer, whatever they might be, were not important. As long as Tatsumi was free of Hakaimono in the end, I would risk everything to see the demon sealed back in the sword once more.

A tremor went through the ground beneath my feet, a ripple of sheer black anger that seemed to emanate from the very walls. The shadows around me grew long, like grasping talons reaching out, searching for me. Hakaimono was close. I had to keep moving.

I saw flickers of movement within the cells as I continued through the dungeon, flashes from the corner of my eye as I passed. Sometimes voices drifted to me, snatches of words or hints of a conversation I couldn't quite make out. I kept moving, feeling guilty as I hurried past Tatsumi's hidden fears and darkest memories. The emotions he kept locked away even from himself.

After a while, though, the cells grew silent, empty, and it began to grow cold. My breath writhed into the air, as ice started to form on the walls, coating the bars and hanging in glistening spikes from the ceiling. Shivering, I pressed on, a globe of kitsune-bi the only light in the pitch-blackness, blue-white flames dancing and sparkling off the ice as I continued.

And then, quite abruptly, I hit a dead end: a solid wall of ice at the end of the corridor. I turned and gazed back down the hall, wondering if there was a side passage. Had I missed a door that led to another part of this frozen labyrinth? No. I knew that I hadn't overlooked anything, just as I knew that Tatsumi's soul was here, somewhere.

Facing the wall of ice, I reached out and put a tentative hand on the frozen barrier, feeling a burning cold sear my palms and fingertips like a flame.

And I felt it. A pulse. A glimmer of emotion, somewhere on the other side.

My heart leaped. He was here. Beyond this last barrier, just out of reach. But how was I going to get to him? If I had the means, I would chip away the ice wall bit by bit until I had broken through, but our time was running out. Hakaimono would soon be here. I had to reach Tatsumi now.

Here, in the realm of dreams, your foxfire is as deadly as you need it to be.

Taking a few steps back, I raised both arms, fingers spread wide toward the obstacle blocking my path. I called my foxfire and felt it surge through my body, up my arms, and spring to life in my hands, blue-white flames that illuminated the darkness like a torch. With a mental howl, I gathered up my magic and in one strong push, sent a column of kitsune-bi toward the wall of ice. Where the ghostly flames struck, the wall let out an earsplitting hiss, as if in pain, and steam billowed away like the breath of a dragon, coiling around me and snapping at my hair and clothes. But it wasn't melting fast enough.

Brighter, I thought at it, pouring more magic into the flames.

Brighter, hotter. Cut through this barrier like a sword through a shoji screen. I am so close to reaching Tatsumi, and this will not stop me!

Suddenly, impossibly, the ice itself caught fire, igniting like a sheet of parchment held to a flame. Kitsune-bi roared as it engulfed the entire wall, and steam billowed out until it was impossible to see through the swirling clouds of white. Squinting, I turned away, raising an arm to shield my face until the steam dispersed and the foxfire flickered out, plunging the hallway into darkness again.

For a heartbeat, it was like something had swallowed me. Swiftly, I opened my palm, and a tiny globe of foxfire sputtered to life once more, illuminating a gaping hole where the ice wall had been...and something dangling from the ceiling in the chamber beyond.

Tatsumi. Without thinking, I ducked through the gap into a room as dark and empty as the bottom of a fathomless pit. The ground under my feet glittered like an ocean of needles, and my sandals crinkled against the frozen ground as I hurried forward, sending brittle echoes rippling through the dark.

"Tatsumi?"

My voice sounded tiny in the soaring blackness, the words muffled by shadow and void. An ominous glow burned against the dark, coming from a tangle of glowing red chains that hung from the black of the ceiling and stabbed up from the floor, an evil web that converged in the center of the room. A figure dangled from the chains, held spread-eagle with head down and eyes closed. There were no shackles or cuffs locked around its limbs; the glowing links stabbed *into* its body and disappeared beneath its flesh.

"Tatsumi!"

Sprinting beneath the web, I gazed up at the motionless figure, my heart twisting painfully in my throat. Tatsumi didn't move or open his eyes; he hung limply in the chains, his body flickering with a subtle light.

I swallowed hard and reached for him, feeling evil energy pulsing from the links, as if trying to suck away all life. "Tatsumi," I called once more, though my voice came out breathy and choked. "I'm here. I came, like I promised. Can you hear me?"

For a few heartbeats, there was no answer. Then, a tiny furrow creased Tatsumi's brow. His eyelids fluttered, cracked open, and I saw the faintest glimmer of violet as he peered down at me.

"Yumeko." His voice was a breath, a whisper of disbelief and hope. "You're...here? But, I thought..." Slowly, as if in pain, he shook his head. "I saw Hakaimono kill you."

"Illusions," I told him softly, my voice rather shaky with relief. "Shadows, tricks and fox magic, Tatsumi. Nothing Hakaimono saw was real."

"Are *you* real?" Tatsumi whispered. "Or is this...another dream? I can't tell anymore." A ripple of anguish crossed his face, and he closed his eyes. "No," he muttered. "I don't dare hope... She'll just be gone when I look up again."

My vision blurred, and I blinked rapidly to clear it. "I'm not a dream," I told him, taking another step. "I'm not going to disappear this time, Tatsumi. Look at me." Those piercing eyes fixed on me again, and I tried not to shiver under that intense gaze. "I promised I would come," I whispered. "I'm not going to let Hakaimono win. If he wants you, he's going to have to kill me, first."

Kitsune-bi flared to life in my palms. I glared up at the evil chains, which flickered and spat and curled tighter around Tatsumi, as if knowing I had come to destroy them. I hesitated a moment longer, watching the ominous pulse and flicker, then reached up and wrapped my fingers around the throbbing links.

Pain seared my hand. I gasped, but set my jaw and hung on,

as blue-white foxfire flared and sputtered against the angry glow of the chains. They hissed, sending strands of red-black lightning arcing down the links, making everything pulse wildly. Overhead, Tatsumi cried out, clenching his fists and arching his head back, making my heart twist. Beneath my fingers, I could feel the chain writhing and squirming, as if it was alive. My palm was on fire, burning, bringing tears to my eyes. I wanted, so badly, to let go. I suddenly felt that if I hung on too long, I, too, would become trapped, tangled in Hakaimono's will with no hope of freeing myself or the soul I'd come to save.

With a growl, I flattened my ears and pictured the foxfire in my hands, imagining a white-hot inferno that could melt steel and burn away all the evil in the world. *You can't have him,* I snarled at the web of chains, at Hakaimono himself, wherever he was. *I will fight to the death if I have to. Let him go!*

The kitsune-bi surged up with a roar, stronger than I'd ever felt, swallowing the glowing links in my hand and racing up the length of chain. Beneath my fingers, the chain shook wildly... and then dissolved as the foxfire consumed it, turning to black smoke that coiled away into nothingness. Kitsune-bi raced up the links, engulfing the entire web as, for a moment, the blaze of blue-white foxfire was almost too bright to look at.

With a shriek that sounded almost human, the tangle of chains vanished into the surge of kitsune-bi, becoming dark wisps that curled away into the void. With nothing left to consume, the foxfire flared once more and flickered out, plunging the room into darkness.

Tatsumi, freed at last from the soul-sucking chains, dropped to the ground.

For a moment, he knelt there, head bowed, shoulders heaving with deep, ragged breaths. Heart pounding, I dropped in front of him and peered into his face. His eyes were closed, his skin ashen, but the subtle light that had been emanating from within was growing brighter.

"Tatsumi?" Very softly, I touched his shoulder. "Are you all right?"

The demonslayer took another deep breath and slowly straightened, gazing down at his hands, as if still expecting to see chains stabbing beneath his flesh. "They're gone," he panted, and clenched both fists. "I'm...free. I never thought..." Brilliant indigo eyes finally rose to mine, slowly focusing as all the pain, despair and hopelessness began falling away. "Yumeko," he whispered, still sounding uncertain that what he saw was real. Carefully, one hand rose, the fingertips brushing my cheek, and then his rough, calloused palm was against my skin.

"You're here," Tatsumi breathed, and in that open, soulful gaze, everything I was going to say seemed inadequate. I lunged forward and threw my arms around him, pressing my face to his neck as I hugged him close.

I could feel his shock; for a moment he went rigid, frozen in the sudden embrace. Very gradually, his muscles uncoiled, his shoulders relaxed and his arms came up to wrap around me. Tentative at first, as if he was unsure of what to do. But then, he let out a breath, and it seemed to release all the fear, uncertainty, horror and doubt of the past nightmare. He crushed me to his chest, clinging to me like a lifeline, like I was his sanity and he was afraid I would abandon him.

"Arigatou," he murmured in my ear, and his voice came out choked. I closed my eyes and savored the feel of him in my arms, his heartbeat against mine. "Yumeko...thank you. I won't forget this."

A deep chuckle, low and ominous, vibrated the air around us. "Well," came the cold, amused voice of the First Oni, echoing through the dark and making the ground quake. "Wasn't that entertaining. Congratulations, fox, you found Tatsumi, but there's nowhere left to run. Now, he can watch as I tear your soul into little pieces and scatter it to the winds."

I felt Tatsumi shudder as we pulled apart, his hands curling into fists. My insides twisted with fear, but I rose with the demonslayer and glared into the void, feeling the oni's presence all around us.

A soul cannot be killed, the white fox had said. *A soul cannot be permanently destroyed, but it can be weakened, sickened, injured. And, sometimes, it can be broken. If you want to drive Hakaimono back into the sword, you must weaken the First Oni enough for Kage Tatsumi to force him out by strength of will. But beware; souls are fragile things. If Hakaimono is too strong, if he breaks your spirit, it will flee back into its body, and from then on, you will not be the same.*

"I'm not running anymore," I called, my voice echoing through the emptiness. "On my life, I'm not leaving this place until Tatsumi is truly free and you are sealed back into the sword for good!"

Tatsumi moved beside me. He was glowing brightly now, the halo around him throwing back the darkness, though the look in his eyes made my skin prickle. "Come then, Hakaimono," he said, his voice hard with determination. "There isn't room in here for the both of us, and you've been using my body for far too long." He raised a hand, and light swelled between his fingers, extending into a beam of luminance, before it flared into a sword. "I will not allow you to commit any more atrocities in my name. Show yourself, unless you're afraid to face the true owner of what you've stolen."

Hakaimono chuckled again, and it turned into a deep, terrible laugh that boomed through the void and caused the ice at our feet to crack and shake apart. "Very well, Tatsumi," he rumbled, as I pressed close to the demonslayer, staring into the darkness to discern our enemy. "If you're so eager to watch me shred your fox girl and beat you back into submission, I'll be happy to comply. This time, your spirit will be so broken, you won't even know who you are when I'm done with you. Are you ready for me, little mortals? Here I come."

I felt his approach before I saw it; from the void above, something dropped toward us like a boulder, huge and dark, with eyes like glowing embers in the night. It hit the ground like the tetsubo of a god striking the earth, and the shock wave radiating out from the crater shattered the ice into millions of shards that swirled around us like a crystal blizzard. As the tremors faded and the earth stilled, I lowered my arm and stared up... and up...into the face of a demon.

The First Oni, the great demon general of Jigoku, towered over us, his mouth split into a shining grin that chilled the blood in my veins. He was huge, far bigger than Yaburama, the oni that had destroyed the Silent Winds temple and killed everyone there. His skin was as black as ink, with glowing red runes crawling up his arms, words and symbols I didn't recognize. When I tried to read them, they burned my eyes, making me flinch and turn my gaze away. Ember horns, flickering and pulsing like they were on fire, sprouted from his forehead, shoulders and down his back, and a wild white mane framed his terrible face. One claw-tipped hand clutched not a tetsubo or spiked club, but a curved sword with a blade that shone like obsidian, as dark and evil-looking as its owner.

For a moment, Hakaimono stood there, smiling, letting us gaze up at him in horror. I stared into the face of the greatest oni of Jigoku and felt much like a cricket that had foolishly decided to stand up to a cat.

Hakaimono's ancient, burning gaze met mine, and the First Oni chuckled. "You look surprised, little fox," he said in a mocking tone. "Was this not what you were expecting? Did you think my true form looked like Tatsumi with horns and sharp teeth?" He grinned, and at my side, Tatsumi took a step forward, placing himself between me and Hakaimono, his glare never leaving the monster towering over us. Hakaimono glanced at him and chuckled again. "Tatsumi always knew. He could feel me, like a stain in his soul, a shadow over everything. He knew, that if that shadow emerged, he would be consumed."

He cocked his head, gazing down at us in an almost patronizing manner. "My, but you mortals are tiny and pathetic, aren't you? I could make this sporting, I suppose. Stomping on you like insects seems rather barbaric, something a brute like Yaburama would do. He never understood that the moment of death, when you see the soul fleeing your opponent's eyes, the moment they understand they're dead—*that* is the most beautiful thing in the world." The eagerness on his face made my skin crawl. "I always wanted to fight you face-to-face, demonslayer," the oni continued. "Don't disappoint me, now."

He raised his arms and vanished in a cloud of flame that seemed to burst out of his skin. The conflagration flared for just a moment, making me wince and turn away. As suddenly as they appeared, however, the flames vanished, and I stared at the figure left behind.

A human-sized Hakaimono grinned at my stunned expression. He was much smaller now, but his size wasn't all that had changed. He was leaner, not quite as bulky and massive, though the muscles rippling under his inky skin were like cords of steel. His head was still crowned with glowing ember horns, and his mane hung to the center of his back. He looked...almost human now; a supremely dangerous warrior, his obsidian blade held loosely at his side. And strangely, this form was even scarier than the enormous oni lord that had towered over us a few seconds ago.

"There," Hakaimono said, his voice soft and lethal. He raised his sword and smiled at us across the blade. "Now we will see who is truly worthy to control this body. Because I will never willingly return to that cursed sword. You're going to have to force my broken, bloodied soul back into that endless torture. So, Tatsumi…" He turned that humorless grin on the demon-slayer. "Are you strong enough to defeat me?"

"Maybe not alone," Tatsumi answered in an equally soft voice. "But it's not just me now. I don't have to do this by myself." His gaze flicked to me, and something in that look made my heart pound. With a tiny smile, Tatsumi turned back to Hakaimono. "The question is—are *you* strong enough to face us both?"

Hakaimono smirked. "We shall see," he said, and sank into a low stance, eyes glowing, the terrible black blade held behind him. "Winner takes this body, loser returns to oblivion. Let's play."

28

KITSUNE-BI AND DEMONFIRE

TATSUMI

I would not lose this fight.

Alone, I wouldn't stand a chance. I knew that. I had lived with Hakaimono long enough to know that he was stronger than me. Even here, in the realm of the soul, Hakaimono's will and sheer power would quickly overwhelm my own. Were I to face the demon myself, I would fall, and he would take over once more.

But, I wasn't alone. *She* was here. And just her presence made me stronger, gave me a reason not only to fight, but to win. I could see her beside me, determination outlining every part of her, her golden eyes shining with resolve. Her fox ears stood tall and proud, her white-tipped tail bristling behind her, reminding me of what she was, but instead of being revolting, it filled me with hope. Yumeko wasn't a warrior or a samurai; she couldn't wield holy magic or the power of the kami, but she was a kitsune who had outsmarted everything that had stood against her. She had done the impossible: fooled Hakaimono, possessed a demon lord and freed the soul he held captive. Together, we had a chance.

Though this wouldn't be easy, by any means.

For a moment, Hakaimono was motionless, his blade and inky skin blending into the void around us. His horns and eyes glowed red in the blackness, and I could feel the energy gathering around him, the drawing of terrible power. Raising my sword, I forced my muscles to relax, preparing myself to respond when Hakaimono moved.

I was almost too slow. One second, the oni was frozen against the void, the next he was in front of me, and that obsidian blade was scything toward my face. I leaped back on instinct, bringing up my sword, and felt the jarring screech of the two blades vibrate up my spine. Hakaimono didn't give me time to recover. He pressed forward with blindingly quick blows that set me scrambling backward, desperately fending them off. The clang and shriek of swords echoed around us, sparks flying between the blades and flashing across the demon's savage grin.

With a brilliant flare of light, something streaked toward Hakaimono's back, and the oni spun, ducking his head as a sphere of blue-white flames flashed between his horns, setting a few strands of hair aflame. Spinning back, he blocked my thrust to his heart and responded with a vicious swipe at my head that forced me to retreat a few steps. But then another globe of fox-fire streaked through the darkness, and Hakaimono couldn't dodge quickly enough. As he whirled around, the kitsune-bi struck his sword arm and exploded in a brilliant flash of light.

The oni's snarl of pain shocked me. Foxfire was nothing but light and illusion; it wasn't dangerous unless you did something foolish and let it lure you into the unknown. But as Hakaimono lowered his arm, I saw the curls of smoke rising from his skin, and his lips were pulled back in a grimace of pain. Somehow,

Yumeko's kitsune-bi had turned deadly, deadly enough to burn an oni lord.

"Well. Wasn't that a surprise." Hakaimono's voice was soft, dangerous, as he turned his full attention on Yumeko. His arm was already healing, singed flesh becoming full and healthy in a matter of heartbeats. "You've picked up a few tricks, little fox. I see I'm going to have to take you a bit more seriously, after all."

Yumeko, standing defiant with her ears laced back and her hands glowing with foxfire, met the oni's terrible smile and didn't back down. "Come on then, Hakaimono," she challenged, and suddenly, her body split apart, becoming two, six, ten, twelve Yumekos, surrounding us in a circle. Hakaimono's brows arched, and the ring of kitsune grinned. "Catch me if you can."

I flew at the oni with a snarl, slashing my blade toward his neck, hoping to catch him off guard. With an almost irritated growl, he blocked my sword and surprised me by lashing out with a long arm, sharp claws reaching for my eyes. I dodged back, but not quickly enough, and curved black talons raked four deep gouges across my cheek.

Pain exploded through my face, and the force of the blow sent me tumbling sideways. There was no blood as I rolled upright, though I certainly felt the throbbing agony slashed across my skin, pieces of my soul that had been ripped away. I swiped a sleeve across my face and looked up, just as the ring of Yumeko gave a unified shout of fury and hurled a dozen spheres of foxfire at the oni between us. Hakaimono hunched his shoulders and shielded his face as they all converged in the center, and the globes of kitsune-bi slammed into him with the roar of an inferno. The First Oni disappeared into the blaze, and for a moment, the blue-white conflagration snapped and flickered like an enraged phoenix in the center of the void.

I took a breath and lowered my arm, as the army of kitsune disappeared with pops of white smoke until only one was left.

As the flames of kitsune-bi began to flicker and die, she turned and gave me a triumphant smile, the ghostly light of the foxfire dancing in her eyes.

A low chuckle cut through the darkness, making us freeze, and Hakaimono stepped out of the flames. Kitsune-bi clung to him, blue-white flames snapping around his shoulders and up his arms. He was definitely hurt; ribbons of red smoke rose from his skin, fragments of his spirit coiling away into the darkness. But he was far from defeated, and the grin on his face, lit an eerie blue in the snapping of foxfire, was chilling.

"Is that all you got?" he asked Yumeko, whose ears flattened at the sight of the First Oni, striding out of the inferno seemingly unharmed. "Granted, I'll give credit where it's due—that hurt like hell. But you're forgetting something, fox." He raised his arms, kitsune-bi dancing up and down his flesh. "The fires of Jigoku flow through the veins of all oni. Our very souls are suffused with its power. You can't kill a demon with fire, even obnoxiously bright foxfire, any more than you can drown a kappa. But congratulations, I'll stop toying with you now."

He flourished his sword and raised it in front of him, and the kitsune-bi dancing along his shoulders flared a sullen black and red. Hakaimono breathed deep, as hellish flames erupted from his skin, swallowing the foxfire and bathing the oni in a red glow. They flickered down the length of his black sword, turning the weapon into a fiery brand, and the heat radiating from the demon became palpable. Lowering his head, he gave us a smile over the flaming sword.

"I have a few tricks up my sleeve, too," Hakaimono said, as Yumeko backed toward me, kitsune-bi springing to life in her hands once more. "Shall we see whose fire will burn the hottest? I'm betting it will be mine."

Grimly, I raised my sword, and Yumeko pressed close, her features dancing with foxfire, as the burning, blazing form of the First Oni sauntered toward us. Hellfire snapped along his shoulders, flickering off his horns, and his eyes were a terrible red in the demonic flames.

He was only a few yards away, close enough to feel the monstrous heat radiating from his skin, when the void overhead erupted with light.

A glowing sphere appeared above us all, floating in the darkness like a tiny moon, casting us all in hazy luminance. As we watched, curious and mesmerized, it drifted closer, trailing a long tail behind it before, in a shimmer of light, it changed. A young woman in simple robes hovered before us, her long hair floating behind her like it weighed nothing at all. She was translucent, pale as rice paper, and glowed softly against the void.

I blinked in shock. A hitodama, a wandering human soul that was unable to pass on after its body died. What was it doing here? I had never seen this girl before.

Hakaimono snorted, throwing up his hand in disgust. "*Another* one?" he exclaimed. "Are we giving off a signal somehow? It's getting crowded in here." Curling a lip, he glanced at me. "Your soul is very popular today, Tatsumi. Maybe you should start charging rent."

"I know you," Yumeko whispered, and the yurei turned her gaze toward the girl. "You guided us through Satomi's castle when we were looking for Master Jiro." The floating specter ducked her head, casting her gaze to the ground, and Yumeko took a step toward her. "You...are you Suki?"

Hakaimono gave a dark chuckle. "I don't care who it is," the demon said. "But I'm getting tired of random spirits showing up to interfere. If you're here to possess this one," he pointed his sword at me, "get in line. Otherwise, get out before I rip you into tiny ghost ribbons and scatter you to the wind."

The hitodama raised its head. Her eyes were huge now as she stared at all of us, her gaze lingering on Yumeko. "Ge...Genno," she whispered, making both Yumeko and Hakaimono jerk up. Her voice was shaky, fragmented, but the name was very clear. "Reika-san…sent me here…to warn you. The Master of Demons…his army has invaded the temple."

"Here?" Hakaimono demanded, just as Yumeko asked, "What do you mean?"

"Genno's…army," continued the hitodama, wringing ghostly hands. "They've…breached the temple walls. While you were fighting…they invaded the Steel Feather temple. They're killing everyone right now."

Yumeko gasped as I turned a furious glare on Hakaimono. "You brought the Master of Demons here?"

"No," growled Hakaimono. "That wasn't the bargain we made, and you know it. The deal was that I retrieve the scroll for him. He wasn't supposed to send his damn army. If they're here, he's taking matters into his own hands."

"They're killing everyone," repeated the hitodama. Her pale eyes widened even more, as if she saw something we could not. "They are…oh! Oh no!"

Her mouth opened in fear and dismay, right before the image of the girl shivered back into a glowing sphere of light. Rising into the air, it flew like a frightened bird into the darkness and vanished into the void.

"Kuso," Hakaimono swore. "What is that bastard doing? If he's betrayed me, I'll tear him and his entire army apart." With a curl of his lip, he glanced at me. "Looks like we'll have to put this little duel on hold for now, demonslayer," he said. "I know sharing this body isn't what either of us wants, but if it's trampled by some brainless bakemono while we stand here and argue, we both die."

I gave a short nod. "For now," I agreed, though it galled me to say the actual words. But the First Oni was right; if the Master of Demons had invaded, we couldn't stand here fighting each other while my physical form was in danger of being destroyed.

I glanced at Yumeko. "You should return to your own body," I told her. "Don't worry about me, I'll be all right. But your body will be just as defenseless if you don't return to it soon."

She looked torn, glancing between Hakaimono and me, realizing the truth of my words but clearly not wanting to leave. "Tatsumi, I…"

Hakaimono snarled. "We're wasting time! I'm not going to stand here and yap while there's a battle being fought around us. Stay here if you want—I'm going to see what's happening."

His form shivered, became a glowing crimson ball, and flew into the void as the hitodama had. Returning to consciousness to take control of the body. *My* body. I clenched my fists and looked at Yumeko, who nodded.

"Go, Tatsumi," she whispered, and I went, rising through the layers of thought and memory, back to the waking world.

I opened my eyes…and stared into the face of the Master of Demons.

Genno hovered over me, moonlight shining through his translucent robes, casting him in a sickly light. Aka the Red stood silently at his back, horns and red eyes glinting in the darkness. I noticed a bulging, red silk bag tied to the half-demon's waist, dangling beneath his obi, and wondered if it held the skull of the Master of Demons, the anchor that held Genno to the mortal realm. Around me, shouts and howling battle cries rose into the air, and the clang of weapons echoed off the temple stones. I caught frantic bursts of movement from the corners of my eyes, and smelled the metallic tang of blood on the wind. But Genno hovered over me, tranquil and serene in the chaos surrounding us, his thin lips drawn into a pleased smile.

"Ah, there you are, Hakaimono," he said, gazing down at me. "You seem to have gotten yourself into quite the predicament."

I tried to stand, and discovered I couldn't move. I still lay on my back in the center of the binding circle, though I couldn't see any priests or tengu around the edges. With effort, I managed to raise my head and saw glowing red links wrapped around my limbs and crossed over my chest, pinning me to the stones.

I also noticed that I was alone in the binding circle. Yumeko's body, which would be defenseless and vulnerable without its soul, was nowhere to be seen. I hoped she was safe.

"Genno," I heard myself say, though I wasn't the one to speak. Hakaimono's furious presence crowded mine, glaring at the blood mage through my eyes. "What are you doing? I told you I would get the scroll fragments."

"Mmm. You seem to have failed." The Master of Demons raised a ghostly finger and tapped it against his chin. "But you did show me exactly where to find the Steel Feather temple, for which I thank you. And the guardians here were so concerned with your arrival, they didn't see my army coming until it was too late. You made a perfect distraction, Hakaimono. My army would never have made it up the mountain if the tengu were aware of them. But did you think for a minute that I would actually make a deal with the First Oni?" His bloodless mouth curled. "I will not have my own forces questioning me, nor will I stand for any competition. I am the Master of Demons. I don't make bargains with those who should be my slaves."

"You bastard." Hakaimono gave a low, dangerous chuckle. "So you betrayed me before I could betray you. Can't say I wouldn't do the same, though you do realize I'm going to tear you and your entire little army apart for this."

"I don't think so." Genno raised an arm, making my blood chill. Kamigoroshi was clutched in one pale hand, the blade throwing off a pulsing violet light. Beside me, Hakaimono tensed, and another presence brushed against me, angry and horrified as she gazed through my eyes at the Master of Demons.

Yumeko! I thought. *Get out of here! Go back to your own body before it's too late.* But I couldn't say anything without alerting the Master of Demons.

"You are a liability, Hakaimono." Genno's voice was thoughtful as he held up the blade, a faint smile crossing his face as he observed the weapon. "A loose end. I would be a fool to enter into a partnership with the First Oni. Even more foolish to release him upon the world with no restraints. I think it's time for you to return to the sword, and I'll generously free this body's poor trapped soul, as well. I don't need the Kage demonslayer showing up on my doorstep when I'm about to overthrow the empire."

"Master."

Footsteps shuffled behind Genno, and the Sasori twins appeared wearing matching smirks. Both were covered in blood, their scorpion-tail braids swaying rhythmically behind them. The spiked chains wrapped around their chest and shoulders left spatters of crimson against the stones as they strode up. Genno paused, handing the sword to Aka, and turned his full attention to the scorpion twins.

"Well?"

The yokai on the left grinned and raised her arm. Clutched in her fingers was the severed head of an ancient tengu, prominent red nose pointing like an accusing finger as it spun lazily around. From within, Yumeko gave a silent cry of horror as the yokai snickered. "Mission successful, Master," she said. "The old crow gave us a great deal of trouble but…we found it."

Her sister stepped forward, sank to both knees and raised a long, lacquered case in her hands to the Master of Demons.

"Excellent." A slow, triumphant smile spread across Genno's face as he reached out, ghostly fingers brushing the scroll. Curling his hand around the case, he raised it before him, pale eyes glowing fanatically bright. "Only one left," he murmured. "One more piece, and the empire will be mine. Aka."

The half-demon stepped forward and accepted the scroll from the Master of Demons with a bow before making it vanish into his robes. Genno gave a satisfied nod. "Find the other," he told the sisters, who immediately bowed and began backing away. "It's here somewhere. Tear this temple apart and kill every living soul until you find it."

Gathering my strength, I surged upright, straining against the bindings holding me down. They seared into my skin, burning and agonizing, but Hakaimono added his strength to mine, and a flood of power filled me. With tiny screams, several of the chains snapped, fraying into coils of mist before vanishing on the wind, and Genno looked back, raising a brow in amused surprise.

"Hakaimono." He shook his head. "You *are* as strong as the legends say. More's the pity. You could have been a powerful asset to my new kingdom." I struggled to my knees, gritting my teeth against the burning of the chains while trying to gather the strength I needed to break them completely. Genno observed my struggles calmly. "Still, I would never be able to trust you, and I have no interest in demons who will not bend to my will. If you are not my subject or a servant, then you are an enemy."

"You're a fool, Genno," Hakaimono growled, as we fought against the chains holding us back. *Almost there. Just keep him talking a few more seconds.* "You do not want me as an enemy."

"I'll take my chances." Genno nodded in satisfaction and drifted back. "Perhaps in another four centuries I'll allow you to come out and play again. Though by that time, the world will be vastly different than the one you know now. Aka, if you would do the honors?"

"Gladly." The half-demon stepped forward, smiling. His red eyes glimmered with anticipation as he stared down at me, and he shook his head. "Pity you didn't recognize me before, Hakaimono," he stated, and I felt a ripple of shock and fury from the demon sharing my body. "After all the good times we shared, I was almost hurt that you didn't even say hello when we finally meet again."

"Rasetsu," Hakaimono growled, as I felt the same flutter of shock. Rasetsu was the name of one of the Four Oni Generals of Jigoku, the most powerful demons in existence. Rasetsu, Yaburama, Akumu, and their leader, the most feared, famous oni of them all: Hakaimono. "Why are you working with Genno?" Hakaimono demanded. "And how did you get stuck in the body of a pathetic mortal?"

"You're asking me? That's rather ironic." The half-demon sounded amused, cocking his head in a mocking, quizzical manner, before growing somber again. "The world has changed, Hakaimono. You've been away from Jigoku for quite some time, and O-Hakumon has made plans without you. Maybe next time, don't get yourself sucked into a cursed sword and you can be part of it all instead of standing in our way."

I tensed, feeling the chains stretch to their breaking point, moments from snapping, as Hakaimono growled: "O-Hakumon? What is the ruler of hell planning without me?"

Rasetsu smiled. "Ask him yourself," he said, and stabbed Kamigoroshi through my middle. I felt the point explode out my back, and heard someone, perhaps Yumeko, cry out in horror. Stunned, I gazed down at myself, where the glittering length of the sword was shoved halfway through my chest, just as the half-demon yanked it out again, releasing a spray of crimson that hissed through the air and spattered against the stone.

As I collapsed, I heard Genno's voice, flat and disinterested, already turning away, returning to the slaughter. "Sayonara, Hakaimono. You've outlived your usefulness, and I have no more need of you. May your next millennium in the sword be a peaceful one."

My vision went dark.

29

MERGING SOULS

Yumeko

Tatsumi!

I felt the sword enter Tatsumi's body, felt the hideous rip and tear of the blade sliding through flesh, felt it lodge between muscle and sinew, and it took everything I had not to flee the mortally wounded demonslayer for the safety of my own body. Every instinct shrieked at me to run, to abandon the dying host and return to myself. I couldn't feel the pain, but I could feel the body's reaction to it, the screaming of nerves and the seizing up of muscles, and it was almost too much. As Tatsumi's body slumped limply to the stones, I spun and found myself back in the void, a stunned oni and a human soul appearing against the darkness.

Tatsumi grimaced and fell to his knees, making alarm shoot through me like an arrow. He flickered once and turned ghostly, as the subtle glow around him grew bright against the darkness.

"No!"

Rushing over, I threw myself down in front of him, grabbing his arms. "Tatsumi, no," I pleaded, as his sad, strangely calm gaze flicked up to mine. "You can't die. Don't disappear now. Stay with me."

"I can't." He raised his hands, gazing at his transparent fingers, and closed his eyes. "I can feel...something pulling me," he whispered. "Meido, or maybe Jigoku, is calling. I'm sorry, Yumeko." One hand rose to my face, his eyes soft as they met my own. "Arigatou," he breathed. "For a little while, my world was brighter...because I met you."

Tears blinded me, but with a snarl that shook the void around us, Hakaimono strode forward, eyes blazing with fury and—I blinked in shock—desperation.

"Dammit, human!" he snarled, looming over us. "Don't you dare give up and die. I refuse to spend another minute back in Kamigoroshi. I will stay in this body and on this realm, even if I have to keep your fragile, pathetic mortal soul here by force."

"You can't stop it, Hakaimono," Tatsumi said quietly. Unexpectedly, the faintest of smiles crossed his face. "This body is nearly gone, and you can't stay here once the soul departs. At least I'll die knowing you'll be sealed back in Kamigoroshi, hopefully forever this time."

"And what happens to the empire when Genno wins?" Hakaimono demanded. "What happens to your clan? And your precious little fox girl?" He shook his head and stepped closer, teeth bared, eyes blazing and furious as he leaned in. "Listen to me, demonslayer. I won't pretend to care about any of that, but I know you do. And right now, our survival depends on both of us. I plan to track down Genno and rip the traitorous head from his body, but I can't do that trapped in a sword." He paused a moment, as if struggling with himself, then growled a curse and held out a claw. "My soul is stronger. Merge with me, and we might still live through this."

I stared at Hakaimono in shock. What did he mean? Could a mortal soul and a demon join together? And, would Tatsumi be saved if they did?

"Become one with a demon." Tatsumi's voice was flat, and a humorless smile twisted one corner of his mouth. "I have very little honor left," he said, "but at least my soul will be clean when I arrive in Meido, or even Jigoku. Unlike you, Hakaimono, I have never been afraid to die."

"Hakaimono." I stared at the demon, still standing with his claw outstretched, until he met my gaze. "You can save him?"

"No," the First Oni growled. "I'd be saving *us*. I can't possess a corpse. Once the soul departs, I'll be forced back into the sword, and this body will be nothing but a shell." He gestured angrily to Tatsumi. "His body is dying and once it does, Tatsumi's soul will be pulled to Meido or Jigoku or wherever he's headed. If it merges with me, if our souls join together, I might be able to heal the damage done to the flesh—enough to save his life, anyway."

"But what happens to Tatsumi's soul if the two of you join?"

"I have no idea," Hakaimono snapped. "But I'm sure of what will happen if we *don't*. We both lose, Genno summons the Dragon and the empire is overrun with demons and blood magic. Lots of people die. Is that what you want, demonslayer?" He glared down at Tatsumi. "Your little fox girl came all this way to save you, and now she's going to watch Genno slaughter her friends and everything she cares about, before she dies, too. Because you failed to save her. Can you live with that for the rest of eternity?"

"I..." Tatsumi's tortured, anguished gaze flicked to me. "Yumeko," he whispered, "if I do what Hakaimono suggests, I...I don't know what will happen. I don't know if I'll be myself anymore. If I hurt you..." His words faltered, his eyes flickering shut, as if that thought was too painful to continue. "I am not the Kage demonslayer," he murmured. "I have fallen to Hakaimono, and am no longer worthy to bear Kamigoroshi. Even if I survive here, the clan will call for my death. I can hope only that they will be merciful and allow me to take my own life with honor." His gaze met mine again, resignation settling over his features. "But until then, until they come for me, my life is yours. What do you wish me to do?"

The glow suffusing Tatsumi grew brighter, almost blinding. His body flickered, becoming transparent, and coils of light began drifting upward, vanishing into the black. Hakaimono growled a curse.

"We're out of time, demonslayer," the oni snarled, and held out his claw once more. "Give up, or keep fighting? Decide, now!"

"Tatsumi." I framed his face with my hands, and though I couldn't feel him anymore, his eyes pierced the distance between us. Bright and soulful as I whispered the final word. "Stay."

Tatsumi bowed his head, and for a moment, my heart sank. But his eyes flashed open once more, hard with determination, as he spun toward Hakaimono and grabbed the outstretched talon.

The light surrounding Tatsumi flared, expanding outward, and both human and demon vanished into the glow. Shielding my eyes, I squinted through my fingers, trying to see what was happening, suddenly terrified that, when the light faded, Tatsumi would be gone and Hakaimono would be the only soul remaining.

The glow faded to almost nothing, and I drew in a sharp breath, my heart seeming to stop in my chest. A body knelt where Tatsumi had been a moment before, shoulders hunched and head bowed, breathing hard, as if in pain. Human-sized. Human-looking...almost. Hakaimono's evil-looking tattoos crawled up his arms and shoulders, and a pair of glowing ember horns curled from his forehead, but that was the only sign of the demon. No void-dark skin, no white mane or claws or fangs. He looked like Kage Tatsumi.

Then he raised his head, and a jolt went through me like lightning. I was looking at them both, two entities somehow merged into one. Their souls overlapped, tangled with each other, but they were still separate individuals. I could see both Hakaimono *and* Tatsumi gazing back at me, and the surrealness of it all made my head hurt.

The figure before me slumped, bowing his head, and my worry spiked. "Tatsumi," I whispered, dropping beside him. "Are you all right?"

He gave a painful nod. "Almost didn't make it in time," he murmured, and I couldn't tell if it was Tatsumi's voice speaking to me, or Hakaimono's. Or both. Raising his head, he looked me in the eye and jerked his head. "Go, Yumeko," he said. "The Master of Demons is still out there, with his army. Find your friends, see if any of them are still alive. You have to keep Genno from getting the last piece of the scroll."

"What about you?"

"I have to...recover a bit." Raising a hand, he clenched a fist, before letting it drop. "This body is still weak—it took everything I had to keep it alive. I don't think I can move yet." He reached out again and grabbed my shoulder, making me jump. "Go," he ordered again. "Stop Genno. Don't worry about me. I'm not...going to disappear. Not this time."

I bit my lip, paralyzed with choice, feeling torn in several directions at once. Worry for my friends and everyone at the temple was twisting my stomach into knots. I desperately hoped Reika, Daisuke and Okame were all right. To find them I had to return to my own body before a hungry demon or yokai ripped it apart. I might already be too late, but I was reluctant to abandon the soul I had come to save, leaving it with the demon I had sworn to drive out. "Do you promise?"

"Yumeko." His gaze met mine, and for a moment, it was just Kage Tatsumi kneeling before me and no one else. Leaning forward, he touched his forehead to mine, closing his eyes. "My life is yours now," he whispered. "After you came so far to save me, I'm not going anywhere, I promise."

My vision flooded with tears. Grabbing the back of his head, I squeezed my eyes shut and held him a moment, feeling his glow surround us, pulsing faintly against the dark.

Abruptly, he pulled back, breaking free of my hold. "Go on," he ordered harshly, sounding uncomfortable now. "I'll join you if I'm able. Stop Genno—that's all that matters." I still hesitated, and his voice became a guttural snarl. "Move!"

Lacing my ears back, I reverted to my fox spirit form and fled, feeling Tatsumi and Hakaimono's gaze on me the whole way. Leaping out of the void, I flew straight up, passed through Tatsumi's outer shell and came back into the world.

It was eerily empty. The courtyard where we'd staged the ambush was abandoned, though the signs of battle were everywhere. Bodies lay scattered about, bleeding and motionless on the stones, demons, yokai and tengu alike. A winged tengu warrior slumped with his spear thrust through the chest of a minor oni, though it seemed that the demon had landed a fatal blow as it died. Horrified, I gazed around at the carnage. The bodies of a shrine maiden, a noble and a ronin were not among the dead, that I could see. A group of amanjaku lay on the ground, familiar black-feathered arrows jutting from their chests and between their eyes, indicating my companions had taken part in the battle. Where were they now? And where was the Master of Demons?

When I glanced over my shoulder, my heart went cold. Tatsumi lay on his back in the middle of the binding circle, the front of his shirt and the stones around him covered in blood. Kamigoroshi lay beside one limp hand, the blade dead and dull, and his eyes were closed. He looked wholly and completely dead, and I barely stopped myself from plunging back into his soul to see if he was still there.

My body, I noticed, was also gone. It had been lying beside Hakaimono when my spirit left it to possess Tatsumi, but now the binding circle was empty save for the motionless demon.

Well, that's going to be a problem. Where did my body get to?

A boom from the main hall of the temple made me jerk up, just in time to see a cloud of fire explode through the wall, scattering wood and stones everywhere. Smoke poured out of the main doors, billowing into the sky, and tongues of orange flame flickered through the holes in the wall and roof.

And suddenly, I was there again. At the Silent Winds temple, surrounded by flames and blood, watching a demon army slaughter everyone I cared about.

Flattening my ears, I raced across the courtyard toward the main hall, realizing halfway there that I was actually *flying* over the stones in spirit form. The thrill of that discovery was overshadowed by the roar of the fire and the sounds of battle through the open doors, shadowy silhouettes darting back and forth within. I glided up the steps of the temple and into the main hall, then halted and gazed around in horror.

More bodies littered the ground, scattered among flames and streaks of blood, tengu warriors, yokai and demons alike. The once elegant, spacious hall had been destroyed—enormous pillars snapped like kindling, the statues of human heroes fallen from their plinths and lying broken on the floor. Fire burned, filling the air with smoke, and hazy figures darted through the clouds, blades and teeth glinting in the hellish light. A tengu swooped between two pillars, landed behind a giant snake and plunged its spear through the yokai's back. The huge snake hissed as it died, and the tengu spread its wings to take to the air again, but a horde of amanjaku demons swarmed over the pillar and flung themselves on the warrior before he could escape. Biting and stabbing, they bore him to the ground, and blood spread over the polished wooden floor as the warrior died.

No, I thought, seeing demons swarming the Silent Winds temple once more, dragging Satoshi to the ground. Master Isao, rising to face the murderous oni as the temple burned around him. *This can't be happening again.* Flying up to perch on a snapped pillar, I searched frantically for my friends among the chaos. *Please be all right, everyone. Please. I couldn't bear it if any of you d—*

My heart dropped. Against the far wall, beneath the mural of the great dragon, Reika stood beside Chu, ofuda in hand, her once spotless white haori stained with red. The komainu crouched beside her, snarling and baring enormous teeth at anything that got too close, but unwilling to leave his mistress unguarded. The floor around them was littered with bodies, some missing heads or limbs, a few burned and several riddled with arrows.

Among the carnage, Okame and Daisuke fought side by side with a handful of tengu, perhaps the last survivors of the brutal massacre. Okame's bow lay discarded in the corner, the quiver empty, a spear held in the ronin's hands.

Behind them all, half-hidden and seemingly forgotten in the chaos, a familiar body slumped against the wall in a shadowy corner. Her chin rested on her chest, and her fox ears and tail were visible in the smoke and flickering lights.

Relief and terror shot through me. Leaping off the pillar, I dove into my body, plunging back into myself. There was a moment of dizziness as I sank into my consciousness, and then, a sensation of completeness engulfed me from the inside, the mortal shell welcoming its missing soul.

With a gasp, I opened my eyes. The roar of flames greeted

me, as did the smell of blood and the acrid stench of smoke. I struggled upright and nearly fell as a sudden light-headedness made my head spin. Putting my hand on the wall, I clenched my jaw and took a staggering step forward.

Reika turned then, and her eyes widened as she saw me. "Yumeko," she cried, hurrying forward. "You're all right. Thank the kami. We were afraid you were gone."

"Reika, what…" I gritted my teeth as the floor swayed under my feet. Flames danced around us, the heat pulsing against my face and bare skin. The shrine maiden reached out and put a hand under my arm, steadying me. "What happened?"

"Genno's army attacked not long after you possessed Hakaimono," the miko answered. "The oni must have led them straight to the temple. We held them off as best we could, but there were too many of them. We were forced to retreat here." She glanced to where Okame and Daisuke battled side by side, their faces grim and determined. "We couldn't leave your body lying defenseless next to Hakaimono, but…did you find Kage-san's soul? Were you able to drive Hakaimono back into the sword?"

I winced. "Not…exactly."

Reika shut her eyes, and she leaned into Chu as the komainu pressed close. "Then, I fear we are all lost."

I started to answer, but a hush suddenly fell over the hall, the sounds of battle fading as the demons and yokai retreated a few steps. Breathing hard, Daisuke, Okame and the last of the tengu stood together, weapons raised, as something floated through the smoke to hover over us. A man, a yurei, in billowing white robes, his long black hair flowing behind him.

A chill went through me, and I felt my tail bristle like a terrified cat. Unlike the few other yurei I had encountered, this man radiated evil; I could feel the taint emanating from him in waves, choking and sickly. His eyes, flat and pitiless, gazed down at us, and one corner of his mouth curved in a small, cruel smile. A trio of figures followed him, and each one caused a new shiver to run up my spine. The twin yokai girls with scorpion-tail braids and matching smirks looked dangerous, but it was the third figure that made the hairs on my neck rise. A tall, lean warrior in black, his crimson hair tied behind him, would have been frightening even without the telltale horns and fangs that marked him as a demon. The hilt of a sword poked over his shoulder, and his cold red eyes observed us without a hint of mercy.

The color drained from Reika's face, and for a moment, she looked like she might faint. Her eyes were wide and horror-filled as she stared up at the ghost, a shudder going through her as she staggered back a step.

"Genno." The whisper seemed dragged out of the darkest part of her soul. The shrine maiden hit the wall and sank to the floor, her expression blank. Chu whined and shoved his blocky head into her side, but she didn't appear to notice. Heart pounding, I looked back to the ghostly Master of Demons, floating over us like a wraith.

"Well." Genno tilted his head as he observed us, still smiling. "This seems to be the last of you. I don't suppose any of you will tell me where the final piece of the scroll is?" He raised both hands in an almost generous motion. "Your daitengu has already gifted us with one part. I will make your deaths quick and honorable if you save me the time."

My insides churned. I could feel the weight of the scroll beneath my robes, heavy and agonizing. The demons and yokai surrounding us drew closer, bloodlust shining from their eyes, blades and teeth bared. Okame, Daisuke and the last few tengu didn't move, though I saw the warriors stiffen. A heartbeat of silence, and then Tsume, the young tengu with the feather-like mane of hair, stepped forward.

"No," I whispered, as another memory floated before my vision, overlaying the scene in front of me. Denga, proud and defiant, facing Yaburama, proclaiming that they would never bow to evil, right before the oni crushed him and the aman-jaku swarmed into the hall. The beginning of the end. And I couldn't do anything to save them.

"Master of Demons." Unaware of my horror, Tsume brandished his sword, as Genno gazed down at him in amusement. "Unholy abomination!" he spat. "Your name is a curse, a blight on the land. We will never bow to you. We will never give up the scroll. I will die before I allow you to possess the power of the Dragon!"

He spread his wings and lunged through the air at the Master of Demons, sword raised high.

Genno just smiled.

Before Tsume could reach his target, two spiked chains shot up from the pair of female yokai on the ground. Lightning fast, they wrapped around the tengu like snakes, circling his body and tangling his wings. The warrior faltered in the air, straining furiously against the chains, his wings unable to hold him up. He started to plummet, but before he hit the ground, the yokai twins yanked their weapons back, and Tsume's body exploded in a cloud of feathers and blood. He hit the ground in pieces, his head rolling back to gape at us, as the mob of demons and yokai howled with excitement.

My hands flew to my mouth to keep from screaming, and to keep my stomach from surging up my throat. It was happening again, just like before.

"If that is your wish," Genno said, and the yokai sisters stepped forward, grinning. "Then we will certainly grant you a painful, honorable death."

The deadly chains shot forward again, this time toward Daisuke and Okame. As I gave a cry of terror, one wrapped around the ronin and pinned his arms to his sides as it cut into his skin. Okame let out a startled curse, his spear falling from his grip, as the scorpion girl yanked the chain taut, bringing him to his knees. The other, stabbing toward Daisuke, was struck aside by the noble's sword. Instantly, the yokai girl yanked the chain back and sent it at him again, and once more, Daisuke's sword flashed, knocking it aside. But this time the weapon coiled around and came at him from behind, wrapping him in its barbed links. Daisuke managed to grab the chain with his free hand before it could coil around his neck, but his sword arm, bound to his side, was rendered helpless. Grinning, the yokai's shoulders tightened as they prepared to yank back and eviscerate their victims.

"Stop!"

Foxfire exploded, surging up in a blue-white blaze, engulfing my whole body. Most of the army flinched, cringing back from the brightness, and the scorpion twins froze, their eyes wide as they fixed on me. I ignored them, my gaze seeking the Master of Demons as I raised the last piece of the Scroll of a Thousand Prayers over my head with one arm, a burning torch held in the other.

Genno's eyes widened and he held up a hand, stopping his yokai army from lunging forward. They obeyed, though I could feel the bloodlust radiating from the crowd and knew that only Genno's will kept them from surging forward to devour me. My hands shook; I could feel the ancient roll of parchment in my fingers, brittle and dry, but forced my voice not to tremble. "This is what you wanted, isn't it?" I asked, holding the flames of the torch only a few inches from the bottom of the scroll. "Call off your demons, or I'll burn this piece of the prayer right here." Glancing at Okame and Daisuke, my eyes narrowed and I glared back at the Master of Demons. "Let them go and...and we can negotiate."

"Yumeko!" Reika surged to her feet, as the remaining tengu whirled around, their eyes wide with shock. "Do not speak to him! Do not negotiate with the Master of Demons! We will not give up the scroll, under any circumstances."

"Yumeko-san," Daisuke added, his voice soft but strained, "Listen to Reika-san. Do not bargain with Genno on our accounts. Let us die with honor, protecting the scroll."

The Master of Demons laughed. His deep, cruel voice rang off the rafter beams, rising over the howl and snap of the flames. "You cannot destroy the Scroll of a Thousand Prayers, kitsune," he told me, but his army did not come any closer. "It is a sacred text from the kami themselves. Why do you think the scroll has been separated and not destroyed by your peace-loving fanatics? Because sacred, holy and ancient artifacts always have a way of returning to the hands of men. Burn it, bury it, toss it into the sea—the prayer will simply appear in the world again."

My heart plummeted, but I kept my voice firm. "That might be true," I said, "but not here. And not now. If I destroy it, you'll have to start your search all over again, and time is running out. You might not find this piece of the scroll before the night to summon the Dragon is past." Genno didn't say anything, and I knew I had struck a chord. I took a deep breath and played my last card. "This is my offer. I'll give you the prayer, if you swear on your honor to take your army and leave. No more death. No more bloodshed. You leave us alone, and no one else is killed. What are a few human and tengu lives if you have the final piece of the scroll in your hands?"

For a moment, Genno didn't answer, and both sides held their breath, the demons poised to lunge forward and rip us to pieces, the tengu and humans braced to die. Daisuke and Okame were frozen, their faces tense and their bodies rigid against the lethal chains, knowing that one word from the Master of Demons would mean a very bloody death.

Finally, Genno smiled. "Very well," he said calmly. "You have a deal, fox. Give me the scroll, and I will take my army and depart. My lieutenants will not kill you, at least, not today. You have my word."

I glanced at the yokai twins, still holding on to their captives, and frowned. "Let Okame and Daisuke go first," I said. "Then I'll give you the scroll. Not before."

The two yokai scowled at me, but Genno simply nodded and raised a hand. Immediately, the twins relaxed the tension on the barbed chains, letting them fall to the ground. With another gesture from the Master of Demons, the third lieutenant, the terrible crimson-haired oni, stepped forward and held out a claw to me, the meaning very clear.

I took a deep breath and stepped forward, trying to ignore the furious glares from the last of the tengu, the feathers on their wings trembling, as if they were fighting the urge to fly forward and stab me through the heart. Anything to keep me from giving up the scroll. I understood their dismay; they were ready to die to protect it, to keep it from falling into the hands of evil. Just like Master Isao, and everyone at the Silent Winds temple. But I couldn't watch that again, especially now. Daisuke, Reika, Okame...we had come so far. I wouldn't let them die. This time, I could do something to stop it.

"No tricks, kitsune." Genno's voice echoed quietly overhead, a subtle warning. "No illusions, no fox magic. I will know if what you give me is real. Play me for a fool, and your deaths will not be quick."

The demon loomed before me, his cold red gaze making my skin crawl. Heart pounding, I put the scroll in his outstretched hand and watched his claws curl over the wood. Stepping back, a sick sense of betrayal gnawed my insides; I could suddenly sense a hundred disappointed gazes boring into my soul. But I wouldn't regret my decision.

I'm sorry, Master Isao, everyone. I know I failed my duty. But what does it matter if I stop the coming of the Dragon, if everyone I care about is gone?

With the scroll in hand, the half-demon turned to Genno and, with a faint, self-deprecating smirk, sank to a knee and held the case up to the Master of Demons. Genno descended slowly, hovering a few feet from the ground as he ran ghostly fingers along the length of the wood. His eyes gleamed, and a triumphant smile spread over his face as he nodded.

"At last. The power of the Dragon's Wish is mine." With a soft chuckle, he floated back, the glee in his eyes truly frightening. "Nothing will stop me, now. Aka, make ready the ship. We depart for Tsuki lands immediately."

Without a word, the half-demon rose, tucked the scroll into his obi and trailed his master out of the hall. The two yokai girls immediately turned and followed, twin scorpion braids swinging in tandem behind them. The army, however, remained.

At the door of the temple, Genno turned back, his gaze meeting mine across the rubble-strewn floor. His three lieutenants walked on, vanishing through the frame, but the Master of Demons gestured casually, like he was tossing a plum pit into the weeds.

"Finish them," he ordered, and was gone.

My heart turned to ice, as the army of demons and yokai gave a deafening roar of bloodlust and surged forward.

Time seemed to slow. I watched the approach of the demon army in a daze, as the circle of steel, fangs and claws closed around us. In my peripheral vision, I was aware of Daisuke, Okame and the last of the tengu raising their weapons for a final stand. I heard Chu's defiant howl, and saw Reika reach into her sleeves for an ofuda, shouting something to either me or the demons. Then a shadow fell over me, and I gazed up into the distorted face of a blue oni, eyes glittering as it brought a spiked club down at my head.

Time jerked into motion again, and I flinched back, bracing myself to die even as foxfire surged to my fingertips. Knowing it wouldn't be enough.

Blood splashed over my face, hot and disgusting, making me cringe. *I've been hit. I'm dying.* But there was no pain, no indication that I'd taken a fatal blow, and after a moment of waiting to see if I would topple over dead, I opened my eyes.

The blue oni still stood before me...but only his bottom half. As I watched, numb, the thick hairy legs crumpled, and the eviscerated demon collapsed to the floor, thumping next to his severed top half, brutish face frozen in shock.

Kage Tatsumi turned to face me, eyes blazing red in the hellish light. Horns curled from his forehead, and glowing tattoos crawled up his arms, coiling around his chest. One hand gripped Kamigoroshi, the blade flaring and snapping with purple fire. He gave me a terrifying smile, then slowly turned to face the army in front of him. The demons and yokai stood frozen a few feet away, staring at the newcomer with eyes gone huge with recognition and fear.

"Yumeko." I jumped at the sound of his voice, neither Hakaimono nor Tatsumi, but echoes of them both. "Are you hurt?"

I shook my head.

"Good. Stay there, I'll be right back."

Hakaimono roared, the sound making the pillars around us shake, and lunged into the midst of the army.

What happened next was hard to describe. Hakaimono moved through waves of enemies like a scythe, savage and unstoppable. Kamigoroshi flared, cutting through limbs, heads and bodies, splitting demons and yokai apart. Amanjaku hurled themselves at him, clawing and biting, and exploded into small clouds of gore before swirling away into mist. A hari onago backed desperately away, slashing frantically with the dozens of barbs on the ends of her hair, but the demonslayer ignored the hooks scraping his flesh and lunged forward, cutting off her head with one swipe of his blade. A minor oni howled as it swung an iron club at him; the demonslayer raised his arm, taking the blow without a grimace, before severing the demon's legs at the knee. Shrieking, the oni collapsed in a puddle of its own blood, and Hakaimono didn't even look down as he drove Kamigoroshi through its back.

In the space of a few heartbeats that felt like seasons, it was over. The last enemies, a trio of rat yokai known as nezumi, tried to flee the raging oni of death as he cut through the final demon. With a snarl, the demonslayer lunged after them, cutting two down just as they reached the exit. The third managed to scuttle through the frame, but an arrow zipped through the air, just missing the demonslayer, and struck the nezumi in the back. It pitched forward with a squeak, tumbled down the steps and disappeared. A few yards away, Okame lowered his bow with a grim smile, the side of his face covered in red, before he swayed on his feet and collapsed.

Daisuke caught him and lowered the ronin gently to the floor to kneel beside him. Both men were breathing hard, their clothes torn and bloody, and Daisuke's fine robes would never be the same. But they ignored their wounds, and the mounds of dead piled around them, their eyes only for each other.

"Sorry, peacock," I heard the ronin murmur, as Daisuke took his hand, holding it to his chest. "I didn't…manage to die a glorious death for you." His other hand rose, catching a strand of silvery white hair between bloody fingers. "Looks like you won't get to compose that poem, after all."

"Okame-san." Daisuke's voice was thick, and he shook his head in an almost rueful manner. "That day will come soon enough," he whispered, holding the ronin's gaze. "There will come a time where we will die a glorious death, and I hope to be at your side when it happens. But right now, we have fought this battle, and we live still. That will have to be reason enough to celebrate."

My stomach tightened. Turning away, I observed the horrific aftermath of the fight with Genno's army, and clenched my jaw to keep from losing my meager breakfast. The inside of the temple was now a blood-soaked battlefield, choked with ash and smoke and strewn with gore. Tengu and yokai lay scattered across the wooden planks, with coils of red-black demon mist drifting around them. Everywhere I looked, I saw nothing but death, blood and failure. We had failed. *I* had failed. The scroll was gone, and Genno would soon summon the Dragon. I had lost this battle.

But you haven't lost everything.

"Yumeko."

Reika picked her way over the carnage with Chu behind her, his huge paws creaking against the wood. The shrine maiden was white, either with horror or anger, or both, her eyes snapping furiously as they met mine. "How could you?" she whispered, as Daisuke pulled Okame to his feet and began limping toward us. "You gave Genno the scroll. Now all of Iwagoto will be lost when he summons the Dragon."

"We'll stop him," I said, meeting her rage head-on. I gazed at my friends, bloody, exhausted, but still alive. Okame leaned against Daisuke, one arm draped over his neck, the noble's arm wrapped around his waist. A few yards away, the last of the tengu were shuffling through the hall, taking stock of their wounded and dead, and would not look at me.

"We'll stop Genno," I said again. "We'll track down his army and use everything in our power to take back the scroll. We still have a little time. The Dragon hasn't been summoned yet."

"And what about me?" asked a soft voice at my back.

My heart leaped. I turned to face Tatsumi, or perhaps Hakaimono, standing a few feet away. His sword was sheathed, and the burning crimson in his eyes had faded, as had the claws, fangs and the tattoos crawling up his arms and shoulders. He looked like Kage Tatsumi again, except for the small but conspicuous horns curling from his brow. Reminding us that, even now, he wasn't human.

"That depends." Surprisingly, it was Daisuke who answered, the noble's hand resting easily on the hilt of his blade. "Who are you? You destroyed Genno's army, but I am not certain of your motivation. Is this Hakaimono we're speaking with, or Kage-san?"

Tatsumi paused, then shook his head. "I don't know, exactly," he replied, and his voice was resigned. "Both. And...neither. Pieces of each of us, perhaps. I'm not entirely certain myself."

"That's not exactly comforting," Okame muttered. "No offense if this really is you, Kage-san, but how do we know we're not dealing with a demon who will tear out our throats the moment we let our guards down?"

"You don't." Tatsumi's bleak gaze met mine. "You shouldn't. A demon's words can't be trusted. But, maybe this will be enough."

And before them all, he lowered himself to his knees in front of me, bowing his head. "Yumeko," he murmured. "If you truly believe a demon still threatens you, kill me now. Or order me to do it myself. I will obey, as long as I have control of this body. My blade belongs to you, as does my life, until the Kage decide to take it from me. Or until my mind is not my own." I saw the faintest of tremors go through him, as if he had to struggle to get that last part out. "Until then, do with it what you will."

"Tatsumi..." I swallowed the lump in my throat and shook my head. "Get up," I told him, and he obeyed instantly, rising to his feet, his gaze on the ground between us. I wished I could touch him, even for a moment, but he was different now. I didn't know how much of Tatsumi, the real Tatsumi, was left. And, much as the thought of Hakaimono still lurking in Tatsumi's soul frightened me, we needed his strength if we were to stand a chance of stopping the Master of Demons.

"You can't die yet," I told him firmly. "We need your help to find Genno and get the scroll back. No matter what it takes, we can't let him summon the Dragon."

He nodded gravely, and I caught the red spark of fury in his eyes as he raised his head. "I have a score to settle with Genno," he said in a lethally quiet voice, and there was no question as to who was speaking now. "I'm not concerned about the scroll, or the Dragon, but the Master of Demons will die screaming for mercy, I can promise you that."

"If we can find him," Reika said, eyes hard as she watched the demonslayer, as if afraid he would suddenly leap at her, fangs bared. "He'll likely be heading to the place to summon the Dragon, wherever that may be. There is only one spot where you can call on the Harbinger, and the history scrolls aren't entirely clear where that is, or they've been deliberately lost. But we must find it as quickly as we can. I fear there's not much time left."

"I know where it is," Tatsumi, or perhaps Hakaimono, said. "Of the three times the Dragon has been called on using the scroll, two of them have been by the Shadow Clan. It's one of the secrets the Kage keep close." He turned away and gazed out the door of the hall, his voice grim but triumphant. "I know where Genno is heading. The place where the Harbinger first appeared—by the cliffs of Ryugake, on the island of Ushima."

"Moon Clan territory," Daisuke said.

Okame grimaced. "Looks like we're going to need a boat."

EPILOGUE

Dawn was breaking over the horizon, driving away the stars and tinting the clouds pink. Standing motionless atop the snowy mountain cliff, Seigetsu lifted his face to the first rays of the sun and closed his eyes.

"She did it," Taka murmured at his feet. He sounded relieved but unhappy, as if still uncomfortable with the deception Seigetsu required of him. "She saved them."

"Yes," Seigetsu agreed. "Exactly as you foretold. The fox girl would possess Hakaimono, Genno's army would attack the temple and the lost soul would warn them all of the destruction to come. She just needed a tiny nudge to find her courage."

"What do we do now?"

"Genno has all the pieces of the Dragon's prayer." Seigetsu gave a nod of satisfaction and stepped back from the edge. Out of habit, he almost reached into his sleeve for his ball, before remembering it was no longer there. "He will be heading to Ushima Island posthaste for the Summoning. The kitsune girl and her demon will follow, of course. The board is set. The last play is about to begin."

For just a moment, perhaps the first time in centuries, Seigetsu allowed himself to feel a tiny glimmer of excitement. Years of planning, watching, waiting, were coming together at last. It was almost time.

"Come, Taka." With a swirl of robes and silver hair, Seigetsu strode toward the carriage perched in the snow a few yards away. Taka scrambled obediently after, hopping from footstep to footstep to avoid the snowdrifts.

"Where are we going now, master? Ushima Island?"

"Yes." Seigetsu shook white powder from his robes and stepped into the carriage. "There is one last item, one more piece to acquire, before the final maneuver." He watched Taka scrabble into the carriage, furiously brushing snow from his trousers, and smiled. Fitting that the game would reach its conclusion in the place where it all began. The kitsune girl had no idea of the storm she was heading into, or what she would find when she got there, but it would be interesting, to say the least.

"Make ready, Taka. We travel to the island of the kami, to the birthplace of prophecy itself, to find the splinter that will madden a god."

★ ★ ★ ★ ★

We hope you enjoyed your journey through
the fantastical Empire of Iwagoto in
Soul of the Sword!
Look for book 3 of the Shadow of the Fox trilogy.
Only from Julie Kagawa and Inkyard Press!

GLOSSARY

amanjaku: minor demons of Jigoku

arigatou: thank you

ashigaru: peasant foot soldiers

ayame: iris

baba: an honorific used for a female elder

baka/bakamono: fool, idiot

chan: an honorific mainly used for females or children

chochin: hanging paper lantern

daikon: radish

daimyo: feudal lord

daitengu: yokai; the oldest and wisest of the tengu

Doroshin: Kami; the god of roads

furoshiki: a cloth used to tie one's possessions for ease of transport gaki: hungry ghosts

gashadokuro: giant skeletons summoned by evil magic

geta: wooden clogs

gomen: an apology; sorry

hai: an expression of acknowledgment; yes

hakama: pleated trousers

hannya: a type of demon, usually female

haori: kimono jacket

Heichimon: Kami; the god of strength

hitodama: the human soul

inu: dog

ite: ouch

Jigoku: the Realm of Evil; hell

Jinkei: Kami; the god of mercy

jorogumo: a type of spider yokai

jubokko: a carnivorous, bloodsucking tree

kaeru: copper frog; currency of Iwagoto

kago: palanquin

kama: sickle

kamaitachi: yokai; sickle weasel

kami: minor gods

Kami: greater gods; the nine named deities of Iwagoto

kami-touched: those born with magic powers

kappa: yokai; a river creature with a bowl-like indention atop its head filled with water that if ever spilled makes it lose its strength

karasu: crow

katana: sword

kawauso: river otter

kitsune: fox

kitsune-bi: foxfire

kitsune-tsuki: fox possession

kodama: kami; a tree spirit

komainu: lion dog

konbanwa: good evening

kunai: throwing knife

kuso: a common swear word

mabushii: an expression meaning "so bright," like the glare of the sun

majutsushi: mage, magic user

Meido: the Realm of Waiting, where the soul travels before it is reborn

miko: a shrine maiden

minna: an expression meaning "everyone"

mino: raincoat made of woven straw

mon: family emblem or crest

nande: an expression meaning "why"

nani: an expression meaning "what"

neko: cat

netsuke: a carved piece of jewelry used to fasten the cord of a travel pouch to the obi

nezumi: rat yokai

Ningen-Kai: the Mortal Realm

nogitsune: an evil wild fox

nue: yokai; a chimerical merging of several animals including a tiger, a snake and a monkey that is said to be able to control lightning

nurikabe: yokai; a type of living wall that blocks roads and doorways, making it impossible to go through or around them

obi: sash

ofuda: paper talisman possessing magical abilities

ohiyou gozaimasu: good morning

okuri inu: yokai; large black dog that follows travelers on roads and will tear them apart if they stumble and fall

omachi kudasai: please wait

omukade: a giant centipede

onikuma: a demon bear

oni: ogre-like demons of Jigoku

onmyoji: practitioners of onmyodo

onmyodo: occult magic focusing primarily on divination and fortune-telling

onryo: yurei; a type of vengeful ghost that causes terrible curses and misfortune to those who wronged it

oyasuminasai: good night

ryokan: an inn

ryu: gold dragon; currency of Iwagoto

sagari: yokai; the disembodied head of a horse that drops from tree branches to frighten passersby

sake: alcoholic drink made of fermented rice

sama: an honorific used when addressing one of the highest station

san: a formal honorific often used between equals

sansai: edible wild plant

sensei: teacher

seppuku: ritual suicide

shinobi: ninja

shogi: a tactical game akin to chess

shuriken: throwing star

sugoi: an expression meaning "amazing"

sumimasen: I'm sorry; excuse me

tabi: split-toed socks or boots

Tamafuku: Kami; the god of luck

tanto: short knife

tanuki: yokai; small animal resembling a raccoon, indigenous to Iwagoto

tatami: woven bamboo mats

Tengoku: the celestial heavens

tengu: yokai; crow-like creatures that resemble humans with large black wings

tetsubo: large two-handed club

tora: silver tiger, currency of Iwagoto

tsuchigumo: a giant mountain spider

ubume: yurei; a type of ghost who died in childbirth

usagi: rabbit

wakizashi: shorter paired blade to the katana

yamabushi: mountain priest

yari: spear

yojimbo: bodyguard

yokai: a creature with supernatural powers

yokatta: an expression of relief; thank goodness

yuki onna: snow woman

Yume-no-Sekai: the realm of dreams

yurei: a ghost

zashiki warashi: yurei; a type of ghost that brings good fortune to the house it haunts